STERLING BROTHERS LTD. II

I0653895

The Price

of a Future

JACKIE ROSS FLAUM

Boldness be my friend.

William Shakespeare, "Cymbeline"

Published by Jackie Ross Flaum
ISBN 978-1-7364729-2-7
Printed in the United States of America

ACKNOWLEDGEMENTS

I'd like to say I did all this whole book of fiction by myself, but I can't lie.

The research started over a year before the first words went on paper. Books, photographs, Internet searches, questions to friends who had lived in the places mentioned in the book took longer than I thought. Some places have been altered a bit—I hope discerning readers will forgive the poetic license.

The story and wordcraft were honed, sharpened and refined by members of my Malice in Memphis group. I especially want to thank my Malice editors and readers: Richard Powell, Lynn Maples, and Angelyn Sherrod.

When I thought it was ready, I turned it over to my Boston editor Ann Hall to find remaining plot holes and other errors. She did an amazing job.

The book cover was designed by Caerus Kourt, using a photo taken by Sandy Johnson Vandenberg, a talented Tennessee photographer and longtime friend. Sandy also shot the photos that Elisabeth Zguta turned into chapter headings. I never imagined I could find images that fit the story so perfectly. Thanks to Reedsy for hooking me up with Caerus.

This book follows Madeline Sterling and Socrates Gray who were introduced in *Justice Tomorrow*. I dedicate them to all those who worked in the civil rights movement of the 1960s and all those who continue that good work.

CHAPTER ONE: THE LAST ESCAPE OF 1964

S ocrates Gray barreled through the Georgia trees listening for baying hounds. Gunshots, an angry posse, tracking dogs, and miles of God-forsaken woods had marked his last few escapes from Justice Tomorrow undercover assignments.

His heart pounded against his chest as he ran through the forest, pushing his way past barren trees, tall pines, and shrubs that offered no hiding places. The wind hissing through the evergreen needles sounded like the whispers of lost souls, other Black people who had fled through these Southern woods. Gray ran until his vision blurred.

Hell.

An apt word for the whole ugly South and for his life's work as an agent in the civil rights organization lately. He glanced around to find his brother. Aristotle Gray ran a step behind him.

A gush of cold wind blew against Gray's back as though urging him forward and he grew angry. The spirits of his ancestors needed to leave him alone. He was tired of carrying their burdens, weary of being the responsible brother, and worn out from being the reasonable partner.

Gray slowed, regulated his breathing, and stopped.

"One time—one lousy time—I want to ride out of a jerkwater Southern town in the back of a chauffeur-driven limousine," he said to the man behind him.

His younger brother drew next to him and guffawed.

"Whites would gawk, and everyone would see Blacks could have a limousine life too," Gray went on. "It's what our parents promised us if we got an education."

Investigations for the covert organization Justice Tomorrow used to be easier: collect evidence against people who killed civil rights workers, then slip out of town on a bus or in a pickup. At least for this trek out of Crossville, Gray's companion walked instead of riding across his shoulders. After their last case, Gray had carried his unconscious partner, Madeline Sterling, for miles before he'd found their extraction point.

"You really think we're ever goin' to live a li-mou-sine life?" his brother asked.

Gray's brother Silver, who had ditched his legal name of Aristotle in favor of that ridiculous nickname at a Justice Tomorrow training camp, strode through the dead underbrush with his teeth clenched. He trampled twigs like they caused all his trouble.

"Goddamn it!" Gray stumbled, cursing the weather, the woods, and the people making him flee. He paused to listen for any trouble that might be following them.

Someone had breached Justice Tomorrow's most closely guarded secrets. The extensive network of agents and collaborators had been destroyed. Lives lost and upended. Gray clenched his teeth and growled low in his throat. Finding out what happened and who caused the organization to break apart would be his new life's work.

"Maybe those narrow escapes Sterling and I had were warnings. Maybe they were signs of cracks in Justice Tomorrow," Gray said.

Silver grunted.

Gray refused to think about all the evidence Justice Tomorrow had stored against people who murdered civil rights workers. Carelessness or treachery might have thrown away years of work by young Black and white investigators working in Southern towns.

"Hell's fire."

His nineteen-year-old brother asked, "When did you start swearing?"

The two fugitives didn't look like brothers except for their rounded chins and oval-shaped faces. Gray had light skin like their father and Silver was dark like their mother. Gray's shoulders were so broad he could rarely find off-the-rack shirts to fit, a problem Silver didn't share.

"How much further?" Silver asked.

"Oh, just a little way more." Gray took a good look at his brother. Younger by four years, Silver bragged he had grown an inch in Crossville, although Gray remained taller at six feet two inches.

"You said that an hour ago."

Silver had filled out. He no longer owned the slim, undefined body of youth. His goofy, carefree grin had disappeared too, replaced by a fire in his brown eyes that never quite went away. For that, Gray would always be sorry.

In retrospect, Gray should never have allowed his brother to join Justice Tomorrow. He had hoped to channel Silver's righteous rage, but he wasn't sure he'd succeeded.

"Let me see where we are." Gray consulted a hand-drawn map that his landlady had given him after two white men tried to shoot up Crossville. Silver and other young Blacks had joined a few whites in town, found guns, and returned fire. It was as hopeful a moment as Gray had felt in months. Afterwards, Gray's landlady had handed him the map and a rusty flashlight then shoved him out the backdoor.

"So many goddamn pine trees," Gray said.

"What did you expect?"

"A limousine."

Silver chuckled.

Gray searched the darkening sky and woods for a landmark, a distinctive tree or formation of trees. They all looked the same, black and sinister. He strained again to catch a sound out of place in the woods. Nothing.

Silver sat on a fallen log and wiped his forehead with his coat sleeve. It had turned cold after an unseasonably warm start to December, but they had worked up a sweat running for miles.

"Here. Can you make heads or tails of this thing?" Gray thrust the crude map at his brother.

Silver studied it a minute. "We passed this grove of pines about ten minutes ago. One of 'em looked like a question mark."

"Damn." Gray joined his brother on the log. For a moment they sat close, touching shoulders and hips, drawing comfort from each other. They were doubly orphaned, once by the death of their parents at the hands of a lynch mob and now bereft of their Justice Tomorrow family.

"You ain't no Black Daniel Boone, but how'd you miss this?" Silver said.

Gray chuckled. "I should have shown you the map before, but we were flying through the woods."

"What's that!" Silver jumped to his feet.

Fear zipped through Gray. Nothing. He heard nothing and whispered, "Where?"

He took a step in the direction of Silver's nod, heart in his throat.

Suddenly a squirrel skittered up a tree in front of Gray.

"Goddamn," Gray said and released a breath.

"I guess we're both a little jumpy." Silver went back to the log they'd shared.

"I'm tired, my man," Gray sat next to his brother and his shoulders slumped. "We're both jumpy. And I'm just weary to my soul."

"Sterling?"

Gray huffed.

"Uh! I don't know why the both of you aren't dead already," Silver said.

"Hope she's safe."

"Nah, that girl can take care of herself," Silver said. "If her mouth seizes up, no doubt in my mind Tom Foster can talk them out of jail or hell."

"Let's go." Gray rose. He didn't share Silver's conviction that Tom Foster would protect anyone but himself. The rookie agent seemed to have hoodwinked both his brother and Sterling. "We've got to get on it, or we'll miss our ride to the safe house."

"Where is this place we're going? East Tennessee?"

"In the middle of no place. In the mountains," Gray said. "We're gonna lie low for six months like Justice Tomorrow ordered."

"Nah, I'd rather fight." A growl rose in Silver's throat.

"Violence never did the Black man any good."

"I'd rather kill a bunch of whites and go out in a blaze of glory than die of starvation or freeze to death in Tennessee," Silver said.

"Sterling's white. The driver we're running to meet is white," Gray said.

"This the start of the 'not-all-whites-are-bad' speech?"

"Don't have the breath for it." Gray started back the way he'd come. "Man, I'd love a brandy, a bath, and a hot fire."

He didn't dare hope for the love he really wanted.

"Why do I get the feeling we aren't going to be living high on the hog in East Tennessee?" Silver said. He rose and followed his brother.

Days of hard traveling lay ahead before they reached their safe house, but Gray didn't tell that to his brother. Instead, Gray focused on placing one foot in front of another.

Six months underground. Six months until he could see Sterling. Six long months. They would start the private investigation firm they had planned and maybe something else they had never planned.

"I'm tired of this shit," Gray muttered.

In the distance, dogs barked.

Gray grabbed his brother's coat sleeve, and they ran.

CHAPTER TWO: A GUT PUNCH

A single blast of December wind rattled a warning against her bedroom window. Justice Tomorrow agent Madeline Sterling's eyes flew open. Car tires crunched on the driveway outside the suburban Maryland safe house where she'd been since fleeing Crossville a few days before.

Sterling bolted out of bed and thrust her feet in shoes. Always put on shoes before trying to escape, her instructors had told her. A mass of red curls fell across her face, and she brushed them aside on her way to the door. In the hall, the scuff of house slippers alerted her to her hostess. Sterling opened the door and made her way to where the older woman stood with a shotgun in her hands.

The two women pressed their backs along the wall and inched forward with the gun trained on the kitchen. With a nod of her head, the taller woman motioned Sterling forward. Lights from the driveway flashed through three glass panes in the kitchen door, then everything outside went dark.

Sterling darted across the hall for a better vantagepoint. Thanks to a nightlight over the counter near the sink, she could see that no one had come into the kitchen. A moment later someone's short strides crunch-crunched across the gravel between the garage and the side door.

Something wasn't right. The visitor didn't seem concerned about noise. Perhaps the kitchen door was a diversion.

"I'll check the front," Sterling mouthed and pointed over her shoulder.

Before she could move, the door latch rattled once, and Sterling glimpsed a flash of white—a cap or a head of hair—through the door windows.

Heat sizzled through her. She'd been discovered. Despite her precautions leaving Crossville, whoever destroyed Justice Tomorrow had found her. Sterling's mouth dried and her heartbeat nearly drowned the noise of her hostess cocking both hammers back on the shotgun.

A whooshing, crackling sound filled her ears.

She felt overtaken, helpless in a whirlwind of senses and surrounded by brambles like the ones she'd fallen into as a child while escaping an angry crowd. This time, while the noise of the brambles growing around her was loud or frightening as it had been in other episodes. This time Sterling could hear a harmony of night colors as blacks, blues, and golds sang to her. She saw the soft huff-puffs sound of someone's breath outside. In December, the mishmash of color and sound spun around her like a warm spring day.

"No!" Sterling slammed her hand down against the shotgun barrel as the side door swung open.

"Oh, my, I woke you." For once, the woman who pushed through the door looked slightly disheveled. Sterling's handler, Mrs. Woolworth, always pinned her hair in a tight bun behind her head, but now her hair sprouted white wisps here and there. Lipstick applied hours before had faded and her face had lost all color.

Her hostess leaned her gun against a wall and heaved a sigh of relief.

"I should have known I couldn't slip in. I must be more exhausted than I realized," Mrs. Woolworth said. "Hello, Sterling."

"You could have been killed." Sterling collapsed onto a kitchen chair, feeling slightly sick from the upending of her senses, something that had happened only twice before. The episodes left her shaky and disoriented. On the other hand, they gave her insights—like knowing to pull down a street to avoid a trio of cop cars and realizing that tonight's visitor was a friend.

"Is everything all right? Should I be worried?" The owner of the safe house glanced around as though others might be coming, people not as welcome as Mrs. Woolworth.

"No, no. I may have bungled my entrance, but I know how to lose a tail. Yours remains one of our secure homes," Mrs. Woolworth said.

"Gray?" Sterling's hands gripped the arms of the chair. She forgot that she was sitting in the kitchen in sneakers and pink pajamas. "What about Gray?"

"Your partner and his brother are fine as far as we know," Mrs. Woolworth said. She hesitated, "Gray's handler has been killed. We also lost Sarah Feinberg and Marquis Dark as well as the evidence they'd gathered in their last case in Mississippi."

"Dear Lord," their hostess said.

Tears pooled in Sterling's eyes. She didn't know Gray's handler — nobody in Justice Tomorrow knew each other's mentor, the person who took evidence agents collected and put it in a secure location. But she had trained twice with Sarah and Marquis, however.

"I'll put on the kettle. Everyone could probably use some tea, and maybe something more bracing." Sterling's hostess turned the light on over the stove, moving about the dimly lit kitchen with practiced efficiency.

Mrs. Woolworth removed her heavy wool coat, draped it across the back of her chair, and sat erect with her hands clasped in her lap. The first time Sterling saw Mrs. Woolworth she was sitting like that in her parents' living room.

Sterling had returned home from afternoon classes at Radcliffe College when she found her parents Katherine and Alan Sterling at the front door. Katherine's eyes looked red, and Alan wore an uncharacteristic scowl. Since Sterling had only seen her parents like that on the day her brother Danny enlisted in the Army, alarm had gripped her. Had something happened to Danny?

Instead, a proper Bostonian woman in a tailored black suit waited for her by the living room fireplace to offer her an investigator's position with Justice Tomorrow. Her dream job. Sterling had been thrilled. Mrs. Woolworth, who never offered a first name, said the organization's leadership had read about Madeline's capture of a thief and her civil rights activity in *The Boston Globe*.

"She came to our attention first because we so admired your Pulitzer Prize-winning book on racial segregation in America, Alan," Mrs. Woolworth said. "Harvard is lucky to have you on its history faculty. I understand you have another book coming out next fall?"

"Madeline is too young for this kind of work," Katherine had said.

"She's perfect for undercover work. Look at those freckles, those blue eyes, that cute smile . . . no one would suspect her of investigating a murder," Mrs. Woolworth had said.

The tea kettle whistling on the stove pulled Sterling back from her memories.

"Thank you," Mrs. Woolworth said as she accepted her cup of tea. Her hostess handed a cup to Sterling and excused herself.

"Is it all you dreamed, Sterling?" Mrs. Woolworth asked when they were alone.

"What?"

"Being an investigator," Mrs. Woolworth said.

Sterling blew across her cup to cool the tea and think about her answer.

In her three years with Justice Tomorrow, she had lied to people who thought she was a friend, killed a man in self-defense, and witnessed abuse that gave her nightmares. She had been shot. Tom Foster, a rookie agent she thought she loved, had betrayed her.

What had she gained? An enduring passion for mysteries and justice. And lately, some kind of voodoo spell she couldn't control. She wasn't sure she had come out ahead.

"I read too many Nancy Drew books as a kid. Detective work wasn't as glamorous as I imagined," she said at last.

"You do have a talent for investigations. Your schemes for getting out of trouble are too bold for my taste, but I'd like to help you continue a career in detective work after this fuss dies down," Mrs. Woolworth said. "Your mother told me you once slid into a purse snatcher in Copley Square like you were trying to steal second base."

"My older brother Danny taught me to play baseball," she said. "Thanks to him, I was a pretty good hitter, and I upended a few boys on base during those pickup games we played as kids. Wherever we moved, Danny and I could always count on finding friends at a sandlot baseball game."

Mrs. Woolworth winced as though something pained her. "Go get your things. We have to leave." She straightened her blue cardigan before sipping her tea.

"You said it was still safe here."

"I was going to let you sleep and leave early in the morning, but . . ." Mrs. Woolworth moistened her lips. "I have dreadful news, Sterling. Your brother's been killed in Vietnam."

The bottom dropped from Sterling's heart.

"No, no! I'm going to sneak out in a few days to be with him . . . our first family Christmas in years."

"I'm so—sneak out . . .? Oh, Sterling."

"No, no." Tears rolled down Sterling's cheeks. "It's a mistake."

Danny was too young. He couldn't be dead. Mrs. Woolworth had to be wrong. He was Sterling's advisor, her loudest nag, strongest ally, biggest pain-in-the-butt, personal comedian, and shoulder to cry on.

"It's a mistake," Sterling repeated.

"I am so sorry," Mrs. Woolworth said.

She trusted Danny. Only he knew her secret.

"Your mother called with the news right before the emergency line was disconnected." Mrs. Woolworth took one of Sterling's cold hands. "I'm your ride to the airport. You're going home."

"Home?"

"It's a risk, I know," Mrs. Woolworth said.

"Why? I don't understand any of this. I don't have any of my case files or evidence." Sterling felt like she was floating above her body, watching this tragedy happen to someone else.

"No one knows that agents like you don't keep their collected evidence. You're not thinking straight," Mrs. Woolworth said. "Besides, you could be called as a witness at a murder trial—whenever it becomes possible to hold a fair trial in the South."

Sterling got to her feet, wondering what to do next. Mrs. Woolworth took her arm and steered her toward the bedroom down the hall. Sterling barely felt her handler's touch.

"Get your things," Mrs. Woolworth said. "I'll wait here. We'll talk more in the car."

"Do my parents know I'm coming?"

"Your father will pick you up at the airport," Mrs. Woolworth said.

Guilt washed over Sterling for allowing her parents to bear the brunt of Danny's death alone, for depending on Danny so much when he was in a dangerous place, for—. Suddenly, Sterling had to know how badly she screwed up in Crossville, Georgia.

"Mrs. Woolworth, did Tom Foster destroy Justice Tomorrow? He was my responsibility in Crossville."

"We don't know." Her handler shrugged. "Tom played a role, perhaps unwittingly. Unbeknownst to us, private detectives were tracking him. As it turns out, Foster's father-in-law is a Georgia political boss. We didn't vet Mr. Foster as thoroughly as we should have. A disastrous break in protocol. But we'll discuss more in the car."

The collapse of Justice Tomorrow was not her fault. At least, not all her fault. She tried to feel relieved but could not get past the guilt. Her real mistake was loving Tom Foster.

Danny was going to help her, but he was gone. Her brother's face swirled through Sterling's head as she pulled on jeans and shoved her clothes in a suitcase. She grabbed for her coat and remembered how Danny had yanked her out of a thicket of briars and brambles the night a Louisiana mob had come after the family. Students from the college where her father taught had marched against the professor's stand on integration. Ignoring his own scratches, Danny had thrust her into the waiting family car.

Sterling fell across the mattress, clutched the sheets and sobbed into a pillow.

Mrs. Woolworth handed her a tissue and the car keys when Sterling brought her suitcase out of the bedroom.

"I drove all night and I'm exhausted," the older woman said. "I hate to do this to you, but you'll have to drive the first part of the way. We have a lot to discuss as you won't be able to contact me after today. In fact, after today you'll never see me again. I need to direct you to somewhere to go if you're in serious trouble. You will be safe at Belles Beauty Shop in Kentucky. There is no way to connect this place to me, Justice Tomorrow, or anyone you know."

"A beauty shop?"

"If you find yourself in a dire situation with nowhere to turn, you'll find Belles is much more than a beauty shop. The couple who own it are former Hollywood make-up and special effects artists," Mrs. Woolworth said. "I know this is a great deal to throw at you after receiving such awful news. Take the blue Ford sedan in the garage. We will leave my white car here. Go."

Mrs. Woolworth stayed behind to thank their hostess and give her instructions while Sterling put her suitcase in the car.

Shivering in the cold, Sterling opened the garage and unlocked the Ford's trunk. When the light inside came on, she gasped. Boxes jammed every inch of space. A bubble of fear shoved aside Sterling's grief.

She peeked inside one box marked "Jefferson Davis Pollack" to see a revolver in a plastic bag along with pages of handwriting. The first page began with an account of Pollack's hiding in the brush outside a Black church. In a box labeled "Herbert Holcomb III," she drew out some scanned handwritten pages, the photo of a dead Black man lying atop a picket sign, and cigarette butts in plastic bags. She replaced that box and opened another with Jonathan Cleary's name on the outside. This one held a knife with rusted red flakes on the blade that she examined in the light from the trunk lid. She and Gray had collected similar evidence against the killers of civil rights workers.

"Holy Mother of God." She replaced the box lid and took a half step back.

She slammed the trunk lid shut. Throwing her suitcase into the backseat, she didn't dare think of what she'd seen. Her hands shook so much it took three tries to get the key in the ignition.

Traveling with Mrs. Woolworth might be the most dangerous thing she had ever done.

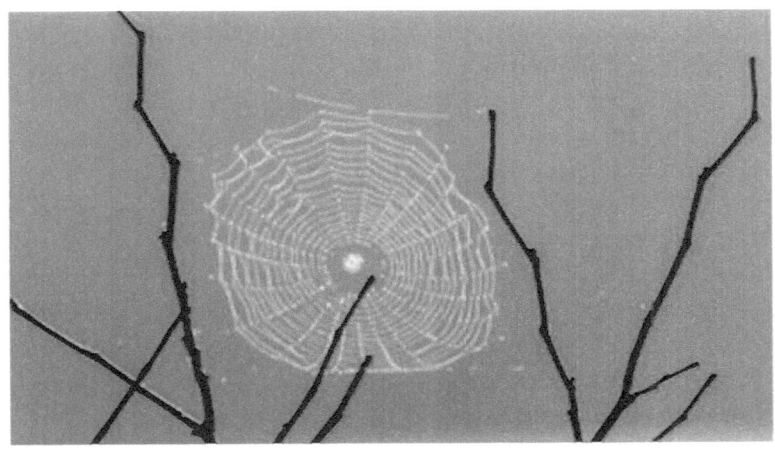

CHAPTER THREE: GRIEVING

The air in Sterling's own home felt strange without Danny. The stripes on the hallway wallpaper looked crooked, the rugs more threadbare, the chairs lumpier with no comfortable way to sit in them. Even though he'd been in the Army for several years, the brownstone home felt emptier since his death. The house itself seemed to mourn.

For her part, Sterling couldn't believe Danny was gone forever. She had flown home to Boston, attended his memorial mass, listened to prayers for the dead. Still, it wouldn't sink in that Danny was never coming back.

She didn't know where to turn. In desperation, she had written to her brother when she learned she was pregnant and asked his advice. Danny had answered that they would figure out what to do at Christmas. Now she was alone. She certainly couldn't tell her parents she was pregnant and add disgrace to their sorrow. There had been no time even if she'd had the inclination.

The last two weeks had been a steady stream of grief. Her parents' weeping, all the food and flowers, the funeral, friends constantly dropping by, and her father's colleagues paying their respects—she had the sensation that she was watching her life unfold on television.

She couldn't bear it anymore. She stood up abruptly.

Two old neighbors visiting with the family in the living room glanced around in surprise when she excused herself. Her mother raised her eyebrows in surprise, the most normal thing Sterling had seen Katherine do since Danny died.

Sterling crept upstairs to Danny's room, sat on his bed, and looked out the window to clear her head.

Instead, images of all the other holes in her life popped into her mind. Gray in hiding. Her lover gone—never really hers to start with. Justice Tomorrow destroyed. Her career as an investigator ended. The empty spaces inside her outnumbered the blood and bones.

Lights on the Christmas tree in the living room shone out the front windows to illuminate a light snowfall. She tossed her brother's old baseball back and forth from her hand to his worn baseball glove then stared out the window at the cars on the street. Watching Danny pitch had always been a treat. She held up the ball. Since she was athletic and Danny's sister, she also became a top choice for those pickup games they played, no matter where they moved.

The last visitors made their way out. Sterling heard their voices in the front hall below then their footsteps on the wooden front porch. She should go downstairs to her parents. A whiff of the pot roast that their neighbors brought over rose up the stairs and her stomach soured. When she got off the bed, something in the street caught her eye.

A tan Chevrolet sedan drove slowly in front of the house. Sterling's head jerked behind the curtains, but the sound of a hurricane followed her, swallowed her in its vortex of briars and brambles. Now the white of the snow outside screamed at her, the noise of traffic looked black, red, and gray. She felt something metallic on her tongue and the Chevy grew to gigantic size.

As quickly as it came the episode vanished.

Sterling clung to Danny's bedpost and fought to settle her stomach, get a hold of her nerves. No mystery about what the voodoo spell tried to tell her.

The car meant trouble.

When she thought about it, she had noticed the sedan before. It had been parked outside the funeral home three weeks ago when the family went to church with an Army Casualty Assistance Officer to plan Danny's service, and across from the church after Danny's funeral mass. Had it been around the house earlier, and she just hadn't seen it? She got closer to the window to catch the license plate number on its next drive by.

Dread filled her as she stood behind the bedroom curtains.

"Madeline? Are you coming to Christmas Eve Mass with us?" Katherine called.

The phone rang in the hallway downstairs.

"Coming." Sterling took air in through her nose and pushed it out through her mouth before she left the window. The relaxation technique she'd learned at a Justice Tomorrow training camp calmed her for a second, but tension tightened her shoulders again. She put Danny's ball back in the baseball glove resting on the nightstand and grabbed the bat leaning against it.

When she got downstairs, her mother stepped from the hall closet with a coat and pointed to where her father stood holding the telephone receiver.

"Madeline, a young man is on the phone for you," her father said.

"What? What young man?" She tapped the bat against her leg as if counting her heartbeats.

"You tell me. He sounds like a nice fellow. Southern," her father said.

For a split second Sterling's heart leapt, thinking it might be Gray. But as quickly as the warmth of the idea came, it fled.

Tom Foster?

Had to be. Justice Tomorrow had assigned her to train rookie Tom Foster while playing his wife for an investigation in Crossville. Gray had warned her not to trust Tom. She should have listened.

She stammered, "T-tell him I don't want to talk with him."

"Tell him yourself, my dear." Her father eyed the bat but said nothing until he thrust the phone into her hand. "I didn't raise a coward."

Sterling buried the phone in her stomach and glanced around for help.

"We're going to church." Katherine handed Alan his coat. "Catch up, Madeline, and this time, don't forget your hat."

Her father thrust an arm into his coat and grumbled all the way out the front door.

As soon as the door slammed, Sterling said, "Hello?"

"Sterling." Tom sighed so softly she could almost feel his breath on her neck. "I am so very sorry about Danny."

"Thank you. It's awful. I—goodbye."

"Don't hang up! Please, Sterling, talk to me. I love you." His soft voice reminded her of the charmer she'd lived with. What started as a platonic friendship evolved over the weeks of the investigation. When the case had heated up, so did they.

"You're a married man," Sterling said. "You knew that when you put your hands on me."

"My wife . . . she was hand-picked for me. I married her to please my father—it was more like a business deal."

"You didn't even have the guts to tell me yourself. You left that to your father."

"I didn't know he was in town! He'd hired detectives to find me, and they found out about the successful garbage dump operation I'd bought into . . . for us."

"Not for us," Sterling said. "Goodbye."

"What about the baby? My baby, our baby. Look, I am still so happy about it, Sterling, and my father is too," Tom said.

A cry of alarm came from somewhere outside, perhaps in the street. Sterling's hand gripped the bat handle in a tight fist.

"Your father must be thrilled to have an heir at last. But neither of you will have anything to do with this baby. I swear it," she said.

"Listen, please! Look, if you won't let me love you—" Tom sounded frantic.

"Do you think the church will annul your marriage?"

"Look, Sterling, please . . . my wife can't have children, but we want a baby. Both of us. This is our only chance to have a child of my blood, someone who will look enough like me to pass as our natural child."

More yelling outside. Sterling dropped the phone receiver and raced for the door. Something heavy fell to the porch with a dull thud. Terror zapped through her like fire under the skin. A scream, a grunt, another thud, then scuffling on the front porch. She opened the door with one hand and clutched Danny's baseball bat in the other.

CHAPTER FOUR: ATTACK

A beefy man in a ski mask shoved Katherine Sterling through the front door. When he followed her inside, Sterling caught a flash of surprise in his eyes as she took half a step and swung the bat at his face. Howling in pain and holding a bloody nose, he pedaled backwards through the door. Sterling followed, prepared to strike again.

On the porch, she drew back to smack the man again when she glimpsed her father struggling with a second assailant. She swung at the first attacker, and he jumped, slipped on snow that had fallen on the front porch, tumbled backwards down all five front steps, and lay moaning on the cement walkway.

"What's going on?" A next-door neighbor yelled.

"Dad!" Sterling cried.

The second attacker, who wore a black watch cap, sat on top of Alan pummeling him with bare fists. Sterling stepped toward him, but Alan's assailant rolled off and sprang to his feet. She side-stepped her father to avoid putting him between her and the attacker. At the same time the assailant pulled a knife from his coat pocket.

Holding his head with one hand, Alan used the other on the porch floor to push to his knees.

"What's all the racket?" shouted another neighbor from his front porch.

Alan twisted to his left as though he meant to answer, and the second assailant reached down, grabbed Alan's coat by the shoulder, and hauled him the rest of the way to his feet.

The unmistakable 'snick' of a switchblade flipping open sounded loud enough to wake the whole neighborhood. Sterling froze. The man in the black cap hugged Alan to his chest.

"Your files. Give 'em to me," he said in an unmistakable Southern drawl.

"I don't have any, I swear." She brandished the bat.

The man put the tip of his knife blade to Alan's throat.

"Alan!" Katerine Sterling screamed from the doorway.

"Listen to me, agents don't keep their files, and I don't know who has them now." Sterling side-stepped a second time to get the man to move in front of the steps.

Alan's captor took a swipe at Sterling with the blade.

"Ah-h-h-h-h!" Katherine raced out the front door, shoved her daughter aside, and ran at Alan's assailant screaming like woman with her hair on fire.

Seizing his chance, Alan slammed an elbow into his assailant's gut, and the startled man shoved Alan at Katherine in self-defense. With a loud cry, the couple toppled onto the porch in a heap.

At the same time, Sterling stepped forward, fully extending her arms as if striding into the perfect pitch. The man threw up both forearms, sparing himself a dead-center crack on the forehead. Instead, the blow landed with such force Sterling heard a crunch. The man grabbed his arm with a scream. His black cap flew off and the switchblade knife danced down the front steps.

The first assailant had rolled over next to the bottom step and used it as leverage to stand. He grabbed the knife and waved it in Sterling's direction.

On the porch, Alan untangled himself from his sobbing wife, helped her stand, and pulled her inside the house.

"Go," Sterling said to Alan's assailant.

"I'm gonna kill you next time—to hell with orders," he snarled as he stumbled toward the steps.

"Don't come here again," Sterling said. "I won't be here, and my parents won't know where I am or how to reach me."

Alan stepped outside again wielding a fire poker.

Sterling and Alan followed his assailant as he cradled his arm, stumbled down the stairs, and nudged his partner to follow. The man with a broken nose kept the knife pointed at Sterling as they made their way to the curb where their car was parked.

"Alan! Is that you?" A neighbor ran off his porch. "I called the police."

As Sterling watched the two men drive off in the sedan she'd seen from her brother's window, she took Danny's bat off her shoulder. Her father put a shaky hand on her arm. She could feel the weight of both pull on her whole being.

As she watched the sedan's tail lights grow smaller in the distance, she felt the responsibility that now weighed on her shoulders – Danny's old baseball bat used for protection to her left and the hand of her father on the other, who now needed protecting.

"We're okay," Alan yelled.

"Robbers. They're gone," Sterling shouted to the neighbor and guided her father toward the porch stairs. Alan sighed and clung to the handrail on his way up the stairs. With one look back at his daughter, he disappeared in the house.

Sterling stood vigil as the neighbors returned to their homes and front porch lights clicked off one by one. Satisfied everything was over, she went inside.

"Mom. Dad."

"Are they gone?" Katherine called from the end of the long front hall.

"Yes," Sterling said.

"We're in the bathroom. B-r-r," Katherine called. "I'm putting antiseptic on your father's cuts—or trying to."

The downstairs half-bath under the center staircase wasn't large enough for three people. Sterling stood in the doorway.

"Is he hurt badly?" she asked. "Are you alright, Mom?"

"Shaken. Terrified. How are you?" Katherine said over her shoulder as she attempted to dab a cotton ball soaked with alcohol on her husband's face with a trembling hand. Her lower lip quivered, and her eyes were red.

"Okay, I guess," Sterling said.

"Take off your wet things," Katherine told her daughter. "Get some house shoes on and wrap up in a blanket."

Sterling's shoes, socks, and the legs of her jeans were soaked from snow. She shivered.

"Do as your mother says." Alan Sterling, who was seated on the closed toilet lid, tried to dodge his wife's attempts to apply antiseptic. One leg jiggled up and down nervously. His lower lip had started swelling, and he sported small cuts on his cheek. Underscoring it all was an angry scowl.

"I don't want these cuts to get infected," Katherine said. "Alan, for the love of all that's holy. Stop moving away from me."

"My God, Katherine." Alan grabbed his wife's upper arms with both hands, pulled her into his arms, and squeezed her tight. "You could have been killed. I could have lost you too."

"I'm fine. We're all fine," Katherine said.

"I'm sorry," Sterling said. "Those men came for me."

"Why?" Alan released his wife, and his voice rose as he stared at Sterling. "Why are people trying to kill my daughter?"

Katherine pushed gently on his shoulder. and he sat back on the toilet seat still gazing at Sterling.

"Madeline . . . you are all we have left," he whispered.

"I know, Dad." Feeling guilty and miserable, she pulled off her shoes and socks and dropped them in the hallway. She used to be scolded for leaving her shoes in the hall.

"Alan," her mother began.

A knock on the front door froze all of them.

"The police," Sterling said. "The neighbors called them. I told them we fought off robbers."

"What?" said her mother.

"When they ask, the thieves got away with nothing." Sterling said. "We can't identify them either. They wore masks. Don't mention me clobbering them with a bat."

A second series of more insistent knocks.

"I'll tell them you're too shaken to talk to them." Sterling said.

"Madeline, if you don't mind, I will answer my own front door and speak for myself." Alan rose, straightened his shoulders, and swept past her.

Katherine pulled her daughter into the little bathroom to whisper, "It'll do your father good to deal with something he can control for a change."

"I'm sorry, Mom. I'm sorry for Danny, for this mess, for everything." Tears ran down Sterling's cheeks.

"Dr. Sterling?" said a deep voice from outside. "We had a report of a robbery. Well, I can see you had some trouble."

"Robbers. Young thugs and cowards," said Alan. "Come out of the cold, officers."

**

"Who were those men?" Her mother whispered to Sterling.

"Amateurs. At least they acted like amateurs, and we got lucky there. Probably hired by someone who wants the evidence Justice Tomorrow agents collected. Judges, mayors, sheriffs, a Senator . . . powerful men were in on some of these murders we investigated," Sterling said, easing the bathroom door shut. "Two agents have died already."

Katherine's eyes widened. "L-let's tell the police we need protection."

"Police are sometimes in on the murders."

"How about all three of us taking a trip?" her mother asked.

"They would follow," Sterling said.

"We'll hire a thug!" Her mother declared.

"Mom," Sterling forced a smile, "do you know how to hire a thug?"

"You must," Katherine snapped. "It seems to be your kind of person."

Sterling gasped. Sounds of her father's voice and the policemen at the door faded. Katherine grabbed her daughter in an embrace that threatened to smother Sterling.

"That wasn't fair. I'm sorry," her mother said in Sterling's ear. "There must be something we can do."

"I have to leave."

"No-no! You can't go," her mother cried.

"Mom . . . sh-h." Sterling strained to hear muttered voices that told her Alan was still talking with the police.

"I won't let you leave us."

Sterling clutched her mother's shoulder. She seemed frailer than Sterling remembered. "I'll find a way to contact you, Mom."

"How will those men know we can't reach you? Are you sure they won't try again?" Katherine whispered.

"I don't know for sure . . . We need to scatter. You and Dad go stay with Aunt Caroline. Didn't she ask you to visit her in North Carolina? We'll all leave together in an hour or so and you drop me off at the bus station. Those guys were clumsy, but someone will be watching. Afterwards, you drive to North Carolina, stop as few times as you can, and stay inside with Aunt Caroline for a few days."

Her mother seemed doubtful. "Will that work?"

"For you?" Sterling shook her head. "I don't know. Honestly, you and Dad need to visit a dozen relatives before coming back home. When you get home, hire a company to set up a security system. I'm sorry to put you in such danger. I didn't know it would come to this. I was naïve."

"What about the baby?"

It was almost a relief to hear that her mother knew. Sterling stared at her cold, bare feet on the fuzzy bathmat as though they could reveal salvation.

"I'll handle it." No use lying to her mother now. "Don't worry. I won't disgrace you."

"'Handle it . . .,'" Katherine muttered. "Holy Mother." She dropped her face into her hands. Her whole body shook.

Sterling had never felt so small, so ashamed. How could she do this to her parents, especially now. Her mother sniffled and swiped away tears.

"I hoped I was wrong," Katherine said.

"Mom—."

"No, let me finish. Madeline, you're a grown woman, and you just demonstrated you can handle yourself," Katherine said low enough to avoid carrying to the men at the front door. "I can't say I'm happy. You broke the church's teachings and the rules of this house. I'm disappointed. That said . . ."

Sterling watched her mother struggle to find her next words and braced herself.

"Ah," Katherine licked her lips. "What will you do when my grandchild is born?"

"I can support us," Sterling said with more confidence than she felt. She summoned more bravo. "I'll be a police officer."

"Really."

"I have references I can use once we shake these—whoever they are."

"Even so, how will you work and care for a baby?" Katherine asked.

"Lots of women do."

"I'm sure," her mother said. "Do you plan to follow a suspect with my grandchild strapped to you like a papoose?"

"No, of course not."

Katherine pointed in the direction of the front door. "What about things like this? Will they happen around the baby?"

"No." Sterling rocked back on her heels.

"How will you prevent it?"

"Don't you think I can pull it off?"

"Oh, honey, you can do anything." Katherine grabbed her daughter's hand and squeezed it. "I have an idea. I mean, something to think about. Would you—would you consider coming home? I could help with the baby. You would be welcome, you know."

"W-what?"

"I'm guessing the birth's seven-eight months off." Katherine's words gushed out of her. "You could go shake these people, return wearing a wedding band, and tell everyone your husband died. We could plant the seeds of that story with our friends, go out of town to your small wedding, come back rejoicing. Show pictures of you and some man. Your new husband is killed in a-a car accident. Once this trouble blows over, you and my grandchild come home to stay."

Holy Mother of God, Katherine Sterling had thought about it, planned it.

Hope shone in her mother's eyes. Katherine wiped away Sterling's tears, caressed her cheeks, and gave her a smile. "We can turn Danny's room into a nursery. He would like that."

Sterling nodded, unable to speak. Pieces of her life clicked into place. She always thought she was most like her father, the dedicated historian, a fierce New Englander, and logical thinker. Now she saw her daring and imagination came from the Mississippi woman she'd underestimated all her life.

"It's settled. Your father and I will go away. Later I'll tell everyone we went to see you married. A small affair because of . . . Danny."

It struck Sterling that her talent for deception also came naturally.

The front door slammed shut. Alan's footsteps echoed on the wood floor of the front hallway, then he opened the bathroom door. He stood straighter, calmer, more himself.

"I handled the police." Alan's chin had a familiar lift to it. "I told them the two robbers jumped us at the end of the walk, followed us to the porch where I thrashed them and sent them scurrying away empty-handed. We couldn't possibly identify them. I said my wife and daughter were too traumatized to talk about it further."

"Excellent," Katherine nodded solemnly.

"Good, Dad."

"Hum-m." Alan studied the women inside the bathroom. "I trust you two have finished conspiring against me."

Sterling and Katherine burst into laughter at the family joke, a tiny but wonderous drop of something normal.

CHAPTER FIVE: NEW YEAR, OLD LIFE

Silver walked into the road and picked up a glass Coke bottle. He'd get a few pennies for it at the store. Maybe buy a candy bar. From the church window across the road, Gray watched his younger brother, who used the alias Ezekiel Tone, pull his jacket around him against the wind. Christ, it was like being a kid in the Missouri boot heel again. Orphaned and poor. Scared of his shadow, living with his aunt, and praying nobody killed her too. Always looking out for his little brother.

Silver walked by the bent metal city limit sign that listed the Mullinsville population as eight thousand. Gray bet that three-quarters of the population lived in poverty on the Black side of town, just like every other place Justice Tomorrow had sent him.

As he watched, a Buick convertible full of young whites drove down the street with the top down in spite of the cold. Red. Shiny. Maybe a new Christmas gift. Honking the horn and showing it off to people who could hardly afford a mule. The whites whooped and laughed as Silver jumped a pothole in the street, raced to the curb, and paused to gawk at the new Buick Spitfire. He faced the church with clenched fists, flaring nostrils, and lips pressed tightly together.

Silver made no secret of how anxious he was to leave Mullinsville. Now this. Groaning to himself, Gray couldn't think of anything good to say about this town either. He posed as out-of-work kin to the preacher and worked in his church, while Silver was a helper for an invalid white man. Silver walked around town with a sullen expression, downcast eyes, and slumped shoulders. He clearly hated the town, loathed his job running errands for a sick man with a foul temper, and didn't act fond of Socrates Gray either.

When he walked onto the porch of the Missionary Rescue Baptist Church, Gray hurried from the window in the vestibule and began sweeping the center aisle of the sanctuary. A moment later Silver opened the door and Gray nodded to him. Silver plopped on a creaky pew, set the Coke bottle beside him with a clank, and stomped his heel on the cracked wooden floor. He sat facing the altar and the large wooden cross that dominated the wall behind the communion table. Gray kept going with the broom.

Back and forth, back and forth.

No good was going to come from the next conversation.

Silver chewed his bottom lip, fumed, said nothing. The silence drifted on and on until Gray began thinking about something else.

"Are you even gonna stop?" Silver said finally. "I mean, I know you aren't doing any work here. You swept that same square three times. Brother Dixon must be pleased that you are so thorough cleaning his church."

Gray's head jerked in surprise. His mind had wandered.

"You wearing the same ratty-ass coat and pants you had on yesterday morning." Silver observed.

Gray checked his clothes.

"You sick or something?" Silver went on.

Gray rubbed the stubble on his chin. He shrugged and resumed sweeping.

"You haven't been yourself," Silver said. "What's going on, brother? Is it Sterling? She's okay. I'm sure she got her to a safe house too."

"I know. Yeah, you're right. I haven't had my head on straight."

"No kidding." Silver knocked his knuckles on the back of the pew. "What do you want, Gray? I mean, I know this work we did is important, but what do you want down the road? Maybe our time with Justice Tomorrow is over. Is that what you're worried about?"

26

Gray leaned on his push broom. His brow furrowed as he thought about Silver's question.

"I haven't imagined life outside Justice Tomorrow in a long time." He grinned at his brother. "Guess I should start. Sterling and I want our own private investigators agency—you change your mind about joining us? You planned it with us. What do you want to do?"

"Get a place with indoor plumbing and shower twice a day." Silver laughed and Gray did too. "When did you last have a good laugh?"

Gray resumed sweeping. "Not much to laugh about."

"Oh, my God. I know what's ailin' you. It really is Sterling. No. No, no." Silver's jaw dropped, and he whispered, "Look, man, not that I don't love her too. She's good-looking, smart, funny, kind. Tells great stories and can toss a grown man on his ass. But, my brother, she's white. You may be educated, and light-skinned, but you are still a Ne-g-ro." He drew out the last word.

Gray stopped sweeping, sick to his stomach. He couldn't bear that his brother guessed his secret.

"You hear about Billy Dodson?" Gray said. "White men jumped him at his own doorstep last night, dragged him into his front yard, and beat him to a pulp. His wife sent their eldest boy to get the pastor. Billy might not die, just wish he had."

"Billy! I-I was with him yesterday."

Gray felt trouble rising from the ground he stood on.

"Were you with him at The General's Store?" Gray asked referring to the white-owned grocery and dry goods store in town.

"I left out the back when things got hot. Y-you mean, he got beat up over pocket change?" Silver shook his head. "All Billy did was ask that white store owner to count the change again. Billy said he gave a five-dollar bill for a pack of cigarettes and got pennies back as change."

"Were you involved at all?" Gray's eyes went wide, fearful.

"Nah. There was three or four brothers in the store, though. We all heard the argument," Silver said. "Since we're all big bad Justice Tomorrow agents, maybe we should find out who beat up Billy."

"Let it go," Gray mumbled.

Silver stood, stood sideways in the pew, and lifted his jacket to reveal a pistol stuck between his waistband and belt. The Detective Special handgun had a piece chipped off the black grip—Gray recognized the gun from the remarkable day in Crossville when whites and Blacks had joined to stop two killers from getting to Sterling.

Had Silver carried it the whole time they'd been running? Jesus Holy Christ. A gun, particularly one that distinctive, could be trouble. He started to tell his brother to throw it in the woods but figured it would do no good.

Silver withdrew the gun from his belt, held it in his hand with his thumb on the hammer, stepped out into the center aisle, and turned his back to the cross.

"We should stand with Billy like men, Gray."

"Stay away from it! All of it!" The command cracked through the empty church like a whip in the air.

Silver slipped the gun back in his belt, covered it with his jacket, and picked up the pop bottle on the pew seat.

"Here. Want this bottle? I got to go to see about Masta George. I got to flip that poor old drooling white man in his bed at least two or three times a day. I got to sit him up in his chair so he can watch his co-l-or T-V in his warm house while I shiver in the shack out back."

Gray took the bottle and put down the broom. "If we find another, we can get a nickel like we did when we went to live with our aunt. Come on, I'll walk with you part-way."

"How long are we stuck here?" Silver groused.

"Until we're safe," Gray said.

"What's safe?" his little brother asked.

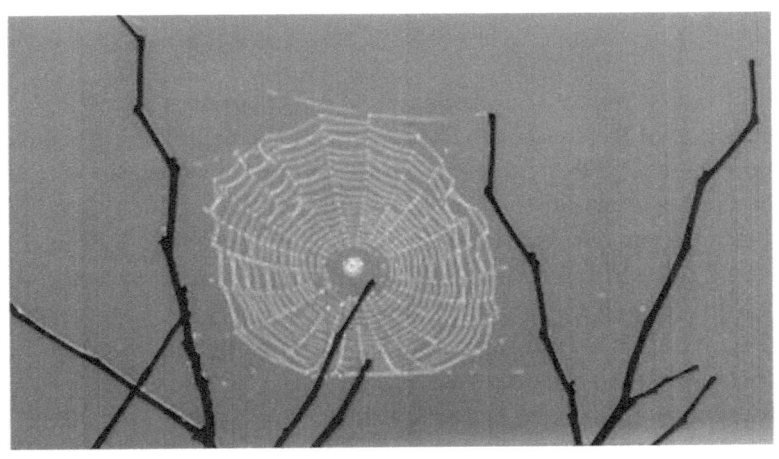

CHAPTER SIX: A NEW ASSAILANT

Aburly man with a black mustache wearing a blue muffler around his neck was one of a dozen people to join Sterling on the bus from Boston to Norfolk. He and Sterling stood out among the passengers who were mostly Blacks and sailors returning to the naval base after a long Christmas leave.

Seeing all the servicemen dragged on Sterling's already low spirits. Her sweet brother Danny should be returning to base after a holiday.

Instead of mourning Danny, Sterling thought of something happy, like her reunion with Gray in a few months. She'd always been fascinated by him. He was several years old and more sophisticated than she, someone her trainers at Justice Tomorrow camps often cited as an example of a good detective, and one of the smartest people she'd ever met. As the bus bumped and swayed along the road, she admitted she still wanted more from him than a working partnership. He'd slammed the door on that back in Crossville.

Sterling fell asleep with an ache in her heart. A polite sailor woke her when they arrived at the brick Trailways building in Virginia and directed her to the grill next door where she could get coffee in the pre-dawn hours. Thanks to the money her parents gave her, she could afford to jump on a number of buses and trains to shake any tail.

That was as much of a plan as she'd come up with so far.

She noticed the man in the reflection of the grill window but only thought he was a fellow passenger. The brightly lit shop was crowded with travelers from other buses, so Sterling sat at a table that hadn't been cleared yet. From the look of it, the previous customer had enjoyed steak and eggs for breakfast. Sterling's mouth watered as she set her duffle under her feet.

The man with the mustache took the booth facing her, removed his coat, and asked a harried waitress to bring him coffee in a Southern drawl. The two of them seemed to be the only civilians other than the wait staff. Everyone else was in a Naval uniform. The man fingered his silverware, scowling as he eyed her.

Sterling's stomach rumbled and she turned to the menu. Bacon and eggs sounded good to her. An uncomfortable feeling gathered around her until a loud wind whistled in her ears.

"No," she whispered.

The black and white lines of type on the plastic-coated menu blurred and the air inside the grill engulfed her in a whoosh. Stifling a gasp with her hand, the bramble wall grew around her. She saw burnt grease and stale coffee, tasted the rock and roll playing overhead, and heard the red, yellows. and purples of the shop slam into each other. Her hand touched the knife on the table and the wind around her vanished.

Sterling blinked to get her bearings. Where was the danger this voodoo vision wanted her to see? She slipped the steak knife smeared with sunny side up eggs into her sleeve, rose with her duffle in hand, and left. Her abrupt departure startled the man with the blue muffler. He struggled to slide out of the booth, leave some money, and grab his coat. She ran out the front door and around the corner with the duffle over her shoulder. Instead of finding a departing crowd to hide in, the street was deserted—and dark. The streetlight was out.

Panic zipped through her. She wanted to scream for help. That would bring the cops, however, and they might have an alert out for her.

Heavy footsteps on the empty street behind her sent Sterling running into an even darker place. An alley.

Maybe that long bus ride wore him out enough to be careless.

30

Sterling glanced around the alley for a weapon and settled on the closest thing. A garbage can lid. Her self-defense instructor's warning rang in her ears.

You lose all the fights that take more than four seconds.

She grasped the metal can lid, crouched behind the trio of cans outside a doorway grasping for rocks or cans—anything she could roll down the alley to make a noise. A rancid smell came from the garbage she'd left open. Her fingers found an empty beer bottle that she sent rattling down the concrete. As she hoped, the sound attracted the pursuer, and he tore by her without looking.

As he ran by, she turned the lid sideways and threw her whole body behind a blow that struck the base of his neck at a forty-five degree angle. He pitched forward and hit his forehead against the brick wall of the alley. The momentum against the wall caused his head to snap back. As the assailant bent backwards, Sterling used a downward motion to strike his temple with the edge of the lid. A perfect hit. With a grunt he dropped to the pavement. Panting, she watched him lay still.

Four seconds.

Sterling rested against the wall to listen for trouble. Nothing. Grunting and tugging she removed the man's shoes and socks, as well as his pants and underwear. By holding it up to the faint light from the street, she read on his driver's license that he was Marshal Cooper from Albany, Georgia. Cooper's wallet also held an employee health card from Bellamy Warehouses, $300 dollars, and a picture of Madeline Sterling pressed next to one that might be his wife and two daughters. She took $200 for any extra travel expenses, stuffed her photo in her coat, and dropped the wallet.

Opening her duffle, she managed to stuff all his clothes but one shoe inside. Since most people were right-handed, she took a chance her attacker was too. With a grimace she used the steak knife to draw blood from her forearm, smeared it on the man's right hand, and placed the knife in his palm. Her coat sleeve would hide her wound until she needed it to show it off. First, though, Marshal Cooper would have to explain why he was in that alley with a blood-stained knife, no pants or underwear, and only one shoe.

Taking a deep breath, she straightened her clothes, fluffed her hair, calmed her racing heart, and returned to the bus station. For seven dollars she bought a ticket on the first bus out of town.

All things considered, she had gotten off easy with a scare and an empty stomach. Her small wound was insurance. If asked, she had something to prove the man had attacked her with a knife.

At a rest stop in Virginia, Sterling noticed a pay phone booth in the Crossroads Country Store, a solitary building by the road that also served as a café and bus station. Maybe she had time to satisfy her curiosity about her assailant, Marshal Cooper. She got some change and went into the booth to ask the information operator for the daily newspaper in Albany, Georgia.

When she called *The Albany Herald* claiming to be a reporter from Norfolk, the reporter who answered sounded eager to trade information for a story about a local man. Sterling told him how Marshal Cooper was found naked in an alley. The reporter put her on hold while he searched for the name in his newspaper's morgue.

Come on.

What was taking the reporter so long?

Come on!

Her fellow passengers began boarding the bus.

Get back on the line.

Sterling started to hang up and run to her bus when the reporter came back on the line.

"Only got one thing on him—picture taken a year ago when The Bellamy Warehouses sold," he said. "Caption reads: 'Foreman Marshal Cooper welcomes J. D. Masterson of Atlanta Investments Inc., Bellamy's new owner, to the main warehouse.'"

"Thanks. Check with the Norfolk police and see if they don't have a report about Cooper being found with a bloody knife too," Sterling said and opened the door of the phone booth.

Who was J. D. Masterson and what was Atlanta Investments? Did they have anything to do with Cooper following her from Boston? Excitement born of relief flooded her. For the first time she had leads in figuring out who was after trying to kill Justice Tomorrow agents. Three leads, really: Marshal Cooper, J. D. Masterson, and Atlanta Investments.

When the bus reached Huntington, West Virginia, Sterling had her fill of air that smelled like dirty feet and a world that rocked side to side. Thanks to Marshal Cooper, she could afford to fly to her next destination. Wherever that was.

She consulted a folding paper map of the United States in the bus lobby and smiled. Philadelphia. She'd head there as soon as she could be sure no one could pick up her tracks. For a moment she wondered where Gray was, if he and Silver were safe. If he thought of her.

Since she needed the exercise, Sterling walked to the U.S. Post Office, rented a box under an alias, and headed for the Pritchard Hotel to catch a cab to the airport.

Tri-State Airport outside Huntington, which had been carved from the top of a mountain, was a small building with no porter service and only two gates that Sterling could see.

Fearful of going South, Sterling stewed about her next destination. She bought an Eastern Airlines ticket for the flight to St. Louis and kept her duffle instead of checking it. The flight wasn't direct so she could get off at any stop they made.

At a small newsstand near the Eastern Airlines counter, she bought a Coke and waited to board. After a few moments she'd even forgotten where she was going.

An arriving family caught her eye, not only because their anxious chatter seemed off the charts, but because the young woman in the middle of it all had red hair. Probably a college girl. She walked with a bounce to her step and a smile on her face, obviously eager to leave. Her parents acted ready to yank her back to Huntington or Bluefield or wherever they came from. Sterling's parents had behaved much the same way when she left for Justice Tomorrow training.

"There's the Eastern Airlines ticket counter," the mother said and lead the way.

The young woman's father put the bags he carried on the scale and said, "One way to Wilmington, North Carolina. Uh, name of Emily Blanchard." When the three-part ticket came up, he paid for it and handed it to his daughter.

"Now put that somewhere safe," Mr. Blanchard added.

Sterling watched Emily roll her eyes and insert the paper into the right pocket of her wool coat without glancing at it. "Right here. I'm gonna be fine, stop worrying."

"Your Aunt Sophie will meet you in Wilmington and you can stay with her until you start school, get settled, and all," Mrs. Blanchard said. "Come on, let's sit over there." A list of instructions, often repeated judging by Emily's reaction, followed.

Katherine had been just like that, Sterling remembered. She wondered if all mothers were this anxious when their children left the nest. She smiled as she caressed her stomach.

I'll probably be like that too.

Sterling flexed her fingers, sat next to Emily, and pretended to doze. She used to be a decent pickpocket, but she hadn't practiced lately. Gray was far better. Conditions weren't ideal either. However, more people arrived to send off or pick up passengers. That helped a pickpocket. It was even more helpful that the airline ticket was hanging halfway out of Emily's pocket. Sterling could steal it with no problem. She also bet Emily's parents would hang onto their daughter until the last minute.

The family held hands as they sat for their last face-to-face conversation in a while. Sterling waited for her chance.

"I've got to go to the bathroom," Emily whispered to her mother.

Sterling roused, bent down to fiddle with her bag, and dropped her own airline ticket to St. Louis in front of the seat beside her. Then she stood, yawned, and ground her foot on her ticket. Foot still on the ticket, she stretched, pivoted to pick up her bag, and managed to slide the ticket under a seat further away from her. As she walked toward the bathroom she glanced back to see her ticket rested on the floor near a discarded candy wrapper. She smiled.

"Go to the bathroom, but hurry. They're about to board." Emily's mother said. The girl rose and passed Sterling. Between the restroom and the boarding area, Sterling lifted Emily's ticket and stuffed it deep in her own coat.

When she returned to the boarding area, travelers for Wilmington, and those sending them off pressed toward the gate for departure. Sterling wriggled in line, fumbled in her pocket, put her thumb over the name on the ticket, and presented Emily's ticket to the agent with a yawn.

"Let's go," muttered a man behind Sterling in line.

"Didn't get much sleep," she said the ticket agent. "Say, you ever been to Saint Louis?"

"Maybe you can sleep on the plane," the harried Eastern agent muttered while reaching for the next person's ticket.

As Sterling figured, Emily's clinging parents refused to let her go to the tarmac until the last minute. They were probably still issuing final instructions when Sterling climbed the steps to the airplane. She ducked inside the aircraft and didn't hear the cry of alarm when Emily couldn't find her ticket.

Sterling settled in her seat and shut her eyes, pretending she'd fallen asleep. Instead, she counted off the seconds.

One-one thousand, two-one thousand, three-one thousand . . .

The airplane door closed. After what seemed like hours, the plane took off and Sterling relaxed. She felt guilty about lifting Emily's ticket. The poor girl had seemed excited about starting a new adventure. Sterling hoped that her own escape hadn't derailed Emily's.

She drew in a deep breath, smelling citrus as though someone in the back had just pealed an orange.

Better.

Sterling folded her arms across her chest and closed her eyes.

If Emily had managed to stop the plane, the whole thing would all be dismissed as a mistake when Sterling showed her Eastern ticket and demanded a search in the terminal. The agent at the gate might even remember Sterling had mentioned St. Louis. More important right then, someone may have found her St. Lous ticket, so Sterling needed to get off the airplane the moment it landed and run.

The bump of the wheels on runway in Wilmington woke her.

As she left the terminal nobody followed her, she was sure. She had left one pursuer in an alley without pants. Now she was positive he hadn't been replaced. Time to settle. People got lost in a city, a big city like Philadelphia. She hopped a bus to Pittsburgh and took a train into Philadelphia.

Sterling didn't want her baby born in the South, and her destination was big and close enough to drive home to Boston in five or six hours if she needed to. She whispered an apology to Danny, who had hated all Philadelphia sports teams.

Besides, she had an important contact there—a master forger she'd used once while in Justice Tomorrow. She'd debated the wisdom of contacting him, but she needed several quality forged documents in a hurry to get a job and a room. She could make passable drivers licenses, but for marriage licenses and death certificates, she needed a pro.

Once she had several new identities, Sterling picked one and found a cheap apartment. With money running low, she should look for a job, but figured she'd find one quick enough. Instead, she set off to find out more about the man who had followed her.

Sterling took a city bus to the massive white Park Central Library on Vine Street. Using the microfiche and a reader machine, she poured over copies of the *Atlanta Journal* and *Constitution* newspapers as well as a dozen Atlanta magazines and smaller publications. Thanks to a librarian's help, she found City Directories of Atlanta to see if she could find Atlanta Investments. It wasn't listed.

After more searching, she finally gleaned that J. D. Masterson, the man in the picture with Marshal Cooper, appeared in business news sections occasionally, as did newcomer Tom Foster and dozens of old Georgia gentry. She wrote down the names of the men who appeared in stories or photos with the Fosters or J. D. Masterson. One or two sounded familiar, but she couldn't imagine why. Jefferson Davis Pollack's name probably stuck out because it was so old South. Other names nudged at her memory, but she shoved them aside. All the names and faces began to blur together.

The same circle of men golfed together, joined the same civic clubs, belonged to the same political party, and attended the same charity balls. She could find nothing about the new owner of Bellamy in Albany. The previous owner was a long-time Albany native who sold the company because he wanted to retire.

Brian Foster, Tom's father, worked as president of First National of Atlanta. She wondered if the bank had an account for Atlanta Investments or if it was connected at all. Sterling would bet her last dime someone with Atlanta Investments was hell bent on destroying Justice Tomorrow.

As it turned out, she didn't have a dime to waste on betting. Finding a job wasn't that easy.

Sterling needed to find work or starve, and the next two weeks of job searching shook her. Getting employment should have been easy—after all, she wasn't interviewing to be vice president of General Motors.

No one wanted to hire a pregnant woman.

Walking home from another futile job interview, she noticed a Help Wanted sign in the window of a local bar and grill: "Short order cook needed." She pushed the front door open.

The place had a homey feel. Pennants from every Philadelphia sports team dangled from the ceiling over the bar and framed snapshots of athletes dotted the wall. In the four corners of the place, big old televisions had been set on large shelves. Each dining table had a green and white checkered tablecloth, some more stained than others, and an artificial flower in a clear vase. The wood panels made it seem dark, but the lights—old enough to be labeled antiques—provided a warm glow.

A short man whose belly drooped over his belt greeted her with a nod. He didn't move from his chair at the cash register at the front door, but his sad eyes followed her. Those eyes and his drooping jowls reminded Sterling of the Deputy Dawg cartoons she had once watched on television, and she warmed to the man at the counter.

"Madeline Stevenson," Sterling said, using the alias on her forged driver's license. "I've come about the short order cook job."

"Horace DelVecchio." He glanced over the bar at her slightly rounded stomach and shook his head.

"I'm a good cook . . . fast and clean. I can even fry chicken if that's on your menu," she said. To call attention to it, Sterling played with the gold band on her finger that she'd picked up in a pawn shop.

"Burgers, cheesesteaks, pastrami," Horace said. "Some fancy salads for da ladies."

"Even better. I can turn those out in a hurry. I worked in a kitchen down in Georgia for a while before my husband took a job here . . ." She took a long pause after that lie and licked her lip for effect. "My husband and his parents died in a car crash about a month after we moved here. I just found out about . . . I need the job."

"You're hired," called a voice from the back of the house. Horace and Sterling turned to see a brunette with grey streaks in her hair striding to the front. She untied her dirty cook's apron as she walked and tossed it at Horace.

He looked stricken as he caught the apron.

"I'm done, Horace DelVecchio. So-long, bye-bye, tootle-loo. I'm out. I can be a short-order cook in that hole or a wife at home but I ain't gonna be both no more." As she passed, she grabbed her coat off a nearby hook and flounced out.

In the silence that followed Sterling cleared her throat and held out her hand for the apron. "I can start now."

The bar and grill kitchen produced a lot of food for its space. Horace employed a dishwasher, two waitresses, and a college student who waited tables on weekends.

While the waitresses hurried back and forth with trays of food, the swinging doors let in the sounds of friends talking, laughter, and whoops of delight. Horace's bar and grill was a place where men could bring their families to eat and return at night to drink in peace.

Behind the doors, however, the wait staff shouted orders, swore at each other, pounded on the counter to hurry Sterling, rolled their eyes when she asked them to help, and complained about Horace.

With a sigh Sterling reached for an order, read it, opened the refrigerator, and grabbed for beef slices to put on the grill. The smell and feel of raw met hit her. Suddenly, the wind swirled, and the crackle of twigs gathered around her, a bramble bush grew around her. She saw Gray's face, heard him whisper to be still.

"No!" She staggered into the counter.

"Hell yeah, two more," Donna, the oldest waitress, said. "You drunk?"

Sterling tossed the steaks on the grill without a word. Her mouth had dried up.

"New girl, youse slow as Christmas," the youngest waitress said and tossed an order slip next to Donna's.

Was Gray in danger? Maybe not, since she was able to shake off her voodoo spell. Or maybe she was getting better at controlling those visions. As she flipped beef strips, she tried to imagine what had triggered it. Fear? Exhaustion? The urge to strangle the wait staff?

Donna pounded the metal countertop next Sterling. "Hey! You workin' here or what?"

"Damn, this place stinks," Toni muttered.

Sterling sluffed off everything for a few weeks, but swollen feet and exhaustion toppled her.

"If y'all hate it here so much," Sterling snapped to the waitresses, "quit!"

Donna cocked her hip. "I got a husband with no job and two teenagers that eat like wolves."

"How long you look for a job before you landed here? Or was this your first choice?" said Toni, the high school drop-out who lived with her mother and cleaned house for a neighbor.

Orville Mason, the Black dishwasher, said nothing. Sterling thought she heard him chuckle under his breath, however.

"Ahh-h!" Sterling squawked. She tossed her spatula across the grill, slumped on a nearby stool, and rubbed her hands over a clean corner of her apron. The smell of burning peppers filled the kitchen. The kitchen staff screeched to a halt in shock. Orville ran over to save the scorched meat and a few onions on the griddle.

"Ah, look, it ain't you," Orville told her as he flipped the meat and pepper strips. "Tips are bad, everything back here's half-broke, and Horace's wife was a bitch."

"Nobody wants her back," Donna said.

"I can't get the smell of meat and onions out of my clothes," Sterling moaned, unable to spit out everything that aggravated her about the bar and grill. "Dogs follow me home."

"Like the two-legged ones that follow Toni?" Donna asked.

Toni gave Donna a cheery middle-finger salute.

The kitchen staff laughed for the first time since Sterling's arrival.

As the weeks went by, Sterling gave up walking to work and spent the extra money to ride the bus. She pushed to keep up with orders during the rush. Once she dropped off to sleep on the cot in the bar's storage room after closing. Orville woke her when he finished his own work, handed her a spare key to the back door, and left without a word. She kept forgetting to return it.

Earning a living shoved Atlanta Investments and its president J. D. Masterson to the back of her mind.

"Later," Donna called one night as she searched for her coat.

Instead of answering, Orville banged pots in the deep wash sink.

"Hey, what's happenin' with you?" Donna asked.

"My wife got canned," Orville announced.

"Geez. Sorry. Dat's tough. Nuthing's getting any cheaper." Donna said.

Sterling's coat no longer buttoned around her. The sole of Orville's left shoe flapped loose.

"Orville, how long were you a Navy cook?" Sterling asked.

His forehead furrowed. The lines around his mouth deepened as he stared at her.

"Your tattoos," Sterling said. "Plus, half the time you mimic my movements at the griddle."

Orville grunted. "Eight years."

"No kidding, Orville," said Donna. "You was a cook in the Navy? They have some good eating on ships. See you guys, I'm outta here."

Orville's wet fingers took the cigarette out of his mouth, and he flicked ashes in the nearby trash can. "Your tip share's on the counter over there."

Donna scooped up a pile of bills and change, counting as she headed for the door. She stopped short. "Hey!"

Sterling checked her own tip share. The bar and grill had been bursting with customers. Tips should be better.

"Where's all the money goin'?" Donna asked.

Orville rolled his eyes toward the front of the house.

"I'm sick of being short-changed. I'm gonna figure this out," Sterling declared as she untied her apron. Donna slammed the door as she left.

With a sigh Sterling searched for her coat and wished for Gray. He had a logical mind that could find the problem in half the time it would take her.

"Wait. I'm walking youse to the street. Saw another guy pissing in the alley when I took out the trash," Orville said.

40

CHAPTER SEVEN: A STORM BREWS

The usual gathering of men in the small Mullinsville grocery on the Black side of town mourned the injustice of Billy Dodson's death.

One by one, men with furrowed brows and taut lips came to the store after supper. Most brought whiskey or homebrew. Tobacco wasn't enough tonight. The pot-bellied stove smoked a little, making their eyes burn with bitterness and sting with helpless rage. They sipped in silence, sharing the kind of communal grief Gray had known too often.

That February afternoon the Warren County inquest had ruled Billy's death accidental. Two deputies and a couple of the young Black men got into a dust-up afterward, but Sheriff Jim Taylor had cooled things down.

"Them fools could of gotten themselves killed today," said a man with a huge gap between his two front teeth.

"I seen it all. I expect the deputies ain't gonna forget it neither," said Moses McKay, a local farmer. He stomped his heels against the outside of the front door sill to get the mud off his shoes and searched for a place to sit.

"I reckon we need to gather up a little more money for the widow," the storekeeper said.

"Pastor's doing that Sunday during services," Gray said. "Least that's what he told me after the hearing."

"Looks like it gonna rain again tonight," said the storekeeper.

"It ain't right!" Moses cried. "None of it!"

Several of the men muttered. One pounded his cane on the floor hard enough to rattle the cans on the shelf next to him.

"Spring's gonna be a stormy one. Kin feel it in my bones already," said the storekeeper. He probably knew, as Gray did, that his store—the one people in the Black community depended on—would be the first place whites would trash if trouble came.

Something flashed outside the window. Gray sat up straighter on his seat and strained to see into the dark.

"I'm thinking those crops we—" a man in faded red suspenders began but stopped when he glanced out the window. "God Almighty!"

A group of young men burst into the store. They seemed to move as one, with one purpose. The store regulars shoved back their chairs. A few got to their feet. Others half rose and went back into their seats again.

"Lord God, boys!" cried one.

The oldest man around the stove shoved someone aside and grabbed a young man's arm.

"Booker, put that gun away!" he cried.

"I cain't," Booker said as he shifted his weight on his other foot and covered the pistol with his coat. "We tired of waiting for justice. We gotta take us some now. Those white men gotta pay for what they did to Billy."

"Well, if it isn't Ezekiel Tone." Gray stared at his brother when he used the alias. Silver gave him the kind of sly, mischievous smile Gray had seen so often right before his brother jumped in the mud or swiped a piece of pie. Only this time he had that gun with the chipped handle in his belt.

"Nobody gonna stop us," Silver told Gray.

"How many guns you got?" Gray asked.

The young man in the front answered for Silver, "Tru's gone home to get his shotgun, so even if none of y'all joins us, we got a dozen."

"'Joins you," an old man repeated. "You want us to join you?"

"That's good you got so many of them guns." Gray pursed his lips and rubbed his chin. "That's real good, because I counted more than a dozen on the deputies at the courthouse today. How many you count, Moses?"

"At least that many. Every deputy I seen had a shotgun and a handgun," McKay said.

"That's not counting the city pigs," Gray said.

"Hm-m, a dozen or more there," Booker's grandfather said.

"Say, who you gonna go after first?" Gray pointed to Booker.

"The two white men testifyin' at the courthouse today," shouted the teenager standing by Booker.

"They's the two done the killing," another added.

"There's a dozen more helped 'em out," muttered an old man with freckles across his cheeks. "Gonna kill them too?"

"You got a plan, my brothers?" Gray asked.

"We gonna grab 'em and kill 'em!" shouted a young man with a crooked nose.

The old men groaned collectively and shook their heads. The man with the cane thumped it on the floor.

"Then we grab a couple more," another young man added. He clenched his fists.

"Okay. No plan. Any you been in a gunfight?" Gray asked.

Silence.

"Well, sir, there's a first time for everything," Silver sneered and fingered his gun.

His friends cheered.

"You're starting a war. Don't make no mistake about what's you're doing." Gray stood.

"You goddamn fools!" the store owner growled. "After you kill them white men, you gotta be watching your house and your wife and your mother and your chilun ever' minute. Sure as you're living, they'll come at you and ever' other Black!"

"We ready!" shouted one young man. Only one or two voices joined him.

"Tell him he's wrong, Booker!" The man who held his grandson's forearm shook it to catch Booker's attention. "Go on, boy, tell him how you're gonna protect yur mama."

"I'll keep my gun cocked and ready," Booker said.

"When you gonna sleep?" McKay asked.

"Who's gonna save my store?" The storekeeper turned to one of the young men. "You?"

"This ain't no game, boys," another old man said. "People gonna die. People right here in this room."

The fire in the stove popped and two of the young men flinched. The air in the store felt as hot as the coals.

The store door eased open, and someone slipped out.

Booker dropped his eyes from his grandfather's. "Maybe we need to get us a plan first."

"Maybe we need help getting our justice. From people who ain't afraid," Spittle from Silver's mouth shone in the firelight from the stove belly.

"Brother Booker, I heard you talked once about a voter registration drive . . . and a march to the courthouse," Gray said.

"Getting our people to the polls—things bound to change then," McKay said.

"We could elect us a sheriff and a town council," another man added.

A few scattered murmurs in the little store sounded for it. The older men remained silent.

"He might be right, Booker," Silver said. "White folks in Washington talking about ways to loosen the hold Southern whites have on the ballot box."

"You get Black politicians, things will change," Gray said. "The Reverend Martin Luther King Junior already showed the way."

"You mean, voting?" Silver's eyes grew wide, and his mouth curled in a half-smile.

"Voting." It dawned on Gray that a voting rights drive may have been Silver's goal all along.

The young men murmured: "He's right," "Good idea," and "Let's get the vote."

"Let's get all our people voting," Booker hollered. "We'll organize, march to City Hall and register."

"I'm with Booker. Who's with us?" Silver smirked at his brother before he backed out of the door, the last of the young warriors to leave.

The young men piled out of the store still shouting about voting rights and Billy Dodson's death.

For a long time, the men in the store shuffled their feet and studied the floor. The sound of their deep breathing filled the air. Gray felt a nudge against his shoulder.

"Have a pull." Booker's grandfather offered him a bottle of Tennessee sipping whiskey.

Gray helped himself, feeling the heat spread from his throat to his toes. Silver and the other hot heads needed a place for all that anger. He supported Silver in the voter drive efforts even though he doubted the pastor would. What else could he do? He only hoped the drive wouldn't attract the kind of attention that would get them both killed.

CHAPTER EIGHT: THE SWITCHEROO

On her breaks Sterling made an excuse to walk around the front of the bar and grill and finally saw the thievery in action. A familiar zing raced through her. Solving a mystery, even a small one like how Horace stole tips, made her feel like herself again.

"Every so often he slips his hand into the cigar box where everybody puts their tips and eases the folding money between the pages of the phonebook under the bar." Sterling demonstrated it to Orville and Donna.

Orville scrubbed the spatula in his hand and took the cigarette out of his mouth. "He missin' steaks and booze."

"I can't use whiskey, and I don't want steaks," Sterling said. "Sorry. I'm not mad at you."

"I'm mad at Horace, the big idiot." Donna slapped her plump hand flat on the kitchen counter.

"I gotta fix this," Sterling said almost to herself. "I can fix this."

"How?" Donna asked.

"Youse gonna get us all fired." Orville's head bopped in the direction of the big refrigerator. "Take a steak home."

"I got a better idea." Flipping onions and green peppers wasn't Sterling's only skill. Gray may have the more analytical mind, but she was the master of clever solutions to the problems he saw. "I'm gonna need this big empty pickle jar."

The next evening Sterling enlisted Donna in her plan.

At the height of the rush Sterling walked out of the kitchen waving two ten-dollar bills pulled from an apron pocket of jangling coins and folding money. Talking a blue streak and gesturing wildly about paying a debt, she handed it to Horace for change.

Grumbling, he adjusted himself on the stool behind the register and dipped into the cash. Several customers eyed Sterling's protruding belly, so she gave them a friendly wave. The women smiled back.

When Horace handed her the change, she clucked. "I gave you two twenties. Look here, would ya? Ya gave me a bunch of ones and two fives, I need two tens and four fives." She figured diners at two or three tables could hear.

"Not four fives."

"Four tens and four fives, Horace. What's the matta with ya?" Sterling said.

Horace became more flustered. "Get on back to da kitchen."

"Give me the right change." Sterling noticed customers had stopped eating to listen.

Donna strolled up with money in her hand and stopped beside Sterling. "Got a check here. What's da hold-up?"

"Let me help." Sterling came around the edge of the bar to the cash register, knocked over the tip box, spilling its contents everywhere and sending the telephone book it was sitting on sprawling upside down. Donna crowded behind her.

"Sorry. Clumsy," said Sterling.

Horace scrambled to pick up the money on the floor, Sterling squatted awkwardly to help, but not before letting her right hand wander through the money in the drawer. She slipped a wad behind her and another into Donna's apron.

"Oh look, at all the tip money," Sterling squealed as Horace squatted to pick bills and coins from the floor. She stood and began to count. "Wow! Good night, huh?"

Horace scowled at her and nearly bumped his skull on the edge of the open register as he stood.

"Yo! What's goin' on over here?" One of the regular customers piped up. He half-rose from his seat at a nearby table.

Sterling announced to the packed restaurant. "We appreciate your tips, and you guys coming to eat with us. Don't we, Horace?"

"Uh, sure," Horace stammered.

Sterling grasped the gallon pickle jar she'd left behind the counter and set it up on the end of the bar. "We all work hard to be good to you. I think we ought to put this tip jar on the counter so you can all see how good you are to us!"

Donna beamed and nodded to the patrons. "Youse the best, guys. Right, Toni?"

Toni, who was busy serving drinks across the room, jerked up and grinned like she understood what was going on. "Hell, yeah!"

Everybody cheered like the Eagles had scored a touchdown.

Grabbing at money in the till with barely a look, Horace thrust two twenties and two fives at her. "Get to work. We got customers here."

Sterling and Donna counted the take back in the kitchen.

"Dat rat," quipped Donna, "he's been cheating us something crazy."

The staff took home extra cash that night, and Horace never said a word to anyone about missing money from the cash drawer. However, he gave Sterling the stink eye every time she came near. After that, the kitchen staff had more tip money because Horace could not fudge the amount that came in. Customers became more generous tippers with the glass jar of money on display.

"I owe ya," Donna told Sterling.

Sterling bet Horace thought the same thing.

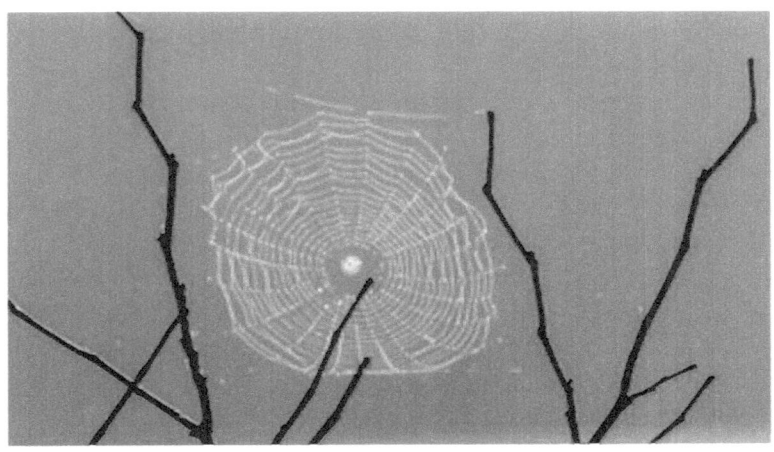

CHAPTER NINE: BLOODY SUNDAY

Gray loved Sunday nights, although this Sunday in early March was damp. The boarding house where he, Pastor Charlie Dixon, and two boarders ate dinner served ham and beans on Sunday. Afterwards, Gray settled in with the pastor for their regular finger of whiskey and the *ABC Sunday Night Movie* on television.

The whiskey served by the pastor went down smooth, tasting mellow and expensive. The conversation ranged from baseball to the rainy weather that kept farmers from the fields to Ernie Terrell's unanimous decision over Eddie Machen in the heavyweight boxing title to the bombing campaign in Vietnam.

After a few Sundays, Gray wondered why Pastor Dixon never mentioned the civil rights marches roiling the South or figures like the Rev. Martin Luther King Junior and Stokely Carmichael. In fact, he refused to discuss the movement at all.

Worse, two leaders of the voter registration drive had come asking for the pastor's blessing from the pulpit and been refused.

"You're not going to keep a lid on those young men for long," Gray had said.

"I'm sheltering you and your brother," the pastor had said. "That's all I got in me."

Gray waited for a Sunday night to raise the issue again.

Occasionally, the pastor invited another man to join their Sunday after-dinner soiree—the storekeeper, the man who clerked at the small dry goods store, a farmer down the road, or a clergyman who was passing by. Most homes didn't have color television sets much less fine liquor, so the men prized Pastor Dixon's invitation. During the week and on Saturday, the pastor opened his home, and anyone could come in to watch television even when he wasn't there.

Sundays were by-invitation-only.

As they dodged mud puddles on their way to the pastor's house after the ham and bean dinner, Gray stopped in the middle of the street.

"Pastor . . ." Gray pointed to the man's small, two-story house where a light burned downstairs. "You expecting company tonight?"

The pastor hurried across the street.

Gray's stomach lurched. Someone dead? Had he been identified somehow? His first instinct was to run, but he forced himself to walk.

Pastor Dixon strode in his front door and thrust a hand on his hip. A faint smell of cigar smoke lingered in the air.

"I could've sworn I locked my back door."

"Well, it was open when I pushed it in," said Sheriff Jimmy Taylor. He stood flat-footed in the middle of the room, both hands stuffed in the waist of his jeans.

Gray gripped the newel post of the staircase in the pastor's foyer. Sweat broke out all over him.

"I guess since you're the big bad county sheriff you don't bother to knock anymore?" Pastor Dixon said.

"You don't knock at my door—you just come on in and take a seat," laughed Jimmy. He walked across the living room and slapped the pastor on the back. Pastor Dixon grinned and hugged the big white man. The sheriff looked as solid as an Army tank.

Gray gaped.

"Jimmy, I been wanting you to meet Joe Peters from Ocala, Florida. He's my late cousin's oldest boy and he's helping around the church. You remember Fervis, that real short cousin of mine from Memphis?"

Jimmy eyed Gray. "You look too tall to be Fervis' son."

"I'm a throwback." Gray forced a smile. The sheriff didn't offer to shake hands. Instead, he used one of his palms to smooth his brown hair that had grown long enough to curl in places.

"You need a haircut, Jimmy. You lookin' like a girl," Pastor Dixon said.

The sheriff grunted. "My boy says I'm 'cool.'"

"Well then, 'cool.' Guess that's all there is to say," chuckled the pastor.

"That must have been a mighty fine supper, Charlie," Jimmy said. "I've been waiting here for ten minutes. Martha baked an extra pound cake, and I left it on the kitchen table. She said if you don't send me home reeking of cigar smoke, she'll have roast beef next time you sneak in my back door. Say Thursday?"

"We'll not be lighting up tonight, gentlemen," Pastor Dixon announced.

"Now that's a shame," Gray said.

"Have a seat, folks, let me pour," the pastor said.

"Your congregation know you smoke cigars and serve liquor?" Jimmy laughed and confided to Gray. "Some of the best I've tasted."

"A chosen few," chuckled Pastor Dixon.

Everybody knew. Gray heard the older women of the church fussing about it all the time. Besides, on Mondays anybody who came over complained the pastor's home smelled like a barroom.

Gray accepted a glass of whiskey without ice, took a seat near the sheriff, and wondered if he could plead exhaustion to slip away. He gulped his first taste.

"You two been friends long?" Gray asked by way of conversation.

"Ever since I can remember." Jimmy leaned back in the chair and moved the ottoman over to rest his feet. "Charlie's the finest man I know—colored or white. I love him like a brother. But don't tell him."

The pastor handed Jimmy a glass with ice and whisky and took a seat nearby. The ice in his glass rattled as he kicked the ottoman.

"You can't have my footrest, Jimmy. I'll share, but you can't hog it."

"Oh, all right." Jimmy leaned over to shove the ottoman closer to the pastor.

The pastor winked at Gray. "He's trying to be a good man. It just comes harder to some."

"Whoa now." The sheriff chuckled. "Here's the man who swept floors and tended bar in a whore house to earn his way through seminary."

"God forgive me." The pastor shook his head as the two men laughed. "At least I repented my sinful ways, Jimmy."

The sheriff smirked. "Saturday somebody stole two chickens from Angus Martin up on Oak Ridge. You know anything about that?"

Pastor Dixon sipped from his glass. "I repented most of my sinful ways."

Ah, now Gray understood something that had puzzled him after service today. As she came out of worship, a woman who had been burned out had thanked the pastor for two hens that her rooster was glad to see. Gray saw Pastor Dixon in a new light.

For a long time, Pastor Dixon and Sheriff Taylor reminisced, recalling their boyhood days when Mullinsville prospered. The three of them deplored the rainy weather, the closing of the town's only hardware store, the potholes on Main Street that were deep enough to swallow a man whole, and pondered the ways Mullinsville could rise from the dead.

Jimmy Taylor had an easy laugh and quick wit. Gray began to relax.

"I hear there's gonna be a voter registration drive," Jimmy said.

Gray's heart dropped to the floor. How had the sheriff learned about it?

"Everybody got a right to vote, Jimmy," Pastor Dixon said.

Jimmy tossed back his drink, and his friend poured another round. Pastor Dixon hoisted his glass to his friend.

"You're taking up more than your share of the footstool, Charlie."

"You've got big feet." The pastor got up to turn on the big boxy television set positioned across the room and consulted *TV Guide* magazine. "Let's see, tonight we have *Judgment at Nuremberg* starring Spencer Tracy and Burt Lancaster."

"I miss the old Capitol Theater downtown. There's nothin' like a big screen at the movie house," Jimmy said as the logo for *The ABC*

Sunday Night Movie came into focus. "The velvety soft feel of the seats . . ."

"Hard as rocks chairs in the colored balcony," the pastor said as he turned off the overhead light.

The only lamp that remained burning threw enough light to see the three faces. Jimmy had his head laid back against the chair. The march-style drums and echoing trumpets of the movie's theme music matched Gray's heartbeat.

"Last call," the pastor declared.

Gray couldn't decide if that buzz through his body was a warning or if he'd down his liquor too fast.

A German march song filled the screen as the movie began. The screenplay showed Nazi persecution of Jews, concentration camps, and people the Nazis had marked as inferior being beaten. Gray found it riveting from the start and glanced at his companions to see what they thought.

Jimmy slumped in his chair. The pastor rubbed his chin.

Suddenly a news bulletin from ABC broke into the movie. News anchor Frank Reynolds began reporting on a peaceful voter registration march in Selma, Alabama that had turned violent. The film footage taken earlier that day focused on the five hundred marchers crossing the Edmund Pettus Bridge.

"My God," Gray said.

As two of the marchers knelt in prayer, Alabama State Troopers plowed into a peaceful, unarmed line of marchers at the foot of the bridge. Mounted horsemen, led by the Selma sheriff, rode into the crowd beating marchers with clubs. Black bodies, men and women, lay on the bridge. Blood flew everywhere. Officers fired tear gas into the retreating crowd of Blacks and charged them with nightsticks.

The television footage picked up the sheriff's voice telling his posse, "Get those goddamned niggers. And get those goddamned white niggers."

"Jesus H. Christ," Jimmy groaned.

Pastor Dixon rose as though someone had pulled a string attached to the top of his head. Gray's hand covered his mouth to stop a cry and found tears rolling down both cheeks.

The three men stared at the televised mayhem in silence. At some point Jimmy gravitated to Pastor Dixon's side. At the end, Pastor

Dixon flicked on the overhead light and seemed to freeze by the switch.

"Almighty God. There's no turning back after this." He heaved a sigh of resignation, as though no one else was around.

The sheriff cleared his throat. "I hope to God this ugliness don't come here."

"After my Darlene was killed, I swore I'd never get involved in the integration fight again," Pastor Dixon mumbled.

"They had no call to kill your wife, Charlie." The sheriff leaned close to whisper in his friend's ear.

The kitchen phone rang, and nobody moved to answer it.

"I almost lost my mind. You got me through it, Jimmy," Charlie Dixon said with tears in his eyes. "But we're coming to vote. After today . . . better help folks accept it."

Jimmy shook his head. "It won't sit well. Up to you and me to see nothing gets out of hand."

"We're coming," the pastor intoned.

"Charlie, don't. Let this blow over. You know I looked away on a lotta things." The sheriff glared at Gray. "A whole lotta things."

The telephone rang.

"Ain't no turning back," the pastor said.

The two men stared into each other's eyes for a moment. Jimmy swiped tears off his cheek.

"Guess I'd best be getting on home. Martha's baking your favorite cake for you—devil's food."

His joke fell flat.

"See ya Thursday night," Jimmy said.

"I'll see you at the courthouse," the pastor said to his friend's back.

The telephone rang again.

CHAPTER TEN: HOPE SPRINGS ETERNAL

Could she go home to Boston? The birds were chirping about the warmer weather of late April and a few crocuses were blooming. Spring and a feeling of rebirth filled the streets and the back of Horace's bar and grill. Things were different in the front of the house, however. After the tip jar incident, Sterling got frosty nods from Horace at best.

The joyous idea of going home to have her baby made Sterling forget to be afraid. She still watched for anything out of the ordinary and took a different bus to work once a week. Still, like the flocks of birds flying north to nest, returning to the nest seemed possible.

It was time for her to go home.

She hummed as her shift started at the bar and grill. Customers piled in before noon and she hardly had time to breathe between orders.

"New customers." Toni reported the news with a big smile as she pushed through the black swinging doors. "Heavy tippers, too."

"Oh, yeah. I seen them guys yesterday," Donna said. "Walking up and down the streets like city workers."

Sterling stopped, frozen between the hot stove and griddle. She started to untie her apron and run.

"Good lookin" too," Toni warbled.

Heart in her throat, Sterling tried to sound casual. "What were those handsome guys doing?"

"Seachin' for some pregnant woman wandered off from her rich husband," Donna said as she carried an order out the swinging doors.

Toni's eyes fell to Sterling's belly. "You ain't rich, are ya?"

"Loaded." Sterling rolled her eyes. "I work here for the fun of it. Order up, Toni."

Sterling inhaled sharply. She couldn't leave in the middle of her shift. But she would vanish tonight. Where could she run?

She couldn't concentrate. Half the time she made stupid mistakes on orders. Hot grease popping from the griddle burned her hands and arms. She mixed up orders. Donna came back through the doors waving two sheets off her order pad.

"Hey," Donna groused. "Where's the peppers?"

Sterling fumbled her spatula and nearly spilled beef strips onto the floor.

"What's going on here?" Donna dumped out some overdone French fries from the fryer and fixed a side order herself. Sterling thanked her with a small smile and turned some sausages so they wouldn't burn. Where was Orville? He was late.

She had started to worry when he crept in the back room and hung up his coat.

"Hey, Orville? Man, are we busy tonight," she called as she sliced more onions.

"What's that! Yeah, well, I see my sink all piled up." He pointed at it and roared, "I told nobody to pile dishes in both sinks!"

Work in the kitchen stopped. Donna licked her lips. Toni stopped chewing her gum and put one hand on her hip. Sterling's mouth dropped.

"What the hell you lookin' at?" Orville snarled.

"Looking for the dog that bit your ass." Donna picked up two sandwiches and fries then threw her hip against the swinging doors to get out.

A crash in the front of house paused the kitchen labor for a split second. Sterling jumped toward the outside door. Nobody yelled for help, and nobody rushed in to grab her, so she went back to her routine until closing.

"Tonight was a bear," Donna muttered as she left for the night.

"I can't wait to get home," Sterling told Orville when they were alone. "I'm beat."

"C'mawn, go home," Orville said. He turned from a full sink of dishes. "Horace needs to hire somebody to help ya."

"Oh yeah? Where'd I get da money? From youse?"

Sterling and Orville raised their eyebrows when Horace pushed open the swinging black doors. Their boss had never entered the kitchen the entire time Sterling had been at the bar and grill. Now he leaned on the countertop she had just cleaned to take the weight off his feet.

"Look, girlie"— Sterling never believed Horace knew her name— "I didn't care who you was long as you could cook. But the guys that came in asking about a pregnant girl? I know their type. I don't want trouble." Horace handed her an envelope full of cash. "Here's your pay. Go."

Her heart and her feet throbbed in a painful, panicked rhythm. The image of a tan sedan in Boston rushed back. Where could she go?

"Now what am I gonna do?" Horace flung his hands in the air. "I gotta get another cook."

"Orville," she said. "He was a Navy cook."

Horace gave Orville the once over and muttered something.

Orville stood tall, his hands dripping over the sink.

"What about the dishes?" Horace said at last.

"Hire that worthless nephew you bitch about," Sterling snapped.

Horace shuffled toward the front of the house. "Start tomorrow, Orville."

"How about money?" Sterling called.

"What about it?" Horace said.

"Orville's an experienced cook. He should get more than you paid me."

"You ain't the Teamsters, girlie," Horace snarled.

Orville dried his hands, untied his apron, and tossed it aside. Horace glanced at him before turning to Sterling.

"Yeah, yeah. I'll bump it up ten dollars a week. But you!" He pointed at Sterling. "Get outta here."

Horace took out his frustration on the swinging doors. They rocked on their hinges long after he waddled out.

Sterling collapsed on a nearby stool. How had those assailants traced her to Philadelphia? She'd been careful, never walked the same way home, never stayed in a routine. Sterling gave her forehead a slap. The forger she'd used when she came to town was a Justice Tomorrow contact. From now on, she would take the time and make her own licenses and papers. She was a decent forger.

Going home wasn't possible now. She couldn't drag trouble back to Boston. Her bankroll wasn't enough to carry her through the birth, so wherever she landed had to be cheap. Plus, what about the weeks after? She sighed and swiped at the griddle with a wet rag.

"Leave it. Shit," Orville said as he fiddled with something on the sink. "Go home."

Sterling's mouth felt full of cotton.

"Now what?" she said, almost to herself.

Orville grabbed her coat off the hook and tossed it to her. "Here."

Where do pregnant women go when they're poor and alone?

Her chin dropped to her chest. Her chest heaved as she caught her breath.

Orville opened the back door wide.

"Thank you, Orville. Good luck." The words came out in gulps.

"I'm sorry," he muttered, slammed the door behind her and locked it. The click of the lock on the door startled her.

Sterling headed toward her bus stop across the street. She wouldn't miss passing by all these rancid garbage cans or the men like that drunk pissing against the brick wall. Maybe she'd splurge on a taxi.

Too late she realized the man leaning against the wall wasn't relieving himself. His feet crackled and crunched faster and faster on the broken glass and pebbles in the alley behind her. When he got close enough, Sterling stopped, swung around, and kicked him in the groin. While he bent over double, she ran.

As she exited the alley, another man stepped out from nowhere and grabbed her arm.

"Help! Help!" She managed to scream before the man clapped his hand across her mouth. The thug from the alley kept one hand on his groin and grabbed her arm with the other. The two men dragged her toward the street where a black car waited, its idling engine sending white puffs out the exhaust pipe.

"Hey, what's going on here? Get away from her," a man's voice yelled.

Sterling twisted and bit the bare fingers as they slid across her mouth. The man yelped but continued pulling her toward the car. The door opened. She dug in her heels.

"Police! Hey, help!" called the man again. He sounded closer.

Sterling freed an arm and used it to brace herself against the car.

"Who's there?" called a woman from a second-floor apartment. A light came on, spilled from the apartment upstairs to the car in the street below.

"Let's go! Leave her!" called a man inside the black car.

Her captor shoved her to the ground. The attacker she'd decked in the alley hobbled to the car and got in. The car sped down the street.

"Sonsofbitches," cried Horace. He stood over Sterling shaking his fists at the departing car. "Girlie, you okay?"

She put both hands on the wet, dirty sidewalk, rolled over, and shoved herself to her feet.

Horace had both hands on his knees panting, and finally found enough air to swear hot enough to melt the concrete.

"Youse know dem guys?"

She shook her head. "I never saw them before. They . . ."

"You better get lost fast." Horace said.

She nodded.

"Sons of bitches," Horace said.

Sterling bent off to wipe blood off her leg with a tissue from her coat pocket. "Scraped my knee."

"I don't like you much, girlie. You cost me money," Horace spat out. "But I won't hold still for hurtin' pregnant women."

She needed to get ice on her knee.

"Streets pretty empty this time of night," Horace muttered. "I dropped my paper on the front stoop, or I'd be inside. Well, I'll go call the cops."

Heart still thudding in her throat, Sterling brushed off her coat.

"No, you'll be here all night and so will I. You think those guys will come back?"

He shook his head.

A city bus squeaked and hissed to a stop across the street.

"I'm gonna catch my bus. Thanks. For everything," she called as she hurried across the street.

She got on the bus and sat behind the driver. As the bus pulled away, she saw a light appear in the alleyway by the bar and grill kitchen as though a door had opened. Her heart fell as she realized who had told the men where she was, how to find her, and when to find her alone. Then locked the door behind her.

Her bottom lip trembled, and she bit it to keep from crying.

She had to clear out of her apartment. Orville probably told her assailants where she lived. She hopped off the bus and hurried down the blocks to her apartment. As she reached the apartment building and grabbed her keychain, she touched the spare key to the bar and grill.

Suddenly she knew where she could spend the night in safety. She only had to grab her things and wait until Orville left work. She'd use Horace's phone to call Donna for a favor. Before the bar and grill opened in mid-morning, she'd make some other calls.

She would go where pregnant Catholic girls could find help.

CHAPTER ELEVEN: MARCHING TO VICTORY

April Fool's Day. The date was not lost on Gray as he marched with 50 other fools from Missionary church to the Mullinsville courthouse. His stomach burned and his nerves screamed at him to turn back.

Under a dark sky that spit rain, Pastor Dixon led the singing and marching from the church along Main Street to register to vote. On a tall white pole beside the steps of the courthouse, the American flag and the Tennessee state flag flapped in a stiff wind. Gray gazed over the twin turrets of the stone courthouse as the marchers approached. All he could see of Pastor Dixon was the back of his head. An hour ago, he'd seen fire in the man's eyes and heard brimstone in his voice as Dixon preached to the marchers about the brighter America they were destined to inherit.

Everyone had piled out of the church full of courage and conviction—he saw it in the eyes of his fellow marchers and his own heart soared.

"We shall overcome. . ." the marchers sang.

A white family dragged their little daughter across the courthouse square to avoid the marchers. Gray had seen the girl jumping rope with the seven-year-old girl marching in front of him. He had tried to discourage parents from bringing their children on the march, but her mother wanted her to be part of it all. The woman held tightly to one of the girl's hand, but the child paused to wave at her friend with her free hand.

"Hey, Donna," she called.

The white girl turned at the sound of her name and grinned. Her mother yanked her arm down before she could wave back.

Gray's heart broke.

"Come on, baby girl. Eyes on the prize," said the woman marching in front of Gray. The tone of her voice was firm, but kind. Gray imagined she'd also learned the hard way that white friends didn't stick. He hoped it wasn't a lesson Pastor Dixon was about to learn too.

"Go home!" a white teenager stepped out of the crowd to yell.

". . . overcome someday." The marchers sang louder.

Gray sang along. Nothing would happen today. If they were turned away, or driven away more likely, the marchers would return. Perhaps in greater numbers.

Most marchers were young men and women led by Silver's friend Booker. Singing and waving signs that demanded their rights or mourned Billy Dodson, the protesters moved slowly, ignoring the catcalls and horrified gasps from the whites who had gathered. Gray swallowed hard as he noticed the marchers were outnumbered two to one.

Gray craned his neck to see what was happening in front of him.

Sheriff Jimmy Taylor, flanked by four deputies in tan uniforms, blocked the courthouse door. They must have been there a long time since their uniforms looked damp and drops of rainwater dripped from the bill of their hats. Two other deputies pushed back against the white crowd, which included men armed with rifles and shotguns. The officers were useless in stopping the unruly white crowd, but the sheriff probably knew that. Gray recognized one of the armed white men as the owner of the town's grocery and dry goods store where Billy Dodson's trouble began.

"What's goin' on, Pastor?" Jimmy asked from the top of the steps.

"We came to register to vote," the pastor said.

The white crowd muttered, hollered threats and profanity. Some of the men shook their fists or hoisted the rifles they carried.

"Coons!"

"Jungle bunnies!"

The woman marching next to Gray flinched and hunched her shoulders.

"Hold on," he told her as the march stopped at the foot of the stairs.

Jimmy waved at them all to hush, but he still had to shout to be heard.

"I'm warning ya, don't come up here," he told the pastor. "Y'all go on home now."

"We have a right to vote," Pastor Dixon said, and his supporters murmured in agreement.

"Amen," said the woman beside him. She sang soprano in the church choir, had a quick temper, and two children. Silver had taken a shine to her when they first arrived.

"Preach!" cried the woman behind her.

"Amen!" other marchers yelled.

Pride bloomed in Gray and nudged aside his fear.

"Go back to Africa!" a white man in worn overalls yelled.

"Sonvabitch!" hollered another white man.

More curses and profanity came from the whites. Someone threw an empty glass Coke bottle that Silver dodged. A few rocks thrown by whites landed harmless in the grass in front of the courthouse.

"Step back!" One deputy made a half-hearted attempt to push the whites further to the side.

"Get out, coons!" shouted another white man and added a profanity. The crowd took up his cry.

A few of the older marchers exchanged panicked glances.

"Take one step toward this door and I'll arrest you," Jimmy warned.

"We shall, we shall not be moved." the soprano at Pastor Dixon's elbow began the song and other marchers took it up.

"Go home!" Jimmy cried.

In the distance thunder rumbled, and around the courthouse the charged atmosphere crackled like heat lightning.

Before anyone could stop her, the soprano lifted her chin, stepped around the minister, and climbed the stairs singing more of "We Shall Not Be Moved."

Gasps ran through crowds on both sides of the courthouse square.

"No!" Gray's heart leapt into his throat, and he reached out as though he could stop her.

The soprano's audacity stunned everyone into a momentary silence that erupted into cheers from the marchers and more debris-throwing madness from whites. When the soprano reached the third step, she turned and raised her fist. A crack like a penny firecracker exploded amid the chaos, and the woman crumpled to the stone steps.

Screams, wails, shouts, and cries mixed with the rain that was starting in earnest. People fell over each other in a rush to escape or used their bodies to protect loved ones from gunfire.

"There! There he is!" Silver yelled as he rose above the chaos and pointed to his left. "Over there!"

"Over there!" yelled another marcher as he waved his arms in the same direction.

"Silver!" Gray jumped from the ground and followed his brother's eyes to a flat-faced white man in bib overalls with a rifle in plain sight. The killer had frozen with the stock of his gun resting against his shoulder and his face contorted in hateful rage.

"Get down!" Booker yelled. A rock hit his head, and he reeled back two steps from the blow as he grabbed his temple.

"Help!" Pastor Dixon raised both hands stained with blood from cradling the dead soprano.

"Get him!" Jimmy pointed at the shooter.

Instead of surrendering, the shooter wheeled and ran towards the far side of town. The whites parted to let him by.

A bottle thrown across the courthouse square clipped Silver's forehead and blood dripped down the side of his face.

"Stop!" yelled a deputy as he pursued the shooter at a trot. He left the other deputy struggling to hold back the whites who surged toward the protesters. At last, he stood aside as club-and-bottle-wielding white men raced across the courthouse lawn.

The marchers who hadn't scattered now scrambled to escape the onslaught.

"Goddamn it, stop!" Jimmy commanded his men. "Push that bunch back." Three deputies leapt to obey and waded into the crowd.

"Jesus, help us!" Cries of pain mixed with the marchers' prayers for help as the rain picked up.

A young Black woman with a bandana on her head dropped to her knees in prayer at the base of the steps. A man with scrapes across his cheek put his arms around her and prayed with her.

"Help! God Almighty!" Pastor Dixon wailed, his face turned up to let the rain wash his tears.

"Drop your guns!" Jimmy shouted at the white mob. He held his rifle at the ready but didn't point it or move from the courthouse door.

Screams and curses in the courthouse square nearly drowned out the thunder and lightning overhead. Rain fell harder. The angry whites began to drop back in the face of nature's fury and melted into other streets of town.

Gray staggered through the remaining marchers, dodging the injured. Sobbing, he followed a stream of blood mixed with rain flowing down the courthouse steps. Pastor Charlie Dixon cradled what remained of the young soprano's head and wept.

"Charlie." The sheriff squatted by Dixon's side. "God damnit."

The pastor raised his eyes to Jimmy Taylor. "No going back."

Jimmy pushed his cap brim and repeated, "God damnit."

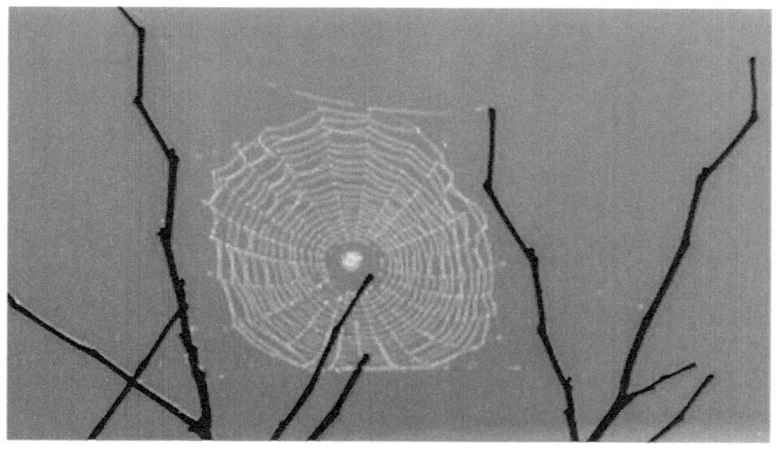

CHAPTER TWELVE: UNWED MOTHERS

In the brilliant light of the late April afternoon, Sterling gazed up at Mary Magdalene House, a large three-story grey stone building set on a hill.

She'd stuffed all she owned in one small blue American Tourister suitcase. After riding five different buses to confuse pursuers, Sterling had reached the end of her money when she got to Trinity, Tennessee. This grim home for unwed mothers on the hill was the furthest place from Philadelphia she could afford.

This had better not be a mistake.

Donna, pretending to be a Mother Superior in Pennsylvania, had called to give Sterling a fine recommendation for a place in the Mary Magdalene House for Unwed Mothers. Sterling hoped it had worked. She came without any assurance she'd be welcome.

When she learned the price of a taxi ride from the bus station to the maternity home, she opted to walk. Besides, trudging between the cracked streets and dodging college students on the sidewalks would do her good after sixteen hours on a bus. She was down to her last $50 and her last fake driver's license—the one she made herself that used her middle name and her mother's maiden name: Margaret Sawyer.

The walk convinced her that this busy college town in the mountains must be beautiful in the summer when all the trees and flowers bloomed. On the other hand, the home for unwed mothers was a monstrosity that no blossoms or blue summer sky could fix. She stopped at the front gate and her upper lip curled in disgust.

The Magdalene House resembled an incongruous mix of 1940s style architecture and a castle from a horror movie. A wrought iron fence encircled the home and protected it with spiked slats. A large, ornate gate opened to a cement staircase that led to the stone house. Big oak and maple trees leaned branches over the fence as though gasping for air and light. The stone, the still-barren trees dripping from a recent rain shower, the faint yellow light through a dirty window upstairs all added to her sense of doom as Sterling trudged toward the gate.

She bet a vampire lived in the basement.

Something struck her shoulder. With a yelp she whirled around, raising the hardbacked suitcase as a shield in front of her. A carload of teenage boys leaned out a Ford Mustang's windows.

"Whore!" yelled one.

Sterling hunkered down near the gate of Magdalene House.

An ear-piercing yell echoed off the stone steps behind her.

"Shoo, boys. I see you, Buddy Tolliver!" cried a nun.

Sterling peeked around the swirl of the nun's black skirt. The car squealed off down the street. With both hands on her hips the woman huffed. "Lord, forgive them for they are but simple-minded, boys."

Sterling lowered her suitcase. "T-thank you, Sister."

"Margaret Sawyer?"

"Yes."

"We've been waiting for you. I'm Sister Agnes. Come with me."

Sterling heaved a sigh of relief that came from her soul.

The home's metal gate screamed like a living creature when the nun opened it wide. As she navigated the wet stone stairs, Sterling rehearsed her story once again. She was a single woman, a victim of rape, a cook from Philadelphia who got in trouble, and needed help. She promised herself the first thing she would do is fall asleep for a week under a mountain of blankets.

"I believe Mother Florence in Philadelphia called for me. A place for someone like me is hard to come by." Sterling was glad to see Donna had played the part of Mother Florence well.

"Oh yes. Mother Florence was real persuasive," Sister Agnes said. The heart-shaped face that peered out of her wimple had staircases of wrinkles on each side.

Huffing and puffing, Sister Agnes ushered her up the two flights of stone steps and into the bleak-looking house. The nun's blue eyes were level with Sterling's and seemed to study the newcomer.

"I run the kitchen here. You want a snack?" Sister Agnes asked.

"Sister, I'm so tired I couldn't eat," Sterling said. "Is there somewhere I can rest, sleep, first?"

"Rest? It's almost suppertime prep time—." Sister Agnes's chins fell over the bottom of her wimple in dismay, but she recovered. "Well, let me take you to Sister Elizabeth. She runs the home."

Sterling followed her down a hall with a threadbare runner on the floor which might once have been red. The smell of scorched meat from a kitchen made her nose wrinkle but roused her stomach. In the hallway, black walnut paneled walls proved perfect showcases for the silver, gold, and alabaster crosses hung on every space not occupied by a portrait of a Pope or Archbishop. At a juncture of two halls and a big staircase, Sister Agnes flung her arm out to direct Sterling into a large comfortable room with thick carpeting, walls that were covered with paintings of the saints, and several comfortable armchairs.

In the back of the room a thin, wisp of a woman in a black nun's habit rose from behind a small desk. When she turned off the light there and came around in front of the desk, she limped as though surprised that old age had overcome her limbs so completely.

"Sister Elizabeth Ann, our new resident has arrived," said Sister Agnes.

"I am so glad to see you, my child." Taking Sterling by the elbow, Sister Elizabeth Ann guided her to the most comfortable chair in the room. The nun might be thin, but her hands felt strong.

"I spoke with Mother Florence about your situation. I'm so glad to meet you in person. As I told her, we usually require families to pay a fee for our program, but she tells me you're an orphan with no money." Sister Elizabeth took her seat across from Sterling and placed her hands in her lap.

Sterling whispered, "I would be glad to do whatever work I can."

The older nun's small brown eyes never left Sterling as she put her hand out in Sister Agnes's direction. "Sister, I forgot my enrollment book and papers. Could you fetch them?"

"Do you have your glasses, Sister?" Sister Agnes asked.

Sister Elizabeth patted her pocket and withdrew a pair of reading glasses. "Yes, thanks."

While Sister Agnes did as she was asked, the older nun stared at Sterling. She remained silent and thoughtful as though taking Sterling's measure.

Finally, Sister Elizabeth said, "We don't accept girls from outside Tennessee, but Mother Florence tells me you are a cook."

"I worked as a short order cook at a bar and grill."

"Hmmm-m." Sister Elizabeth's lips pursed in disapproval at the word 'bar.'

"A cook." Sister Agnes turned from the desk, clutched the book to her chest, her eyes as wide as the smile on her face.

"Philly cheesesteak sandwiches, fried chicken, hamburgers. French fries, salads—those sorts of things. I can also cook a full Thanksgiving dinner."

Sister Agnes sighed wistfully.

"We need a cook at Magdalene House," Sister Elizabeth announced. "To help Sister Agnes in the kitchen."

"What a blessing you've come to us," Sister Agnes said. "That kitchen . . ."

"You will work in our kitchen cooking meals for the girls and the women on staff," Sister Elizabeth broke in. "It's an excellent fit. You'll never have to leave the grounds."

Sterling found that dreadful news. Being cooped up in this grim place until she had the baby might be the literal definition of hell.

Sterling squeaked out, "Cook for how many?"

"Twenty girls and five nuns," Sister Agnes said.

Footsteps and incoherent chatter could be heard from the direction of the wide, ornate, wooden staircase Sterling had seen opposite Sister Elizabeth's office. Someone laughed and others joined her. Sister paused and smiled in the direction of the noise.

"Our girls have free time until supper," Sister Elizabeth said and folded her hands. "Sister Agnes is so happy to have experienced help."

"Just so you know, there's only one cook in the kitchen and that's me," Sister Agnes said.

"Yes, Sister." Sterling rubbed her eyes.

"Oh, gracious, I was so excited about this opportunity for you and for Magdalene House that I forgot how tired you must be," Sister Elizabeth said.

"Exhausted." Sterling nodded. "And nervous."

The nun patted one of Sterling's hands. "Nothing to be nervous about. All the girls here are in the same position of sin and desperation."

Sterling could feel her cheeks grow hot and red.

"You'll find childbirth as natural as breathing," Sister Elizabeth went on. "You'll be fine. You appear strong and healthy."

The enrollment book Sister Agnes handed the older nun was a substantial binder with hundreds of pages and colored tabs. Sister Elizabeth flipped to a form then took out her reading glasses.

"I need to get some information about you and the father of your child, if you know who he is."

"I was raped," Sterling said. "I don't know who the father is. I was too ashamed to report it to the police."

"We will need to discuss expenses," the nun said.

"I have no money. Well, what I brought." Sterling reached for her purse. She felt a twinge of guilt for lying to a nun.

The nun shook her head. "No, no. In lieu of our usual fee, you will be our cook, plan meals, buy supplies, and train a new girl to take over. In addition, we will pay a stipend of two dollars a day for your service."

"B-but what will I live on when I leave?" Sterling asked. Two dollars a day wasn't much.

"All our girls must work to supplement the care they receive, although it doesn't cover the actual cost," the nun said firmly. "When you leave, you will have confidence in your soul, and a sense of peace and righteousness to replace your shame. You will be ready to reclaim your place in society. You can marry someday."

Panic hit Sterling. She and the baby couldn't live on peace and righteousness. When she and the baby met Gray and Silver, she needed something to live on.

The smallest of knocks interrupted Sister Elizabeth before she could continue.

The door opened to admit a younger woman in a brown A-line skirt, brown heels, and white blouse. Her head sported a large animal skin-patterned barrette that held back a voluminous amount of black hair. She wore a blouse with a Peter Pan collar and a sorority pin. A welcoming smile crossed her face, but the hazel eyes that landed on Sterling seemed filled with disdain.

"I'm sorry I'm late, Sister Elizabeth. I just learned we had a new resident."

Sister Elizabeth greeted the newcomer as a penitent child. "Humph, well, we were just about to finish. Helen Abernathy, meet Margaret Sawyer. Miss Abernathy is our counselor. She'll be helping you along your journey to motherhood."

Sterling rose and extended her hand to Helen. The woman's hands felt soft and limp. "Margaret Sawyer from Philadelphia."

"Philadelphia? Sister Elizabeth, you know we don't accept out-of-state women no matter how dire their state." Helen raised one eyebrow.

Who questioned a nun? Sterling cringed, waiting for Divine Retribution.

Instead of a lightning bolt attack or a rap on the younger woman's knuckles, Sister Elizabeth tucked her head down, rearranged some papers on her desk and explained, "We have an opening. She had a need. As it happens, she also has a skill we can use."

"Sister, we do not—."

"Our new client is a cook." Sister Elizabeth lips became a firm line.

"Oh." Helen smiled in understanding. "Margaret Sawyer."

"My friends call me Sterling."

"Do they? How odd," said the counselor.

"A nickname from the school playground," Sterling said.

The older nun cocked an eye at Sterling, rolled a pen between her fingers, and gave her an amused look.

"Well, I hope you will soon feel comfortable," Helen said as though Sterling hadn't spoken. "Here our clients do not have names. Only numbers. Everyone's privacy is protected that way."

"Numbers?" Sterling felt her cheeks burn. "Am I a thing instead of a person?"

Sister Elizabeth appeared to write in her book, but Sterling thought she heard a chuckle.

"You will be One Hundred," Helen announced.

"Easy to remember." Sister Elizabeth handed a slip of paper to Sister Agnes. "Sister, you have a helper."

"Good, the kitchen's been neglected for too long," Sister Agnes said.

"The doctor comes to see all the girls on Tuesdays," Helen said as though Sister Agnes hadn't spoken. She sat down in a chair next to Sterling. "You are about seven or eight months along?"

Sterling nodded.

"Seen a doctor?" Helen asked.

Sterling shook her head, feeling miserable. "No."

"Hmm-m. Well, the doctor can tell us if the baby is healthy," Helen said. "Most of our girls are seven months. We have a long list of Catholic couples eager for a baby to love who will—."

"Sister, I want to keep my baby."

Helen waved her hand at Sterling in dismissal. "Oh, many girls think that in the beginning. That's the reason our counseling sessions should begin at once."

Sterling rolled her eyes.

"As you get closer to delivery you will see it is best for the baby to have a complete family," Helen said a little firmer. "A girl on her own can't provide what a child needs."

"My baby and I will be a complete family."

Sister Elizabeth released a great sigh. "Please. One Hundred, nothing must be decided now. Here is our daily and weekly schedule, sign please. You see we have confession three times a week here at Mary Magdalene House. Chapel is at five every morning and six every evening. Diet and nutrition classes as well as religious training are held before chapel. I'm sure Sister Brigid or one of the girls can help you with the schedule until you get used to it."

"Speaking of schedule. If we want to get One Hundred into the kitchen for dinner prep, we better get at it," said Sister Agnes.

Sterling's jaw dropped.

"Sister Agnes, this poor child looks like a strong wind would blow her over. Let's let her out of kitchen duty tonight," Sister Elizabeth said. "I'll talk with you later, One Hundred."

"Call me Sterling, please. I don't want to be a number."

The old nun studied her a moment. "I understand. We insist on using numbers for your protection and the baby's. This house has been helping girls in trouble for decades. Allow us to help you, One Hundred."

Helen rose and handed several pieces of paper to Sister Elizabeth. The nun sighed, "Oh, yes, sign these other forms. Here's one agreeing to our house rules, another to consider adoption for your child, one to be seen by our doctor, and still another gives permission for Our Lady of Hope Hospital to treat you. Most of our girls deliver there."

"Sister, I want my baby."

Sister Elizabeth smiled so slowly Sterling could trace it from her mouth through the wrinkles on her cheek to the heavy-lidded eyes. "It only says 'consider' adoption, One Hundred."

Sterling took the papers and tried to read them in the poorly lit room as Helen Abernathy peppered her with questions about her home, her parents, her education, her finances. Miss Abernathy snickered when she said she had attended Radcliffe College— information she hadn't meant to give. She couldn't think clearly. When she rubbed her eyes for the third time, Sister Elizabeth held out her hand for the forms.

"Come, One Hundred, let's get you to bed." Sister Elizabeth said. "Sister Agnes, would you show her to her room? She'll be rooming with Fifty-one on the first floor."

"Once you get settled into a routine you will move upstairs with other girls in their third trimester. Girls in the second and third trimester are on the second floor. You will like it here. I hope you brought something from home to hang on your wall," Helen said. "Makes it nicer, I think."

"You'll find a maternity dress on your bed," said Sister Elizabeth. "We give them to all the girls."

"Like uniforms? As in Catholic school?" Sterling hated the idea.

Helen nodded. "We are a Catholic school of a kind. We teach girls who have fallen to be righteous children of God again."

Sister Agnes huffed. "Come on, One Hundred. If you don't get a rest now you'll be of no use in the kitchen after dinner."

Sterling's feet dragged across the worn carpet as Sister Agnes led her around the staircase and down a short hall. She put one hand on the wall to keep her balance.

"We didn't used to have social workers here," Sister Agnes said with a trace of bitterness. "A couple of years ago our board decided we needed professional help. Now we have numbers instead of names. Now we're farming pregnant girls out for work. Huh! Now we have modern thinking that adoption is best for babies. I thought thirty years of helping girls become good mothers was 'professional,' but what do I know?"

She stopped and lifted Sterling's chin up with one finger. "Delivering a new life into this world is noble, my child. Remember that. Your sin will bring such joy to some couple. Here we are."

Sterling blinked to clear her vision. Making love with Tom hadn't felt like sin, it felt like heaven.

The nun knocked and opened a door. Sterling gasped in delight. Deliciously warm and inviting, shades of yellow, pink, and blue twined on the twin bed comforters and pillow shams. Two grey and pink shifts lay across them and a pair of black shoes sat at the foot. A small battered green chest painted in the floral pattern of the bedspread rested at the end of each twin bed. One nightstand in between held the only light, a short wood lamp with a pink shade.

A hollow-eyed girl in her early teens stood beside one bed in a shapeless shift that covered a bulging belly. Her long arms dangled by her sides.

"Fifty-one, meet One Hundred," said Sister. "Now, the bathrooms are down the hall. First floor showers at nine, second floor at nine-thirty until we get the bathrooms fixed upstairs. Lights out at ten."

The girl's smile never crawled past her lips. "Welcome."

"Well, I'll leave you with God's blessing," Sister Agnes said.

When the door closed the teenager pointed to one of the garments on the bed. "That's your shift. It's really comfy. Towels over the rack by your trunk. Your dress is hangin' on the back of the door. I'll show you the bathroom."

Fifty-one smoothed the comforter on her bed before she sat down.

"Sister Elizabeth and Miss Abernathy like order. Acceptance. Repentance," the girl said. "You'll get used to things."

Sterling closed her eyes. She was back in Catholic high school.

"We're lucky to be here. Care, food, friends, chances to worship God, and prepare to bring another life into the world."

Her words barely reached Sterling. The bed. It looked so comfortable. She crawled between the sheets. Sterling felt her muscles scream at the glorious rest. She closed her eyes.

"Oh dear, well, I see. Okay, ah, I'll wake you in an hour so you can go to the kitchen." Fifty-one fled like a scared mouse.

Sterling burrowed deeper under the covers. Warmth seeped into her, and she thought of Gray. Was he comfortable and warm? Did he think of her as often as she thought of him? Where was he?

CHAPTER THIRTEEN: RESURRECTION AND CRUCIFIXION

At the last "amen" of morning chapel, the Magdalene House women rose as one, genuflected in the aisle, filed out of the chapel and down a dim hall with no pictures or carpeting. Finally, it opened into a large dining hall with three long tables. Four of the girls broke line and disappeared into the kitchen along the far wall. They reappeared, along with a nun, all in in aprons. A moment later, a large window rolled open, and the girls filed by to get breakfast. The line proceeded as if the girls were receiving a Holy Sacrament.

Like wooden soldiers they all thanked the servers and God then sought places around crowded dining tables in silence. Fifty-one found a friend and abandoned Sterling, for which she was eternally grateful.

Sterling sat in the first open space she found. After helping with dinner clean-up and sleeping like the dead, she thought she could eat two plates of breakfast. The blonde across from Sterling watched the plate of scrambled eggs and fried potatoes disappear.

"Glad you're enjoying them eggs," she whispered. "Don't get 'em often. Mostly it's hot oatmeal or cold cereal. Where'd you come from?"

"Philly," Sterling replied between bites.

The girls around her gasped.

"Philadelphia! Wow, I ain't never been there. Heck, I never been nowhere!" chirruped a brunette across from Sterling. "I'm Thirty-two. I know, I don't look that old."

Everyone chuckled except a stocky girl whose dark hair had blond streaks. She nudged Sterling with her elbow.

"Don't laugh—makes her go on. I gotta listen to her after lights out," she said over the giggles. "I'm Sixty."

"You shouldn't oughta tell folks where you're from," the girl sitting by Fifty-one told Sterling. "And fur sure not your name. Against the rules." She glared at a girl to Sterling's right. Everyone fell silent again.

"The goddamn rules—ph-eff!" The girl on Sterling's right laughed. She tossed her long auburn hair over her shoulder and pointed down the table at Sterling's roommate. "I'm Angela. You stuck with Fifty-one?"

"So far," said Sterling, trying not to stare at the long scar along Angela's jawline. The wound must have happened long ago and marred an otherwise beautiful face.

"Too bad. Miss Abernathy loves her," Angela confided. "Never met a rule she didn't follow."

"How'd she end up here?" Sterling chuckled.

"Ask her stepdaddy," Angela said and bit into a burnt piece of toast. "Damn nuns make her think that's her fault."

"How do you know?" The fat girl across from Angela gasped.

"Sh-h!" hissed Fifty-one. Everyone fell silent for a moment. Whispers broke out again.

"I'd kill for a cigarette. Anybody?" Nobody spoke so Angela turned to Sterling. "New girl, you got smokes?"

"Never picked up the habit," Sterling said.

"Guess I'll wait and steal one from the woman I babysit for," Angela said.

"You have a job outside Magdalene House?" Sterling asked.

"Most of us do. I'm babysitting two boys. Christ, I hope this kid I'm carryin' ain't as big a brat as those two."

One of the nuns came in the dining room ringing a bell. "Time to get ready for work. Bring your plates to the kitchen. God bless you all. One Hundred, Sister Agnes would like a word. Afterwards, Miss Abernathy needs to see you."

"Hold onto your ass with Abernathy," Angela told Sterling as the girls scooted their seats back from the table and fell into a silent line.

The dining room began to empty. Sterling made her way to the back of the dining room and through the swinging kitchen doors. Her stomach turned over the minute she walked inside. The sounds and smells hit her at once—disinfectant, raw onions, rotten food, mold, and a nerve-clattering clanging pots and pans. Years of caked-on grease and overused disinfectant assaulted her nose. The floor felt sticky as she walked across it.

Sterling wrinkled her nose in disgust. The stained walls were institutional green, but they felt tacky to the touch and dingy to look at. She cringed at the stained countertops. Sterling's breakfast threatened to come up. Everything needed scouring from ceiling to cabinets to floors.

Presiding over two young pregnant women who washed the pots and swiped at the metal countertops stood Sister Agnes.

"Cook, do ya?" she asked Sterling. "Let's see. . ."

The back door slammed and everyone in the kitchen turned to look at a young Black woman wearing a pale flowered dress.

"You're late, Layla," called Sister Agnes.

"Sorry, Sister. Car broke down again," Layla said as she adjusted her long braids.

Without waiting for the nun to reply the woman tied up her braids in a red scarf, hung up her coat in a corner pantry, and dragged out a mop bucket.

Sister Agnes murmured something like, ". . . got her hands full."

The mop bucket in the back rattled. Layla got to work.

"One Hundred, take that soup pot and start cutting up vegetables to throw in. See if you can find two or three that aren't rotten. Twenty-two, hand her a pot. Eighteen, start chopping onions."

Sterling watched everyone jump to obey.

Sister Agnes barked at Sterling, "What're you standing there for? Get going. Knives are on the counter. Cut all the rotten spots outta the potatoes too."

"How do you pass a health inspection?" she murmured.

"Sister Agnes?" Helen Abernathy stood by the swinging doors. "I'm afraid One Hundred has a counseling session."

Sister Agnes' face colored to a bright red faster than anyone Sterling had ever seen.

"She is here to help me," the nun said.

"That's true," Helen said with a condescending smile. "But she has to come to me first. Rules. Sister Elizabeth's rules."

"Board of Directors rules, ya mean," Sister Agnes growled.

"Nevertheless. . ."

Sister Agnes nodded at Helen, probably realizing it might not be a good idea to show disdain for the governing board.

"Sister," Sterling said, "I can come right back after meeting with Ms. Abernathy and help you clean on this place before dinner prep? I mean, how long can it take me to repeat 'I'm keeping my baby'?"

Helen shot Sterling a glare and opened her mouth to say something, but Sister Agnes interrupted.

"You think it's dirty in here?" growled the nun to Sterling.

"Yes," Sterling said. "But second, how can anyone prepare a meal in such clutter and disorganization? It's a wonder you manage. Saucepans shouldn't be half-way across the kitchen from the stove."

The nun grimaced then she said, "Fix it."

"I'm afraid we have to—." Helen began.

"You're right, One Hundred, the place needs an overhaul. Skip counseling for now. Get it done." Sister Agnes brushed past a sputtering Helen and called to a few of the girls loitering outside to follow her inside the kitchen. "Sixty-one, Thirty-three . . ."

"You can't suspend her counseling," Helen said.

"Missing a session with you won't matter with this one," the nun said.

Helen gasped.

Angela waddled into the kitchen with two other girls.

"You don't leave until noon for work assignments so instead of loitering, today you will work," Sister announced.

"Thirty-three has a counseling session in an hour," Helen said.

"I'll try to see that she's there," Sister Agnes's eyes seem to dare Helen to say more.

"What the hell is going on here?" Angela whispered to Sterling.

Sterling didn't quite know.

Helen's mouth opened but nothing came out. She retreated from the kitchen and left the doors swinging violently. It reminded Sterling of Horace's exit from the bar and grill kitchen.

A fire burned in Sister Agnes' eyes, and she seemed filled with new spirit.

She called for Layla's assistance, and they finished pots of vegetable soup for lunch. A cadre of pregnant women under Sterling's direction—with occasional barked orders from Sister Agnes—scoured the kitchen and all the cooking tools. When they stopped to eat lunch, Sister Agnes recruited more helpers.

"Hope you're happy," Angela muttered to Sterling as they took a break.

"I should have kept my mouth shut."

"Damn right," Angela said.

Sterling's feet and back ached. The work detail went on for hours and ran through a dozen young women. At last Sister Agnes turned on the stove vents, opened the outside door to air out the place, and stood back to survey her kingdom. Sterling took in the clean, reorganized kitchen and the change made her smile. All the young women wore the same satisfied smile.

"I wish we had some new paint," someone said.

Sister Agnes wiped her hands on her apron. "We don't have paint and can't afford any. We barely have money for food."

"I know where there's paint, Sister."

The nun seemed surprised Layla was still around.

Layla shrugged. "I mean, I reckon it's still in the basement."

"Can we paint the walls?" Angela said.

"You. You go to your job," Sister ordered. "Now."

Angela opened her mouth to say something but took one look at Sister Agnes and said nothing.

Sister huffed. "All right. That's enough. One hundred, go with Layla and see what's downstairs."

"Paint? Now? We just put up the pots and pans," wailed one girl.

Angela elbowed the whiner. "New paint would be good."

"No talk of this today." Sister held up her hands for quiet. "Time for dinner prep."

Everyone groaned.

"Go, my children," Sister Agnes thundered. "One Hundred, hurry back." She clapped her hands and pointed to the refrigerator and listed the vegetables and pork to pull out.

Layla motioned for Sterling to follow, but before anyone could move Sister Elizabeth appeared in doorway, followed by Helen Abernathy. The old nun wore a scowl that turned to wonder as she took in sparkling stoves, gleaming pots, and brightener walls. All the young women held their breaths.

"Well! A miracle," Sister Elizabeth said.

The women in the kitchen beamed.

"Soap, water, and elbow grease," Sister Agnes said. "Nothing fancy."

Sterling tugged on Layla's arm, and they slipped out the back into the sunshine.

"Oh, this feels so good," Sterling said as she lifted her face to the sky.

"Feels hot when you're hoeing," Layla said and motioned Sterling to follow. They walked around to a wooden cellar door.

"Hoe! Do you have a garden?" Sterling asked, letting her eyes wander over the long backyard that the weeds had taken over. The neglected yard matched the theme of Mary Magdalene House.

"Me, my mama, my auntie, everybody I know has a big garden. We done planting. Now we got to keep the weeds out. That means hoeing."

Sterling nudged her, and her touch made Layla flinch. "See that yard? Waste of space."

"I see it. Lookee at the weeds." Layla grinned, turned her eyes to the sky for a moment before she walked on.

"How do you know Sister Agnes? Were you one of the girls here?" Sterling asked as she followed.

Layla shook her head. "Colored girls aren't allowed. Sister found me laying on the ground by the side of the road. I was with a man with a bad temper, and he nearly beat me to death. She hid me here. He tore up the town looking for me."

Sterling shuddered.

"I was fourteen," Layla said. "Sister Agnes and Sister Elizabeth kept me hidden down here weeks until he stopped looking. They give me a job so my Mama wouldn't go hungry that winter."

"Sister Elizabeth?"

"Now, don't you go thinking bad of Sister. She's got troubles keeping this place open." Layla yanked on one side of the cellar door. "There's a flashlight on a nail somewheres over here. Got it."

"Everybody you know has a big garden?" Sterling looked over her shoulder at the overgrown backyard.

"Corn, beans, tomatoes, potatoes, squash." Layla climbed down the first step into the basement. "Gots to or we'd starve come winter."

"That backyard . . ."

"Watch your step!" Layla cried.

The air in the basement became cooler with each step down. Sterling was tempted to grab onto Layla to be sure she didn't fall on the rickety wood steps and bash her head against the stone walls of the basement. Layla stopped at the bottom and offered her hand to Sterling as she stepped into the musty darkness.

"Wait here." Layla took the flashlight to help her see further down the wall. With a click an overhead light bulb came on.

Sterling let her eyes roam over the floor of the basement. It was wide, tall enough for her to stand, but probably not for someone as tall as Gray.

"What's in all these boxes and things?" Sterling asked and brushed by a rake and hoe.

Cartons and boxes lined the walls and, at last, she saw twenty or thirty paint cans against the far wall. Sterling opened one of the boxes.

"Mason jars. A whole box full."

"Good for canning. I could put up a whole mess of beans with those jars," Layla said.

"I'm sure Sister would give them to you," Sterling said. "There."

Layla bent down and pulled out some cans. "Most of these look no good. They've rusted shut."

"Only way to tell is open them all up," Sterling said. "Let's take them upstairs, find a screwdriver and pry off the lids."

"Here's some brushes. Look pretty good. My, my, here's a roller here that ain't been used." Layla sounded excited.

By the time they brought up the tenth can, Sister Agnes was in the doorway of the kitchen calling for them. She eyed all the cans with suspicion before she ordered Layla home to her family and Sterling into the kitchen to help with dinner.

**

The next morning at Matins, Sterling noticed two of the Sisters had green paint under their fingernails and on their hands. When the dining hall doors opened the distinct aroma of fresh paint warred with the smell of baked cinnamon rolls in the air. Sterling pushed open the swinging doors and laughed.

"Wonderful, isn't it?" Sister Agnes said. She looked comical with blood-shot eyes, rows of wrinkles and dots of pink paint across her face. She placed a tray of rolls on a metal countertop.

"Holy God!" cried Angela, who stood behind Sterling.

"Get an oven mitt and get the second tray out of the oven, One Hundred. I'll put this one in the serving window," Sister Agnes said.

Sometime in the night, the walls of the kitchen had been repainted using whatever paint the nuns could salvage from the rusty cans. One wall was pink. Another red. Another dull green. The fourth wall was half red and half green with pink splashes of color. The ceiling, which hadn't been finished, would be white.

"Wait until Sister Elizabeth sees this," Sterling murmured.

But it wasn't Sister Elizabeth who drew back in horror when she saw the kitchen. Helen Abernathy gasped aloud.

"It's so fresh and clean," Sterling said and swung a large pan of rolls from the oven onto the stove. "Isn't it wonderful?"

"Did the board approve this?" Helen wouldn't back away.

"Excuse, please. Let me set out the bacon," said one of the sisters as she brushed between them. She pushed up her sleeves to reveal a streak of white paint on her forearm.

**

Helen Abernathy disguised her counseling office at Magdalene House as a place of peace and tranquility. Her small desk occupied a corner of the carpeted room, and two straight back chairs sat in front of it. The rest of the room resembled a family living room with a gold plush sofa, a green paisley chair, a trunk used as a coffee table. The walls held oil and watercolor paintings of various families with children. Sterling caught the scent of lavender the moment she came in.

Helen smiled at her. She offered Sterling a seat in a comfortable armchair and folded her hands on top of her desk.

"Do you feel rested?" she asked.

"Much better, thank you. Yesterday was a long day. My feet aren't swollen either."

"Good. You should prop them up from time to time during the day." Miss Abernathy withdrew some papers from her desk drawer.

"If Sister Agnes lets me."

Helen grinned. "Sister Agnes has a good heart. Her bark is worse than her bite."

"I hope so," Sterling said and drew a chuckle. "Layla seems nice."

"Poor Layla had no one to help her. Why, without Sister Agnes that colored girl would have died," Miss Abernathy said in an absent-minded way as she continued to look for something on her desk.

Sterling rolled her eyes. Layla was probably better off than the girls in Magdalene House. The vegetables she'd seen in the kitchen shouldn't be eaten.

Finally, Miss Abernathy found what she needed and folded her hands in front of her on the desk. "I want to discuss your future, One Hundred."

"Won't you call me Sterling here?"

The notion stopped Helen, but only for a moment. "Have you thought about the future seriously?"

Sterling said nothing.

Helen rose and leaned on the front of her desk. "Let's talk about what will happen to your baby."

"I plan to keep my child and start a promising new career."

"Do you?" Helen's eyebrows rose. "What promising new career?"

Sterling hesitated. "I have several options that I would be foolish to discuss with you."

"I see," Helen smothered a smile. "'Several options.'" Well, let's say you do keep your baby. What do you have to offer your son or daughter?"

"Love. A mother's love." She felt the conviction of it in her soul.

"Do you believe you are the only person on earth who could love this baby?" Helen asked, her voice soft and earnest. "Do you honestly think yours is the only love this child could have?"

"I-I want this baby," she said.

"YOU want."

"The baby will be better off with me than anyone else." Sterling hated Helen Abernathy with all her heart.

"Better off than with two parents who love him? You can give him more time than a doting mother who has all day to read to him and play with him, prepare him healthy meals, and keep his clothes clean? You can give him more than a father who will protect him, teach him to fish, and provide for him?"

"It-t's a girl," Sterling choked out.

"I'm asking you to think this through," the counselor went on. "You are single woman who must work, and you'll have to farm this baby out to a caretaker eight to nine hours a day."

"I have someone who wants to help," Sterling seethed.

Helen brightened. "Oh, your mother. How old is she?"

"I didn't say anything about my mother."

"No, you didn't." Helen smiled. "So, a stranger or a relative? Someone with little time for your baby. Can you be sure you'll have a safe and secure home for her?"

A soft knock at the door interrupted the counselor. Gratitude washed over Sterling when a young woman from the kitchen poked her head in. Helen's words had begun to crawl under Sterling's skin and into her heart.

"I am terribly sorry, Miss Abernathy. But One Hundred must be off to the kitchen. Sister Agnes said . . ."

Helen stiffened. "Every day? When is she available? No matter. I'll schedule her counseling for afternoons before dinner prep." The counselor took out a black appointment book.

"Don't bother. I won't be back." Sterling swore she'd never suffer through another session like this.

"That's not how it works, One Hundred." Helen's eyes reflected a predatory glare from the desk lamp. "Counseling is part of what you agreed to when you joined Magdalene House."

CHAPTER FOURTEEN: MARCHING IN MAY

After the first deadly march, it seemed to Gray that every young Black in the county wanted to register to vote in Mullinsville. The next time they marched to the courthouse, the sheriff announced they had no permit to march and ordered them to disperse. Almost immediately white men rushed the marchers, beating anyone they could find with bats and broken bottles as the overwhelmed deputies stood by. When Sheriff Taylor finally ordered his men to stop the rioting, the deputies attacked the marchers and drove them away with clubs and pepper spray.

"We're coming back," the pastor shouted at his friend, Jimmy Taylor, as the marchers helped their wounded back to the church.

The next time Black citizens came to register, the older members of the community fell in line with young people. They prayed at the courthouse steps as deputies watched. By Gray's count, Sheriff Taylor had fewer deputies.

In late May, a few white college students who had finished with classes for the year had heard about the voter registration march and showed up to help. The local Black community didn't know what to make of the white students until Silver stepped up to welcome them and hand one a sign that called for peace.

More angry whites from Mullinsville also gathered every time there was a march too, sometimes joined by a few men that nobody recognized. Gray didn't know their names, but he knew their grim expressions and the profanity they spit out. He also knew that the warmer the weather, the hotter tempers would become.

Sheriff Taylor had learned from his mistakes. He lined disciplined armed deputies along the white side of the street like a wall of rifles. Officers had quit over how Sheriff Taylor had handled the protests, so the line was thinner but tougher. Other officers stood along the steps to the courthouse. Every white face scowled and frowned, their hate and fear living things that leaped from person to person in search of a home.

After the first horrific march and the brutal one that followed, Gray and his brother chose to walk right behind Pastor Dixon and monitor anyone who moved beside him. Gray also figured his pastor needed the moral support. His parishioners thought Pastor Charlie Dixon wore the death of his friend and choir member like a cloak of thorns around his shoulders. Only Gray and the pastor's friend Sheriff Taylor knew that the marches had also awakened Pastor Dixon's memories of his wife, killed in a violent attack on a peaceful civil rights march before Charlie Dixon returned to Mullinsville.

In contrast to the first rainy march, today the demonstrators had to wipe the sweat off their brows and roll up their sleeves. The sun bore down, and listening to Pastor Dixon preach before the march, Gray felt a sense of finality settle over the protesters.

As always, Sheriff Taylor held his rifle at the ready on the courthouse steps. Pastor Dixon climbed the steps slowly with his eyes on his friend, took his hand, lay it gently on the sheriff's gun barrel, and pointed that rifle at his heart. The marchers stopped chanting for peace and justice. Even the white protesters shut up.

"We're gonna end this today," the pastor cried. "Choose this day who you will follow, God or man."

"Jesus Christ," Silver said.

Gray's stomach turned over. He didn't realize he was praying for a miracle until Silver told him later.

The pastor and the sheriff stared at each other for what seemed like a long time before the miracle arrived. Jimmy Taylor lowered his gun and stepped aside so his friend and the marchers could go inside the courthouse.

Sheriff Taylor turned to the white crowd. "The law says these people have a right to vote. Now you may not like the law, but I am sworn to uphold it."

"Or else what, sheriff. You gonna shoot us all?" yelled the same white loudmouth from the first march.

"Damn right. Now if one of these people over here breaks the law, I'll come for them too," Sheriff Taylor said.

"You're a dead man," the man hollered, his face red as one of the stripes on the stars and bars flag flying overhead.

"I'll die at peace and see my Savior. You'll just die," Sheriff Taylor said.

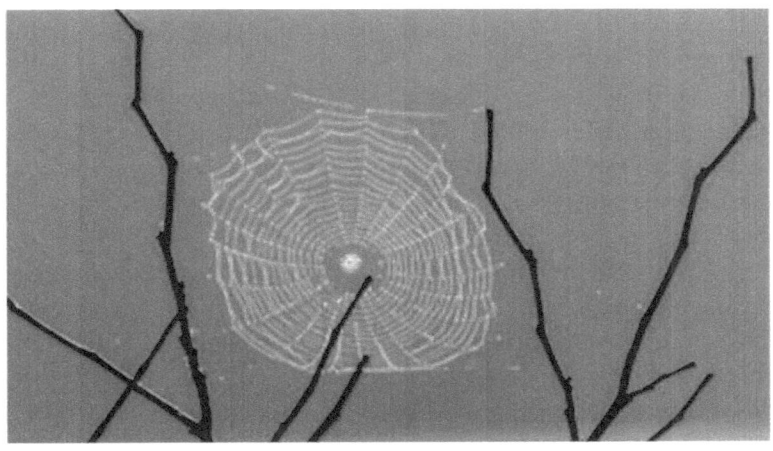

CHAPTER FIFTEEN: LOVE AND HATE

Sterling stopped on the sidewalk and turned her face to the sky, grateful that Sister Agnes had sent her for groceries on such a warm summer day. The nun always seemed to know when Sterling needed a break from the house.

The June sun had shaken off its winter haze and made Sterling forget the oppressive cold of winter and the drabness of early spring. The sun caressed her cheeks and buoyed her spirits. Spring rains had swept the streets clean of winter dirt and stones embedded in the blacktop road sparkled like stars in the summer night sky.

The red wagon Sterling pulled caught on a rock in the sidewalk, and she twisted the handle to dislodge it. She had talked the grocer into donating more meat than Sister Agnes ordered. Sterling couldn't wait to see Sister's face. Moreover, Sister Agnes now bought fresh vegetables from the Black farmers instead of the local stores. Layla's family had tilled most of the backyard and turned it into a late-blooming vegetable garden that they would share with the residents of Magdalene House.

One of the sisters had started a gardening program for the residents too, although Sterling wanted nothing to do with it. Half the side yard of Magdalene House had been dug up and planted in vegetables.

"Hey, Sterling, hold up," came a voice from across the street.

Sterling grinned at her only friend at Magdalene House, the only one who called her by her name and not a number. Angela panted across the street. She looked like she might be carrying a baby elephant.

"I'm gonna cut this thing outta me with a kitchen knife," she said.

Sterling laughed.

"Bad thing to say." She touched her scar. "Kitchen knife's how I got this."

Angela's abusive mother had taken a swipe at her and sliced open her jaw. Angela had never wanted children, but she'd fallen for an Irishman, who told her the scar didn't matter to him.

"What do you think it's like to deliver a baby?" Sterling asked. "Everybody acts like it's some big secret."

"It must be the worst kindda pain and suffering," Angela said. "That's why nobody talks about it."

"Nobody talks about it because it's about sex."

"Before the state took me to the Children's Home, I overheard my mother say having me split her wide open," Angela said as they started walking. "Down there."

For the millionth time Sterling wished she'd asked her mother more questions about love and childbirth. She had no idea what to expect.

"I read about it in some books at the public library, but it was all—well, it was nothing about how it feels," Sterling said, although the clinical description had made her queasy. "I don't know why I didn't think of it before."

"I bet the librarian looked at you funny when you asked for the books."

Sterling rolled her eyes and chuckled.

"You still gonna keep your baby?" Angela asked.

"Oh yes. I'm a Helen Abernathy failure." Sterling knew it was a girl. She had picked out a name too, Katherine Gray Sterling.

"I don't know how to be a mother," Angela said. "Abernathy's had no problem with me."

Do I know how to be a mother? It seemed to Sterling that being a mother would come naturally.

"Abernathy says being a mother's a lot harder than it looks," Angela said.

"Is it?"

"How the hell would I know?"

In the distance Sterling heard the snap-crackle of someone tossing penny firecrackers and wondered if her baby girl would hold off being born until July Fourth. She'd be late, but with first babies the doctor said nobody could tell when they'd arrive.

"Wouldn't it be fun to have a Fourth of July baby? She'd share a birthday with the USofA."

"You're nuts," Angela said.

Pulling the red wagon of groceries behind her Sterling waddled like her former boss Horace—she could think of it no other way—as she and Angela approached the towering iron front gate of Magdalene House.

She felt a spark of anger. What she and the other young women needed was information about childbirth and delivery, not lectures on sin. Given what she heard from whispered conversations of the young women, they were all woefully ignorant.

Still, the nuns had sheltered her when she had come in desperation. She felt safe there even when the good sisters urged her to think what might be best for the child and give the baby up. She wasn't what they saw: a young woman with no skills, no prospects, no hope for a decent life for her baby. Only Sister Agnes refused to dismiss her claim that she could raise her child.

"I would not bet against you, One Hundred. You're a tough one. But you have no idea how hard it can be," Sister Agnes once said. The wistful look in her eye made Sterling wonder whether the nun spoke from personal experience.

Sterling caught her reflection in a puddle of water as she crossed the street. When was the last time she wore lipstick? Her hair had lost most of its curl, her skin looked greyish, and she hadn't seen her ankles in months. Her pregnancy was like a runaway train. Her moods swung from desperation to exhilaration. The shapeless shift she wore didn't help her bedraggled appearance. Most of the time she felt like a sack of flour on legs.

"Lookee here," Angela said with a whistle.

They paused to admire the long blue limousine with tinted windows parked in front of the house. A childless couple had come to adopt, no doubt. They came all the time in Fords, Chevys, and, once in a while, in big town cars. Sterling prayed they were good people ready to love someone else's baby. Maybe they'd leave a contribution to repair Magdalene House. At the top of the stairs, she saw the figure of a man, his face shrouded in shadows.

The gate squeaked with its usual unholy noise, and Angela swore.

"That damn thing needs oil," she said. "So much oil."

Sterling, busy with dragging the wagon over the rough stones toward the stairs, grunted. This time, she promised herself, she would get a gallon of oil and fix those gate hinges. At the last minute, the back wheel caught in the swinging iron gate and stuck.

"Let me help you."

Sterling stiffened, abandoned the wagon, and ran for the steps.

"What the hell!" Angela cried.

"I just want to talk, Sterling," Tom Foster said. "Please. I've been searching for you everywhere. I've called every Catholic home for unwed mothers in America."

"Shit!" Angela ran up the steps as fast as she could and passed Sterling. "Sister Agnes! Sister Agnes!"

Sterling whirled on the third stone step and glared down at him. He had filled out, grown his hair longer, let a mustache grow. He wore a white shirt and fine-tailored suit of dove grey with a squared off pocket handkerchief to match his rose-colored tie. He reeked of men's cologne and dollar bills.

"I can't imagine what we have to talk about."

"My baby," Tom snapped.

"Are you pregnant? I thought you'd put on some weight." Sterling turned and lifted one foot to take the next step.

"Please, I just want to talk, to-to see you."

"Here I am. In all my glory."

"You look . . . amazing. I want you to know I love you," he said. "I will always love you."

"Go away."

"If you won't have me, give me our baby. Sterling, please. I can look at our child every day and see you. And love you both. Grace and I will be the best parents ever. The child will never want for anything in this world. We will take him to church, send him to the finest schools, get him a hunting dog . . . Sterling, you can't do any of those things."

"I will love her. The baby's a girl, I know it."

Tom stepped closer and Sterling's hand clutched the cold iron handrail. "Grace will love her. She's . . . she's a good person. She's already fixed a nursery with this mobile thing on the side of the crib that plays 'Rockabye Baby" over and over and over."

Sterling hated the tears puddling in the corner of her eyes. She had nothing like that for her child. Did she have the right to deny her baby the life Tom offered?

"My father is inside with Grace and Sister Elizabeth. We're talking to the sisters about a donation to fix this place. We will give you enough money to start your own agency just like you've always planned. You can look out of glass windows from the top floor of your agency as you dreamed. Our child—"

"Stop!"

"Sterling, please, listen."

"One Hundred!" Sister Agnes stood at the top of the stairs with pinched lips and a furrowed brow. "Stop making a scene and come inside." Sterling had never seen the nun so rigid, so angry. "Mr. Foster, would you mind bringing in the red wagon?"

"Oh, no, of course not, Sister." Tom backpedaled down the stone stairs and grabbed up the wagon. As he dragged it up the stairs, Sister Agnes took Sterling by the arm into the hallway toward Sister Elizabeth's office.

"You lied to us," she said, the wound of it glistening in her eyes.

"I am a cook. I am pregnant. I came from Philadelphia. I told you nothing about the child's father. Margaret is my legal middle name— what did I lie about?"

"You never said the father of this child and his wife wanted the baby," she said.

"What difference would it make? I am keeping my daughter." Sterling gritted her teeth.

"It makes a difference to the child, to the baby you claim to love. That baby would have a complete family and a life of privilege in a Catholic home. Stop thinking of yourself for a moment," Sister Agnes said.

"Sterling? Madeline Sterling?" A slender blond in a short sleeve navy shirtwaist dress stepped out of Sister Elizabeth's office in white high heels. She wore a pearl necklace, a white cardigan with mother-of-pearl buttons, and white gloves. Behind her, Tom's father Brian glared at Sterling.

"Please, might I have a word with you?" Grace said. "Alone."

As Grace Foster walked down the hall toward them Sister Agnes turned her back and spoke to Sterling. "You should hear her out for the baby's sake. I'll wait right here for you. Ah, thank you Mr. Foster. I'll take the wagon and show you back to Sister Elizabeth's office. One Hundred, take Mrs. Foster to the chapel."

Wordless, Sterling led the way down the hall to the chapel. The usual peace she felt when she entered didn't come to her today. Instead, Sterling was trying to figure out how she could escape Mary Magdalene House. The chapel doors closed behind her, her heart thudded, and she faced Grace Foster. They gazed at each other for an awkward moment.

"You must hate me," Grace said.

"Until the day I left Crossville, I didn't know you existed," Sterling said.

"You don't love Tom?"

"How can you love a man you can't trust?"

"I love him with all my heart. I know he's got a wandering eye, but . . . well, Tom's been my weakness since seventh grade. He ran for class president, and I helped him win." Grace's perfectly lined lips curled into a smile. "We are a fit, Tom and me. We have the same dreams, goals, habits. He'll be a force in Georgia politics someday. The Foster name will open doors."

"I am glad for you if that's what you want. Truly," Sterling said.

"Our son—," Grace began.

"It's a girl."

Grace moistened her bottom lip. "What I truly want is something I can never have. You have what I've always dreamed of and can't have. Tom and I tried for a baby before he, well, lost his mind and went off to join the revolution."

"You mean, Justice Tomorrow."

". . . but we can't have children. I mean, I can't give Tom children." She collapsed into the back pew.

Sterling caught the scent of fresh roses. Bouquets of them in containers sat all around the chapel.

Grace followed Sterling's gaze. "My favorite flower. We donated them this morning. Do you like roses?"

"Very much," she said.

Grace scooted over in the pew to make room and Sterling sat down on the edge of the seat. Now that she was close, Sterling could see the unshed tears in Grace's eyes. The woman's body seemed to tremble with the effort of holding them in.

"I want you to consider the joy it would bring me, a barren woman, to hold a baby in my arms and know she was mine to raise," Grace said. "What a gift you would be giving Tom and me. Not just to me, but to this baby. She will be the jewel in our crown of life. Nothing and no one will come before her. She will have two loving parents. This I promise if you will sign the adoption papers."

Sterling rose and faced the cross in front of the chapel. Did she have the right to deny her baby the kind of life Grace Foster was offering? Wealth, privilege, the love of a mother and father? Not exactly, she reasoned. Tom would be an absentee father as he was an absent and unfaithful husband. Whether she gave up the baby to Tom and Grace or kept her, Sterling was certain the baby would be raised by a single mother. Suddenly, she knew the right choice for her child.

"Do you think it fair to deprive me of the same joy you want?" Sterling said. "There are a dozen women in this very house who have already signed over their child for adoption. Why not choose one of their babies?"

"Those babies are not Tom's, not his blood."

"Is that so important to you, to Tom?" Sterling's stomach grew sour.

"It is everything," Grace said. "Don't you see?"

"My baby is more than just Tom's heir. She has to be." Sterling whirled to the chapel door, planning to go back down the stairs and run for Layla's new vegetable stand. No one would think to look for her there.

"One Hundred?" Sister Agnes waited for her at the head of the stairs, looking alarmed.

"She doesn't want a child. She wants a trophy," Sterling said.

"Wait!" Grace called from the chapel door.

"What are you talking about?" Sister Agnes demanded. She grabbed for Sterling's arm, but by that time Sterling had started down the steps. Sister Agnes caught her on the shoulder and threw her off balance. There was no railing for Sterling to grab and her toe caught the edge of the crumbling stair. Her arms whirled in the air as she yelped and fell.

With a crack that rattled her whole body, her back and head struck the second step. She moaned, rolled, and fell to the bottom. The rusted gate, the honking car horns beyond, the hollering of men in the street, and Sister Agnes' screams all blended into one noise inside her head. Water gushed from between her legs.

"What's happening?" she mumbled when Sister Agnes reached her.

"Oh, no! I'm so sorry," the nun kept repeating.

**

The irritating ring of the telephone next to her hospital bed dragged Sterling from a deep sleep. Labor and delivery had exhausted her. Eyes half closed, she smacked dry lips and fumbled for the telephone. In the process she knocked papers off her bedside table and sent a small plastic tray bouncing off the linoleum floor. Everything hurt, but especially her back, her incision, and the stitches from the delivery of her daughter.

Where's Kate?

Her eyes flew open, she gasped and sat up as quickly as she could manage.

Brian Foster stood in a stream of sunlight from the far window consulting his gold wristwatch. Tom's father looked more dapper than the first time she'd seen him. Dressed in a three-piece dark blue business suit, he carried a bouquet of flowers in the crook of one arm.

The insistent phone kept ringing. Fear rippled through her.

"Aren't you going to answer? That's the third time the phone's rung. It might be important," said her visitor.

She grabbed for the receiver through a wall of wind. Suddenly, the air grew still.

"H-hello?"

No one said anything on the other end for a second, although she could hear grunts and groans.

"Hello? Who is this?"

"S-sterling? Sterling!"

Gray! He sounded weak, hurt.

"They grabbed Silver and me and . . ."

"Are you okay?" she said.

"Where . . .? Are you okay?" Gray said.

"I'm fine. Gray—."

"Run! Don't come!"

A scream in the background. The phone went dead.

"Gray! Wha-what's happening?" She whirled around to Brian. "What did you do?"

CHAPTER SIXTEEN: AN UNIMAGINABLE CHOICE

The ransom demand snatched the breath from her body.

"Did you understand what I just told you?" Brian Foster looked like a banker explaining terms for a mortgage on her first home. Part of that was true, Tom's father was an Atlanta banker.

A sudden rush of wind in her ears swirled her senses as the cracking of brambles knitting together up her body threatened to strangle her. The greenish walls yelled at her, and she tasted the sound of screaming.

"I'll never give her up. Never!" The smells of sweat tasted bitter, and the sight of Brian Foster enraged her.

"What is going on in here?" The door to her hospital room flung open. "This ain't labor and delivery."

Brian smiled at the nurse, who glared back. "Sorry. I believe a twinge of pain overcame her."

"Huh." The woman took a few steps away from Brian, her eyes full of suspicion.

The wind in Sterling's ears vanished, replaced by a deadly calm that came from knowing what she had to do.

"Huh." The nurse said again before she turned to Sterling with a smile. "Here she is, Miss Katherine Gray Sterling. All cleaned up and checked out. A healthy, hungry baby girl."

"May I—." Brian began.

"Neither of them needs visitors right now," the nurse said as she placed the baby in Sterling's arms.

Sterling sighed in relief. This nurse had been outraged to discover that the day shift left the scared young patient to labor alone for hours. She had stayed with Sterling through the long night, a peppermint candy in her mouth perpetually going from one cheek to the other.

"I understand. I'll leave in a minute," Brian said. He handed the flowers to the nurse. "Perhaps you can put these in water."

"I'm not a florist," the nurse said. "I'm getting a bassinet so the baby can stay in here. Your visitor better be gone when I come back, little girl." She allowed the door to close gently behind her.

Brian stepped closer to the hospital bed. His eyes glowed like the devil inside him wanted to grab Sterling's throat. She searched frantically under the covers for the call button to get the nurse back. Her curly hair, still matted from the sweat of labor, felt damp again.

"You look tired," Brian said. "I know this is upsetting. We can call it all off, release your friends."

Sterling gave him a faint smile.

"Give Kate to me now," Brian suggested. He took another step toward his granddaughter.

"She's too little to leave the hospital." Sterling picked up a water glass on her bedside table and threatened to throw it at her visitor.

Brian stopped.

Sterling placed the glass back on the table and tucked her bedcovers around the infant in her arms. Her free hand found the nurse call button hidden by her hip and pressed it. Foster took a step closer.

Please someone show up this time.

"Stop right there or I'll scream 'fire' at the top of my lungs," she said.

"I only want to see my granddaughter." Brian took another step closer.

"Look from over there."

The bedside light cast an eerily yellowish glow on Brian's face when he paused. He raised his arms in surrender and cooed at Kate from a distance.

"She has Tom's mouth and cleft chin . . . but that wispy red hair and small nose are yours," Brian said. "I know who to look for when you bring her. I don't want a doll or someone else's child."

"I'm not . . ." She stopped. Gray had sounded desperate and in pain.

Brian shrugged.

"I'll think about it. But if I say yes, I'll only give her to Tom and Grace. I never want to see you again." Sterling heard the words come out of her mouth and couldn't believe what she'd said. She adjusted the covers to hide her daughter's face and glanced at the telephone.

The idea that someone captured Gray still shocked her. He was so cautious. Yet, Gray's own voice had confirmed it. He must have been protecting Silver.

"After you think over the proposal, you'll need this. Here's where we'll make the exchange. It's about four hours away. You come alone now, hear?" Brian Foster tossed a folded paper onto the bedside table. "Bring my granddaughter to this farm outside Memphis—look for a broken weathervane over the hayloft. I'll leave these directions. If you and Kate don't show, I will slaughter those two coons like spring hogs."

Who did Brian imagine she would bring along? A nun from Magdalene House or a Justice Tomorrow agent? Sterling still had no idea who survived the destruction of Justice Tomorrow. The last she knew someone still hunted its agents. Every emergency number her employer had given her rang and rang.

"Get out," she snarled.

"Sterling, I'm sorry it had to come to this." Brian's tone softened.

"Does Tom know you're here?" she said. "Does your son know you kidnapped Gray and Silver?"

"Kate will enjoy a comfortable life with Tom and Grace in Atlanta," Brian went on as though she hadn't spoken.

"Tom doesn't know," Sterling said flatly. "He's basically a con man. Violence isn't his bag."

"He knows . . . oh, he knows." In a sudden fury, spittle shot from Brian's mouth along with his words. He inhaled deeply. "Tom would be here, but I'm much better at, ah, negotiations. Sterling, you know Kate will be better off with Tom and Grace."

"No one is better off with Tom," Sterling hissed. "I bet Grace agrees."

Brian laughed long enough to make her wonder what she'd said to set him off.

"One week," he said finally. "Kate ought to be out of the hospital."

"Two weeks. She has jaundice. She must stay here for treatment," Sterling lied. "I'll need a car."

Where was her nurse?

"And gas money," she added.

His eyes grew wide then narrowed. A satisfied smile pulled at the corners of his mouth. "Two weeks. If you're not there with Kate at noon, I'll sic my hounds on you and watch them tear you limb from limb."

"These the same dogs that hunt Justice Tomorrow agents?"

"Agents?"

"Like Tom pretended to be."

For the first time Brian hesitated and clasped his hands before answering. "I have no idea what you are talking about."

His uncertainty scared Sterling more than his arrogance. His answer suggested two different people had been after her: one looking for information about Justice Tomorrow and the Fosters looking for her baby. The notion terrified her.

"Holy Mother of God."

Brian tossed his car keys onto the bedside table under the lamp. He pulled out his wallet and counted out one hundred dollars to slip under the keys. He had plenty of bills left in his wallet.

"It's a 1965 silver Buick LeSabre. Parked in the front lot, first row. It's full of gas too," Brian said.

"Leave me a bill of sale in the glove box," she said. "Wouldn't want some policeman to haul me in for stealing your car."

"Clever girl," Brian grinned. "You'll have it. I'll have someone watch the car until you pick it up."

Money meant serious business to Tom and his father. Best for everyone if Brian believed she was the same kind of person.

"No need to have me followed, Mr. Foster." Sterling forced herself to sound calm, even carefree. "I have a few demands of my own: one hundred thousand dollars and letters of introduction for Sterling Brothers Limited, private investigators. Bring it to the exchange point and, if my friends are alive, you'll have a granddaughter."

Merely saying the words made her sick to her stomach. Kate kicked against Sterling's arm as though she hated the idea too.

"You want money?" Brian sounded surprised, but his tight shoulders relaxed.

"My friends and I need a fresh start." Bile rose in her throat.

"A fresh start . . . with colored boys?" The idea plainly disgusted him.

"Can't you get the cash?"

"Well, yes." Brian hesitated. "I can get the money."

"Good. Get out. Oh, leave a carrier for Kate in the LeSabre," Sterling added.

A quick knock and the door opened. Sterling's nurse strode in pulling a plastic and metal bassinet. She looked at them in surprise.

"He's leaving." Sterling tightened her grip around her newborn daughter.

"See you in two weeks." Brian saluted her casually, aimed a winning smile at the nurse that wasn't returned, and left. Before he closed the door, he laid the bouquet of flowers on a nearby chair.

When the door closed, Sterling dropped her head and whimpered against her sleeping newborn.

"Humph. Who the hell was that?" the nurse said.

Sterling kept crying.

"Okay. Speaking of hell, well, I just caught it." The nurse fluffed Sterling's pillows and straightened the covers. "We aren't supposed to let girls from Magdalene House touch their infants before they're adopted."

"I'm never letting Kate go. Never," Sterling said, embarrassed by the trembling of her chin and the tears streaking her cheeks.

"I got it. She's yours. You signed the adoption forms under duress."

"What adoption forms? I don't remember anything like that," Sterling sat up, eyes wide in horror.

"Here." The nurse reached in her pocket and handed over several sheets of paper. "I hope there's not a copy floating around somewhere. You want Kate. You keep her."

Sterling took the papers and ripped them up. "How dare they ask a woman to sign legal documents when they're in labor!"

"Oh, they dare. They dare a lot of things with Magdalene House girls." The nurse took her patient's wrist to count her pulse, held Sterling's hand a moment longer than necessary. "You're from Philadelphia, little girl, how'd you end up in Tennessee?"

"I needed a place to stay . . . for the baby."

"I went to Philadelphia once on one of those bus tours," said the nurse. "Wasn't much. I liked the Liberty Bell, though. I'm gonna roll this bassinet in here by your bed."

"Put it where I can touch Kate, please."

"Close enough so you can touch her," the nurse said and thrust a thermometer under Sterling's tongue. "You need to eat something after the night you had."

Afraid and in agony, Sterling had begged all night for relief. Instead, as Kate split her open the doctor had muttered: "You girls like to play then whine and cry about the pain."

"Everybody's gigglin' about you telling Dr. Turney you were going to take his medical license," the nurse said.

Sterling mumbled something. When the nurse removed the thermometer, Sterling said, "I will get him too."

"Good," the nurse whispered and adjusted the peppermint in her mouth. "He treats all the girls from Magdalene House like shit, mostly because you girls are too ignorant to know better. Don't the sisters at the home tell you girls what to expect in delivery?"

Sterling shook her head.

"Good God." The nurse helped Sterling get Kate to latch onto a nipple and bustled out of the room. A rancid odor that turned Sterling's stomach drifted in from the hallway.

Alone with Kate, the room grew quiet, but the undercurrent of fear lingered. The only sounds came from carts rolling in the hall outside, an occasional laugh, and rubber-soled footsteps squeaking on the linoleum floors.

"What are we going to do, Kate? I can't think straight right now," Sterling asked her little girl as she nursed. "Gray sounded like he was hurt." She tried to shake the memory.

Kate opened her eyes for a second.

"Don't worry. Your mother's good at getting out of trouble. I'll think of something."

Her words sounded flat. Truth is, she and Kate should vanish today, now, before whoever stalked Justice Tomorrow agents found them. She couldn't imagine they would be far behind if Tom and Grace Foster could find her at Magdalene House.

Holy Mother, I'm so tired.

She gazed around the cream colored walls, wondering idly how a charity case from the unwed mothers' home got a private room. She figured Brian Foster had something to do with it. He would want their conversation to remain private.

After a few restless minutes, she murmured to Kate, "First thing I've got to do is trade that Buick to Sister Agnes for the home's Chevy that she drives to market. She'll figure she owes me—and Brian Foster won't be looking for that car."

A crushing weight dropped on Sterling's chest.

Am I really thinking of risking Kate? Never. No, I'm not.

Kate whimpered and went back to nursing.

Gray's and Silver faces flashed through her mind. The words Gray said over the phone sounded like they'd been beaten out of him, except for the last two.

"Don't come," she repeated. Gray imagined her life was at stake.

I can't let them die.

Sterling's sobs racked her thin body until stomach cramps made her stop. Exhausted, she rolled down the head of the bed a little, winced at the burning around her incision, and laid there staring at the cream colored ceiling and the portrait of a white Christian Jesus on the far wall.

Jesus was a dark-skinned refugee . . . and a Jew.

When she had parroted that information gleaned from her father's colleagues at Harvard, Sterling had created an uproar at her church's confirmation class. The memory made her grin.

"Are you going to get your mother called into counseling at church, Kate?"

If she remembered correctly, Jesus was also a risk-taker. At least the Jesus she'd learned about from the nuns at St. Catherine Girls School in Boston who were regulars at civil rights demonstrations.

Her door banged open. Sterling gasped and put her hands over a sleeping Kate to protect her.

"Here we are," her nurse said as she carried a tray in front of her. "A sandwich and juice to tide you over until dinner." She held out her arms for the child.

Sterling hesitated.

"I'm not gonna steal her. I only want to put her to bed right here beside you. She'll be looking for another meal in a couple of hours. I'd eat and go to sleep if I were you."

The nurse swaddled the newborn and gazed at the baby. "She's gonna have your curly hair. I bet those eyes stay blue too. Like you. That's a mighty rare combination, red hair and blue eyes."

"I'm sore," Sterling said, aware of a growing discomfort where she'd been stitched up. She bit into the ham sandwich and chewed without enthusiasm.

"You've got a large episiotomy," the nurse said. "You'll have cramping too. I'll see what I can get to help. I'll show you how to soak witch hazel into a sanitary pad. Smells a little like sassafras or maybe cinnamon. That'll do you good later."

"C-can I call my mother?" Sterling said. Her tears dropped onto the top bedsheet. "I want. I want my mother."

Her nurse's eyes grew soft. "That's your post-partum hormones rushing around, sweetie. And some homesickness, I bet. There, now. Your mother would want you to feel better. You have to go down the hall to the pay phone for a long-distance call and I don't want you out of bed. When Miss Kate wakes up to eat, ring for me and I'll get you a proper dinner."

The nurse left Sterling to sniffle and snuggle down in bed. In the stillness of the room, she gazed at the ceiling, reached over the bassinet, and rubbed her finger lightly over Kate.

Sterling felt like she'd just fallen asleep when Kate cried to be fed. At the first mewing noise, Sterling jerked awake with one fist clenched and both eyes scanning for danger. Kate's crying grew louder. Sterling rang for the nurse and fumbled to pick up her daughter.

"Three whole hours. I was about to go off shift," the nurse said, clacking a peppermint around her mouth. "Let me help you settle Miss Kate here and I'll bring you something from the cafeteria. Hamburger steak or fish?"

"Is it Friday already?" Sterling mumbled.

"No, sweetie, you got a few more days before you have to eat fish." The nurse laughed, took Kate away, changed her diaper, and handed her back to Sterling to nurse. Kate knew what she wanted and went after it.

"I'll get you hamburger steak," the nurse said.

As soon as they were alone Sterling told Kate, "We have to sneak out of here soon. We'll take a trip to Memphis to see if we can help Gray and Silver. We may get there only to turn tail and run to Boston."

The idea sickened her, panicked her. She would think of something, she always did. Gray would never leave her to die—he'd carried her through the Alabama woods unconscious and bleeding for hours. He'd held her hand, let her cry on his shoulder, embraced her when she nearly fell apart. The only thing he hadn't done is tell her what she longed to hear.

"Who do we know in Memphis?" she asked her daughter.

Since Justice Tomorrow's contacts were blown, Sterling didn't know who to trust. It had to be someone she knew personally. She couldn't think of anyone. Panic flushed her cheeks. Who? There had to be someone she'd worked with before in Memphis, even the cousin of someone. Her stomach cramped again.

Sterling's eyes darted around the room looking for help, for inspiration or comfort. They lit on the telephone by the bedside where she'd last heard Gray's voice and she prayed to St. Jude that Gray would call to say he and Silver had escaped. The phone remained silent.

Instead, St. Jude sent her a memory, the face of a man in Memphis that she and Gray had worked with before. His name? Her head seemed full of wool. He was a Black pastor who had helped them with a case. Gray had spent months under this man's care and slipped out of town without notice, the way Justice Tomorrow intended. Gray had even lived in the back of his Memphis church.

His name? What is that man's name? He pastored Mt. Sinai Baptist Church. Ah, Pastor Jacob Warren.

She and Gray had been undercover in Memphis. She hoped she lived long enough to see their work convict the killers of a Black sanitation worker who had the audacity to register Black voters. One murderer was a city official.

Important people. People with money to spend on assassins.

Kate's eyelids drooped and Sterling jostled her to get her to nurse. When Sterling rang the call button, her nurse returned with a plate of hamburger steak, mushy white mashed potatoes, and greasy green beans. While Sterling ate, the nurse burped Kate on her shoulder then laid her back in the bassinet. She stayed a few minutes making small talk but also watching her patient force down some food.

"You'll start feeling better," the nurse said. "See you tomorrow."

When the door closed, Sterling reached for the phone, got an outside line, and asked for long-distance information and wrote down the number she was given for the Memphis church. Tomorrow, Sterling would call her mother and Reverend Warren.

Thinking of Katherine Sterling made tears start again. Her mother would tell her to come home. But she couldn't put her parents at risk again. Sterling cried until she rolled the bed to a prone position and pulled the covers over her. She hiccupped and closed her eyes.

As she faded into sleep, Sterling asked St. Jude for one more favor.

Send me a really good idea.

**

The scent of musty hay, old horse manure, and sour sweat filled Gray's nostrils. He hung by his wrists from the rafter of an old barn, watching one kidnapper read a newspaper while the other whittled a long stick. Dust mites floated in the sunshine that oozed through the cracks in the barn wall.

Gray pretended to be unconscious since his kidnappers didn't seem amused by beating men who could not feel anything. He kept his swollen eyes opened far enough to keep his captors in sight. While he wanted to know what they were doing, closing his eyes shut only made him focus on the throbbing, burning pain radiating through him. Drops of sweat dripped from his back and face. He would have sold his soul for a swallow of water.

From somewhere behind him Gray heard a moan. At least his brother was still alive. Hope. While they were alive they had hope. That made him think of Sterling and he almost smiled. She'd dare anything. Once he'd run to the house where she was living in South Carolina with a pair of angry white men a dozen steps behind him. She'd known one of the men from the church she attended and stopped them all in their tracks. Hands on hips, she'd launched into a furious assault on them for trying to take 'her' nigra before he finished with her yard work. After that, she had told them, they could do whatever they wanted to him. She'd been so persuasive, the men had come inside her house to get lemonade, and when they returned Gray was practically in the next county. From what he'd heard later, she'd convinced the men Gray's escape was all their fault.

A shrill ring startled him. The sound of the telephone stirred the two kidnappers. As far as Gray could remember, it had only rung once before. The older kidnapper put all the legs of his chair on the ground and rose. The phone was attached to the wall next to Gray so he could hear the conversation.

"Yeah?"

"It's time," a woman caller said.

She'd spoken so softly during her previous call that Gray had only caught a few words. Who was she? From her accent he'd pegged her as a white woman born and raised in the South. Educated, judging by her word choice. She didn't sound elderly, but not young like a teenager. Was she a secretary? A messenger? He couldn't decide, but the kidnappers spoke to her with respect.

This time the woman spoke loud enough to open graves. Excited. Determined. Cold.

The orders she dictated chilled him. His stomach clenched and he swallowed hard.

"Do not kill them," the woman's voice said. "I repeat, your orders are to keep them both alive."

"Both them coons 'bout half-dead now," the kidnapper said.

"Our success depends on their remaining alive . . . for a time. If they die later, so much the better. It's a fine line but follow your instructions to the letter."

The man kicked at the straw on the barn floor like a kid who'd been told he couldn't have dessert.

When the first kidnapper hung up, the second put down the stick he'd been whittling. "We rolling?"

The first man grinned and turned to Gray.

Gray closed his eyes and steeled himself.

CHAPTER SEVENTEEN: A DESPERATE PLAN

S terling had to hold on to Kate at all costs. Her plan would work but it rested on keeping her hands around Kate.

Clouds of dust billowed around the car as she drove to the barn on Triangle Farm outside Memphis. As Brian had told her, a broken weathervane in the shape of a triangle sat atop a cupola on the roof, an unusual decoration over the hayloft that the earlier landowner had fancied. Heat rose in waves across the surrounding Tennessee cotton fields, and a lazy breeze stirred the grass in the turnaround in front of the barn.

Holy Mother of God, what am I doing here?

The place looked deserted. She parked the car near the split rail fence opposite the barn doors but kept the motor running.

Breathe in, breathe out. Hey, I've been tight spots before.

After months on the run, Sterling had learned how to assess her surroundings for danger. It came naturally to Gray. She wished he were beside her.

When Sterling's eyes finished a sweep of the ground, she turned to look over the barn. She noted telephone poles with electrical wires running into the barn. Her eyes lingered at the silo silhouetted against a cloudless blue sky, then she reached over to touch her daughter.

"When you're older," Sterling whispered to Kate, "I'll explain why I had to do this. You'll love the men we're saving as much as I do. You'll be part of our world-class detective agency. God, why is it so hot in here?" Sterling pushed the air-conditioning to high.

She smiled at Kate and rolled her window up tight. The car engine hum drifted in the air. Birds swooped through the sky over the fields.

The farm looked just as Brian Foster had described. He had told her it was isolated when he gave her directions and in this, at least, he didn't lie. To get to it, she'd driven by one rural grocery store, two horse farms, a half dozen shacks barely visible from the main road, a handful of cotton fields, and a plantation home straight out of *Gone with the Wind*.

Sterling squinted into the sun bouncing off the car's hood and wished she'd brought a hat. Her pale skin burned easily and, as her mother always reminded her, too much sun made her freckles stand out. Her back ached, her middle bulged, and nothing fit her, not even her skin. She felt old and wired together with caffeine.

To soothe herself, Sterling caressed the light pink blanket over Kate that she had scrimped to buy in Philadelphia. Her stomach rumbled to remind her that she hadn't gotten to eat breakfast today and she rested a hand on her middle to apologize. Kate came first, and Sterling was pressed for time.

The baby wrinkled her nose and dozed off. Sterling hoped she'd go on sleeping through this nightmare.

I can make this work.

She usually owned an unshakeable faith in her schemes. Sometimes she had frightened Gray with the way she brazenly defied an angry crowd, pulled a sleight of hand to keep an incriminating document from a suspect, or slithered under bushes to overhear conversations.

If things went screwy, she would drive off with Kate and renegotiate. She would save Gray and Silver later.

Judging from Sterling's scouting yesterday, only one thing appeared different at the barn. The red Ford that had revved its engine like a drag racer had disappeared. It was probably waiting behind the barn's two large front doors, ready to roll. The prisoners would come out that way too.

Then it gets real.

With Silver and Gray safely in the backseat, Sterling would drop into the driver's seat with Kate held against her right side. She would pretend to be shifting the child over to Tom. Instead, she'd throw the car into gear, clutch Kate against her right shoulder, and punch the accelerator. She'd clear Tom quickly, slam the driver's door closed with her left hand, lay Kate in the carrier, and hit the gas again. She'd be gone, with a good head start, before anyone could react.

Nothing more to do but wait.

She checked her mirrors again. The great-grandson of a Ku Klux Klan Grand Wizard owned the cotton farm where Gray and Silver were prisoners, but he lived in Memphis. He only showed up to supervise the planting and picking.

Sterling had gleaned those tidbits from Reverend Warren. Her contact had done more than tell Sterling the history of Triangle Farm, he'd taken her to visit a farmer who lived down the road and arranged her get-away. Then he'd gotten a ride back to Memphis and told her to never call again.

"Ah-h-h!"

A scream from the barn galvanized Sterling.

What the—? An animal?

An agonized cry, louder this time.

Mother of God! Gray!

Heart in her throat, her eyes darted around the barn area while she tried to think of what to do next.

Suddenly her gaze halted at the cupola atop the barn. Below it, a wiry Black man stared at her from the hayloft opening. He ducked inside, but not before she noticed his mutton chops and bushy mustache.

Stomach churning, Sterling laid her palm on the car horn hoping the racket would stop whatever was going on in the barn. The commotion woke Kate. Sterling stopped honking to shush her baby back to sleep. At last, the only sounds came from the car engine and a flock of blackbirds flying overhead.

Sterling looked in the rearview mirror. No dust rose from the road she'd just traveled, which meant no car was coming. She checked her watch. Her arm quivered so much she could hardly read the time.

Tom and Grace were late.

Maybe Tom planned to rush the exchange and catch her off guard.

Sterling lifted her daughter out of the baby carrier on the passenger side, gave her a kiss on the forehead, and made sure that the passenger door was locked. She spent one extra second enjoying her daughter's tiny smile before she made sure the driver's door and the one on the passenger side in the back were open. All windows were rolled up completely except the one left half-open behind the driver.

Sterling noticed Kate's red face, removed the pink blanket swaddling her, and tossed it aside. It fell across the baby carrier.

"Better? Little cooler?" She rolled down the back window on her side of the car halfway. "Okay, Kate, let's go. Let's hope St. Jude's got his eye on us."

She opened the car door to prepare for the phony exchange. She had decided not to put Kate in the carrier she'd strapped to her front yesterday when she checked out the barn. She would have to pull the baby out to pretend to make the exchange and taking Kate out was awkward. Kate would be left open to Tom's snatching her.

Instead, Sterling would hold her daughter against her chest with both arms around her. With another wince, Sterling hoped she wouldn't have to endure these childbirth wounds much longer. When she applied the cinnamon-smelling solution her nurse had given her, the worst of the burning and itching felt better, but Sterling always felt the stitches were about to pop. She opened the car door and stood, testing her weight and the sturdiness of her stance.

O-ouch. Okay. Let's go.

She reached inside the car to grab a pink diaper bag filled with enough formula and cloth diapers to seem genuine, then took Kate in her arms. She left another diaper bag with a giraffe on it in the car for later. After marching off fifty large steps from the Chevy Sterling dropped the pink bag to mark where Tom should stop for the exchange. Then she quickly back-pedaled to the car.

The Chevy sedan had plenty of gas, so Sterling could keep the motor running. Once she started her escape, her hope rested on everyone expecting her to follow the turnaround circle in front of the barn and go back out to the county road.

She had parked in the curve of the turnaround, however, with her car pointing toward an overgrown tractor road.

Hardly more than a path, no one could see it through the weeds and cotton plants unless they were looking. When she had pulled into it from the state road yesterday, she'd been overjoyed to see the overgrown farm road filled with bone-jarring ruts. She'd walked—or crawled—most of it with Kate strapped to her chest. It wound through the field, a gate, and finally emerged among some trees onto the state road to Nashville. Even if the kidnappers realized she planned to drive down it, they didn't know where the pitfalls and potholes lay.

She did. Throughout the night, she'd practiced the drive in her mind to avoid the worst potholes. The route was hotwired in her brain and muscles.

Where is Tom?

Holding Kate in the front carrier, Sterling had mapped out all but a few feet of the tractor road yesterday and taken several screws out of the gate's hinges so she could crash through it without too much damage to the car. She didn't want to risk breaking an axle or ruining her radiator.

Kate had been a good little detective. She had only cried once when Sterling was crawling along the road with the baby and filling some potholes with rocks. She'd even been quiet when Sterling scouted the area around the barn. But Sterling had hustled to the car to nurse at the first whimper. Kate never fussed unless she was hungry or startled.

Finally, dust rose from the main road to the barn. Sterling stiffened. Tom and Grace Foster were coming.

From the nearby field the odor of meat, maybe a dead animal, wafted to her on the breeze.

Suddenly, a black vortex swirled from her feet toward her head. "No-o! Not now!"

Helplessly, Sterling watched as the spiraling darkness around her feet turned into brambles that scratched her legs and arms. She saw a scream and heard a calliope of bright colors. At the center of her upended senses, Gray held her tightly in a dark night. When he lifted her in his arms to carry her to safety, he nodded toward the barn door.

The bramble wall disappeared.

Sterling staggered and banged against the car's frame. She didn't need a voodoo spell to tell her Gray had saved her after she'd been shot. She wasn't going to let him die.

Her eyes scanned the barn to make sure nothing had changed while the voodoo briar held her. This time she checked out the bottom of the old place. Amid the grass and weeds she saw a wooden bar leaning against the side of the barn. The bar was used to slide through the handles in the two doors and lock the barn from the outside. It would bottle up the Ford for a few precious seconds.

Her knees could barely hold her, but Kate remained secure in her embrace. Sweat soaked her face and shirt. Sterling gazed down the road and tasted the lingering acid of her morning coffee and her fear.

Don't let Tom get too close. Hold onto Kate. Dodge the first pothole to the right.

Her pursuers—and she was sure there would be some—might hit a few potholes in the tractor path and be slow to follow them.

A breeze kissed Sterling's face and cooled her cheeks. Suddenly filled with confidence, she smiled.

She watched Tom drive closer.

His black Cadillac stopped well short of the diaper bag. Sterling turned away to shield Kate from the swirling dust. The Cadillac blocked most of the entrance to the road they'd all driven. Sterling made a show of craning her neck to see if she had enough space to drive down the main road. In a pinch, she could.

She wouldn't need it.

A tall, black-haired man got out of the Cadillac, took off his sunglasses, squared his shoulders, and faced her.

"Morning, Sterling," he called.

"Where's Grace, Tom?" Sterling held out the palm of one hand to stop him then wrapped it around Kate again.

"Here, like you asked." He smiled as though he expected her to melt in his arms again.

Sterling swallowed hard. A lifetime of regret for a moment of weakness.

Oh, it was more than one moment.

She had resisted his gentle teasing, his back-handed compliments, and piercing hazel eyes until the night Gray told her—

"Now what," Tom called.

"Your wife should see this exchange," Sterling said. "She should witness the depravity you've stooped to."

Tom tapped the large envelope in his hand against his tan slacks.

The Cadillac passenger door opened, and Grace Foster got out looking more like a Southern debutante arriving at a tea than a woman coming to exchange prisoners for a baby. She adjusted her wide-brimmed straw hat with a ribbon band that matched her green dress and came toward the front of the car.

"No further." Sterling wiped one sweaty hand on her jeans.

Grace took two more steps and held out her arms. "Sterling, you are doing the best thing for Kate"

"What? I can't hear you," Sterling said.

Grace took a deep breath. "I said, you are doing the right thing." Sterling huffed.

A little softer Grace said, "Kate will be loved. She will have the devotion of both a mother and a father. A-And she'll have two adoring grandfathers."

Sterling lifted Kate to her shoulder. "I know Brian Foster, so that doesn't thrill me."

Grace lowered her arms. "You've made the right choice for Kate."

"What choice?" Sterling cried.

Grace's green eyes pooled with tears. Pity wormed into Sterling's anger again. Grace took a hankie from her pocket to dab her eyes. Sterling felt a little sorry for Grace, a woman who couldn't bear children yet wanted them desperately.

Kate would be happy with a mother and a father. The home for unwed mothers had harped on the need for a child to have a father and mother. Even an absentee father was better than none.

"I'll get the baby, Grace," Tom said to his wife, "you take the bag."

He strode toward Sterling with the brown envelope in his hand, pausing only long enough to yell toward the barn, "Get 'em out here."

One of the large doors of the weathered gray wood barn cracked open.

"Stop, Tom!" Sterling said.

"I love Kate," Tom said when he reached the trunk of Sterling's car. "I'll protect her. I will."

Sterling believed him, and it made her hate Tom a little less. A little.

"Throw the envelope in the backseat." She stepped back as he tossed the envelope through the open window.

"Don't you want to count it? It's all there—everything you asked for. The money and a stack of letters of recommendation." Tom's *English Leather* aftershave danced on the breeze, as if to remind Sterling of those glorious nights in his bed.

"I trust you," Sterling snapped. "You were always trustworthy about money."

Tom angled his body to block his wife's sightline and leaned against the trunk of the Chevy.

"Say the word and I'll divorce—"

Old familiar patter. She curled her lips into a sneer.

"We're both still Catholic, aren't we, Tom?"

He dropped his head.

"Sterling. . ." Tom's soft voice beckoned, "can you blame me for wanting a piece of you? Kate will always be part of you too."

"If you really cared for me, you wouldn't be doing this," she said.

"I'm not doing—." He stopped and cleared his throat. "I mean . . . I have to know, why are you here?"

"Honor is nothing to you, so you wouldn't get it," she said. "Grace must not have a backbone."

Tom's laughter cut her off.

"No, that's not it," he said. "It's Gray."

His question shocked her. "You're jealous?"

"Of a colored boy?" Tom's upper lip curled in disdain. "But you . . . you always seemed attached to him."

"Of course," she said. "He saved my life. More than once."

"No, you came to me on the rebound."

He opened a gash in her heart that Sterling thought she'd closed.

"Tom?" Grace sounded impatient.

Sterling looked over Tom's shoulder to discover Grace standing with a hand on her hip. In her other hand, the diaper bag swayed away from her body like a sack of garbage.

"For once in your life, take some advice," Tom whispered to Sterling. "Don't use those letters of reference. Go underground. People are coming to kill you."

"What people?"

"Is there a problem?" Grace's voice carried a command.

Tom turned to his wife. "Honey, why don't you get in the car and get out of this heat?"

116

"I'm fine." Grace's words landed like stones on Tom's back, and he grimaced at the sound of each one.

He licked his lips and glanced at the sky. One of Tom's tells. He was about to lie.

Tom leaned in a little closer. "The people who destroyed Justice Tomorrow are still out to get you."

What was the lie? Sterling frowned.

"Tell me the rest, Tom," she said. "You claim to love me, prove it."

"Hey, I'm the one keeping you alive." Tom shuffled his feet. "Okay . . . Okay. My father's always wanted a grandchild. Goes double, no triple, for Grace's father. Atlanta society's all about bloodline, money, power. Her father—and everyone back home—thinks Grace is pregnant. I arranged an extended business trip in Europe so Grace's father would never find out about you and Kate. Nobody better find out. Bet your life on that."

"Tom. Let's go," Grace called. The woman's eyes, which had so moved Sterling with their silent desperation, appeared narrow and menacing.

"I don't have our share of the bargain, now do I?" Tom whirled to tell Grace.

"Bring those two boys on out here," Grace shouted at the barn, although she locked eyes with her husband.

One barn door thudded wide open against the backstop. She thought she caught the glint of a silver fender. No doubt the red Ford was ready to race out after the exchange. No sign of Gray or Silver, however.

"How do you know about the people who are after Justice Tomorrow?" Sterling grew more anxious at the delay. "Did you sell us out?"

Tom shook his head. "What I told you came from a former FBI agent, a colored detective who tracked down Gray."

"You hired a Black detective?" Her bitter jab seemed lost on Tom.

"He's a big fan of Justice Tomorrow. . . when he found out why I really wanted to find Gray and Silver, he—." Tom ran a finger down his jaw and winced.

"Where are Silver and Gray?"

"What's the hold up?" Tom yelled toward the barn and took a step.

The second barn door swung open and hit the side of the barn with a crack.

"Give Kate to me, Sterling," Tom said.

Sterling angled her body and the baby away from him. "Once Silver and Gray and I are safely in the car."

Tom glanced back at his wife almost vibrating with fear, as though he was playing a part that scared him. Sterling took a half step away from him.

From inside the barn, three men dragged Gray and Silver through the open double doors and into the sun. Gray's head hung down between his shoulder and his toes made furrows in the dirt as two men hauled him to her car. Both agents looked so bruised and bloody, Sterling hardly recognized them.

"Holy Mother of God!" Sterling cried. "What have you done to them?"

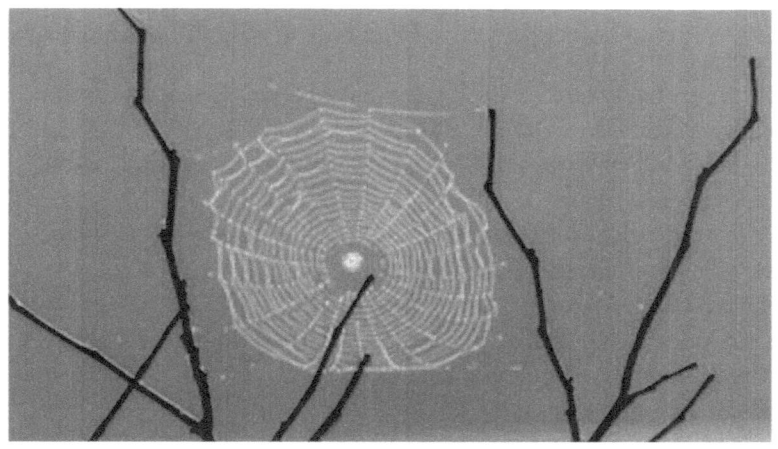

CHAPTER EIGHTEEN: ONE MOMENT IN ETERNITY

Three men dragged Gray and Silver to Sterling's car.

"You sonofabitch!" Sterling yelled at Tom. Kate whimpered.

"No, I—." He flinched, retreated from her fury, and turned to Grace speechless.

One of Grace's hands touched her neck in a graceful poise.

Two of the men opened the rear door of Sterling's car, tossed Gray across the backseat and rolled him to the floor. Another man loaded Silver on the seat. From the open window the smell the sweat, urine, and rotten meat drifted out. When they folded Silver inside, the third man slammed the door and dusted off his hands.

Sterling bit back a scream.

"You men get back in the barn," Sterling snarled and edged close to the driver's seat. Her eyes, however, burned into Tom's before she glanced at his wife. "Grace! Get that bar leaning against the side of the barn and lock the door behind them."

"W-what?" Grace's eyes blinked.

The three men looked at each other, uncertainty on their faces.

"You men, get in the barn! Grace, lock them inside!" Tom bellowed.

The men backtracked until they disappeared inside the barn. Grace moved to do as she was told.

"Now, back in your car, Grace," Sterling commanded. Slowly, Grace obeyed.

Tom came closer. Sterling inched away until the driver's side doorframe hit the back of her knees.

Almost there. Almost time.

Tom leaned closer. She couldn't slide into the driver's seat yet and shuffled closer to the car. He followed.

"Back away!"

Tom paused, inched closer. "It's you she wants."

A sharp cry of anguish split the air behind her.

Sterling turned toward the sound in the backseat. As she did, her arms swiveled and put Kate near Tom. In one quick move he slipped his hand between the baby's bottom and Sterling's chest, then flipped his other hand between the baby's head and Sterling's arm.

He yanked.

Kate shrieked.

Sterling tightened her grip on the baby.

"You're hurting her! Let go!" Tom said. "You're hurting Kate!"

Kate screamed. Sterling released her hold.

Tom ripped the baby from her arms and clutched Kate to his chest. He wheeled and headed toward his car. Sterling pounced on him like a lioness.

"No! No, give her back. No, no, no!" Sterling jumped on Tom's back and clawed at his face.

"Jesus Christ, Sterling." Tom backpedaled until she hit the side of the Chevy hard enough to make a loud crack against the door frame. With the wind knocked out of her, Sterling's grip on his neck loosened enough for him to twist around and stiff-arm her into the driver's seat.

"Crying's a waste now. You can't ever have her. If you come for her, I have a copy of the adoption consent you signed in the hospital. It's over, Sterling." He jogged toward his Cadillac with their wailing daughter.

Sterling's worst fears unfolded in slow-motion. Through her tears, she watched Kate, clasped in Tom's arms, disappear into the blackness of the Cadillac. She heard an engine start. Suddenly, the passenger door of Tom's car opened, and Grace's high heels stuck out. Her feet kicked as though struggling to find the ground and her arms waved about until she got out of the car.

From the back, Silver groaned, "He-lp."

With her hat flopping on her head and a venomous look on her face, Grace sprinted for the barn door and struggled to lift the bar that was across the barn doors. Behind the doors a car engine revved.

"God, no. Kate!" Sterling straightened in the seat and put the car in drive before she fully closed the door. She hit the pitted path through the cotton field at twenty, thirty miles an hour. The car crashed into the first pothole, bounced until the axle touched ground, and someone in the back cried in agony. The car kept going, but Sterling didn't want to risk that again. She focused on the map in her mind and not the searing rip in her heart.

Pothole to the right, now left, and left again. She dared not look to see if a car followed them. Right, right, and left. She twisted the wheel and ventured one quick glance in the rearview mirror. The red Ford followed. She jerked the wheel left, right. Another glimpse backward showed the red Ford had stopped with its nose pointed down and its hood up. One man jumped out while another hung out the passenger window. When Sterling crashed through the rickety gate and dodged two more potholes, she drove onto the state road with no one behind her.

Sterling slowed, crying so hard she relied on her instincts to stay between the lines on the road. Two cars passed on the other side, but no one pulled in behind her.

She failed. Failed.

"How did I let this happen?" She swiped at her wet cheeks. "My baby. My God, she's gone. I lost her. Holy Mother Mary, help me."

Her fear of capture melted into grief.

Four miles down the state highway, she turned onto another farm road flanked by trees and marked by a newly painted black mailbox with its red flag up. She followed the winding driveway and passed the Black farmer and his teenage son who waited outside a metal garage. A police siren wailed in the distance. As they had agreed, she drove straight into a garage attached to a white clapboard house. The door slammed down behind them.

CHAPTER NINETEEN: SORROW

Sterling cut the motor. A truck engine started outside, and gravel crunched in front of the garage. The farmer, Rufus Allen, shouted something about a jack for the tire. She listened carefully and heard something heavy land in the metal truck bed outside. A tire, perhaps. Her pounding heart slowed. They sounded like they were following the plan to back a pickup half-way across the front of the garage, jack up one wheel and remove the tire. If anyone came to the house, they'd see the farmer working on his truck and a garage nobody could have entered.

Sterling rested her forehead on the steering wheel.

How did things go so wrong?

She shook from the enormity of what had happened and couldn't open the car door. How could she get her daughter back?

A roar like a tornado blasted through her mind, and she began free-falling into a black hole. She let herself fall toward oblivion.

"Sterling." Silver gasped from the backseat. "St-erling."

With some effort, she raised her head. At first, she remained frozen in the stifling heat, staring into the garage without seeing, lost, unable to move, gulping for air. Silver called again.

She lost Kate. The words in her head made little sense. She looked at the empty car seat where Kate had slept. She fingered the soft pink blanket and buried her face in it to catch Kate's scent.

A primal scream of agony rose from deep within her and she emptied it into Kate's blanket, the piteous sound pouring out until her throat hurt. A hollowness grew bigger and bigger until it left nothing inside her. She had no substance. No feeling. No life.

She lost her daughter.

Half of Silver's face appeared dimly in her rearview mirror.

"Sterling! Gray's . . . breathing." Silver managed to gasp.

Sterling pulled herself out her mental abyss. In the glow of the dome light, she found her way out of the driver's seat, fumbled around to the side of the car, and yanked the back door open.

"Can we get him off the floor?" she asked Silver.

Her first good look at Silver made her gag. Besides his swollen eyes, blue-black bruises colored his dark skin. His nose angled oddly to the side of his face. She tore her eyes away, afraid of what she'd find on the car floor.

"Gray!" She touched his shoulder and when he didn't move, she shook him. Sterling took one hand and pressed it against the artery of her partner's neck.

"Thank God." His pulse felt strong.

She cast about for help and found a jug of water sitting on a workbench. Her hosts had remembered to leave water for them in the garage.

"I'll get water." She couldn't think what else to do. "Can you sit, Silver? Gray? Gray!"

Nothing came from the man on the floor, but Silver moaned as he struggled to sit. When she gave him the water jug, he proved too weak to hold it to his lips alone.

"Phew! You stink. Your Yale classmates wouldn't eat lunch with you now." She climbed into the back, careful not to step on Gray's hand or touch his side.

"Wouldn't eat with us anyway," Silver murmured. Water dripped down his chin to what remained of his shirt.

"Sit up," Sterling said.

"Hurts."

"Okay." She dribbled water on Gray's neck before she tilted Silver to the right and rested his head against the opposite car door. Every motion made him gasp. When she took his hand away from his shoulder, it had blood on it. She wiped her hand on the seat and turned to Gray.

"Hey, ya'll okay in here? Ain't nobody come up the road behind you—so far. Your other car be here directly, and we got them boxes out back cut just like you say." Rufus stepped into the garage from the side door and a puff of cooler air followed him.

A compact but muscular-looking man with freckles peppering his face, Rufus had taken an enormous risk hiding them in the garage.

"Help me," Sterling called.

Rufus pulled a chain on the light overhead and hurried over to the back seat.

"Sweet baby Jesus." He covered his nose.

"We need a doctor," Sterling said.

Rufus shook his head. "You need to git. You know they blockin' roads to Nashville right now."

"I'll go another way," she said. "We need a doctor."

"Nuh, huh," Rufus said. "No doctor coming here."

"Then help me get them into the house. I've got to see how badly they're hurt."

Rufus hemmed and hawed. "What if the sheriff come?"

"The longer we're here, the less likely they are to find us," she said with more confidence than she felt. "It's getting out of town that will be worrisome."

"You gots to git," Rufus said.

"Not until I know how badly they're hurt."

With a huff, Rufus said, "Soon's the new car gets here."

"Okay."

They helped Silver first, and all but carried him out of the garage. Then Sterling hovered over Gray, applying cloths dampened by water from the jug to his head and neck, even his feet to cool him down. At last, her partner moaned and raised himself off the car floor with one hand.

Gray opened one swollen eye, focused on her, and gave her a little smile.

"Sterling," he breathed as if her name was a prayer.

"I'm here," she said, and they looked into each other's eyes.

He held one arm cradled against his chest. She got under his arms and tried to help him rise to his knees.

"You smell good," he murmured as his head rested against her leaking breasts. He tried but failed to get off his knees onto the car seat. "I knew . . . you'd come . . . you're that crazy."

"How badly are you hurt?" She held the jug of water to his lips. He gulped it down.

"My arm . . . probably broken. Silver's worse." He hauled himself toward the seat, then collapsed against her again. "Damn! Goddamn."

She tried to haul him onto the seat, but he was too heavy, and her episiotomy stitches felt like they were shredding.

Rufus and his son returned after several minutes. "Uh, that first fella wanted to get clean. First time we saw how bad he got hurt, my boy ran behind a tree and got sick. We still poured buckets of water over him. Lord Almighty."

"Can barely breathe, but he wants to smell nice. Sounds like my baby brother." Gray tried to chuckle, but his voice dissolved into painful gasps. He gazed at Sterling, and she caressed his cheek with one finger.

CHAPTER TWENTY: IN A FARMHOUSE

By late afternoon, Gray and his brother had fallen asleep on the bed in the biggest bedroom of the house. The small house smelled like rubbing alcohol, the only antiseptic Rufus and his family owned, and the filthy clothes the two men had worn. After shooing three younger children into the yard to play, Mrs. Allen found some penicillin pills left from a bout of pneumonia the previous year. Sterling gave each man two to swallow. That left one more.

Silver already had a fever. All the movement seemed to have sapped his last reserve of strength. Sterling had no idea how she would maneuver both men in and out of her car in their present conditions.

The only good news appeared to be how well her escape worked.

Mrs. Allen called a friend to gossip and the first words out of her friend's mouth concerned the sheriff's search for two "escaped colored killers." They believed the men were headed north.

All day, no one came up the Allen's drive except the man who sold Rufus a 1960 blue Pontiac Catalina station wagon with only fifty thousand miles on it. All the way from California, he told Rufus. The man exchanged money and keys with Rufus, signed the papers, and laughed about something that happened at church Sunday, before he got in a car driven by his brother to go home.

The moment he left, Sterling heaved a sigh of relief.

Rufus and his teenage son folded down the back seats, spreading an old quilt over the back and brought out pairs of cardboard boxes in different sizes. Six of the cardboard boxes had false bottoms and semi-circular holes cut in two sides. Silver and Gray would lie across the back of the station wagon. The cardboard boxes with semi-circle holes for their necks and torsos would fit over them, then light items like empty cereal boxes and bedsheets went inside the false bottoms. The boxes were glued together to form a line, biggest to smallest, from the front seat to the rear. Other boxes packed with paper on the bottom and an assortment of sheets, towels, books, empty boxes of macaroni, and laundry soap on the top would fill the back, too. The big boxes had gashes in them for air that looked as though the cardboard had been damaged in transit.

Rufus applied a Greek letter sorority sticker to the back window and left a blue and white pom-pom inside the front passenger-side windshield. The driver of the station wagon would seem like a college student packed to move into a dorm.

"I'll be ready to go in a minute, Mr. Allen." Weariness nearly overtook her.

She stepped back into the garage and went to the Chevy's backseat. The brown envelope Tom threw through the window had wedged under the driver's seat. She took out some of the money and thrust it in her jeans pocket. The Allens had given her more help than she asked for and she had used sheets, clothes, and medicines they couldn't afford to lose.

Next, she opened the trunk. Kate's pink diaper bag lay there. She outlined the yellow giraffe on it with one fingertip and felt sick. She swallowed hard, opened the bag until she found Kate's real birth certificate and the fake identities. The enormity of her loss threatened to pull her under, and Sterling rested her forehead against the upraised lid of the trunk. She grabbed her suitcase, a brown paper sack with blonde and brunette wigs, and slammed the lid. Before she left the garage, she paused to collect the pink blanket.

The Memphis heat and humidity made her feel like she hadn't showered in days. But she had washed and soaked her episiotomy only this morning before she and Kate left the motel.

Kate. Sterling grasped the blanket to her nose. Her breath hitched as the pain of losing her daughter sliced through her again. She tried to focus on what she must do instead of what she should have done.

Mrs. Allen appeared at her elbow outside the garage door. "You don't look good."

"How could humans treat another like this, Mrs. Allen?" she said.

"People been abusing' each other since Cain and Abel," Mrs. Allen said. "No use to ask why we cain't all change our sinful ways."

"I left some things in the Chevy's front seat and trunk. Please find them a good home. I hope the Chevy is good to you," Sterling said and pressed the money from her pocket into Mrs. Allen's hand. "You didn't ask for all this trouble, and I'll never be able to repay your kindness. I hope we meet again in better times."

"I do wish you well," Mrs. Allen didn't look down, but wrapped one hand around the money and transferred it to her apron. "I put you some snake bite medicine in the back. Might come in handy."

Getting Silver and Gray in the car and covered by the boxes took all three Allens and Sterling. By the time it was done, it was late afternoon. Sterling took her bag inside the bedroom to change.

Stained towels covered the small bathroom floor and blood streaks showed in the tub. Since she had no washing machine, Mrs. Allen would have to wash everything by hand. Sterling closed her eyes and shook her head. At her next confession, she would tell the priest she had doubts about a God Who would take her big brother Danny in a senseless war and allow Black people to be treated so badly. And take a baby from her mother.

Stupid, stupid, stupid. Kate was all my fault. My fault.

How could she have let Tom get hold of Kate? She couldn't bear it. Gasping from her sorrow, she took off her shirt to change clothes. Her full breasts ached with no baby to ease them.

When she emerged from the bedroom, Sterling wore a blue skirt, a white collared blouse, a string of pearls, bright pink lipstick, fake eyelashes, and a brunette wig. The skirt felt tight, the wig itched, and her soul hurt.

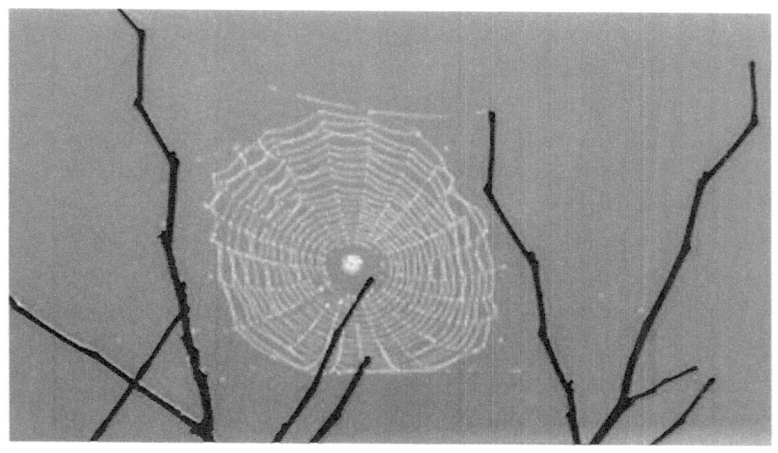

CHAPTER TWENTY-ONE: ESCAPE ACROSS THE MISSISSIPPI

As she searched for the street that led across the Mississippi River bridge, Sterling thought of reporting her daughter's kidnapping to the police.

And tell the cops what? Two well-respected people held two Negroes for ransom, and I risked my daughter to save them? No? Maybe I can tell them that the adoption papers these pillars of the Georgia community have are fake, and I never intended to give them my only child.

The reality was, Sterling could never get the authorities involved. Kate was gone and Sterling's grief turned to rage. Tom and Grace had a different problem. They couldn't let anyone know they were anywhere near the barn. They couldn't afford to get Sterling involved either or the secret of Kate's birth might come out. They couldn't afford to involve the cops any more than she could.

Sterling pounded the steering wheel with one hand.

"What's happening?" Gray sounded alarmed. "Where the hell are we?"

She scratched her head and longed to snatch off the wig. The cotton pads she wore in her bra to soak up milk leaks needed changing, but she had no more pads.

"It's okay. Everything's fine." When had Gray started cursing? She'd never heard it from him before. "How are you and Silver?"

"Hot."

"I'll turn up the air-conditioner. I haven't seen any cops for half hour or so. The ones I saw passed by without a second glance. I don't think you should sit where anyone could see you, though."

"H-How'd you do it?" Gray gasped in pain. "How'd you find . . .? How did you get us out?"

He sounded so fearful, she tried a joke. "Why, kind sir, I work for Justice Tomorrow. Until we were betrayed, we were real smart."

"Get real, Sterling. Justice . . . Tomorrow . . . fell apart. How'd you do all this?"

"I had a plan. It worked." Her eyes darted to the glove compartment where the brown envelope of letters and cash rested. Angrily, she bit her lip.

Her plan would have worked if only she'd paid attention. She lost her focus and let Tom get close. She smacked the steering wheel again. Letting Tom get close was the source of all her problems.

"Tom Foster did this. I could hear the men at night when they thought they'd beaten Silver and me unconscious. It was Foster paid them and Foster ordered —"

"Brian Foster, not Tom," Sterling said. "I got the ransom demand from the father, not the son."

"A family of vipers. The whole damn bunch. I'm going to kill them all." Gray knocked against her seatback.

"What did you hear in that barn?" She tried to sound curious and not like someone who was afraid of his answer. Had he learned about Kate?

He mumbled something she didn't understand, and she heard the boxes rustle as someone moved. Then silence.

Gray must be miserable lying on his back the length of the station wagon. Periodically, she heard a moan and groan but couldn't tell which man was in pain. When his captors dragged Gray out of the barn, the beautiful, penetrating, brown eyes that haunted her dreams had swollen shut. She and Rufus Allen had managed to get Gray's left arm in a sling, but she knew it was broken.

She tried to squelch her renewed outrage. A new, putrid odor made her roll down the windows.

"Water," whispered Silver.

"There's a water jug back there," she said.

From the radio, Elvis Presley sang "It's Now or Never," and she joined along to give her mind something else to think about. It was a popular song from her training camp days.

She thought of all the Justice Tomorrow agents she had known, the young investigators she had grown close to in their training and re-training camps. Her heart ached to think of her friends who had died, Sarah Feinberg and Marquis Dark. There were probably more she didn't know about.

Sterling felt lost and flailing. She couldn't count on Justice Tomorrow's resources and had no idea where to go for supplies, safe houses, or medical attention along the way. She'd learned her lesson in Philadelphia using a contact she barely knew. Now she had no idea what to do. She had planned on Silver and Gray spelling her at the wheel while she nursed the baby or slept in the back. That was impossible.

Finally, she pulled onto the bridge across the Mississippi River.

Kate. She'd lost Kate. Sterling made the sign of the cross as she drove across the bridge.

Holy Mother, you lost a child. You know this grief. Is this the price I must pay for being careless with the most precious gift I ever had?

The bridge seemed endless. Inattentiveness made her slow the car.

Her eyelids drooped, her head slowly dropped until a truck whooshed by and she jerked upright. She'd almost drifted off. Driving further would be dangerous. Between her anxiety over the exchange and Kate's feeding schedule, she'd hardly slept the night before.

Gray seemed to read her mind. "We need to find a place to stop. All of us. Especially Silver."

"I'm okay," Silver whispered.

What was that putrid smell?

"I'll look for some place safe to pull over." She raised her voice so Silver and Gray could hear in the back.

"Okay." Silver's answer dissolved into a sharp cry of pain.

"Hold still, Aristotle!" Gray grunted. "You're making the boxes fall over."

"Don't. Don't touch anything." His plea made him sound like a little boy lost and far away. "Every motion hurts."

When the conversation behind her didn't bring her a surge of adrenaline, Sterling knew she had little more to give. There must be some place off the bridge to pull over. She leaned over the wheel to get a better look at what lay ahead.

They had almost reached the Arkansas side of the Memphis bridge. Not many lights shining from houses, trailers, gas stations or truck stops over there. Instead, it looked like a lot of dark farmland stretched out before her on either side of the road until they got to a few filling stations in West Memphis. Good and bad. Good, because Sterling could stop and see someone coming. Bad, because anyone coming along could see them too. She needed cover.

Like an answered prayer, she saw it. As she got off the bridge, straight ahead on the right side of the highway, her headlights caught a shiny new metal gate. It opened half-way onto a dirt road in a field with trees close to the riverbank. She saw what looked like a haystack. Perhaps a shed or barn that leaned slightly. Hard to tell in the night, but she took a chance that cover was at the end of the road.

"Hold on."

She slammed on the brakes, yanked the wheel, and turned hard off the highway. The station wagon bucked and bumped. Silver screamed.

Her heart leapt into her throat.

CHAPTER TWENTY-TWO: PAIN BY THE RIVER

The scream made Sterling slow down.

"Silver! Talk to me! Gray!" Sterling's voice vibrated with the bumps in the dirt road. "I think, I hope, I found a place to rest. Answer me!"

"Oh God," Gray groaned. "Stop."

She turned on the bright beams for a second to see far ahead in the night and her heart jumped. Perfect. She cut off the lights, got out of the car, opened the gate, and drove through. The gate remained unlocked but propped in the closed position by a few rocks. The undercarriage of the car thumped a few times along the road as she slowly navigated by the light of a half-moon. She stopped beside a tumbled down shack and a stand of trees by the Mississippi River.

In the back, Silver moaned.

Sterling ripped the wig off and threw it on the car floor. With both hands, she fluffed her curls and lifted her hair off her neck. Ah, cooler. Her nose curled at the rotten smell. She grabbed a flashlight, got out, and looked around. The lights of the Memphis skyline lit the waters of the Mississippi that lapped the shore a few feet from where she stopped. On Sterling's left, the shack leaned precariously. On the right a dozen trees skirted a field that had been planted in what seemed to be neat furrows.

She opened the back door of the station wagon and lifted the weightless boxes outside until she freed Gray. He lay across the back of the station wagon without moving. She took all the boxes off Silver and nearly gagged.

"My God."

The flashlight shone on what should have been Silver's face. He had looked better five hours ago. The mass of cuts, bruises, and place where his nose should have been resembled a Hollywood horror mask. One hand rested near a bulge under his torn plaid shirt.

"Is he okay?" Gray sat, shoved himself out the opposite door and struggled to stay upright by leaning against the car.

"He needs a doctor. Rufus Allen was right. I think his rib is broken. Gray, he needs a hospital. We have to take him back to the Negro hospital in Memphis."

"He'll be arrested. Hell, we'll all be arrested!" Gray said.

Sterling came around the car next to Gray. "Silver could die."

"No, he won't." Gray said. "You treat him."

"I got a first aid kit, but I don't know where to start," she stuttered. His hand grasped hers and squeezed gently.

She kept her hand on the car to guide her to the front seat, where she pawed around the brown paper sacks and finally found a first aid kit that she'd brought. She took out the ointment, and grabbed a bottle of alcohol that might disinfect the wounds. Before she did anything else, she dug in another paper bag for a bottle of warm Coke, used the bottle opener she always carried, and took a big drink.

By the time she returned to the back, Gray had eased back into the station wagon and rested his head against the front seat. All the car doors stood open to let in a breeze. With one hand, Gray patted a wet cloth, torn from his tee shirt and dampened with water from the water bottle, across his brother's face.

She leaned into the passenger side and handed Gray the Coke. "This may perk you up."

For a second their fingers touched, they looked at each other, and Sterling flushed.

"H-he's on fire," Gray sounded a little flustered. He took a sip of the Coke. "I gave him the last penicillin pill. He needs a doctor."

Gray looked so wounded and frightened in the moonlight that she turned away, not wanting to see him like this. Too many of her illusions had vanished in the months they'd been apart. She wanted to keep one.

"Sterling?"

She turned on the flashlight to study Gray's body in a more clinical way. Cuts and bruising covered his soft features and light brown skin.

"Lift your shirt," she said.

He had dark blue spots on his abdomen and cuts on his side. She opened the ointment, squeezed some on her finger, and reached for Gray's side.

"What did they do to you?" she asked.

"Ow! Jesus Christ, Sterling, you're the worst nurse I ever saw."

"Then stop getting hurt."

"Don't poke me!"

"Show me your back." When he did, a hand flew to cover her mouth. "Mother of God."

"Rufus didn't tell you?"

"How can you stand to lay on your back?" She felt his forehead, nodded, and realized he probably couldn't see her. "Fever. You need a doctor too. Except for the hospital, I don't know where to find a doctor. I didn't think of it."

"Thought of hiding us under boxes, changing cars, going west instead of east. You knew they would try to stop us, didn't you? And sic the police on us?"

To her surprise, Gray touched her cheek and caressed it. "You found us, came for us. Seeing you . . . is good enough for me."

She leaned against the hand on her cheek. She felt light-headed from the rush. Suddenly she caught a whiff of something rotten. Raw meat, perhaps, a sandwich in one of the sacks in the backseat.

Without warning a whirling tunnel of grape vines or brambles grew around her. She gasped in panic then reeled as colors became loud and sounds turned yellow and red. In the center of the vortex, she saw the exchange at the barn.

"Do you love Gray," the Tom in her vision asked.

"Yes," Sterling said to the vision.

"Yes? What are you talking about?" The real Gray took her arm.

Suddenly the Tom in Sterling's memory grabbed Kate and disappeared in his Cadillac.

"No," she gasped.

"Sterling? What the hell?" Gray shook her arm. "You checked out for a while."

"No big deal." Sterling stammered, trying to remember what they'd been talking about.

"No big—?" Gray repeated. "Hey, look at me." His fingers took her chin and turned her face toward him.

"It's a like a voodoo spell comes over me sometimes. My senses get mixed up." She put her hands on his.

"Voodoo?"

No control. That's what she hated most about these spells. She never knew when she'd be entangled in the brambles and chaos inside her head. The brambles she recognized. Her father, mother, her brother Danny. Her mind skittered back to the screaming, hollering, terror-filled night her family fled the Louisiana mob and her tumble into a tangle of prickly bushes.

"I have no power over it, and I had to figure out what the visions mean," she said as though Gray been privy to her thoughts.

"Visions?" Gray sounded even more concerned.

"Gray, let's focus on Silver. His injuries—geez, look at him. We've gotta go to that Memphis hospital for Negro patients. I'm afraid—"

"No!" Silver said. A painful hiss came out of his mouth.

"We can't go to Memphis." Gray released her arm. "You think the police won't come in there after us?" He left what would happen after that to her imagination.

"No hospital." Silver whispered. "I feel better . . . . since the car's not moving."

"Silver." she protested.

"You need sleep, Sterling. That voodoo spell, or whatever just happened, makes me nervous," Gray said.

"You're just now getting nervous?" She forced a laugh.

"That ever happen before?" Gray asked.

"A few times. I don't know why it happens or how to stop it. I hear this wind, see these brambles, and my mind sees visions," she said. "When I come out of it, I've got a message or something."

"Jesus Christ," Gray said, wincing as he adjusted his left arm. "That's crazy. Go to sleep. I can watch things."

"Know of any hospitals for Black people in Arkansas?" Silver said softly.

Before she could answer Gray said, "How would a white girl explain driving up to a hospital with two wounded Black men?"

"Leave us in the parking lot and drive off," Silver said.

"Leave you?" she said. "Not after it took me so long to find you. I suppose I could—"

"No," Gray said. "Tomorrow we'll drive to St. Louis and find something along the way."

Silence. She carefully made her way around the car to Silver's side. She turned her back to the river and shone on the flashlight on him so she could apply ointment to the worst of his wounds. Twice she gagged and had to step away.

"I'm going to wipe your face with alcohol on a gauze pad. It might cool you down some too," she said. "I'll try not to hurt you. Show me what's under your shirt."

She flicked on the flashlight and aimed it from his waist to his face. He shook his head. "Hurts . . . to . . . breathe."

"I bet." She managed to pull his shirt out of his pants without his screaming. When she lifted it, the putrid odor assaulted her. She closed her eyes until she could fight back nausea.

"I'm goin' to pour alcohol on this to kill the infection." Sterling acted before he could object, catching the drips of blood and alcohol with his shirttail. He sucked a long pull of air through his teeth.

"I don't care if we all go to jail," she said. "I'm taking you to that hospital in Memphis."

"I care," Silver whispered. "I didn't do all this to end up in jail. You know. . .one of those men in the barn was a deputy sheriff."

"What? A deputy?"

"You're so naïve," Gray grunted. "Saw his badge."

Sterling sighed, torn between what she knew she should do and what her friends wanted. No matter the consequences, she couldn't let Silver die. Gray's hand touched her arm.

"Don't do it," he said. "I know you think you'll take us to a hospital anyway, but don't."

Since that was exactly what she'd been thinking, Sterling sighed.

"Okay, if y'all don't get worse tonight, we'll go on. I got aspirin. Let me come around to help Silver take them." She backed out of the car and felt her way around the car to the other side in the dark. As she walked on the uneven ground, her eyes adjusted to the light from the stars and moon. She stood facing the car to shield the light from the river and turned on her flashlight to find the aspirin bottle from the first aid kit.

So many aspirin were gone already, the new bottle felt light and useless in her hand. A jolt of panic shot through her. Her friends needed more help than she could give.

Uncertain how to make Silver more comfortable, she remembered Mrs. Allen had given them snake bite medicine. She reached between the seats and found the Mason jar. When she opened it, the scent of whiskey filled the air.

Helping Silver sit up enough to swallow the aspirin and whiskey took a while. She had to crawl inside the door and sit close to him. While his head rested against her shoulder, she could feel heat from his infected wounds.

"All my fault. I got him in Justice Tomorrow . . . Tom, I mean," Silver whispered.

White hot rage sizzled through her. She swallowed it. "You may have gotten Tom into Justice Tomorrow, but he fooled everybody. Me too." Especially her.

"Not Gray." Silver gasped. "He always knew."

Gray grunted.

"You know, Tom had no skills as an investigator," Sterling said, "but he believed in the mission of Justice Tomorrow. He cared about all of us until he saw a way to make a lot of money."

"Feel better that you got played too." A glimpse of the old Silver. "Nice."

She meant it as sarcasm, but somehow the word triggered sweet memories of how it felt to be swept away by Tom's promise of undying love. Stung by Gray's rejection, she had fallen into Tom's bed. On the rebound. She admitted it. Tom had gotten that much right.

Sadness swelled in her, and she stomped down the tears. Tom was right about another thing: crying and regret solved nothing.

"I knew you'd get us out . . . somehow," Silver said. "Gray told me to have faith."

"I didn't know you were in trouble for a long time." To her surprise, Silver took her hand. From his uneven breathing, that slight gesture hurt. She leaned down and kissed his forehead.

"Should a seen Gray in our safe house. Once he gets something in his head, he's like a tree that won't be moved."

She already knew that about her old partner.

"You need to shut up, little brother," Gray said.

Sterling held the jar of whiskey to Silver's lips.

"He beat this white man so bad—the cracker had shot a woman from the church choir. She just wanted to vote," Silver said.

"Give me that liquor," Gray said. "You're not old enough to drink, Aristotle Gray."

Sterling handed over the bottle, spilled some, and the aroma of whiskey grew stronger.

"Gray's not been right since you left," the younger man whispered to Sterling.

He was wrong about Gray. The air of violence she could always feel swirling around him had burst into the open in Crossville when the local sheriff had been killed and white killers had stalked her. Afterwards, she had been heartsick, but the corrupt sheriff's death released something in Gray.

"You gotta look out for him . . ." Silver began.

"Look after him yourself." Sterling said. "How could I have a world-famous agency of private investigators without you and Gray?"

Gray snorted. "Oh yeah, the White Chick and Two Brothers."

"Gray, Silver, and Sterling?" she countered.

"Sterling Brothers Limited," Silver whispered.

"'Cause we're a limited edition," Gray said. It was an old joke.

"Somebody besides me has to keep the company books," she said. "I can't add or divide."

"I always thought that was an act," Gray muttered.

His fingers brushed hers and warmth rush over her.

"No laughing . . . Sterling. Hurts." Silver drew a few shallow breaths. "I want to write books."

"You can write about the cases we investigate," she said. "Somebody should and you can still be our financial officer."

"Gray made me major in math," Silver wheezed. "I liked history."

"You always copied me," Gray teased.

"Gray knew we'd need someone with business knowledge one day," she said.

Silver gazed into her eyes. "You think . . . he knows everything."

"Hm-m." She urged him to sip water. Most of it ran down his chin. "Our agency will have a tall New York skyscraper for its offices. The whole building. My office will have a balcony. You can have a corner office."

"Gray?"

"You know he'll be in the basement or the lab or someplace getting our employees to invent better binoculars or smoke bombs o-or invisible ink."

"Right on." For a moment Silver seemed to stop breathing but picked it up again slower. "I love . . . you, white girl."

"We're a great team. Have another sip." She reached over and took the whiskey bottle from Gray and held it to Silver's lips.

"Feeling better." Silver jerked as though a sudden pain gripped him, then settled back against her. "Gonna break Gray's heart I got to you first. His own damn fault . . . for not speaking when he should have."

"You're drunk," Gray observed.

Sterling closed her eyes. She couldn't agree with Silver more. Over and over, she had replayed what Gray had once told her.

Hundred years ago, the world wasn't ready for a white woman to love a Black man. It still isn't. Probably never will be.

The worst part of that awful moment? In some sliver of her heart, she had agreed with him then. The knowledge still filled her with shame.

"You need to sleep," Sterling told Silver. "Wake up feeling better."

"I . . . wanna drive."

She settled Silver against her chest. "Not until you sober up."

He started to laugh. "Ow!"

"Sh-h-h," she said and glanced over. "Gray's asleep. Don't want to disturb our watchman."

How long she sat holding Silver's head against her and staring dully into the dark car she didn't know.

"I heard a baby cry," Silver whispered suddenly. "After they threw us in the car."

Sterling's heart nearly leapt out of her chest. She licked her lips. "I thought it was a cat."

"Maybe," he drifted back to sleep.

Her head bobbed and she jerked awake again. A mosquito buzzed, and she swatted it away. Occasionally she dabbed at the cuts on his face with alcohol-soaked gauze. It was so hot. Her stomach churned from exhaustion. Her muscles screamed for mercy. Silver seemed to relax, so she cradled him until she could lower him down flat.

"I'll check on you in a minute." The words of the lie slurred. Weariness dragged on her so heavily she knew she was in danger of sleeping a long time. At that moment, she didn't care.

She scooted out and stepped around the rear of the car to be greeted by a small welcoming breeze off the river that carried the scent of dead fish, decaying weeds, and rancid mud.

In the distance, she could see lights from Memphis across the bridge. To her right, darkness. A few lights in West Memphis looked so dim and far away they might have been stars. Occasionally, a car or two crossed the bridge. She could barely hear them. Instead, crickets and frogs called to each other in the stillness.

Nights used to be like this at her grandparents' house in Mississippi. As a child she loved visiting her mother's parents and the small furniture factory they owned. She stumbled on her first crush, the furniture plant manager, forcing himself on a Black employee. She informed her grandfather, and he told her colored women liked that sort of thing and she should forget it.

The breeze blowing across the Mississippi River felt heavy and full of the promise of rain. Sterling retreated to the driver's side. She pushed aside the doughnut pillow she'd sat on for driving and used it as a headrest when she stretched across the front seat. The fake leather interior stuck to her skin.

They'll be on us if we stay here. I can't sleep for long.

Behind her, Silver's rustling to get comfortable, and Gray's light snores lulled her to sleep.

CHAPTER TWENTY-THREE: A WATERY GRAVE

"No,no, no-no-no!"

Gray's desolate cries dug low and deep into Sterling's sleep-drugged brain. She pushed herself off the seat and her eyes swept around the car. How long since she laid down? No lights. No sound but Gray's piteous chorus.

Driven by his desperation, Sterling half-crawled over the front seat and snapped on the flashlight.

A sob caught in her throat. "Holy Mary Mother of God!"

From the passenger side of the bed, Gray clutched his brother in his good arm. Silver's head lolled to one side. Somehow, Gray had pulled the body halfway onto his lap. He raised his head from Silver slowly to meet her eyes. His mouth opened in quiet, agonized cries. Tears streaked down his battered cheeks and landed on his shirt.

"He's dead." Gray crushed the body closer to him, holding her eyes and shaking all over with the force of silent mourning. His head collapsed onto Silver's chest and his wails echoed inside the dead man's chest. She turned off the light.

A scream filled her throat, her head, her mouth, and she stuffed it inside with a hand slapped against the lips. She scrubbed her face, moaning low instead of letting her grief fill the sky. She reached for Gray, touched his shoulder, stroked his cheek, and mumbled her sorrow against his shoulder.

"Eternal rest grant unto him, Oh Lord. And let perpetual . . . May he rest in peace. Amen." Sterling mumbled what she remembered of the prayer from her brother Danny's funeral and made the sign of the cross.

Suddenly, her stomach revolted. She skittered out of the front seat, stumbled into the weeds, and vomited. Nothing but bitter regret and useless bile. She came back to the car, washed out her mouth with warm Coke.

She should have listened to good sense and taken Silver and Gray to the hospital.

She located her flashlight and went around the car to shine it on Gray. He still held his brother, rocking back and forth. A ragged hum of grief surrounded the men and seemed to close them off from her. Sterling crawled in so close to Gray that the heat of his skin burned her. After a moment she reached across Gray to caress Silver's forehead, his hair.

"He was trying to grow an Afro," she said. "H-he seemed better when I went to sleep. Oh, God. Gray, I am so sorry. I shouldn't have left him—."

The humming stopped. Gray turned and when she looked into his swollen eyes, he shook his head at her.

"Not your fault. I should have watched over him closer. I should have carried him into the hospital and let you go. He was my responsibility. My fault."

Mosquitoes buzzed in chorus. A bullfrog croaked. She moaned and held onto Gray's shoulder as he sobbed.

"What are we going to do now?" It was more a question she was asking herself than one for Gray. "We can't leave him."

"I don't want him buried in some white cracker's field," Gray said.

Sterling nodded, though she knew he couldn't see her. Besides, neither of them was strong enough to dig a grave.

Gray shifted Silver from his one good arm to the floor of the station wagon. Then he heaved a ragged sigh. "We'll give him into the arms of Old Man River."

"Y-you want to put him in the Mississippi?"

"Let's pull him out on the quilt."

She crawled out of the car and swayed, her arms and legs wobbling under her.

Gray made his way to the back to grab the old quilt by the edges nearest the rear bumper.

"Help me." He used his right arm, pulled, and one side of the quilt moved.

Sterling took hold of the quilt's other edge as well as Silver's foot. Together she and Gray pulled the body until she could lower Silver's shoulders and head gently on the ground.

With a whimper that sounded like a wounded animal, Gary crossed his brother's arms across his chest, folded the edges of the Allens' old quilt over the body and stood with his head bowed.

"I am going to kill Tom Foster. Slowly. He orchestrated all this," Gray said as though discussing plans for a party. "I will kill everyone he holds dear down to his last son and daughter."

Kill everyone?

A drop of sweat rolled down the right side of Sterling's face. She stifled her fear and shock by clearing her throat. He didn't know. Gray didn't know about Kate. How could he? They had fled Crossville before she could tell him she was pregnant. They were apart during the last five and a half months of her pregnancy, and he was unconscious during the exchange.

"Will you help me?"

"Of course, anything." She blurted out, "You should know, Tom found me and told me where to get you."

Gray's rage flew across her like a meteor and disappeared. "Y-you weren't with Tom the time we were apart?"

"What? No." She wished she could see his face, although she should be glad he couldn't see hers and pick out the half-truths she spoke. "Back in Crossville, we played at being married. That was our assignment, that's how we fit into Crossville society."

"Why do you defend him?"

"I'm not defend—I am telling you the way it was. His father found him and got hold of him. It was like a watching a snake charmer."

Abruptly Gray fell to his knees by his dead brother. "I should have taken better care of you, Aristotle. Mother said to watch over you, and I failed her again."

Sterling allowed the air in her lungs to seep out. Gray would ask again, demand more information about her time away from him, but she must be better prepared. Her grief at losing Kate and now Silver rose in her throat and threatened to choke off her air. Gray must never know the real price of his freedom. He already carried too much guilt and sorrow about Silver.

"Help me drag my brother into the river."

"You want to do that?"

"This flesh and bones isn't him. Not anymore. I have to accept that." Gray's voice became gradually deeper. "We'll put rocks in his pants and in the quilt, so the body will sink."

In the distant sky over Arkansas, she heard a rumble of thunder.

"I don't want anyone to find him like this." Gray stood by Silver's head when she returned. "Help me."

She took off her loafers, forced the barrel of the flashlight into the waistband of her skirt, and went over to the quilt barefooted. Together, they tugged on Silver's ankles and the edges of the quilt until Gray doubled up in pain and rested against a tree.

"Let me." Sterling held Silver's feet wrapped in the quilt, dragging the corpse over the weeds and rocks of the field toward the river. She winced at the rocks that dug into her bare feet. At first, the body was hard to move. Gradually, the body slid over the grass into the muddy ground of the water's edge.

Gray sat on a log and rested. He finally rose and began tossing rocks from the riverbank onto the quilt. She found a few rocks and stuffed them in Silver's jeans pocket. She watched Gray stand, grasp a sapling for support, and peel off his clothes. It was too dark to see much, but he turned away from her with a "Sorry" when he shucked his pants.

They waded into the water together. When it got over their knees, the water helped them carry the body.

Gray stopped and weaved in the water for a moment, panting. "I got him." He took the body out further, alone, and vanished behind a pile of brush along the river.

"Gray?" She couldn't even hear water splashing. "Gray!"

Her nervous stomach kicked, making her risk clicking on the flashlight. She glimpsed him chest deep in the river, leaning against a gentle current, his outstretched arm carrying his brother like an offering. He kept walking. Worried, she flicked off the light and called to keep track of him, to make sure he wasn't drowning.

At last, his splashing back to shore made her exhale. She shielded the light with her hand so she could find her way back to the car in a hurry for something to wrap around him. On the way, she snatched up his clothes. She listened to him moving through the water, struggle toward the shore. Weeping. She put her shoes on and hurried back.

"Gray, here's a sheet to wrap in, get dry." She walked toward the river with it spread wide before her, wrapped him in, pausing to savor the feel of her arms around him. While he stumbled to the car, she scuffed her feet to mess up the smooth path made dragging the body to the river. To show him the way, she shielded the flashlight's glow and pointed it to where she'd put his clothes. From there, she heard him crying.

She waited for him at the water's edge, marveling at the calm out there when there was so much storm on the shore. Drawn in the night sky with flashes of lightening, the faces of her brother Danny, Kate, and Silver slammed into her heart. The lost ones stole her breath and left her with tremors.

No tears. She would never waste time on tears and what-ifs ever again.

Gray moved so quietly she didn't realize he stood by her. She could see the outline of his cheeks, nose, and mouth as he gazed over the Mississippi. He spoke as though thinking out loud.

"Silver was so full of hot air all the time—you'd think he'd float. Body sank right down, settled into the current as nice as you please. Might be in New Orleans in a day or so. He always wanted to go there, listen to the jazz and Dixieland."

Sterling's head dropped a little, and she put a hand over her mouth to keep herself from screaming. She moved back, away from the water. Memories of her own brother's funeral mass smashed into her. Danny died in Vietnam—she still couldn't wrap her heart around it. Now Silver was dead too. She grabbed for Gray's arm.

She tried concentrating on things she could see, things that were real. A river barge came downstream in the middle of the river, its progress marked by dots of light fore and aft. Across the river, lightning lit the Memphis skyline.

Suddenly, Gray punched the air viciously with his left fist and took a step toward the river. He cried to the heavens, "What kinda man am I? Huh? Answer me that, God. You're the evil one, You know that? White man won't let me eat, sleep, or piss where I want. Whites lynched my daddy and made my mama crazy enough to die. White men beat my brother to death. You let them do this! You stood by and did nothing!"

The outburst startled Sterling. Her arm slid off Gray.

"After all that," Gray went on, "all that, God, You twisted around, connived, and made it so the only woman, the only woman, I could ever love is white."

Sterling's heart squeezed in love and pity. She moistened her lips. "Not exactly how I hoped you'd tell me, Gray, but I'll take it and treasure it."

He turned to her and drew her into the circle of his embrace. His words ruffled the top of her head. "God damn all of it. God damn everything and everyone but you."

A sense of completion settled over her, and she knew the rescue was the only thing she could have done. She should have held onto her daughter, but she had to take the risk. It was her decision to attempt a rescue, her crazy plan to take Kate along, and her arrogance that cost her Kate. Gray would never bear the burden of guilt that she carried. He would never know what she sacrificed for him.

Dizziness swept over her as he released her and took a few steps toward the water. She raised her chin to see him standing there, both hands over his face. A tree swept by, caught helplessly in the river's rush. Thunder roared.

"Gray. We gotta get out of here."

The lightning from the coming storm revealed him moving toward the car. Slumped over. Broken. Lost.

"Gray, look at me." She grabbed his hand. "We will make life, a good life. You and me. Together. Don't you think Silver would want us to be happy?"

She saw the first stirrings of the man she loved when Gray gave her a crooked smile. "Not much of a choice: drown in hate or keep you from getting killed."

Sterling put her hands on his cheek, his forehead, and slid them toward his chin. When her fingers touched his lips, he pulled her close, leaned over, and buried his face in her shoulder.

"We've got to go," she said, hating to end his touch. "I'll fix these boxes over you when you're comfortable."

When she'd made sure Gray was hidden, she placed the doughnut pillow under her and climbed in front of the steering wheel. She found the brown wig, wiggled it on her head, and tucked her red curls under it. Using the hand mirror from her purse, she applied makeup as thick as she dared to cover dark circles under her eyes, and pink lipstick. The wig looked fine for a drive-by look. She hoped nobody checked her out her closely.

With a satisfied grin at her image in the mirror, she started the car and backed out. Thunder rumbled. She would have to drive to St. Louis through a rainstorm. From there she'd figure it out.

The field gate near the highway closed behind her car and she scurried around to the driver's seat as lighting tore across the sky. In its wake, she saw an Arkansas State Police car pull in and park to block her in. She waved at him, reached in the car for her fake license and registration, and whispered to Gray: "Cops."

She stepped beside the car door, cocked her hip, and slipped her documents in her skirt's side pocket, mindful that the trooper watched her. He climbed out of his cruiser as though he was in no rush. An angular face under the brim of his uniform hat was all she could make of his features, but the trooper moved with a swagger. As he grew nearer, he seemed not much older than her.

"Morning, Officer." She leaned against the car and smiled at him.

"Mornin'." He stopped two feet away and shone a powerful flashlight on her. She threw a hand up to shield her eyes and hairline. It was so natural a move, the trooper didn't act like it was anything but a reaction to the light and not a way to keep him from examining the wig too closely.

"What were you doing in that field?"

"Sleeping. I'm moving from Jackson to St. Louis. Got real sleepy, saw the open gate, and drove to those trees." Sterling pointed to the riverbank. "I figured no one would see me and I'd be safe for a couple of hours. A girl traveling alone must be careful."

The trooper nodded. "Driver's license?"

"I know I was trespassing, but I didn't hurt anything, I promise." She handled it over.

The trooper whiffed inside the car and his nose wrinkled. "That liquor I smell?"

A tsunami of panic hit Sterling. She hung her head. "I might have had a little drink in that field. My boyfriend broke up with me yesterday."

The police officer drew in a deep breath and grimaced.

Besides the whiskey aroma, she probably smelled like the underside of a garbage can.

Cry. Make him feel sorry for you.

But she couldn't. Sterling's stomach clenched.

The trooper walked around the car with his light, observing the outside and studying the inside. "How do you like this Pontiac?"

Sterling blinked in surprise. "Drives like a tank. My daddy wanted me to be safe. I wanted a Mustang. You see who won."

With a chuckle, the trooper walked back to the front of the car. Sterling turned to face him, waiting for him to pounce.

The trooper flipped her license between two fingers. "Okay, miss. It was smart to pull over when you got tired but get a room next time."

She dropped her head and played in the dirt with her shoe hoping to avoid a lecture.

"You don't know who might prowl out here," the trooper went on. "We got officers searching the Arkansas and Tennessee sides of the river for two colored boys who murdered three men yesterday—one a Shelby County deputy sheriff. Happened on the other side of Memphis in a barn like the one you slept next to."

"No! How awful . . . and scary." Sterling hoped the quivering in her arms and knees didn't show. "I'll remember those families in my prayers tonight."

"Here's your license. Might be good to pull into a gas station and wait out this storm." The trooper tipped his hat.

No mention of a red-haired white girl at the murder scene or driving the get-away car. Sterling stuffed her license into the pocket of her skirt. Did the trooper merely leave that part out or was that information Tom and Grace didn't want known? They didn't want anyone to connect what happened outside the barn to them or to her. Too many questions might arise about a baby.

Three men dead.

Could Kate's father, the man who stole her from Sterling, be a murderer? A shiver ran down her spine.

Yanking the door open, she scooted under the steering wheel and tried to find a comfortable way to sit.

In a moment, the cop backed away and drove off, leaving her free to get on the highway. A bump and a rock crashed into the undercarriage as the car cleared the dirt road and lifted onto the asphalt highway. The tires hummed on the road. The first plops of rain hit her windshield.

The first chance she got she'd have a sitz bath. She dreamed of it.

"All clear." She checked the side mirror to be sure the cop had left.

"Three men dead?" Gray said from the back. His voice sounded weak, tired. "What the hell happened? Everyone was alive when I blacked out. I remember nothing until I came to in the floor of your car."

"I don't know," Sterling said. "When I took off, all three men were locked in the barn. That's all I know about them until I looked in the rearview mirror to see that red Ford behind me with its hood in the air. They must have hit a pothole. I never saw them again—I think I saw two of them in the car. I don't even know where the third man went."

"Well, something happened," he gasped. "Goddamn head hurts so badly."

"Gray, I'm drinking hot Coke to stay awake, but you can have some. Let me find some aspirin too." She kept her eyes on the road. "Big, dark thunderclouds ahead of us. Can't stop. I'm going to reach my hand back between the seats to hand you the aspirin bottle."

"Won't make a dent in this headache."

"That's all I've got." She glanced in the rearview mirror to discover nothing behind her. "Do you have the water jug back there?"

The boxes jostled in her mirror, and one hit the back of her seat.

"I got this whiskey." More boxes bumped into each other. After a while, he wheezed, "Aristotle Gray is dead. My only brother is floating down the Mississippi River. He's gone. You're all I have left, Sterling."

She swallowed. "I'll try to be enough."

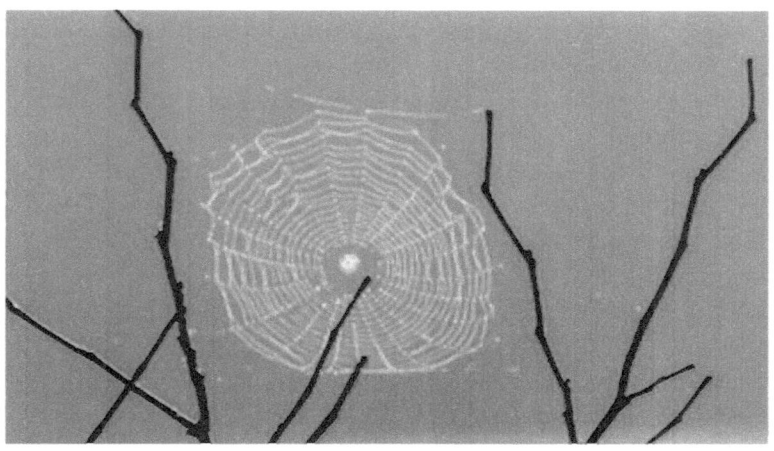

CHAPTER TWENTY-FOUR: FLIGHT TO ST. LOUIS

Gray woke in a panic, in the dark with a sack over his head. The relentless pounding in his head overpowered the burning of slashes along his back and sides. His broken arm radiated pain, and his disorientation grew in a spinning world he couldn't stop.

"Help! Stop!" Gray slung his good arm out to get rid of whatever covered him.

"What's wrong?" Sterling called from the driver's seat.

A woman's voice.

"Let me go!" he cried.

Not the voice of the woman from the barn. Someone else.

"I pulled over, that's all," Sterling said. "Gray, everything's okay."

"Sterling?"

Was it really her? Gray couldn't hear well with a feed sack over his head and his stomach pulsating from the body blows he'd received.

"You're with me now," Sterling said. "I have you covered with boxes."

Now he could see and feel that cardboard, not feed sack burlap, surrounded him. Stifling. He was so hot.

"I've got the car's air-conditioner up full blast. I'm freezing up here," she said.

Had he spoken aloud? What was happening to him? His hands felt the surrounding floor. He was alone.

"Where's Silver? Where's my brother?" he said.

For a long time, he heard nothing. "Sterling? You found us."

"Don't you remember?"

"Where's Silver?"

"It's my fault. I should have taken him to the hospital," Sterling began.

His brother was dead. Now Gray remembered. "No, that's my fault. And his. That's not your burden to carry."

"I knew better." Sterling's voice had a catch in it.

"No!" Gray said. "Where are we?"

"Just the other side of Poplar Bluff. We'll be in St. Louis in two hours, maybe. I figure nobody will think to follow us there. Have to find a road out of town after that. It's hard to read a map while driving, so I pulled over," she said.

"Where's Silver?"

"He died," she said again. "You buried him in the Mississippi River right before the storm."

"Storm?"

"A gully washer. We drove through it."

"My brother's dead?"

"I'm sorry, Gray."

Her words struck him like a knife that ripped another wound in his heart. His back burned like hellfire and his left arm rested in a sling and hurt like the devil if he moved it.

"I'm so sorry," she said again.

The car started and rolled along the road. Another scrap of memory popped in his head.

"The barn. Then we were in a farmhouse."

"Yes."

He didn't tell her what else he had recalled—beatings, hunger, thirst, hanging from his wrists. Silver's smart-mouthing their three captors. The shrill, Southern woman on the phone who had approved the abuse.

"We-we were filthy," he said. "Silver had to get clean."

"He sure did," Sterling said.

"They jumped us. Put feed sacks over our heads as we locked up after Sunday services. In Mullinsville." Memories came to him like bursts of sun through trees.

"How did I get to the farmhouse?" he asked.

"I drove you."

He would have to take her word for that.

"I remember. You've put on weight since I last saw you. Filled out. . .everywhere."

"You're saying I'm fat?" Sterling's outraged sounded fake.

"Not fat. Exactly. Filled out. In the right places," he said.

She chuckled. "Too late. I'm already insulted."

His head hurt. "I can't win."

"Gray, did those kidnappers ask you about Justice Tomorrow files?"

"Sometimes."

Although, the men didn't seem to care whether they got the files or not. Why did he think that?

"I am so sorry I didn't get there sooner." He heard her hesitation. "What happened before your kidnappers dragged you out of the barn to my car? Did you see a Black man with mutton chops and a mustache?"

"Silver and I were the only Black men they captured. The only Blacks in that barn," he said. "Three men shot?"

"There was someone else there," she said. "Someone you didn't see."

The only person he knew about was the woman on the phone who barked orders.

"A woman. A heard a woman's voice," he said.

"Grace was close to the barn. It was probably her."

He shook his head, regretted moving and started to tell Sterling, she was wrong. Something else plucked at the corner of his mind and washed over him in a sickening realization.

"Silver had that pistol from Crossville," he said. "The one with the broken grip. Never got a chance to pull it out of his belt."

"Are you thinking someone used Silver's gun to kill those men?" Sterling's voice rang with alarm. "Can it be traced to him? Did you have fake IDs on you?"

"I was called Joe Peters," Gray lost track of his thought for a moment, "Lots of people in Crossville know Silver had that gun."

"Gray, think. Did people in Crossville know you and Silver were related?"

He shifted around, trying to find a comfortable spot on the hard surface of the station wagon's flat back. His reward sizzled with pain from the wounds on his back. "I don't know. Can't think."

"Let's hope they don't connect the gun and the dead men," Sterling said.

From what little Gray could see through the holes in the box the sky had turned greyish blue. He caught the flash of green leaves on a tree branch. Yellow, blue, green, and dots of white were about all he could see when he looked through cracks of the barn walls, too.

Don't Be Cruel came on the car radio. Sterling tried to sing along but her effort sounded half-hearted.

His head hurt so badly. He closed his eyes against the pain.

"What else do you remember?" Sterling asked.

"A woman—no, a man with a Rebel flag tattooed on his biceps—used a board on Silver. I hollered at him. A woman's voice. Nothing after that." Gray didn't want to remember. Were there two women's voices?

"No Black man?" Sterling's voice sounded urgent. "Sure?"

Gray's stomach hurt all the time when he moved, or something moved him. His captors had pummeled his abdomen and kidneys until blood colored his urine.

Was there another Black man in the barn? Is that what Sterling said?

The car slowed on the pavement and finally hit gravel.

"I've got to get some gas," Sterling said. "Lay still until I drive away."

An attendant came around to pump Sterling's tank full of gas. Gray imagined a teenage white boy with pimples wiping the windows and checking the oil. He remembered himself as a young man at Yale on scholarship, learning to revere Gandhi and the Rev. Martin Luther King Jr.

"Can you get me a copy of the *St. Louis Post Dispatch* and *The Commercial Appeal*? I see their news boxes over there," Sterling said to the attendant. Coins jingled.

"Shore," said a young voice.

Silver was so young. Gray had secretly rejoiced when Silver followed him into Justice Tomorrow training camp. Why had he let his brother quit school and join? Gray snorted, knowing he couldn't have stopped Silver if he tried. But he didn't try. He wanted to keep his brother close and out of trouble. By then, he and Sterling were partners, and he was falling in love. His little brother had a big, toothy smile so warm people naturally wanted to be around him.

Silver's smile. Gray panicked. It wouldn't come into focus. He recalled when Silver's front teeth came out on the same day of first grade and the big hole that had left. But his brother's smile at nineteen wouldn't come to mind. Gray's body jerked against a cardboard box.

"Ma'am, them boxes smell like something died back there," drawled the gas station attendant.

Odd, Gray imagined a faint hint of cinnamon. Maybe Sterling had it on the air freshener that dangled from the rear view mirror.

"Oh, no! Some of my food probably spoilt," Sterling said as she turned the ignition key. "How much do I owe you?"

What Black man would be with the kidnappers? What was Sterling talking about?

"Eight dollars and twenty-five cents, counting the papers," the young man said and handed her the newspapers she asked for.

"Whoa, I was almost empty," Sterling said.

The gas station attendant chuckled. "You pretty near coasted to the pump. Thank you, ma'am, and here's your change."

Sterling had money. She paid for gas, some candy and other items at the drugstore where she stopped, and she must have bought a car, no, two cars. She left one with the Adams, no, the Allen family. Where did all that money come from? Her Justice Tomorrow salary? Somehow Gray didn't think so.

He felt the car hit the pavement again, the tires humming along the road. The radio played mostly static until she turned it off.

"Gray, you have to keep me awake. Talk."

"After Justice Tomorrow collapsed, what did you do? Where did you go?" he asked.

"Well, I went to work as a short-order cook in Philadelphia," she said. "Then I moved on to work in Tennessee."

Gray heard the bitterness in her voice, and it triggered a scrap of memory about Mullinsville.

"I worked in east Tennessee in a mudhole town by the side of the road," Gray said. "People there eked out a living, growing corn and enough vegetables to can for the winter. Black people were afraid to go into that county seat after dark."

The car hit a bump, and he grimaced before continuing.

"Silver and some of the young hot heads wanted to start a voting drive but the pastor—. He and the sheriff grew up together and were quite the scourge of the town as boys. Pastor wanted to stay out of it."

Gray fell silent again.

"What happened?"

"Bloody Sunday. It was Bloody Sunday."

CHAPTER TWENTY-FIVE: PIECES OF THE PUZZLE

Sterling swerved to avoid pieces of a busted tire in the road. A loaded semi-trailer truck cargo rumbled by her, its tailwind shaking the car.

"Huh! What the hell!" Gray cried from the backseat.

"Just a truck passing," she said. "What happened after the Bloody Sunday march in Selma?"

Gray's voice sounded weaker. "Being poor makes white people angry, and they look for someone to blame. Why they want to blame their poverty on folks poorer than they are is a mystery. Ignorant white folks always want to kick down, not up."

Sterling squinted at the sun now streaming through the window after the thunderstorm.

"Somebody shot and killed Jimmy Taylor in his driveway." Gray said and Sterling's heart sank. "Pastor Dixon nearly died himself. Nobody could reach him, he grieved so. He nearly moved in with Jimmy Taylor's widow and son. I tried to keep the church going but wasn't long afterwards that Silver and I were kidnapped."

"Poor Pastor Dixon. His best friend. Do you know who did it?"

"I don't have a clue, or I would have . . . handled it." Gray's words dragged. He sounded tired.

Sterling's throat went dry. Gray couldn't keep 'handling' things. His growing tendency toward violence frightened her.

"What did you do after you left Crossville besides cook in a bar?" he said. "Didn't you make it to your safe house?"

Gray didn't seem to remember what she'd told him a few miles ago? Did he remember her telling him about the Black man with mutton chops at the barn? Sterling frowned at her reflection in the rearview mirror.

"I did get to a safe house. I was there when I got word my brother died in Vietnam." Her voice grew husky, and she cleared her throat. "My older brother Danny—remember how I used to talk about him? Army lieutenant?"

Gray didn't sound like he remembered, but he muttered, "Yes."

"My handler came for me at the safe house and drove me to the airport so I could catch a plane to Boston and told me about a safe place I could stay. A place in Kentucky. Gray? Are you listening?"

He didn't answer. She turned off the radio so she could listen for his breathing. At first, she couldn't catch a sound from him, and panic shot through her. She pressed against the seat and leaned her head back as far as she could.

She heard a snort followed by a soft groan. The highway ahead came back into focus for her, although not for long.

The trip had given her time to think, and she'd remembered things that happened right in front of her.

On her last day in Boston Sterling remembered that the assailants came while she was on the phone with Tom. Perhaps he'd really called to make sure she was home when the men arrived.

Sterling frowned. That didn't sound right. Tom and his father may want the Justice Tomorrow's files, but neither would ever risk harming the unborn baby.

When she told him she was pregnant, Tom had whooped and twirled her around their tiny Crossville living room. He kissed her and planned to buy a cradle the very next day. She had laughed at him, clinging to his arms and soaking in his excitement. Finally, they agreed to keep the baby a secret since Justice Tomorrow would pull Sterling out of the mission if they learned about it.

"Wait until my father hears that I'm about to give him the heir he always wanted," Tom had said. "I did something right at last,"

A car honked as it passed the station wagon, and Sterling concentrated on keeping the car in its lane. In a pasture to her right, a sleek, brown horse raced from the barn and around the pasture, stopped, pranced, and threw up his head. Delighted to be free.

She would never feel that free until she held Kate again.

That baby would have a complete family and a life of privilege in a Catholic home. Stop thinking of yourself for a moment.

Sister Agnes' words echoed in Sterling's ear. Was she being selfish to want Kate? Maybe her daughter would be better off with Tom and Grace. Tom's wife seemed like she would be the perfect mother. She appeared so eager to have Kate and she hadn't lost her poise through the entire exchange, which Sterling grudgingly admired in retrospect.

The exchange scene at the barn replayed in her mind. Tom had made it clear he wanted her to escape alive. He'd bought her time to get away, even as he stole Kate from her arms. She returned to thinking how up-tight Tom seemed. Maybe he knew no one outside that black Cadillac was meant to leave barn in Memphis alive. In her mind's eye she watched Grace run to the barn and lift the bar to free the red car that had chased her down the rutted farm road. Sterling tried to remember, had Grace then stepped inside the barn? Somehow Sterling thought she had.

Were all those people killed to keep the truth about Kate's birth a secret? Did Tom hope to pin the murders on Silver and Gray in some sort of perverted revenge?

"Tom's father is rich and worried about his family name," Sterling said aloud as though Gray were listening. "He has eyes like a cobra."

"You have much experience with cobras?" Gray muttered from the backseat.

"Holy Mother!" She had always assumed the dark shadow behind Tom was his father. She hated Brian Foster, but what if she was wrong? "Gray, maybe someone besides Brian Foster is behind all this murder."

"Who else was there?" Gray asked.

Sterling told him again about the man with mutton chops and a mustache who peeked from the hayloft.

"Huh. Well, he sure kept quiet while those honkies beat Silver and me."

"You're assuming he was with the kidnappers," Sterling said.

"Hmm-m. Aren't you?" The boxes moved as Gray attempted to get comfortable. "Who else could he be? I'm going to roast his ass over an open fire."

Amid the static from the radio, Sterling considered a player she'd only heard about from her Justice Tomorrow handler and read about while searching for something on Atlanta Investment's J. D. Masterson; namely, Tom's father-in-law John Cofield. She turned off the radio.

"Gray, my handler knew John Cofield and his daughter Grace Foster. She told me about them while we were in the car driving to the airport," Sterling said.

"Tom is married?"

"You didn't know? He talked about her often. Loved her dearly," Sterling lied. "Mrs. Woolworth, my handler, had been questioning me about the mission in Crossville when she dropped a bit of information about Cofield and his daughter."

"What did she say?"

"Well, Grace is insufferably arrogant like her father. New money, you know. A beautiful woman with a dreadful laugh and the most exaggerated drawl. Apparently it was quite a joke in society circles when Grace Cofield set her cap for Tom. No Atlanta debutante would date him for fear of Grace's retribution."

"Well, she caught him," Gray said.

"Mrs. Woolworth said that money and power attract money and power, although the scuttlebutt is that Grace is very much in love with him."

"Love can make a person do strange things," Gray observed.

That's the truth. A lump in her throat kept Sterling silent for a moment.

"Mrs. Woolworth also told me that John Cofield's a big player in Georgia politics," she said. "Rumor has it Grace is poised to take over his empire. But Mrs. Woolworth thinks John Cofield's right-hand man will be the most likely successor. Politicians in the South don't tend to like having a woman boss."

"What lovely people," Gray said. "Who's the right-hand man?"

"She didn't say. But she described John as a lumbering fellow with a bulbous nose who sort of looked like a gangster from one of those Humphrey Bogart movies," Sterling said.

"Justice Tomorrow certainly dropped the ball checking Tom Foster's background," Gray said.

Sterling's eyes blurred and she blinked against the sunlight bouncing off her car's hood. She took one hand off the wheel to stretch her fingers and think about that conversation with Mrs. Woolworth. A political leader like John Cofield would certainly want the evidence Justice Tomorrow collected. Several political figures—mayors, judges, policemen—were implicated in murders Sterling and Gray had investigated. No doubt there were other public officials in other Justice Tomorrow case files. Perhaps Cofield knew it. Still, it didn't seem likely he would risk his granddaughter's life to get it.

But Grace's father didn't know about Kate. Tom and Grace are passing Kate off as their natural child.

"Not likely with that red hair," Sterling mumbled aloud.

On both sides of the highway woods, pastures, fields, and towns rolled by as though in a dream.

One thought kept stabbing her awake each time she threatened to doze off: *Holy Mother of God, Kate is gone.*

She prayed for help as the car rolled onto the gravel shoulder of the road.

"Sterling!" Gray cried.

She jerked the car back onto the highway.

"Do we need to stop?" he said.

"No, Gray, I'm fine now," she said. "You fell asleep, so I did too."

The boxes shifted in the back as Gray changed positions. "Can't stay awake."

"Probably a blessing with the way you hurt," she said.

"I'm sorry, Sterling. Listen, I didn't know about Danny. I'm sorry," Gray muttered. "We've both lost brothers."

"You would have loved Danny," she said. "He knew a million puns."

Gray's mentioning Danny made Sterling feel better. Maybe Gray did remember things she'd told him.

CHAPTER TWENTY-SIX: THE NEVER-ENDING ROAD

The road to St. Louis seemed endless to Gray. A forever journey in semi-darkness with pain in his body and torment in his soul. Sometimes Sterling would remark on a herd of cows, green fields, and signs to stop at Joe's Café or drink Budweiser beer. He didn't feel like he was in the same world as Sterling. Perhaps he never had been.

"How did you find Silver and me?" he asked.

"Tom," she said. "I told you. He tracked me down and, ah, told me you were in trouble. Well, he didn't find me personally. He hired a private investigator to do it."

Gray mulled that over.

"What did you have to pay Tom to get us out?" Gray asked after a few miles.

"I made a deal." Sterling's voice sounded heavy from the effort of getting oxygen in and out.

"Seems like Tom was willing to let his men go back on the deal."

"I think those men belonged to his father. Or his father-in-law. I knew going in that Tom had very little say in this, and somebody else—his father, most likely—controlled the rest. Tom did warn me they were coming for us."

"He wrecked Justice Tomorrow and had Silver and me kidnapped," Gray said. "What did they want from you?"

"They were looking for any agent they could lay hands on," she said. "He wanted what I had."

"What the hell was it?"

He heard Sterling gulp several swallows of last night's Coke. At least he figured it was Coke. She always had one.

"Case files. The people who want the rest of those files will still come after us hard."

He heard her picking her words carefully like Silver choosing which rocks to step on in the creek.

"What did those files have that anyone needed?" The cardboard boxes knocked and raged against each other as Gray tried to get comfortable.

After a long silence, he said, "Sterling?"

"Can we leave it at that?"

"What did you do to free Silver and me?" Gray said. "I have to know."

"You don't," she snapped.

A low growl of irritation rose in his throat.

"Don't ever ask me again what it took to get your release." The anger in her voice seemed to melt away, and she added, "Please. Your gift to me."

Gift? He rustled around, letting his rattling the boxes reflect his discontent. She said nothing. The tires on the road hummed beneath him. He settled, exhausted, suddenly understanding. The price of his freedom cut her too deeply to explain. Right then. But she would when she was ready. He cleared his throat.

"I won't ask again."

The words hurt his pride, but his head pounded so badly he needed relief. He groped in the backseat for the aspirin bottle. After washing two down with the last of the water in the jug given to them by the Adams, no, the family's name was Allen, his pain eased a little. He planned to drink the whiskey, but the aspirin took the worst of his headache away, so he waited. Sterling must have cranked the air conditioning on super high. He shivered and watched chill bumps ripple along his good arm.

Where were they going? Gray focused on the question. The answer danced outside his grasp. Kentucky? Someone unknown to Justice Tomorrow or anyone else? Sterling's telling him where they were headed suddenly blurred into the day a mob lynched his father. His mother had taken Silver and run into the woods, but not before making him promise to get his father out of the house. He couldn't make his father stop shooting at the mob. Gray ran out the back as white men were breaking down the front door. He left his father to die. And when his father died, life drained from his mother.

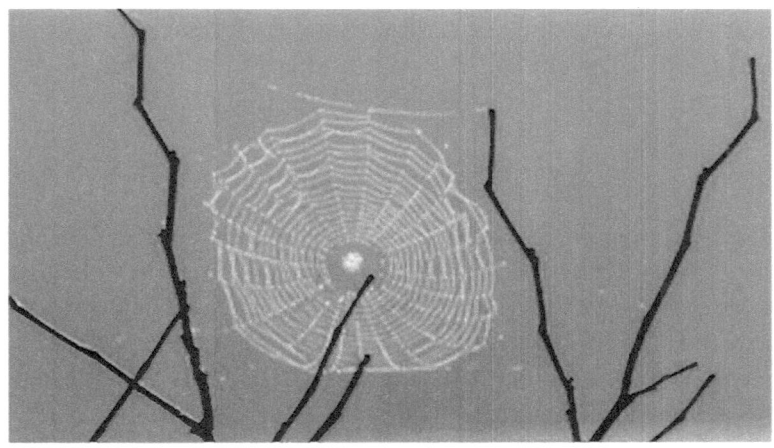

CHAPTER TWENTY-SEVEN: THE CAGE AND KEY

"Gray! Wake up," Sterling said. Her hand tapped the cardboard box and dragged him from a terrifying nightmare. "We're a little south of St. Louis. I pulled off into a little nowhere road so you can stretch your legs."

Woods again? Not St. Louis or Kentucky?

His arms and legs wouldn't obey him.

"Can't . . ."

She got out, lifted the boxes to reveal his face, and touched his forehead. "Holy Mary and Joseph, you're on fire."

Her words, her face, her touch jumbled in his mind.

"Your cuts . . . they look all red—," she said. "They're infected."

"Aristotle. Where's my brother," he whispered.

Something cool on his face, his forehead, the cuts on his chest and side. The all-too-familiar smell of rubbing alcohol. Her hands, Sterling's hands. The feel of them on his skin made him sigh and close his eyes.

"I've got to get you some help. You have to get to a hospital."

Gray didn't care what she said or where they were going. He closed his eyes. The car moved again, and the hum of the tires lulled him to sleep.

**

Gray's condition terrified Sterling. She located Homer G. Phillips Hospital for Negroes and frowned as a white woman in a checkered dress berated a Black man parked near the entrance. As she drove by she noticed a police cruiser near the emergency door. Leaving Gray there would mean prison for him as a murderer if they connected him to the barn in Memphis—and jail for her as an accessory. She drove away with a death grip on the steering wheel.

One thing she'd learned, however. She would risk prison rather than let Gray die as Silver had.

Thank God the rain had stopped. Puddles dotted the streets, making the summer humidity worse. Children cooped up in their homes during the rainstorms now flooded the curbs, vacant lots, and tiny patches of grass in front of duplexes. Others jumped and splashed in puddles on the streets.

Sterling drove up and down streets looking for a secluded place to leave Gray but close enough that she could point people to him. She figured adults watching their children play would be most likely to help an injured man.

This half-baked plan had to work fast, or she'd drop him off at Homer G. Phillips and take her chances. Even if she dropped Gray off near the emergency room door and phoned in a tip from a phone booth, a white woman would be noticed. She had to blend in, to act and sound like a woman driving with Tennessee plates lost in a Black neighborhood, or someone might involve the police. She drove faster.

Had she already waited too long? A lump rose in her throat at the idea of losing Gray. She would drive around this one last street to find what she wanted and if she didn't see it, she'd head to the hospital. She should have ignored Silver and Gray and gotten Silver to a doctor. The fear of the police killing him was real enough, but maybe Silver would have lived. Before the guilt of it strangled her, she shoved the idea away.

A stand of trees in a vacant corner stood against a backdrop of bushes and evergreens. It would be the perfect place to leave Gray if there were people on an adjacent street. It provided a sheltered area to get Gray out of the car unseen, a place for him to sit out of the sun, and it lay in the bend of a street. Now, if only she could find people on the street close by. A white man parked, got out of his car, and walked to the door of a tailor shop. Two Black men strolling by stepped away to let him pass—something she'd only seen in the deep South.

St. Jude, be with me one more time.

She drove around the corner.

Several Black families stood in the front yard and sidewalk talking mere yards from the bend in the road. Five or six children raced around the adults' legs and the trees that grew in the tiny yards. The white duplex behind them stood taller than it was wide, but it had two front stoops. An elderly Black man used a cane to help him down the stoop from the one on the right. She drove by, turned down another street, and returned to the bend in the road.

**

"Gray? Okay, I'm going to get you a doctor. But I have to stay out of it as much as possible." Gray tried to pay attention to Sterling's voice. "Do you understand? First, you've got to get out of the car and under that tree."

Sterling climbed in the back of the station wagon and moved some boxes around. With some effort she poked, prodded, and pulled on him until he climbed out of the car. The world spun and the pain in his arm made him so sick he threw up bile the moment his feet touched ground. She half-carried him to a shade tree and propped him against it in a dry spot.

"Lean your head back and stay right there," Sterling said. Her flushed face and narrow eyes told him she meant business. She slipped something into his shirt pocket. "I've got to get someone to help, someone to get you to a hospital. The driver's license in your pocket says you are Joe Williamson from Jackson, Tennessee. You were attacked from behind."

"No . . ."

"Joe Williamson. You are very ill, your arm needs setting, and your wounds are infected. Gray, I swear I will find you just like I did before." She stroked his cheek and held his gaze. "I will never let you go."

She vanished like a dream he barely remembered. He heard children laughing and calling to each other. For a time, he heard Sterling rummaging around in the car, but he couldn't see her without lifting his head. Gray had no interest in doing that. He closed his eyes, trying to find a corner of the world that didn't hurt.

I'm Joe Williamson.

**

Sterling scanned the neighborhood before she got Gray out of the car and under the tree. No one seemed to be around. He looked so sick when she left him that she almost ran back.

St. Jude, one more favor, please.

She searched for the white duplex again and picked her target carefully. She passed on a harried older man and his wife who kept watch on two young boys playing in street puddles.

They look too preoccupied.

A young man stepped onto the stoop of one duplex and helped a woman holding a baby outside. He took the baby but guarded her steps as they all came outside to the yard and sidewalk. The people in the yard crowded around to see the baby. Sterling braked to a stop near the sidewalk where the young man stood with his back to the street and rolled down the window.

I hate this. I hate the way I have to do this.

"Hey, you. Boy! I'm lost."

"She talking to you, Reilly," muttered an older man and nudged the young father.

"I need directions," Sterling shouted.

Reilly handed the baby to the woman by him and walked a little closer to Sterling's car. Everybody in front of the duplex appeared to look everywhere but Sterling's car.

"Where you want to go, ma'm?" Reilly asked.

With a huff she said, "I've ended up on this street twice. I want to go to King's Highway." Her lip curled slightly and hoped the young man hurried with his directions.

Reilly squatted beside the window and rattled off some directions. She only heard "turn right at the first stop sign" and wished he would finish.

When he stopped talking she pointed around the bend in the street where Gray sat. "You might wanna know, a colored boy's sitting under a tree back there. He looks like somebody beat him to a pulp. I thought it my Christian duty to mention it."

"Thank you, ma'am," Reilly said and took off in the direction she pointed. Two other men ran behind him.

Sterling harrumphed and flipped down the visor to check her lipstick. While she smacked her lips, her heart nearly leapt from her chest and her stomach roiled. She watched Reilly disappear behind the bend in her rearview mirror. Through the open window she heard a man holler somebody to bring a car around.

Thank God.

Driving from the curb slowly, she halted at the stop sign and saw a car back out of the driveway then pull around the bend in the direction of Gray's tree.

Once Sterling knew someone was looking after Gray, it was time for her to become nothing more than an afterthought. She turned right as directed.

She would call the hospital and find out about a new patient named Joe Williamson in a few hours. If he wasn't there, she'd be back to the white duplex to find Reilly.

**

Gray awoke in a clean bed that felt infinitely more comfortable than the station wagon. For one thing it wasn't moving. He vaguely remembered someone—a man—giving him water. The cement walls and cracked plaster ceiling around him made him think of a cellar. Now he looked around in alarm. His arm had been set in a white cast and the other arm lay taped to a board to support the IV in his vein. A bag hung from a stand and dripped fluid into him.

No Sterling. Her face swirled in his memory, the fear in her eyes. Her promise to find him.

"Hello there. Glad to have you back with us. Let's get your temperature." A woman in a nurse's white uniform stood on the side of the bed.

"Where am I?" His throat was sore, and his voice came out hoarse.

"The G—Homer G. Phillips Hospital in The Ville of St. Louie," the woman replied and held up a thermometer. Her white uniform made her blue-black skin seem even darker. "Open your mouth. I'll get you a drink in a minute."

Gray obeyed, held the thermometer under his tongue, and the nurse picked up his wrist from the board to count his pulse.

"My arm's cramping, can you take this board off me," he said, nodding to the IV as she read his temperature.

"If you promise not to thrash around and dislodge the IV. I don't want to replace it again," the nurse said.

"Promise." Gray tried to smile. "H-how did I get here?"

"Three men said you were attacked." She poured a cup of water and held it to his lips. "You look like five miles of bad road, my brother."

He drank deeply. "I don't remember."

The nurse nodded and reached for a tray behind her. "Your memory gets jarred by a blow to the head like you got. It'll come back. You're passed the danger point with that concussion, though. I'll give you a little something for the pain."

"Did I come alone?"

"I told you, some brothers found you under a tree. They brought you in."

A tree? Gray frowned.

The nurse prepared a shot. "Roll over toward your good arm a little."

He tried. She pulled down the cover, pushed him over further, lifted his hospital gown, and stabbed him in the hip.

"You gonna feel better in a minute. I hope whoever did this to you rots in hell," she said.

"Me too," Gray answered.

"Sorry about this room. We're a bit overcrowded." The nurse pulled out an envelope. "Got a letter here and I want to get it to the right person. Who are you?" the nurse said.

Cobwebs cluttered Gray's mind. But something stuck in the web.

"Joe Williamson from Jackson, Tennessee."

"See, you know your name and you didn't when you got here. I'll put the note right here on the nightstand, Mr. Williamson. It was in your shirt pocket when you arrived."

He waited until she turned off the overhead lights and shut the door of his room. The bedside light showed paint peeling off the walls of a room with six white metal hospital beds, all stripped to the bare mattress or springs like he was in a storage area.

His hand with the IV took the note and the hand with the cast smoothed it out to read, "Gray is my favorite color. See you soon."

"Grey isn't a color, Sterling, it's a shade," he said to the empty room as the pain medicine took hold.

**

Getting Gray into the hospital might prove easier than getting him out.

Sterling had found a motel, but before she checked in she wanted to be sure no one followed her. She drove downtown, parked in a lot, slipped down in the seat, and tried to rest.

I could probably pass as a nurse. Until someone asks me to empty a bed pan.

She drifted to sleep and dreamed Kate, Silver, and Gray were locked in an iron cage. Silver and Gray kept telling her to find the key before it was too late. She awoke in a panic and glanced at her watch. She'd slept only half an hour.

What key?

Still trying to shake the dream, Sterling left the car and walked a few blocks to a coffee shop. Heat rose off the empty sidewalks. Since it was near suppertime, the office workers from neighboring buildings had gone home for the day, and the coffee shop had few customers. When she opened the door, the scent of old bitter coffee almost stopped her at the door. The cool air on her skin and her rumbling stomach drew her in. She ordered a bacon and tomato sandwich and bought a copy of the *St. Louis Post-Dispatch* to read while she ate. On page two under a big headline, she found news that made her lose her appetite.

According to the Post-Dispatch, Joe Peters of Ocala, Florida and Ezekiel Tone of Jackson, Tennessee, were wanted in the deaths of three men in a barn outside Memphis, Tennessee. Two of the victims were known drug dealers. The third victim was a Shelby County deputy. Local police believed the deputy discovered a drug deal in progress and was killed trying to apprehend the suspects. Police discovered a gun believed to be used in killing the alleged drug dealers. The FBI had joined the hunt for the two Negroes suspects in their early twenties. The two suspects were wounded, apparently from the fight in the barn that left the others dead.

Sterling glanced up from the newspaper. Somehow the police had the last fake driver's licenses that Silver and Gray had used, the ones with Joe Peters and Ezekiel Tone as aliases. No mention of her or the Fosters. No news of a Black man with mutton chops and a mustache on the scene. No word of her baby. Where was all this information coming from? Anyone who claims they saw these two Black suspects was lying, since Gray and Silver were hidden in the backseat of a car registered to a nun.

What if the Allens got caught?

A flash of horror—the Allen family were innocents in trouble that she brought to their door. But the paper hadn't said anything about arresting a family or finding evidence at a farm down the road from the barn. Maybe the police hadn't released that information.

The newspaper story convinced Sterling that she and Gray had to get back on the road. She signaled for the bill.

As Sterling folded up the newspaper to go, her eyes fell on a picture of a white man, who represented the NAACP Board of Directors, presenting a check to a member of the Homer G. Phillips Hospital Board of Directors. The newspaper photo told her two things: whites did go to the Negro hospital, and she had a safe place to sleep tonight. She read the name under the caption twice to be sure. But she knew the white man. Attorney David Cohen was her father's college roommate, and she hadn't seen him since the families vacationed together at Virginia Beach when she was thirteen.

Sterling may have found the key to her problem. Or at least her immediate problem of safety.

CHAPTER TWENTY-EIGHT: A REPRIEVE

A bored-looking bald man sitting on a stool in a small guardhouse by David and Miriam Cohen's driveway leapt to attention when Sterling drove into the drive. He eyed the dirty station wagon with suspicion.

By the time she reached the walkway to the house, the Cohens were waiting on the front porch. Their smiles of welcome faded when she explained why she'd come. Afterwards, Sterling watched in amazement as they worked like a practiced team of spies.

"This ain't our first rodeo," David said as he closed the garage door on her station wagon. "We've been activists most of our lives. Why, Miriam and I met at a protest."

"That's a very inventive way to hide someone, those hollowed out boxes, I mean," Miriam said. She whisked Sterling inside a homey kitchen painted in shades of blue and gold. Appliances and cannisters competed for counter space with stacks of pamphlets from the NAACP, the Red Cross, and other groups as well as periodicals like *The Village Voice*.

"Sit." Miriam steered Sterling into a chair as though afraid the younger woman would break. Soon the aroma of vegetable soup filled the kitchen, rousing Sterling's appetite.

"Lucky you arrived on a Monday," David quipped when he came in from the garage. "Miriam cooks on Sunday and we always have leftovers. Eat while we wait for my friends to poke around for information."

"Pfft," his wife replied. She ladled soup into a bowl while David searched in the drawers for a napkin and spoon.

"Alan and Katherine Sterling would be out of their minds to see you like this," Miriam said.

"I'm in lots of trouble," Sterling said.

"What kind of beasts are chasing you?" David ran one hand over his bald head and sat opposite the table from her. "I've had to help people to Homer G. Phillips after skirmishes at CORE demonstrations, but nothing as bad as what you're describing."

"My friend Gray and his brother were kidnapped by three men . . . at least three." Both Cohens grew wide-eyed as Sterling added, "I rescued them."

"Of course you did." David's fingers massaged his chin as she told him about the deputy sheriff, the red car that chased her down the farm road, the newspaper article about two kidnappers being drug dealers, and the fake drivers' licenses the police found in the barn.

"When I drove them away from that barn, all the kidnappers were alive," Sterling said.

The hall telephone rang, and David excused himself to answer it.

"I mean, I know for sure that two of the men were in the red car that chased me down the road. I saw them for a split second. I presume they walked back to the barn when their car was wrecked," Sterling told Miriam. "Now all three of kidnappers are dead."

"What? Who got killed?"

Sterling shook her head.

"And who sent the kidnappers?" asked Miriam.

"I don't know that either. Not for sure. I've been too busy staying alive to figure it out."

"The FBI?" asked Miriam.

Sterling's head felt full of fluff. Not FBI. Someone else. But Tom Foster had said something about the FBI. A former fed had helped him track down Silver and Gray. That was it. The man had found Gray and Silver for Tom. He was in the barn too.

"We've made powerful enemies in our civil rights work," she told Miriam.

Miriam covered her mouth with one hand.

Sterling raised a spoonful of soup to her lips, tasted, and ate like a starving child.

"Good, good," Miriam said in approval as David returned to the kitchen shaking his head. She gave him a warning look. "We'll get you a doctor."

"No, no," Sterling said. "I'm not hurt. Just tired. If I could, I want to shower and sleep."

David jerked his thumb over his shoulder toward the telephone. "You should know that a search of the barn produced some clothes and two drivers' licenses for Negro men. Law enforcement thinks the names are aliases since they couldn't find any record of such men. They found the tracks of three other vehicles. One car went along a tractor road to the highway. The other took the main farm road to the barn. The alleged drug dealers' car was found wrecked in the tractor path."

"You have a friend at the FBI." Sterling's jaw dropped.

David smiled. "I cannot confirm or deny. The newspapers must not know, but the gun that killed the alleged drug dealers belonged to the deputy."

"The deputy shot the dealers?" Sterling gasped.

"That's the current thinking," David said. "Now, the weapon that killed the deputy, that's a mystery. It might be traceable if it was used in another crime. Notably, one piece of the grip is missing. The deputy was shot at close range allegedly."

Silver's gun. He had it in Crossville.

Sterling's mouth dried up and she pushed away from the table.

"This is awful. Sounds like there might have been a struggle for the gun that killed the deputy." Miriam shuddered and rubbed her arms as though she were suddenly chilled.

Sterling muttered, "There must have been at least three shots. Whoever shot the deputy must have gotten blood on his clothes or something."

"Did you hear them?" Miriam said.

"The shots? Gray, Silver, and I were gone."

"The good news," David said, "is that your name hasn't been mentioned."

"Still, I'll leave with Gray as soon as I can figure a way to get him out. Who knows when that alias will be connected to him." Sterling scanned the room as though hoping to find the answer somewhere close. "I wasn't as careful as I should have been coming here. I may have put you in danger."

"Don't worry about us," David guffawed. "Miriam and I have been raided and vandalized more times than I can count. It's not easy being right."

"David can help you with Gray," Miriam said. "He has friends at Homer Phillips."

"I have to ask," David said. "How do you know Gray and his brother didn't kill their kidnappers."

"I saw three men put Gray and his brother in my car. Those men were alive and after us in a red car when I saw them last. At least, two of them were in the car. Besides, Gray and his brother were too beaten up to do anything."

Who else was at the barn besides Tom and Grace? She blinked and remembered.

Mutton chops . . . Mustache. The man in the hayloft.

"Maybe someone was hiding in the bushes," Miriam suggested.

"Wait. There was another man." Sterling said. "A Black man up in the hayloft. I thought he was one of the kidnappers, but Gray never saw him. That man could have been there to kill the kidnappers once they'd disposed of everyone in my car."

"Why all the violence?" David said.

She started to tell David and Miriam about Tom Foster and his wife, the importance of bloodline to the Southern power brokers, the loss of her daughter, the hell of that exchange. Instead, she covered her face with both hands and moaned.

"Maybe it was part of a cover-up," she suggested.

"Well!" Miriam sat back in her chair.

David hummed. "Possible."

"Gray and I have to stay out of sight." Sterling rubbed her forehead until a thought struck her. "What about your guard?"

Miriam smiled. "Joshua? He wouldn't say who came here if his life depended on it."

"Oh, good. I can only think that this accusation against Silver and Gray is a way for the killer to cover their tracks." She glanced at David and Miriam to see if they believed her.

"If Gray is in the hospital, where is his brother?" Miriam asked.

Sterling shook her head slowly.

David closed his eyes and bowed his head.

"Upstairs to bed," Miriam said in a way that meant she'd heard enough. "David, please get her bag."

Leaning on the banister in the central hallway staircase, Sterling climbed to the upstairs guest room. She peeked over the railing into the front hall separating the living room from a library so cluttered with books and papers she thought of her father's office. David followed.

"Thank you for taking me in. Gray and I'll be gone tomorrow," Sterling said.

"I understand your haste to leave, but I don't think it's necessary for our sake. Nobody pays attention to us anymore . . . like wallpaper," David said as they walked to the guest room.

Sterling put a hand on the older man's chest to steady herself. "One night."

"Why am I not surprised Alan Sterling's daughter is stubborn?" David muttered. "I'll make some arrangements—cars, meals, safety precautions. A way to get Gray out of the hospital . . . perhaps a visitor or a visiting dignitary. Yes, I'd better get busy."

She hung on the banister when she remembered something from the kitchen. "Red Cross. Maybe that's how I can get Gray out. I'll be from the Red Cross."

David's eyebrows came together. "Well, I suppose. Yes. Getting a Red Cross sign on your car shouldn't be hard. Yes, I can use that idea. We have an NAACP member in the automobile business, and I like using boxes to hide Gray. Let me see what I can do."

Sterling shut the bedroom door behind him, stripped, and tossed her clothes on a chaise. She inhaled the faint aroma of roses from a room freshener on the table. The air was cool, her stomach felt comfortably full, and she ran a hand over the soft robe laid on the chaise for her. Her tense muscles eased. She wrapped the robe around her, gathered her sitz bath supplies from the bag, and padded on thick carpeting to the guest bathroom. The tub soon filled with hot water, and she sank down in the water with a happy sigh. Even her swollen breasts eased.

"Madeline? Madeline Sterling." A knock. Miriam's voice outside the door jerked Sterling awake with a splash.

"Yes. Yes. Coming." The water in the tub had grown cold. She toweled off, slipped into her robe, and opened the door.

A frowning Miriam took her arm. "Come. Climb into bed. David set the alarms on the house. You can rest and feel safe. Is it cool enough in here for you?"

Sterling was half asleep already. "Yes, thanks."

"In a day or so after you've gone, I will call your parents. I'll say you looked wonderful. My lie will become a mitzvah. They must be worried, especially after losing Danny. May his memory be a blessing."

"Amen." Sterling's chest felt tight. "I'll be better in the morning. You'll see."

Miriam turned off the lights and shut the room. "Hm-m. Goodnight."

As they walked down the hall to their bedroom, Sterling heard David teasing his wife, "Such a mother hen."

**

The rose scent disappeared. Sterling searched for it. It reminded her of her mother's old bedroom in Mississippi, the room with a pink and green quilt that had been Katherine's as a child. Pink. A pink baby blanket.

Someone pounded on the front door downstairs.

Sterling smelled smoke. Faint, but enough to drag her upright. The window opposite the bed showed streaks of dawn. Pushing back the covers, she got to her feet. The smell of smoke grew stronger.

"Hey!" yelled David from down the hall.

Sterling opened her door to see David wrestling with a man much taller than he. She jumped on the intruder's back and poked her fingers in his eye, The man hollered, released David, grabbed both Sterling's arms, and bent forward. She flew over his head onto the floor, stunned by the impact. The assailant leaned over and punched her in the face while she still gasped for air.

He might have struck her again, but his eyes went wide. With an 'ooof,' he collapsed. Behind him David, wielding the metal base of a bedside table, panted.

"So there." David managed to say.

Sterling reeled from the blow to her face. Touching her cheek made her wince.

"Fire!" Miriam yelled from downstairs.

"Water! Get some water on it." David hurried downstairs.

Sterling followed the Cohens, holding a hand to her bleeding mouth. Miriam had already directed a fire extinguisher on remnants of a Molotov cocktail thrown through the front window. The red rug under the broken front window burned, and flames engulfed the curtains.

Adrenaline covered over the pain in Sterling's face. She ran into the kitchen, flung open the cabinet doors under the sink, and filled a pot full of water.

At the foot of the steps, David snatched the pot from her. "More."

Sterling raced back into the kitchen, filled a second pot of water, and returned to the living room to hand it to David, and fill his empty pot. After a dozen trips, the fire fizzled out. Smoke filled the central hallway and fled out the broken window.

Sterling and David surveyed the damage.

"It's not too bad this time. The walls will have to be repainted. Curtains and rug replaced. New window." David coughed then called, "Miriam?"

"Here, my dear." She waved from upstairs. "I've secured the intruder's hands behind his back with one of your ties."

"I'll call the police," David said.

"No." Sterling cried. "No police."

"Harrumph. Of course." David stroked his chin. "I'll get ice for your face, young lady."

"I wonder who sent this gentleman," Miriam called out over the upstairs banister. "One of our numerous friends . . . or yours, Sterling?"

"Doesn't matter," Sterling murmured as she started upstairs. "I have to go now."

"How did he get in?" David wondered.

"Let's ask," Sterling said.

"You knocked him out." Miriam said. "Well done, you two. Oh, my! Your face, Sterling. Let me help you." She guided Sterling into the guest bath and pulled out a first aid kit.

"Miriam, I'm—"

"Huh. Yours isn't the first split lip and black eye I've seen." Miriam pulled her toward the bathroom.

"Black eye!"

"Hm-m." Miriam went to work on Sterling's face and lips with cold water and ointment. "You're lucky he didn't land a direct hit to that eye."

"He really got you." David walked into the bathroom with an ice pack for Sterling and another pressed to his cheek.

"Oh, David." His wife pivoted to fuss over her husband.

David waved her off. "He missed my nose. Ladies, your prisoner is waking."

By the time Sterling came out of the guest room ready to go, David had propped the intruder against the hallway wall.

"He seems mute," Miriam observed and brushed an errant strand of grey hair from her face.

Sterling crouched to the man's eye level. "You know who I am?"

He nodded.

"You know I'm crazy enough to peel the skin off your face with a dull kitchen knife," Sterling said.

The man's eyes narrowed. The whiskers along his jawline moved as he clenched his teeth.

"I have several dull knives in the kitchen. I'll be right back." Miriam fled downstairs.

"Who sent you?" Sterling asked.

The man shook his head.

She grabbed his collar.

"Sons and daughters of the Confederacy," The man sneered.

"Where are you from?"

"Georgia," he muttered.

"What do you want?"

He smirked.

"For the love of God. I keep telling everybody, I was one lowly agent. I don't have the files." Sterling dropped his collar.

"Files? You're worth two thousand dollars dead," the intruder said.

Sterling's jaw dropped. "Who wants agents dead that badly?"

He shook his head.

The notion of being hunted so viciously paralyzed her for a second. This intruder had answered too quickly, bungled the fire. He was another average guy, not a professional killer or hunter. Someone behind him was. She punched him in the nose.

Blood flew. The man howled and swore.

Ignoring the stabbing pain that vibrated through her knuckles to her shoulder, Sterling pulled her arm back to strike again.

"That's all I know!" The man listed to one side.

"Was it Marshal Cooper?"

The man grimaced.

"What about Brian Foster?"

The man tried to chuckle.

"J. D. Masterson?"

The man glared.

Bingo. J. D. Masterson.

"He ain't messing around," the man said.

How did you find me?"

"You bought an airline ticket to St. Louis in the Huntington Airport. We've been looking for you here since you lit out from there. We got a list of people here who might know you." The man threw a string of profanity at her. "I saw these kikes on the list. They're always stickin' their noses where they don't belong, so we watched the house."

"You didn't come alone." Sterling jumped to her feet, rubbing her sore knuckles.

The man hung his head.

"David! Miriam!" Sterling hollered over the railing. "There's another man."

She should have figured he'd have a partner. How careless of her. Again.

David hurried through the front door with a baseball bat. Sterling grabbed the intruder's shirt again. "Where is he?"

The man's words slurred. "For some goddamn reason, he pounded on the front door."

David stomped through the house with his weapon. He went outside only to return in a few minutes cradling the bat.

"Sterling, there's a gentleman outside who would like a word."

She leaned over the railing. "Who?"

David merely pointed outside with the bat.

"Listen carefully so you can report," Sterling told her captive. "I'm leaving the Cohens and never calling or coming back. Again, I don't know where the files are."

The intruder spat on the Cohen's carpet.

As she started down the stairs, the intruder yelled, "Hey, baby. See ya later!"

Sterling tried to shrug off the chill that moved through her. "Let him go in an hour or so, David."

He held onto her hand. "You'll need different transportation to get out of St. Louis and help getting Gray away from the hospital."

"You can do that?"

"Oh yes." David flashed a grin and nodded toward the door. "Someone will be at the front of the hospital waiting for you."

"Thank you. Whoever's chasing me knows about my station wagon."

"They know our cars too." David shrugged. "Do the best you can to get to Homer G. Phillips. Go the front of the hospital and look for a white station wagon fitted with boxes like yours and bearing a Red Cross sign."

"David, when you and Miriam talk to my parents, tell them . . .tell them I love them both very much."

"I will." David squeezed her hand, and she went outside.

Two birds tweeted and flew overhead as she stepped off the porch steps onto the front walk. A faint spicy fragrance rose from the large bed of white and red dianthus flowers growing around the house and front walk.

Silhouetted against the pre-dawn sky, a man waited like a thin black apparition. He stood with his hands folded in front of him, head down slightly. Nearby a white man sat tied and seated cross-legged under the broken living room window. The captive's head hung as if it were too heavy to lift, and his shirt had ripped at the collar.

"Let's speak in private." The man's black pants and dark shirt appeared barely mussed.

Sterling followed him off the walk away. His steps fell silent as tiger paws on the ground. Now that he had gotten closer, she could see his narrow face sported a mustache and his bushy eyebrows nearly overpowered his small but piercing eyes. Heat and humidity already made the air heavy like that morning in Memphis.

"You! The hayloft—." She drew back to punch him, but he caught her wrist.

"Hey, lady, I'm on your side. You might have burnt up if I hadn't knocked tonight." His brown eyes flashed as he glanced at her fist and thrust it aside. "You might wanna ice those knuckles."

"Who are you?" she asked, chilled by this new character in her drama. He bore the aura of violence that she often felt around Gray.

"You got reason to hate me, I get it. Hard for me to say, but I got played. You gotta believe that part. Tom Foster hired me to track down his good buddies Aristotle and Socrates Gray. He said he was worried about them and wanted to make sure they were okay. He gave me information about Justice Tomorrow that the FBI didn't have, so I thought he was for real."

"You're the FBI agent?"

"Former agent, but yeah. Anyway, I found the Gray brothers."

"Did you tell Tom where I was?"

The man shook his head. "He must have found you hisself. When I told him where the Gray brothers were, he thanked me, paid me more than I asked, and said he'd take it from there. Throwing money like that, giving up Justice Tomorrow secrets? I thought I'd follow up. The man disrespected me, and the good work Justice Tomorrow did."

A witness. Sterling suddenly floated on the wave of excitement. She had a witness who could prove Gray and Silver didn't shoot anyone.

"You shaved your mutton chops," she said.

He gave her a toothy grin. "I wondered if you saw me in the barn."

"You saw what went on there."

"What they did to those two brothers in the barn . . . Those sons of bitches." His words fairly dripped with a rage that contorted his features into a frightening mask. "Nah, ain't got no tears for those honkies. They deserved killin'. I didn't stick around to see it. Once those two in the car busted it up and walked back, I lit out."

Sterling's excitement lurched into dread. She bit her lip to keep silent.

"See, when the brothers get snatched outside the church, I knew I'd been had. I followed the truck that took them but lost 'em around Jackson. Picked them up again in Memphis, thanks to friends there. Spent some time scouting the place, looking for a way to get them free from the outside. No luck. I waited until one night the white men were drunk or asleep, tossed a rope over the block and tackle in the hayloft window, and climbed inside. Woke one bastard and had to be real still all night. Lost my chance to act," he said. "I still hear those two brothers screaming in my sleep."

Sterling felt sick. "You . . . you shot those three men."

The man's shoulders dropped. He turned over his hands to show his pale palms. "Ah, hell, girl, I'm real disappointed. I—."

"Sterling!" David cried from the front door. "Cops!"

The former FBI agent grabbed her arm. "Rule one in the art of gettin' lost, don't stop at a family friend's house. Sleep in parks, not motels. Keep the brothers outta sight. Don't you be seen with 'em."

"I'm not stupid."

The man guffawed, released his hold on her, and ran toward the far side of the house. "I'll find you again."

"Wait!"

The man vanished.

Across the lawn, the garage door opened, and Miriam backed Sterling's empty station wagon out. She turned it to face the end of the drive, jerked to a stop, got out, and Sterling ran down the front walk to take her place.

"Gray will be waiting at the hospital, go to the front of the building and look for a solitary nurse standing outside. Be sure to take the sack of sandwiches and this thermos. They are here on your front seat." Mariam handed Sterling a blond wig and helped the younger woman wiggle it on her head. Sterling took off down the driveway with the windows rolled down.

In the distance, sirens wailed.

CHAPTER TWENTY-NINE: THE BAIT AND SWITCH CHASE

Sterling drove the empty station wagon into the street and the guard shut the gate behind her. As she started to pull out, the Cohen's neighbor across the street appeared with one hand on the steering wheel and another holding a coffee mug. He waited until she drove by and pulled in behind her, shielding her car from anyone coming down the street.

Sometimes you just get lucky.

The sirens sounded close. She glanced in her rearview mirror in time to see two police cars turn into the Cohen driveway. Sterling disappeared around a corner and unleashed a huge whoosh of air out of her mouth.

Despite the heat, she kept the front windows rolled down and the air conditioner off so she could listen to the noises of the city. Every time she heard a siren in the distance, she pulled into a parking space and ducked down until the police car went by.

Twice she got lost in the neighborhoods around Homer G. Phillips. The hospital campus sprawled across ten acres, and she got caught up in traffic. At last, she turned into the main hospital entrance and parked under a tree and behind a row of shrubs. A white Ford Squire station wagon with a Red Cross logo occupied the adjacent sheltered parking place. Satisfied that spot was safe from prying eyes on the street, she got out.

"Hey!"

A Black woman in a nurse's uniform complete with white cap climbed out of the car beside her. The seats in the back of a Ford station wagon were down flat and piled with cardboard boxes, as they had been in Sterling's Pontiac.

"The Red Cross?" Sterling got out of her car clutching her doughnut pillow, David's thermos, and his brown sack of sandwiches.

"Hm-m, yeah, sometimes whites drive a Red Cross car full of care baskets into the hospital. Sweet Jesus, you stirred up a hornet's nest," the nurse said. "Listen, here. My man's real sick. He shouldn't be traveling, he needs rest and care. I put a note in his bag of medicine with the name and address of my cousin's garage in Wiley Fork, Arkansas. Map on the seat. He fixes cars for whites and his wife's a former nurse. They'll help if you can get there."

"Thank you." Sterling took the white sack that rattled like it was full of pills.

The nurse lingered beside Sterling's Pontiac.

"Any trouble?" Sterling asked, grabbing her duffle and putting it in the passenger seat along with everything else she'd carried.

The nurse sniffled. "Copacetic. Just the usual car of pigs in a plain brown wrapper pulled in front of here."

"I saw another pair near the Emergency Room."

"They park out there all the time hoping to catch somebody who was in a demonstration. Or a Black with a warrant out who comes to get help."

"You think they'll be interested in me?"

"Possible, but we got it covered," said the nurse. "I'll drive out first and speed away. Go down Kennerly to get to King's Highway. Don't signal none of your turns or people will know you're from out of town."

"Once I'm on King's Highway, I can find my own way," Sterling said.

"Hmmm. By then, you'll be alone. Once you get on the road, find a place to ditch the cross. It'll peel off." She demonstrated. "Then wait a while before you drive back on the highway, give the cross marks a chance to fade or maybe rub it with water or soda and wipe it off. Gonna check once more on my man."

Sterling positioned her doughnut pillow and got behind the wheel of the white Ford. The nurse eyed the pillow, shrugged, and checked the area around the parking place for visitors. Satisfied that nobody was looking, she lifted the boxes and spoke softly to Gray.

Finally, she shut the back door and leaned down to the driver's window, "Girl, don't you undo my good work. Now, go on about your business."

"I owe you."

"When this craziness gonna end?" The nurse shook her head. "Sweet Jesus, when?"

Heart in her throat, Sterling backed out of the parking space and headed toward the street again. The nurse had it right—an unmarked sedan with two men in fedoras parked down the street. One read a newspaper.

"Okay. Going about my business." Taking a deep breath, Sterling watched the nurse pull on a long-sleeved white sweater, a blonde wig, and drive off. The police didn't follow. Sterling waited for a break in the traffic and drove out. With her heart in her throat, Sterling saw the cop's car pulled out of its parking space behind her Ford.

To her surprise, once she began driving on Kennerly, a woman with blond hair pulled out of a side street driving a similar white Ford station wagon—a decoy. Sterling smiled. As the cop car tried to pass, the decoy turned abruptly into a side street while another white car, this one a blonde driving a white Plymouth station wagon, pulled in front of them then turned down a street on the right. The nurse driving her old white Pontiac fell in behind the police car. It dawned on Sterling that the decoy cars were crisscrossing in front of the police while she drove straight ahead.

On cue, the first blonde in the Ford decoy car reappeared from the next side street to drive beside Sterling. The cop car dropped away from Sterling's Ford and fell in behind the Chevy decoy. The nurse sped up to get beside the cop car and box it in. From another side street, the Plymouth decoy pulled in the cops' lane, stopped suddenly and turned down a narrow residential street with such a screech of tires, the cops made an illegal U-turn to follow. A glance in her rearview mirror showed Sterling that the cops apparently realized their mistake right away. They turned back onto Kennerly just as the blonde in the decoy Ford peeled off onto Euclid Avenue with the police in pursuit.

Sterling headed to King's Highway alone. She figured the cops would be calling for reinforcements, if they hadn't already.

Sterling weaved in and out of cars down city streets until she found a sign to the highway. Once she took the on-ramp going south, Sterling sighed in relief, feeling tension drain from her arms. She was on her own with some assurance that nobody had tailed her.

"Gray? Are you awake?" Her breasts felt tender and swollen from milk Kate wasn't drinking. They leaked into sanitary pads she'd torn up and stuff tightly in her bra.

"I was happier in that comfy hospital bed," he mumbled. "And my cast itches."

"Well, I missed you," she said. "A fire woke me this morning."

"What!"

"Best of all, I found the killer of those three men," she said. "Or rather, he found me. The Black man in the barn."

"Who?" Gray sounded like he was in a fog.

"Yeah, I met him. For all the good it does us. He's gone and I didn't even get his name." Sterling waited for a response.

She got one groggy profanity.

Suddenly her parched throat ached for relief, and she wished for a Coke in the worst way.

Instead, she pulled off the highway, drove a mile searching for a place to get rid of the crosses on the door and found an abandoned gas station that was perfect. In half an hour she and Gray were back on the road in a car with no sign of the Red Cross insignia. She headed for the next exit and Wiley, Arkansas.

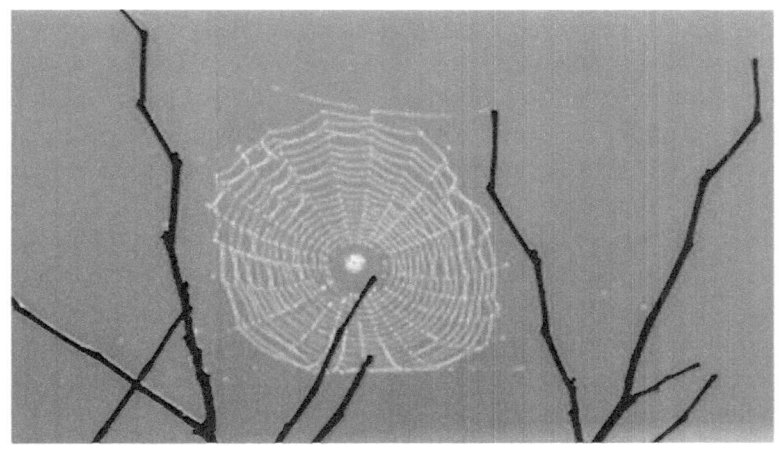

CHAPTER THIRTY: ZIGZAG TO HELP

Gray slept most of the way to Arkansas, lulled by the medicine he'd been given and the Motown songs Sterling favored on the radio. He lost all sense of urgency and fear, drifting instead to his boyhood when he and Aristotle had come to live with their aunt. Before Aristotle became Silver. Their mother had just died of grief, leaving the two boys alone. Their aunt had liked The Four Tops and Marvin Gaye.

Aunt Harriet lived in a white house on the outside of a small Missouri town. She and a hired man raised soybeans and vegetables in two fields and sang what Aristotle called slave songs all day when they were working. Aunt Harriet sang off-key. Gray and his brother had arrived during canning season and the two-bedroom white house smelled of vinegar from pickling cucumbers.

Aunt Harriet put them to work right away. Each boy had a housekeeping chore, and each had a row of the garden to tend. They soon discovered Aunt Harriet was nobody to fool with. She carried a wooden spoon that cracked on their heads or shoulders when they smarted off, failed to get their school lessons, or slacked on their chores.

The walls of her living room had flowered wallpaper and wooden floors polished to a shine. Aunt Harriet had sewn curtains with gold flowers over the windows. She had a silver tea service that resided on a small cart under her front window. The boys weren't allowed near it. Once a month, her church women came over for a meeting and had tea from that silver set.

He should have saved his brother, taken a chance on the police finding them at the Black hospital. No matter what Aristotle wanted, he was the big brother.

"Gray, have something to drink. Time to eat too. Help me here, sit." Sterling's voice drew him away from Aunt Harriet's house. He clawed his way upright and out of the boxes to find her seated in the back of the station wagon with him.

"Eat?" Gray muttered, still trying to wake.

"Yes, it's what people do. This is dinner. Have a chicken leg," she said and thrust one at him.

Gray whistled softly.

"What happened to you?" He took her chin in one hand and gently turn her head side to side. "How'd you get the fat lip and black eye?"

"The two men who set the Cohen's house on fire. One must have bruised my jaw too. It hurts like the devil. He got the worst of it, though."

"Thank God for that." He nibbled the chicken leg warily but was pleasantly surprised to find it was good.

"Have some water?" Sterling offered him water from the metal top of a thermos.

"Are we out of whiskey?"

"Hey. You've got pain pills, I need something to take the edge off," she teased. She tore a chicken breast into tiny pieces then ate the chicken bits one at a time. He doubted she chewed them at all.

A small alarm buzzed through him. How badly hurt was she? The question faded into the fuzzy cotton of his mind, like so many other thoughts.

"Where are we?" he asked.

"I don't know. Some little town south of St. Louis."

South? Gray changed his position slowly for fear something would bleed or throb.

"Just as well. We must stay away from people we know. I think we'll head back south, to Arkansas. We get to Wiley Fork, and we can rest with a contact there," she said and rolled her shoulders. "I almost fell asleep behind the wheel."

"Wiley Fork? Where's that?"

"I think it's a suburb of Batesville," she said.

"You want to go south?"

"Who would believe we'd do that?"

"Nobody smart," he said.

"Gray, you need a real bed and professional care. There's someone in Wiley Fork who can give it to you. We're going south."

He glanced around at the dilapidated wooden buildings that hemmed them in. "What is this place?"

"A little town with an alley where you could sit up and eat. I needed to stretch my legs and look at the map carefully," she said. "Besides, I want to talk about what happened last night."

"Do we have potato salad?"

"Sorry. Coleslaw." She handed him a fork and a heavy plastic tub. Their fingertips met around the tub and a surge of desire shot through him.

"This is a lot of coleslaw," he observed. He wasn't dead if touching her fingers could rouse him.

"It was on sale." Her voice sounded husky.

He sighed. "What do you want to talk about, Sterling? Your voluptuous new figure? Your black eye? The fire?"

"I'm surprised you remember anything I said this morning." She rested her head against the front seat. "And I guess 'voluptuous' is better than 'fat'."

"Whatever they gave me before I left the hospital knocked me into next week."

She filled him in on the fire at the Cohen's house, the mysterious Black man who saved them, and the interview with the captive assailant upstairs.

"The guy who gave me a black eye didn't say J. D. Masterson gave him orders to come after Justice Tomorrow agents, but he looked shocked when I mentioned his name."

"Masterson? Who is he?" Gray couldn't pull the name from his memory.

"President of Atlanta Investments. And before you ask, I don't know anything about him or the company."

"Where did this guy in the hayloft, the ex-FBI agent, come from?" Gray said, hating to ask for fear she'd already told him, and he'd forgotten.

"Don't know. Apparently, his pride got hurt when Tom suckered him, and he wanted to fix the harm he'd caused. Maybe he was furious enough to kill," she said. "We must find out who he is. He's our best suspect in the murder of those three men."

"Murder?"

"Oh, Gray." She sounded scared.

How little he remembered about the last several days frightened him, too.

Sterling licked her lips. "The cops say you and Silver killed those three men—one was a deputy sheriff."

Gray lied. "Yeah, I know."

She put a few more tiny pieces of chicken in her mouth and swallowed.

"Silver and I didn't kill those men," he said, "though I applaud whoever did."

"The deputy got shot at close range . . . like there was a struggle for his gun."

"Silver and I were in no shape to struggle."

"How do we prove that?"

"You," Gray said.

She snorted. "You think anyone would believe me? But yeah, I know two men were in the car behind us."

"The Adams, no Allens. Some more witnesses. We were at their farm." Gray poked at the coleslaw in the tub.

"You know I can't involve them," Sterling said.

Gray tried another bite of coleslaw. The tangy flavor appealed to him. He looked at Sterling and licked his lips.

"Are you okay?" she asked.

His head swam. "Do we own a gun?"

Sterling shook her head.

"We need to get one," he muttered.

"I hate guns," she said.

He snorted.

"People who use guns are too stupid to think of any other way to get out of trouble," she snapped.

"I would have been happy to be stupid just before that honkie hit me with a board."

"I know, but—"

"Sterling, you really believe that Dr. Martin Luther King Junior, the king of civil disobedience, didn't carry a gun for protection?" Gray peeled the last bite of meat from the chicken leg and laid the bone in a napkin on his lap. He knew he had to eat something, but the food landed precariously in his stomach.

"You told me that every time a Black man raised a gun to a white man it brought disaster," she said.

"I know, I know. But sometimes a single Black resistance in self-defense makes the white man back off." Gray suddenly sagged from exhaustion. "What are we going to do?"

"Well, I got the name and address of a safe house," she said.

"Then what?"

"We're gonna drop out of sight," Sterling said. "We're going to find ways to hide for at least a week before we drive to our destination. Live in the car. I've plotted a route through Arkansas to Louisville, and Morehead, Kentucky."

Arkansas? Louisville? Gray grew more confused. "Morehead?"

"Yeah, a beauty shop in Morehead. It's way off everybody's radar." Sterling closed her eyes. Gray thought she'd gone to sleep until she picked up the conversation again. Her words slurred. "Nowhere near the Justice Tomorrow network, not in our web of connections. My handler . . . Mrs. Woolworth . . . she gave me the name of a friend nobody in Justice Tomorrow would know. A contact in case of an emergency."

"Feels like an emergency." Somewhere on the edge of his mind, he remembered pieces of this conversation. He thrust the coleslaw tub at her. "Here, I can't eat anymore."

Sterling rubbed her eyes, sat straight, took the tub, and slid out the passenger door. Gray watched her go, feeling guilty that he couldn't help her drive, plan their escape, dodge cops, or even throw away a goddamn coleslaw tub.

"Damnation!" Gray lay back down across the back of the station wagon, adjusted the boxes over him and tried to find a comfortable spot. Hell, he couldn't hold his head up for fifteen minutes at a stretch. He shouldn't be giving her grief when she was carrying the whole load of their survival.

By way of apology he said, "I know something about Batesville. A year ago, singer Jim Reeves took off from Batesville after he and a business partner closed a real estate deal. He was piloting the plane when it crashed in Nashville. Killed them both."

His storehouse of useless information paid off. Sterling broke into a spirited rendition of *He'll Have to Go,* a Reeves' hit.

Mercifully, Gray fell asleep while she was singing.

The days and nights blurred for him. It was day if the tires hummed beneath him, and the back of the car seat near his head jumped to the sound of anything Sterling could find on the radio without static. He endured more country music than anyone should, dreamed of holding Sterling in his arms, and woke from nightmares of losing his brother.

"Gray!" Sterling called from the front seat one day when rain pelted the car. "Talk to me. Keep me awake."

"I'll tell you what I remember from the time Silver and I fled that assignment in Crossville until now," Gray said. "You have to ask questions, so I know you're paying attention."

The windshield wipers made monotonous swish-thud, swish-thud noises.

Sterling asked, "Do you have nightmares about killing the county sheriff in Crossville?"

Odd place to start. "Do you?"

"You bet your sweet bippy."

He smiled at the wisecrack from a television show. He should have known the sheriff's death weighed on her. "He was going to kill us. It was self-defense. Besides, we don't know exactly how he died or who killed him. There were bullets, knives, and rocks flying all over the place."

"We burned his body." Sterling shuddered

"Nobody suspects we were involved. I have no regrets, Sterling. None."

"I'm not sorry. It was him or us," she said. "Still, it seems everything that happened to us ever since traces back to the Crossville assignment."

Gray doubted that very much. He thought life had begun unraveling in Alabama months before the Crossville assignment when a posse of dogs and murderous drunks had chased him and Sterling into the woods. She'd been shot and he'd hidden them both under a dead deer while the posse circled around them. Afterwards, Sterling had seemed different, withdrawn, no, desperate.

"Do you ever have nightmares about hiding under that dead deer," he asked.

"What deer?"

Maybe she hadn't heard him.

"In Alabama . . . Before Crossville? You got shot. We crawled under a deer that must have been rotting for days. The dogs carried on all around us, but those drunk honkies . . ."

"Gray, I have no idea what you're talking about." She sounded mystified.

He didn't know what to make of that. The smell, the filth—maybe that's why the sound of dogs barking made his stomach roil and his teeth clench. He knew she'd been conscious the whole time, how could she not remember those terror-filled moments?

"We stayed absolutely still while the dogs dug around us," he said. "The men finally pulled them away to run into some other part of those God-forsaken woods,"

She chuckled. "I don't remember anything like that. Okay, getting shot I remember real well, but that's all. I meant the destruction of Justice Tomorrow came from our time in Crossville."

"When Tom sold us out."

"I'm not sure he did . . . At least not directly or on purpose."

Gray whooshed out a mirthless chuckle, instantly regretting it as pain lanced down his sides.

"I know you hate him. But I don't think he's smart enough or ruthless enough to destroy Justice Tomorrow. I see him as a pawn. A weak man who goes along the path of least resistance," Sterling said. "Tom's father is a son of a bitch. He had private detectives looking for him. They discovered his involvement with Justice Tomorrow and dug deeper."

"If Tom's father had detectives clever enough to ferret out Justice Tomorrow, why did Tom have to hire a Black man to hunt down Silver and me? Why couldn't his father's men do it?" Gray asked.

"I don't know. Maybe Tom wanted to break from his father," Sterling suggested. She had already figured Tom had hired the FBI agent to find her baby. Tom would know she'd come for Gray anytime he was in trouble.

"A little late-in-life teenage rebellion?"

"Maybe he thought he should send a Black to find a Black."

"Sounds like Tom," Gray murmured

Sterling went silent, leaving Gray to fester in his hatred of all things related to Tom Foster.

"Did you know Tom's father-in-law is the Big Kahuna of Georgia politics? I think I told you that."

Gray had forgotten Sterling told him Tom was married but he didn't care about Tom Foster's father-in-law unless the man was somebody Tom loved. In that case, Gray planned to kill him too.

"The Big Kahuna might be interested in Justice Tomorrow's files and protecting his friends. I bet my last dollar he has lots of friends in those case files," Gray said.

"Hmm-m. Probably. I wonder if he would care enough to pursue and kill all the agents?" Sterling said. "I had a run-in with someone after I left Boston."

Gray chuckled when she described stripping Marshal Cooper and finding he was foreman of a company in Albany, Georgia that had been taken over by Atlanta Investments. The story had a familiar ring, like she'd told him about it before.

"The question is, who was Cooper working for when he came after me in Norfolk? I can't imagine it was Bellamy Warehouses. More likely it was Atlanta Investments."

From the tone of her voice, that episode riled Sterling. Despite his cobweb of thoughts, he was intrigued.

"I dug through some Atlanta Journal Constitution stories and found all these men connected through golfing, political events, charity balls," she went on. "In that group, the Fosters are the newcomers, the social climbers, or so it seems to me. The rest are landed Georgia gentry from old money. On the social register, you know."

Sterling named Atlanta Investments president J. D. Masterson, Tom's father Brian Foster, and a dozen other Georgia businessmen but none of the other names meant anything to Gray.

"Who is behind Atlanta Investments besides J. D. Masterson?" he asked.

"Good question."

"That's right, you don't know. Call the Georgia Secretary of State and ask for the officers, the headquarters, their net worth—some of those things have to be on file and available to the public even if the company's privately owned," Gray said.

Sterling sounded upbeat. "I knew there was a reason to keep you around."

"Besides my sparkling personality?"

"I wish it would stop raining for five minutes," she said. "Five minutes"

For longer than five minutes, he listened to the beat of the wipers and the splashing of tires on the wet road, as the pain from his headache and from the cuts along his back grew. The pain and the thought of Tom fired his lust for revenge. Gray took a pain pill.

"Sterling . . . Sterling, promise me we will hunt down and kill every single person responsible for killing Silver, starting with Tom Foster and every single person he loves." Gray found words harder to form. "Promise me."

"I promise." Her pledge lacked enthusiasm.

As he slipped into sleep, two things crossed his mind: first, Sterling wanted to please him. Two, Tom Foster had a hold on her.

CHAPTER THIRTY-ONE: FEELING SAFE

The nurse in St. Louis had said they could find help in Wiley Fork, Arkansas but Sterling didn't get a good vibe from the town. For one thing, the place was a long way from the Interstate highway exit, which meant a quick escape might be difficult. Driving around to find ways in and out of town showed her a place with empty storefronts and few pedestrians on the downtown sidewalks. The stoic men in baggy pants and bib overalls who lounged on the wall around the courthouse and the number of Confederate flags flying around town gave her the creeps. In a nearby park, the statute of a Confederate soldier with fresh flowers around the base didn't make her feel any better.

She drove by The Stop on Inn motel and restaurant, which looked like a decent place to stay, and finally stopped at an Esso Station to ask directions to Appling Motor Garage. The attendant looked at her like he wasn't sure he had heard correctly but pointed her to the right address.

Finally, she saw "Appling Motor Garage" in red letters printed on a crooked sign over a three-bay garage. She drove around back. Judging by all the cars parked there, the place was busy.

"We're here, Gray," she said.

Outside the garage, an overweight Black man smoking a cigarette and sitting in a lawn chair by the door watched her come toward him. He set the chair back on all four legs as she approached.

"I need some work done," she said to the man and jerked her thumb over her shoulder in the direction of the station wagon. She hated going into her bigoted white woman role, but she had to fit in.

"Yes, ma'am. Tubby Appling's a good a mechanic," the man said.

Scowling, she waited until he stood and opened the door for her.

A petite Black woman with horn-rimmed glasses looked up from her ledger book when the door opened. Black grime streaked the office walls, which were already plastered with ads for tires, motor oil, and new seat covers. The smell of gas and oil filled the air.

"Mrs. Appling?"

The woman nodded and pushed her glasses back on her nose.

"Your niece sent me," Sterling said.

The woman's eyebrows shot up. She glanced around to make sure they weren't being overheard and patted her hair in the back. "Been expecting you."

"I'm so grateful to you."

"You'll have to leave the car." Mrs. Appling stopped fussing with her hair long enough to grab an order pad. She wrote hurriedly, talking as she did. "Monroe Mitchell outside can take you where you need to go."

"How about The Stop on Inn motel?"

Mrs. Appling nodded her approval. "I'll gives ya a call when the repairs are complete. Give us a day or so. Here's our number if somethin' comes up. Sign here for the repairs."

She shoved a paper at Sterling and held up a pen.

"Call tomorrow," Sterling read. "Do not trust the driver."

She nodded, took the pen to sign, but when she pushed the paper back to Mrs. Appling the woman stopped her.

"Oh, that's your copy," Mrs. Appling said. "Pay on delivery."

Sterling handed over the keys. "Valuable cargo in the back."

"This ain't our first rodeo, as Mister Cohen say." Mrs. Appling whispered. A smile crossed her face and traveled to her eyes for the first time.

Mrs. Appling's warmth boosted Sterling's spirits as she walked back to the station wagon.

Sterling opened the car long enough to tell Gray the plan and get her duffle. Hoping he understood what she told him, she found Mitchell and asked for a ride to The Stop on Inn. He frowned, opened the door of a blue sedan, and she climbed in the back to sit behind him. The car smelled so fresh, and the floors swept so clean she feared she'd get it dirty by sitting in it.

"Where ya from?" Mitchell asked as he started the car and headed down the street.

"Mississippi. You from around here?" For a moment Sterling couldn't remember where she was.

"Born and raised. You have car trouble on the road? Look like you're moving," Mitchell said and turned onto a wider street.

"I was lucky somebody gave me the name of this place," she said and frowned at his face in the rearview mirror. "What a mess! I've got to get to my room and call my husband's office, tell him where to meet me. Are you married?"

"Thirty-nine years." Mitchell said.

"How long have you worked for Appling?"

"I help Tubby some." Mitchell glanced in the rearview mirror and Sterling read suspicion in his eyes.

"How nice." Sterling looked out the window.

"He's a good man. No trouble around him, he won't put up with it."

Sterling's heart leapt into her throat. "You have much trouble here?"

"Some." Mitchell adjusted his seat and put both hands on top the wheel. "From outsiders, mostly, Mrs . . ."

"Thank you," Sterling said as she grabbed her bag and walked into the motor lodge without looking back.

Like the outside, the interior of the Stop on Inn looked like nobody had changed the lighting or furniture since the Interstate highway was built around the town, leaving it isolated. Sterling was sure she'd seen that lobby chair in her grandmother's living room.

With a casual hello to the clerk, she filled out paperwork, presented a Margaret Sterling fake driver's license that she'd changed to read Margaret Beerling. The license wouldn't pass close inspection, so she hurried the clerk into giving her a room key.

A Black man sweeping the lobby floor followed her with his eyes until she swung around to glare at him.

As she walked to her room, the weight of the last few days dragged on her. The inn's carpet looked clean but well-worn, the paneling on the walls was dated, and the baseboards were scuffed. The whole place smelled of old wood and musty carpet, but the glass door to the outside was convenient to her room. She made sure she was alone when she arrived at her door.

Nobody inside. She checked under the bed, in the bathroom and closet, finally using the desk chair to brace against the door. Two windows facing the parking lot behind the motor lodge needed bracing and she put the front legs of the ironing board in the track used to open the window while the back legs fit against snug against the bed frame. Feeling more secure, she headed for the shower. The water pressure left something to be desired, but it felt like heaven. For a long time, she stood under the spray and let the hot water hit her back. She filled the tub, soaked her stitches, and applied hot washcloths to her swollen breasts.

Afterwards, she pulled a clean tee shirt out of her bag and rechecked the chair under the doorknob and the windows to see they were locked. Satisfied she was as secure as possible, she crawled under scratchy sheets and slept.

Sterling thought she'd be good at resting, merely taking it easy for a few days, but she was wrong. By the end of the second day, she had washed her dirty clothes in the tub, dried them across the air-conditioner vents, packed, and paced the room for hours. She only left the room for dinner in the place next door. She watched hours of television and soaked in the tub twice a day.

Every night she thought of a dozen ways to get her daughter back. Every day she rejected the ideas she'd come up with at night. All her plans ended with jail—or death.

Every night she bargained with God to grant her one more day with Kate. Or one more hour until she could get her daughter back for good. She longed for Gray's help and knew she could never ask for it.

Her breasts leaked less, but now they felt tighter, and the nipples more tender. Maybe that was normal after a baby stopped nursing. The onslaught of grief at losing Kate still made her nauseated. She prayed again for just the touch of her daughter's tiny hand.

Once she reached for the bedside phone to call the Atlanta Secretary of State and hopefully discover who was behind Atlanta

Investments. But she stopped, fearful the call could somehow be traced to the motel.

Maybe I'm too paranoid.

She spent her time putting her ear to her door, listening for a sign of trouble coming down the hallway, and pushing aside the drapes to scan the parking lot.

Maybe I have a reason to be paranoid.

Sterling felt like jumping out of her skin.

CHAPTER THIRTY-TWO: ALARM

Mrs. Appling proved to be an attentive nurse and an excellent cook. She climbed the stairs to the room over the garage in the morning before the shop opened and in the evening after closing to bring Gray meals, change bandages, and apply ointment to his back.

"You have a much lighter touch than Sterling," he had muttered to Mrs. Appling the night she and her husband drove him into the garage and half-carried him up a flight of stairs to the room over the garage.

"She your woman?" Tubby Appling had asked. Gray heard the disapproval.

"Partner. Work together. . .long time. Ou-ch." The bedsprings creaked as he eased into the bed.

"What happened to you?" Mrs. Appling had handed him a pain pill from the hospital's bottle. "I never seen anybody so messed up."

"Ran into some KKK folks," Gray had mumbled.

"Huh. Lots of them here too," Tubby had said. "When people are working in the garage, though, don't walk on the floor if you kin help it. If you gotta, huh, well, don't flush 'til evening."

Gray slept and dreamed of his brother, of how he might have saved Silver by taking him to a hospital. The scuff of footsteps on the stairs outside his room jerked him awake. He listened. Nothing from below. No voices or the sound of whirring or pounding as mechanics worked on cars. It must be night. He'd slept a whole day.

"Now look at this," Mrs. Appling scolded as she carried a tray inside the room. "You didn't eat nothing. Your plate still full."

"I slept," he said.

Mrs. Appling frowned. "That's not good. You got to drink a lot more and eat something to build back your strength."

"Where can I reach Sterling?"

"She's at The Stop on Inn. She got there all safe and sound or I'd have heard." Mrs. Appling made room on his bedside table for her tray. Her glasses slid down her nose and she pushed them back. "Your car's already clean, oil changed, and you ready to go. Car key's on the front counter near the register. I keep it handy."

"This ain't your first rodeo."

She laughed and watched him eat before she took her tray full of plates and cups away.

"Drink more," she said and gave him a pain pill.

She must have returned while he slept. He awoke in the night to find a bedside light on illuminating two glasses of water and one of orange juice. He forced himself to drink the orange juice and one glass of water.

When Mrs. Appling woke him the morning to bring his breakfast, she dropped his spoon then spent some time fiddling with her hair.

"How are you?" She hardly looked at him.

"Better, thanks to your nursing and cooking." Gray found that merely sitting up in bed brought pain. He adjusted the two pillows behind his head and that was the extent of his energy.

Mrs. Appling patted the back her hair again. "You'll get stronger. Don't you worry. Be patient. Your body's got a lot to complain about."

"I wish it would stop complaining and commence healing," Gray said.

She laughed and the bare wood walls of the room felt brighter.

"You bring a little cheer everywhere," he said.

"I bet you sweet talk all the girls," she said.

Gray shook his head. "Been a while since I had the chance."

"Uh-huh. I put the boxes in your car back like they were. I finally got it clean inside, but your car, well, it smelled awful."

"Is that your nice way of saying I need a bath?"

"No sir, I would never say that. If you're up to it, though, I'll change the sheets while you're in the bathroom." She fussed with the covers.

"Mrs. Appling, you look nervous. What's going on?"

She dropped her hands with a sigh. "There's men from the local KKK come here asking around about a Black and a white woman traveling together. They say they got a notice . . ."

Gray threw back the covers. "I've got to get Sterling."

"No, no, you can't leave 'til you get a little stronger or you'll make things worse." She turned to the table and shook two pills from a brown bottle. "Time for your antibiotics and a shower. I'll help you to the bathroom door."

**

Early the next morning, voices below his bedroom pulled Gray from sleep. His bedroom, which sat over the three bays of the Appling garage, always smelled faintly of oil and gasoline but now he could also smell whiskey. He opened one eye, drew back the black curtain to look out the window at the fog, and wondered why so many people were below him at such an hour.

The voices weren't loud or shrill, but their conversation sounded urgent. Two or three male voices and one female that sounded like Mrs. Appling. At first, he couldn't decipher anything the people below said. When he did catch a few words he sat up, crept to the bedroom door that led to the steps and opened it so he could hear better. His arm, weighted by the cast, banged against the doorframe, but the noise failed to interrupt the people below.

"Five thousand dollars, baby! Think on it," said Tubby. "You know what we could do with that money. Even splitting it with Monroe, we could fix up the whole garage, give you that kitchen you always wanted."

"It ain't right. I won't," Mrs. Appling said. "Those two folks work for our people. We promised them a safe place. I mean, we owe—"

"We owe ourselves," said a man whose voice Gray didn't recognize. "Come on, man, this is our chance."

"Monroe's right," Tubby said. "Baby, we ain't never gonna see this kind of money again. They offering five thousand dollars!"

"You think he asleep upstairs?" asked Monroe.

"He's real sick, hurt. White people beat him so bad he near to died," Mrs. Appling spat out. "You want to give him over to those same white people? Uh! I don't want no part of it. I might be poor, but I got my pride. That man and his partner—"

"—his white woman," said Tubby.

"I ain't no part of this." Mrs. Appling sounded bitter.

A door slammed downstairs.

"You in?" Monroe said.

"Let's go meet these men," Tubby said.

"You think she'll make a fuss?" said Monroe.

"Nah, my baby's good," Tubby said.

Another door slammed.

At first Gray wondered if he'd dreamed the conversation. Parts of it had drifted in and out like a half-remembered melody. He didn't want to get up and run again. He didn't want to believe he'd been betrayed again.

He'd caught some of Sterling's naïveté.

Gray moved quietly across the room, collected his pants, and struggled to put them on with one arm. A noise on the stairs made him put down his shoes quietly and flattened himself behind the door.

Nobody knocked and no one burst through the door. After a while, Gray released the air he'd been holding and resumed putting on his shoes. His knees trembled from the effort of standing. His hands shook as he fought to get into a shirt. He didn't attempt to button it. Patting his pockets with his good arm, he made sure he still had the paper with Sterling's motel name on a scrap of paper.

When he had dressed and gathered the rest of his filthy clothes in a sack, he crept down the stairs leading to the garage. The bays were closed, but through the greasy windows in the big doors, he could see the station wagon parked outside facing the street. A car went by.

The garage hummed with a mixture of electric and mechanic noises that ratcheted his urgency into overdrive. His stomach threatened to heave last night's dinner, and the smell of oil overwhelmed him, but Gray made his way slowly toward the office. When he peeked in the window of the door, no one was there.

Slipping into the office, Gray bent as low as he could to use the worn plastic couch and a side table to shield him from anyone who might glance in the front window from the street. He crept behind the counter, searching for the keys to the station wagon. There were a million keys in a box and on the wall, none labeled, none that looked like the station wagon key he needed. He could hot wire the car, but his skills were rusty. In frustration, he slammed his hand on top of the countertop and felt a key. He pulled it under the counter and read the tag: "white Ford station wagon" and a license number.

Now he remembered Mrs. Appling had told him where she put the keys.

Heart in his throat, he reached for the phone and asked for information then for the number of Sterling's motel.

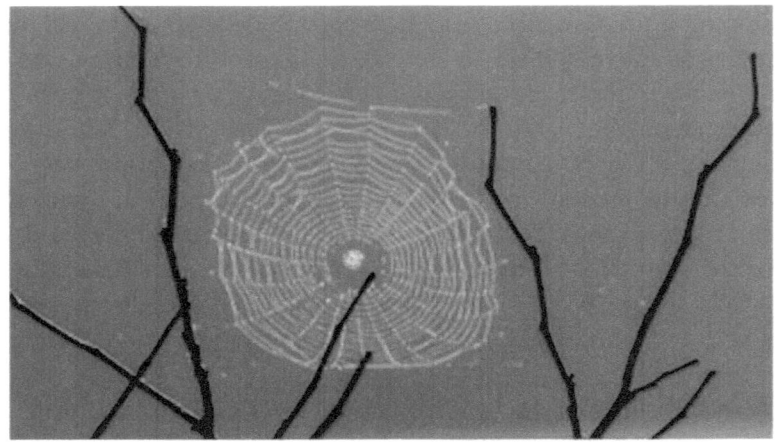

CHAPTER THIRTY-THREE: BETRAYAL

The air-conditioner heaved a mighty blast of cold air that rattled the metal ironing board wedged against the motel window. Sterling woke and turned on the bedside light, suddenly frightened. The cold air grabbed her in a whirlwind of bramble vines. The stale smell in the room turned green, purple, and yellow, the whir of the air conditioner tasted like caramel on her tongue, her clothes looked loud, angry, and dangerous. Then, as quickly as it came, the tunnel of vines left. and her senses came back to normal.

Shaken, she dressed hurriedly in jeans and a shirt and jammed the rest of her clothes into her duffle. She reached for the phone to call Appling Motors, wanting to warn Gray to get out. Sterling figured she'd have to walk back to Appling.

Instead, the bedside phone rang. Sterling fumbled for it twice before she could get a grip on the receiver.

"I'm coming for you," Gray said.

"You know the way?"

"Tell me," he whispered.

She did, adding "Come around to the side door."

Sterling was still shoving a foot in her sneakers when she closed the door to her room with one hand and shouldered her duffle with the other.

What had happened?

Once she stepped outside the glass door and closed it behind her, Sterling shivered in a thick early morning fog. The sun shone fuzzy and weak through the clouds, as though content to let the world enjoy a little cool before returning it to scathing temperatures. For several minutes she leaned against the warm brick wall of the hotel, holding one arm under a tender breast. Had Gray meant for her to run or wait outside the door for him? She squatted and peeked through the glass door to see if anyone was in the hall. No one. She waited several minutes and looked again.

Three white men, including the clerk, strode down the hall toward her room. She stood, sidled along to the corner, looked around in the fog, and turned the corner. From there she could hear anyone who came out of the building from the side door and keep an eye out for Gray. Her heart pounded.

Suddenly she heard a car engine, and a white station wagon burst out of the fog. She waved. Gray stopped in front of her.

"Get in! Under the boxes," he said.

Sterling opened the back door and slid on her back through the first half-circle in a big box. She had trouble getting the other box holes lined up over her body and was still arranging things when Gray drove away. She went sprawling. Boxes flew everywhere.

"What's happening?" she cried.

"Hey!" yelled a man's voice behind them.

The car took a sharp turn and another before Gray slowed and told her, "You were made."

Sterling thought a moment. "The man who drove me to the motel . . . but he was Black."

"You're so goddamn naïve!" Gray shouted. "You're surprised? Half our troubles come from Black people so comfortable in slavery they don't see the allure of freedom. I've had to drag folks to the polls who should come dancing and singing."

"Wrong!" she yelled back. "I'm arrogant. And reckless. Stupidly, recklessly arrogant, and it's cost me more than I can ever say!"

The truth of her outburst stunned Sterling. She had been so sure she could save Gray and keep Kate, so positive her plan was foolproof. Her arrogance cost her Kate. She should never have risked her daughter—Gray would never have asked her to.

She and Gray rode in strained silence. Finally, she grew calm enough to notice the new thicker blankets across the back of the station wagon that made laying the length of the station wagon more comfortable. The stench of sweat and sickness of the back was gone, replaced by a floral scent. The summer fog racing by her peepholes in the boxes gave way to a bright sun. She squirmed to get comfortable. Her swollen breasts felt lumpy.

The car stopped. Sterling tensed.

"I can't drive anymore." Gray slurred a few words. "We're on a dirt road. The highway leads to Tennessee."

"Tennessee?"

"I started north but turned south. Who would think we'd be dumb enough to go back into Tennessee, right?" The front door opened, and she began sliding out of the boxes in the back.

Gray offered his good hand to help her climb out. When she took it, he drew her so close his words ruffled her curls.

"I don't mind your astonishing naïveté," he whispered as he caressed her cheek with his palm, "but your arrogance frightens me."

"Don't worry," she said. "I've lost both."

**

A woman's voice answered on the first ring. "Yes?"

The caller said, "They were here. In Arkansas. Driving a Ford station wagon. Want the license plate number?"

"Yes," said the woman. The caller recited it.

"Should we pursue?"

"Where were they going?" the woman whispered as though she didn't want anyone else in the room to hear her.

"North, best as we can figure. Missouri, maybe."

"Of course. North. We'll take it from here," the woman said. "Everywhere they go we pick up more names, more integrationists. They will eventually lead us to all the Justice Tomorrow agents."

"Okay." The man was disappointed. "If you say so."

"Not my decision," hissed the woman.

CHAPTER THIRTY-FOUR: MILK FEVER

Nights meant darkness, stillness, and peace. Gray lost count of them on this journey, but he did know he felt better. Two days in a stationary, soft bed had worked wonders. His back complained of returning to the bounce and jar of the station wagon until he couldn't stand it any longer. He took pain pills to dull the pain during the days and most of the nights. The last two nights, however, he had left his medicine alone and leaned against the front seats, listening for trouble while Sterling slept fitfully in the front.

A sentry so weak he could not have done more than sound an alarm. Still, it was something.

What day is it?

Monday, it must be Monday. They had been on the road two days since the incident in Arkansas, by his calculations. Going south, then west then north again. He thought they might be in Tennessee again. The idea made him shiver.

How long since he lost his brother? Gray didn't want to think about that.

He strained to see what lay outside his window. A nothingness that slowly morphed into trees at the edge of a clearing. Sterling must have parked on a country road again. She had not backed in for a quicker escape or parked hidden from the dirt road by bushes and trees.

Serious breach of basic security. As he rolled down his window to allow more air, he frowned.

The air outside was alive. Frogs croaked. Insects buzzed. A crow cawed in the distance. Odd quick inhale, exhale breaths came from the front. Sterling's breathing seemed ragged, like she had to fight for oxygen. It reminded him of the odd breath noises she made as he held her in his arms listening to the dogs and men around the dead deer where they had hidden.

There was no danger here. Why was she breathing so strangely?

Gray moved the rest of the boxes away from him. The skin under his left arm itched from the cast, and he longed to scratch it. Sterling had straightened out a clothes hanger for him to stick down the cast, but he couldn't find the damn thing. When could he rid himself of the cast? Sterling would know.

He hated being so dependent on her.

As his eyes adjusted, he could make out drooping leaves on the trees and smell fresh air. He looked through the tree branches into the sky. A streak of light that wasn't a star. Dawn. No matter. He had to get out of the station wagon to attend to an urgent matter. He risked opening the door, hoping she had remembered to kill the interior lights.

She hadn't. He glanced into the front seat.

Despite the light over her head, she didn't awaken. The bright red color of her face highlighted the faint purplish-blue color that lingered around one eye. A tangled mass of curls lay across a doughnut hole pillow. She'd put on a blue cotton dress that had hiked up on her thighs as she curled across the front seat. He reached out to touch her, to make sure she was real. Her skin felt hot like everything else in this God-forsaken place. He drew back in wonder.

Sterling rescued him. She came for him.

He clutched the car door frame, stunned again by the reality. In the hellhole of that barn, he had clung to the hope that somehow, some way, he would see her again. What had she done, he wondered as he watched Sterling sleep. What price had she paid for his life?

He had promised not to ask.

Gray thought about that as he weaved into the woods to relieve himself against a tree. Why had she asked for that promise and why the hell had he given it?

Headlights coming up the lane behind him sent Gray diving among the bushes and hugging the dirt. Not a car, a pickup. His heart thudded against his rib cage.

Shit, shit, shit.

The Ford pickup truck stopped, backed, and pulled behind the station wagon. Gray prayed Sterling would stay low and out of sight. The truck's headlights shone into the car and its motor kept running. Both doors opened. He saw a pair of legs clad in blue jeans come out of the driver's side.

"Lookee here," said the driver. Young and white to Gray's ear.

"Wasn't there last night," said the passenger, who also sounded white. The legs on the other side of the Ford staggered two steps like the boy was drunk.

"Whatcha think?" said the driver.

"We're gonna get skinned for staying out all night, that's what I think. Let's git on home," said passenger.

Gray felt around the forest floor for a club, although he knew the two of them could take him in a fight. He would have given his soul for a gun. His face grew hotter, sweat trickled down his back, and he prayed for Sterling keep quiet.

Stay down, Sterling. For God's sake for once don't try to bluff it. . . Not with drunk kids.

"Ah, come on. Jest take a quick look," said the driver.

The Ford's door screeched as the driver clung to it for balance, and Gray seized the chance to move out of the bushes and get behind the truck. He pressed his back against the bumper and slapped a hand over his mouth to quiet his panting. A glance into the truck bed showed him nothing. Nothing he could use as a weapon. Nothing that gave him an idea of what to do next. He peered around the fender.

The two young men lurched toward the station wagon laughing and whispering so loudly he could hear every word.

"Donnie, there's a pretty girl in the front," the driver cried. "Hey, sweet thing."

"Lemme see," said Donnie and shoved the driver aside. "She's awake."

"Come out, pretty girl," the driver hollered. "Got something for ya."

He unzipped his pants as Donnie tried to open the car door. Sterling must have locked it.

"We wanna meetcha." Donnie laughed and clutched his crotch.

The two men pounded the windows, rocking the car, and hooting.

More sunlight lit the sky, and a faint sunbeam struck the truck's driver side door. Gray blinked to clear his mind. Licking dry lips until they parted in a grin, he crept along the side of the truck.

Damn stupid kids.

With some effort, he climbed into the driver's seat using only his good right arm. To his ears he sounded loud and clumsy, but the drunks made such a racket terrorizing Sterling that any noise he made didn't matter.

He started to push a filthy St. Louis Cardinals baseball cap off the seat but changed his mind. Instead, he slammed it on his head with one hand and dragged it low over his forehead. Pulling the door closed quietly, Gray put the truck in reverse with his good arm and stomped on the gas. The truck whipped backwards into the dirt road.

Steering with his right hand and steadying the wheel with the fingers of his left, Gray turned the truck around and pointed it the way the boys had come, which he hoped was the direction of the highway. He let the truck roll forward slowly, wishing Sterling would pop up from her seat and see where he was going.

The startled boys raced toward the truck, yelling and waving their arms. Gray waited until they got close, but not near enough to get a good look at him.

Before they could touch a fender, Gray pressed on the accelerator and tore down the road. The tires spit gravel and dirt into the young men's faces, but they kept running. He admired their determination. They stopped, hands on their knees and heads down as though winded, and he rounded a curve out of sight. He drove a little further and pulled to the side of the road, trusting Sterling would seize her opportunity to follow him.

He only hoped her escape didn't mean running over the two young drunks. They would probably have enough pain when they got home.

While he waited for Sterling, Gray rummaged the cab of the truck. Cigarettes, a half-eaten Mars candy bar, a dozen empty beer cans, chewing gum, Sen-Sen mints, and the holy of holies: a rifle mounted on the rack behind him. He had just found a box of shells to go with it with he heard a car engine in the lane.

Gray cut the truck's engine but left the lights on. To be kind, he tossed the keys into the bed of the truck instead of the woods. He lofted the rifle from the truck and Sterling braked. As quickly as he could he climbed in the backseat with the rifle.

He was still getting settled under the boxes when the car left the bumpy dirt lane and hit the highway pavement. The tires hummed, Sterling's turn signal flicked on, the car accelerated.

"You okay?" she yelled.

"Yes. You?" More than fine. Taking a page from Sterling's crazy book of escapes had given him a rush.

"Fine."

Sterling whooped and pounded the steering. "That was . . . that was like before."

"About time," Gray chuckled.

Sterling broke into peals of contagious laughter. For the next mile they laughed letting all the worry and pain fade.

Afterwards, Gray didn't want to berate her for her failure to take precautions. He tried to get comfortable while his body complained about the unaccustomed rush of action and waited to hear Sterling crying. Every time they escaped a tight spot, once they were safe, she usually burst into tears.

Nothing.

Maybe she had no more tears left.

"We need to ditch this car," she said.

"Did they get a good look at you?"

She gave him a mirthless chuckle. "All the way up my bare legs."

"Well, then they can't describe the car at all. We were in shadows, and I had a cap pulled down low. I don't think they got a look at me," he said, surprised by the hot rage he felt at someone ogling her.

"You think those guys live up the road?"

"Most likely," Gray said. "Just kids really. I heard one say they were in trouble for staying out all night."

"They were so drunk I'm not sure they could describe anything even in broad daylight," Sterling said.

"Perhaps we don't need to ditch the car, just the license plate."
Gray added, "Besides, I'm not sure those boys will report us at all.
Too embarrassing."

"Still, we need another car. I'd feel better," she said. "Maybe we
will find someone selling their car in their yard or something. But we
need another station wagon."

"Then stop outside the next town. I'll let you out, you walk into
town, get a new car then come back for me," he said. "You have
enough cash?"

"Not enough for a Cadillac, but maybe an old Chevy," she said.
"I'll convince some salesman my daddy wanted me to buy my first
car all on my own with my own money."

"Hopefully you can convince him to get it done fast." Gray began
having doubts about this plan.

"Oh, that shouldn't be hard."

"Then we'll ditch this one deep in the woods somewhere."

The dawn broke bright and warm into the front windshield and
spilled over the seat onto the boxes. It would be a scorcher of a day.

"I don't want that rifle. I hate guns," Sterling said.

He could still feel his helplessness, the thud of his heart trying to
break out of his chest when the two drunks appeared. "Learn to love
this one."

**

After a long, anxious day spent waiting for Sterling to find a new
car then reorganizing the boxes, Gray fell asleep in the rear of their
new 1960 Ford station wagon. The seats were worn and cigarette
smoke from the previous owner had seeped into everything, but it
drove well. The entire adventure had worn him out. His body had
ached until he took a pain pill. A jostling front seat jerked him out of
a heavy sleep. He raised up enough to peer out the window and see it
was dawn.

"Are you awake?" Sterling called from the front seat.

"Almost," he said. They were in another wooded area sitting off
another country road. Gray swore if he lived through all this he
would always live in a big city.

"Want some breakfast?"

"What do we have to eat?" Bacon and eggs sounded good to him. His appetite was making a comeback.

"Peanut butter and jelly sandwich," she said.

"Again?" He chuckled. "Never mind, I've been dreaming of peanut butter."

"It's what Miriam and David packed. They must be stale by now. Sorry," she said. "Do you think you can drive?"

Must be stale—didn't she know? Wasn't she eating? He shoved a box aside and leaned over the front seat to look at her closely. Her pale cheeks, usually dotted with freckles, still flamed red as they had earlier. She looked thinner than the last time he'd really looked at her—he tried to think how long ago that had been. Maybe when they had stopped outside St. Louis? She'd looked like she'd put on weight in Memphis down by the river, but now she seemed too thin. He reached up to touch her forehead.

"Sterling . . ."

"I know. I have to stop somewhere. Get help. I've got the chills too," she said. "A hotel. Deserted barn. Abandoned house."

"How long have you been like this?"

"Hit like a Mack truck last night." She handed him a sandwich wrapped in waxed paper. "I hurt all over."

"Should you go to a hospital?"

"No," she said.

"Private doctor," he suggested.

"Where? How?"

"Drive to a phone booth and find one in the phone book." Anxiety flamed through him. "Where are we?"

"Out of Tennessee. Near Paducah, Kentucky, headed for Evansville, Illinois," she said.

"Is it on our way to Morehead?"

"We're taking the scenic route in case someone else is on our tail."

The peanut butter, like his worry over Sterling, stuck to him. He felt it on the roof of his mouth, his fingers, and lying like a hard lump in his stomach after he swallowed. They stopped several times to locate a phone booth with an intact phone book in it. After several calls, she finally found a doctor who would take an emergency drop-in. Gray moved fitfully in the back, unable to see what was going on and unable to help her.

"Okay, here's Dr. Braxton's office. It's probably just a cold, though. I parked on a city street under a tree so it won't get too hot in here. Plenty of people out shopping today. I'm trying to find change to feed the parking meter," she said. "Oh, geez, I need deodorant."

He heard her footsteps scrape on the concrete outside then the excited voices of children and the patient tones of a woman passing by. Sterling opened the back of the station wagon and rummaged around until she found what she wanted.

"Okay. Be right back."

The wait for her rapidly became hot and interminable. Gray racked his brain to find some way to get out of the station wagon and find Dr. Braxton's office. Casually. A shaggy Black man who looked and smelled like a mangy dog.

He couldn't think of a way to get to Sterling, and that scared him as much as anything else. He calmed himself by dreaming of the day he could strangle the life from Tom Foster, that woman who gave orders to the men in the barn to beat them, and everyone Tom Foster loved.

His fingers searched the backseat for the rifle and pulled it close.

Who gets a cold in the summer? Could it be something more than a bug? Gray flexed his arm and stretched his legs out as far as they would go and dared a peek out his window. He saw the signs directing people to the shopping area, a men's shop, and a doctor's office. Nothing worrisome.

Gray eased down, half on his side. He could drive. He should relieve her. Whatever she had wasn't helped by fear and exhaustion.

A dozen people passed by the station wagon on their way to and from the town's shopping area. Although no one paused or came close to the car, his anxiety ramped up with every sound. A car starting. A dropped package on the sidewalk. He could hear voices, and soon picked out differences in footsteps. Clipped steps belonged to women in heels, shuffling feet were men's, children owned small but irregular footfalls.

A scuff-step-step-scuff-step kept coming closer. He swallowed the lump of fear in his throat. Someone's hand touched the door handle. Without worrying about the boxes moving, he put the rifle against his right shoulder ready to fire.

"Milk fever." Sterling opened the driver's door."

"What?" Gray asked.

"Mild infection. Some kind of bug," she said as the driver's seat back bumped "Doesn't feel mild."

"Damn." Adrenaline drained from him.

"Doctor gave me packs of pills." She continued as the car rolled forward. "I hope you don't catch it."

"Sterling, I can drive. Get us someplace where we can change places."

"Are you sure?"

"I'm much better. I can drive." He hoped he wasn't lying.

"We'll go toward Louisville," she said. "Once I find a safe spot, I'll stop. From Louisville it looks like three-four hours to Morehead. It's a little college town."

"If these people at the beauty shop take us in, what would we do there? I know nothing about hair and make-up," he said, trying not to sound like a petulant child.

"Look, the owners of the shop used to be Hollywood make-up artists and illusionists," Sterling said. "We'll rest, heal, and learn the art of disguises."

The idea of sleeping in a proper bed for more than one night appealed to him more than learning about make-up. The air conditioner began to blow cold air toward him. Gray needed more information, but right now he reveled in cooler air.

Finally, the car rolled to a stop. For a moment he listened to Sterling's labored breathing.

"You sure you're okay to drive," she said.

"Sure," he said. "Do I have a license?"

"In the seat pocket of the car."

Gray pushed some boxes aside. "Damn." They were in the woods again. He got out, stretched, and took a few steps. He did feel stronger.

"Can you drive with one arm?" she asked.

"Many people drive with one hand," he said and offered his right hand to help her out of the car. "Why are you wearing a wedding ring?"

"Part of my role as a married woman with two children who was in town on vacation." She leaned against him for a moment and drew a deep breath. He reveled in the heat of her body next to his before he opened the back seat door to get her inside.

"Yuk, this back seat smells awful," she said and gazed up into his eyes.

"Well, uh,"— he couldn't pull away from her—"Neither of us have had a shower in days."

Somehow, Gray felt colder when she got in the car and moved to the passenger side of the backseat, the side where Silver had once laid. Gray never picked that place to rest.

"Give me an hour or so," she said. "That's all I need. Talk to me so I know you're awake."

"Okay."

Boxes rattled and finally she said, "I'm ready back here. Tell me how you let Tom Foster kidnap you."

As trees, billboards, old barns, new cars, and small towns rolled by, Gray told her stories of Mullinsville, his landlady, and the little store where the men went to smoke at night. At first Sterling laughed and asked questions.

Finally he gave her a detailed account of locking up the church, feeling the air shift around him, then realizing someone had pinned his arms and put a bag over his head. He skipped the gruesome part of being in the barn. Finally, he got to the woman who had called on the barn phone that hung from the wall nearest Gray. She said the boss wanted the men to hurt Gray and Silver so much they'd be no help to Sterling. He could still hear her distinctive Southern drawl and tried to imitate it for Sterling. When she didn't snicker at his performance, he knew she had fallen asleep.

**

The moment she got under the boxes in the backseat, Sterling heaved a sigh of relief. She had to rest. The obstetrician who had diagnosed her mastitis, or milk fever, had been firm about that. No stress either. She had almost laughed in his face.

Time to head for the place Mrs. Woolworth had told her about: Belles Beauty Shop outside Morehead, Kentucky. She wondered as she drifted to sleep how far away it was.

When Gray woke her, it was almost dark.

"Maybe we can make Morehead tomorrow," he said as he came to the back to help her out.

Sterling straightened her skirt. She would have a warm Coke and get a jolt of caffeine. The idea of a Coke with lots of ice made her dreamy-eyed.

"No, I can drive all night if I have to," she said.

He climbed in and didn't shut his door. She paused, pivoted, and shut it for him automatically. Before she started the car she smiled. She'd been shutting cabinet doors and drawers for Gray the whole time she'd known him. He never seemed bothered by the possibility that an open cabinet could make him bump his head or cause someone else to poke their eye out.

CHAPTER THIRTY-FIVE: REFUGEES

Marabelle Carlson, forty-two-year-old owner of Belle's Beauty Shop, passed by the kitchen window of her home behind the shop and did a double take.

She waved both arms at her husband who was still at the breakfast table. "Paul, come look at this. Someone's parked a station wagon out front."

Paul Carlson put aside the lecture he would deliver to his Morehead State University drama class, wiped fried egg yolk off his brown mustache, and walked to the window with his napkin still in hand.

"Looks like they parked and left," he said, adjusting his wire-rimmed glasses.

"No, on the ground. On the passenger side! It—it looks like a body," Marabelle said.

Paul dropped his napkin, pushed the screen door of the kitchen open, and ran around to the far side of the station wagon. "My God."

Gray, who had tripped getting out of the backseat, lay with his face planted on the gravel road. He tried to protect the arm in the cast as he rose to one knee.

"Jesus H. Christ!" Paul slipped his arm under Gray's shoulder. Once on his feet, Gray weaved so much Paul leaned him against the car.

"Who are you? Never mind, you need a doctor," he told Gray.

"Gray. Socrates Gray. I'm not hurt badly."

"Your looks are deceiving," Paul said as his eyes roamed over Gray's misbuttoned shirt, bruised face, and the cast on his arm. "Can you stand alone?"

Gray spared him half a smile. "Not sure."

"Marabelle?" Paul looked across the top of the car at his wife. "This man needs a doctor. He looks like a denizen from Dante's Inferno." Paul leaned down to tuck an arm under Gray's shoulder to help him stand. He drew back from the car and wrinkled his nose.

"Shall I call an ambulance or the po—," Marabelle approached the driver's side.

"No!" Sterling popped upright in the front seat.

Marabelle shrieked.

"Hey!" Paul pressed Gray against the car with one hand.

"Sorry." Sterling rolled down the window. "Sorry. Didn't mean to scare you."

"Who are you?" Marabelle said, her eyes still wide.

"Madeline Sterling . . . Mrs. Woolworth! Mrs. Woolworth sent us," Sterling said.

With one hand on her chest, Marabelle caught her breath. "Well, huh. Mrs. Woolworth." She looked over the top of the car to her husband. "I'll be darned."

Paul shrugged. "Looks like we've got company."

Marabelle gave Sterling an appraising look. "Honey, is that a wig or an ugly hat on your head?"

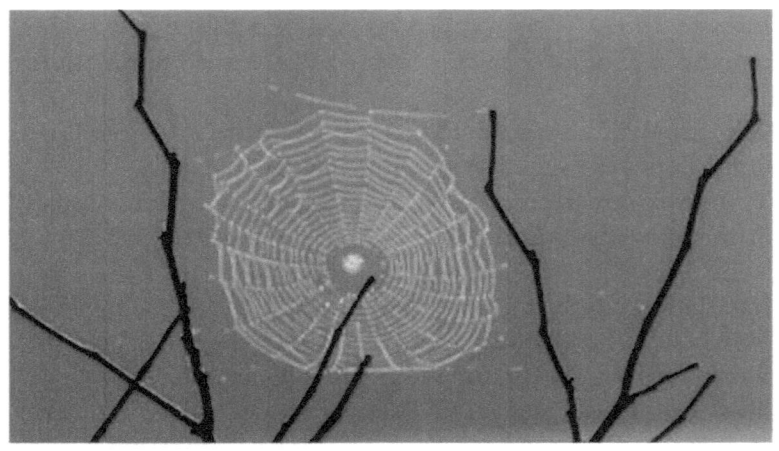

CHAPTER THIRTY-SIX: RECOVERY

For two days Sterling slept in the large master bedroom on the second floor of Marabelle and Paul's house tortured by dreams of losing Kate, losing Silver, and nearly losing Gray.

Feverish and aching, she moaned on the big bed as though her grief had at last found a safe place to pour out. The green vine pattern in the bedroom wallpaper encircled her, taunting her with visions of what she had lost. Her colossal failure, the price of her recklessness.

Her hosts took turns keeping watch during the day and Marabelle slept in the trundle bed across the room from her at night. Several times she heard Marabelle or Paul by the side of her bed or felt their hands—hers soft and his rough—touch her forehead to check for fever. Once she cried out for her mother and the sound of her own voice woke her.

"I lost her. I lost my baby girl." Sterling had said to her parents from a phone booth near the obstetrician's office, leaving them with the impression the baby had died. How could she admit she took a gamble with her own child and lost? She could barely allow herself to think of committing such evil, much less speak the words to her parents or Gray.

Never to Gray.

Until she could figure out a way to get her back, Sterling's resolve to spend time with Kate, even if it was only an hour, grew. The longing became so strong it felt like a living thing crawling inside her.

Her fever broke, but Marabelle didn't let her get out of bed except to shower and use the bathroom. Her breasts had felt hard as rocks but had softened as rest and medication healed her.

Marabelle brought magazines for Sterling to read. Other times she brought a snack, sat and chatted about the shop, her career in Hollywood, her decision to come back home and help her aging parents, whose deaths she still mourned. She said nothing about what Sterling really wanted to know: the connection between Marabelle and Mrs. Woolworth.

Sterling enjoyed the pampering, but it gave her too much time to think.

Gray visited several times a day for a few moments. At the end of one week, he took her hand and sat down on the edge of the bed. He had just come out of the shower and smelled of Ivory soap. His jeans looked new, and so did the blue shirt that pulled a little across his shoulders. She soaked in the sight of him, the feel of his hand next to hers on the bed.

"Now what?" he said. "Are we planning to stay for a while?"

"That depends on Paul and Marabelle," she said.

"I'm better. Paul found a country doctor who checked me out and gave me so many pills to take that I feel like a walking drug store," Gray said.

Sterling cracked a smile.

"He rolled out this ancient X-ray machine—I think he stole it from a museum. Anyway, he checked my arm and made a face." He demonstrated by pulling down his eyebrows and lips.

"What did you tell the doctor? I mean, who did you tell him you were?"

"I am an exchange student from South Africa studying theater and drama at Morehead State University with Dr. Carlson. I was visiting friends in Louisville when I was attacked."

"Not a bad cover story." Sterling found it harder to concentrate. A heavy weight seemed to pull her down deeper into the bed and she didn't resist.

"Thank you. Paul and Marabelle have your cover story ready. Apparently, they've had time to think about what we would need if we arrived. They expected you and were warned that I might be tagging along."

Mrs. Woolworth had thought of everything.

"Where are you sleeping?"

Gray pointed to the ceiling. "Right above you. There's a small room, barely big enough for a double bed and dresser. I think Paul used part of the attic to make the room. It's comfortable. I'll be moving to the workroom when you're better."

"Compared to the station wagon how is it?"

"No contest."

"Where is the car, by the way?"

Gray brought her hand to his lips and kissed it. "Paul cannibalized it for parts and sold the carcass to a junk dealer down the road. Fastest strip-down I ever saw."

"You've been outside with Paul and Marabelle while I've been confined to this bed? I'm jealous."

"Some. I said I felt better, but I don't feel that way for long. Paul took me to his workroom. He's some kind of innovative genius."

Sterling sighed. "We have to stay here until we're strong, Gray. Back to normal."

"Let's talk to our hosts."

Gray got up and put her hand under the covers. The window air-conditioner hummed.

"Go back to sleep," he said as he kissed her forehead.

"Stay." Her fingers grazed his arm, and he smiled at her.

"Nope, you need to sleep."

"I'm not sleepy."

He chuckled.

She huffed to show her displeasure. As she closed her eyes her thoughts drifted to Marshal Cooper, J. D. Masterson and Atlanta Investments, Brian Foster, Tom's father-in-law John Cofield, and the host of politicians, doctors, lawyers, and businessmen who ran in the same circles. They were connected to the destruction of Justice Tomorrow and held the answer to getting Kate back.

Right then it all seemed too daunting. Too big a conspiracy. Too great a risk after the price she and Gray had paid for this scrap of peace.

She glanced at the vines printed on the wallpaper and tried to trace one back to its origins. That task became too taxing, her mind wandered before her eyes reached the corner of the room. She was tired of looking over her shoulder. Would she have to do that all her life?

What had she told Gray about all of these Atlanta elites? She had a suspicion they should take the fight to them.

No. Not him. I learned my lesson about taking chances with people I love.

Sterling turned over in bed and willed herself back to sleep with something else ringing in her ear.

Any fight you win lasts under four seconds.

**

"Home is Where the Heart Is" read the decorative plaque hanging on the wall above Marabelle's head in the breakfast nook. The sage green kitchen walls held calendars, a box for incoming and outgoing mail, and other plaques with sayings like "There's No Place Like Home" on them. Seeing them every morning made Gray miss his brother.

"You should know what you're in for if you let us hang around," Gray told Paul and Marabelle as they ate dinner. Sterling had joined them in the kitchen for the first time. She picked at the food on her plate and her eyes had dark circles under them. Paul seemed oblivious, but Gray caught Marabelle casting worried looks at his partner.

"We've got some idea." Marabelle was a brunette when they arrived but had gone blond since then. On her, the change seemed natural, attractive. "We knew trouble might follow you."

"That's right." Gray said.

"People are chasing Gray and me for the civil rights work we did. You can see what they did to Gray when they found him. We have no idea who these people are or who is behind it all, although we do know police officers throughout South are involved," Sterling said. "These folks seem to have unlimited resources and a powerful thirst for blood."

"That's pretty dramatic," said Paul.

Marabelle's eyes narrowed. "I'd like to see anyone try to come take you. I was Rowan County Sharpshooter Champion at the county fair last year."

Sterling mustered a smile.

"Jest kiddin'. We're ready," Marabelle said.

"You can't see them, but I have motion picture cameras to record intruders who might try to come in. Would you like to see the morning you arrived?" Paul said.

Sterling waved her hands in front of her face to decline the offer. Gray remembered how he felt, and he had no interest in seeing how bad he looked.

"I'm also trying out motion sensors," their host said.

"Motion sensors?" Gray grew alert, fascinated. "Where are these motion picture cameras?"

"In the rain barrels outside. One pointed at the house and the other at the back of the shop. I change the film every two weeks," Paul said. "These new Super Eight cameras only run when we're sleeping thanks to a switch—"

"All that time in the Paramount special effects department wasn't wasted." Marabelle interrupted. She reached around the table to touch her husband's shoulder and smile at him with affection. "Once he starts talking about his inventions, he won't stop."

"You like the motion sensors better since the bunnies and raccoons don't trip the motion wires and scare us half to death," Paul said to his wife. "Oh, you two need to know where the wires are so you don't fall over them."

"Amazing," Sterling said in a flat tone. "How do you know Mrs. Woolworth?"

"She's an imaginary character. The person who created her is a, well, let's say I would never tell her no," Marabelle said. "Taking you in is the first thing she ever asked of me."

"We're a lot to take care of," Gray said.

Marabelle shrugged. "I hope you're gonna be better company."

"The long and short of it is, we are not afraid to help you. We were on a few civil rights marches ourselves," Paul said. "Stay for a semester. I've already gone to the trouble of slipping a file on Simphiwe Gray into the student records at the college. Simphiwe is Zulu name that means We are Fortunate. You made good grades in an English school in South Africa and came here on scholarship. Congratulations."

"Simphiwe. I can pronounce it. Thank you," Gray said in a British accent.

"Ech. We'll practice that accent. I'll bring some books on South African history and culture too. Remind me, I have your student identity card in my briefcase somewhere," Paul said. "Classes start after Labor Day."

"As a Paul's student you can live with us and work at the shop occasionally. Now that you're feeling better, we'll move you to the loft in the workroom behind the shop," Marabelle said.

"You should be comfortable there. I built the loft, put a new mattress on the floor, and added a bath for my students," Paul added. "They use it as a crash pad when we're on deadline to build sets and props for a theater production. You'll be part of that too."

"We'll move you to the room upstairs, Sterling," Marabelle said. "You'll be my cousin from North Carolina here to learn the beauty business. You're divorced with no children. Your ex-husband knocked you around—that'll explain any cuts or bruises you still have. He's huntin' for ya, so women in the shop will be looking out for strangers."

"Gray and I don't want to be a burden. We want to work for our keep, learn disguises and make-up—"

"Gadgets like those sensors and cameras," Gray broke in.

"Do the dishes and sweep up the shop?" asked Marabelle.

"Yes. And buy a used car." Sterling picked up her plate and Marabelle's and took them to the sink. "We only want to stay until we've learned whatever you can teach us. If we stayed until we are safe, we could be here a lifetime."

In the silence that followed, Sterling scraped the plates and put them in the sink full of soapy water.

She hadn't eaten three bites, Gray observed. He'd never seen a white person that pale either.

He wasn't sure how to fix it. When he looked up from the table, his eyes locked onto Marabelle's.

CHAPTER THIRTY-SEVEN: HAVE MERCY

Gray came into Sterling's room the next morning, threw open the drapes, and turned on the overhead light.

"Time to get up. It's noon. You have to get up," he said in a voice Sterling found far too cheerful.

"Why?"

"You need to move around little," Gray said. "Don't overdo it but stretch out. Come look around. "Look outside. It's beautiful."

"It's hot out, and I'm tired of sweating," Sterling grumbled.

"You missed breakfast. Come down and have cereal at least," he said.

"Gray, I still don't feel well. Let me sleep." She rolled on her side and closed her eyes.

He sat on the edge of the bed and tapped her on the shoulder.

"What?" She sounded cross.

"We are going to make it. Things are okay."

"Are they?" She rolled back over.

Stunned, Gray backed out of the room and went to the shop to find Marabelle. He didn't know what else to do.

**

Sterling heard Marabelle's steps outside the bedroom door and braced herself. After a knock Marabelle walked in.

"What's this I hear about you still feeling poorly?"

"I'm so tired. I don't have the energy to sit up."

Marabelle, who sported a new silver blond-haired pixie hairstyle, busied herself around the room fluffing pillows, folding Sterling's clothes, and grabbing her duffle to put on a chair.

"We're going to take your stuff upstairs," she said as she moved around the room. "Gray has already taken his clothes to the workroom loft. You and I can strip the bed, wash the sheets, and put them back on the bed."

Sterling's heart sank. The jobs Marabelle laid out sounded impossible to do in one day. She groaned and pulled the sheets over her head. The bed sagged as Marabelle sat next to her and gently tugged at the quilt.

"I don't know what's going on and I don't wanna know. But you can't hide in here forever. You can't let sadness get a grip on ya."

"I'm still sick."

Marabelle huffed. "You need a little exercise and sunshine. That'll do you a world of good. Come on."

She tapped on the covers under Sterling peeked out. With a sad huff Sterling took the bathrobe Marabelle handed her, struggled to find the arm hole in the robe, and gave up.

"I can't do this anymore," Sterling cried and beat her fist against the mattress. "I can't keep trying and hoping and running and pretending! I'm tired of being afraid to lose anything else."

"Ah-h. . ." Marabelle said. The older woman put her arm around Sterling's shoulder and squeezed.

"I can't."

"I got a little experience being down in the dumps," Marabelle said. "The only way to fix it is the same way you eat a cow . . . one bite at a time. Now, get dressed. We'll get you a fetching new hairdo. We'll tackle the sheets upstairs later."

Sterling groaned, but Marabelle left her little choice.

As she came out of the bathroom and crossed the hall to the bedroom she paused to watch Marabelle preening in the dresser mirror.

"Are you—is that a wig?"

Marabelle turned in a circle so Sterling could get the full effect. "Just came in the mail. Like it?"

"Wigs are hot and uncomfortable. I hate them."

"Oh, honey, you need a good wig, and you need to wear it right. You can't just plop it on that curly head and go. Preparation's everything. If you're that sensitive, you need a wig cap over that red hair. Here, feel this. It's real human hair, not like that fake thing you had."

"The other one got me by." Sterling sounded defensive to her own ears.

Marabelle didn't appear fazed.

Almost against her will, Sterling became interested in what her hostess did with the wig.

"Your skin tone would work well with this silverly blond color," Marabelle observed. "Sit on the bed a minute. Let me get a wig cap and the eyebrow pencil out of my make-up box in the bathroom."

Within the hour Sterling wore Marabelle's wig and marveled that she ever thought they were uncomfortable. The make-up artist had used her pencil to give Sterling darker brows and a few fine lines on her face to age her. Sterling looked in the mirror and giggled at the change.

She felt a tingling of energy.

"Maybe Gray and I need to make some plans," she said.

Marabelle hummed her approval as she stuffed clothes in Sterling's duffle.

"We need a car of our own. I'd like to buy a decent one on the installment plan," she told Marabelle.

"Maybe one of our customers in the shop has a car to sell. Now that I think on it, Mary Graber has a Chrysler she wants to get rid of," Marabelle said. "Since you're feeling your oats again, take your clothes upstairs and let's get you moved."

Marabelle took the sheets off the trundle bed where she'd slept. Sterling took her clothes to the third floor room and caught a glimpse of herself in the dresser mirror upstairs. The reflection changed her mind about how she looked. She didn't recognize herself.

Thanks to Marabelle, her face looked older. Or running for her life had done that. In either case, she didn't look like herself in that wig.

That made her think. Perhaps she could catch a glimpse of Kate. Who would know? No, she couldn't take the risk. Still, she could go to Atlanta and uncover something she could use against Tom to buy some safety. In the process, she might discover the key to getting Kate back. One was connected to the other.

But the plan needed to be safe, sane, and low risk.

"I need to disappear for a couple of days," she said when she came back downstairs

Marabelle's face clouded.

"Gray can't know," Sterling added.

"I thought you were partners."

"Where I'm going would be dangerous for Gray," Sterling said.

"But not for you?"

"Not so much," Sterling hedged. "I can't risk his safety. I'll be certain I have no tail when I return."

Marabelle shook her head. "You just said a minute ago that you were tired of running and hidin.' Now you're headed back into the lion's den?"

"It's the wig." Sterling said with a grin that faded in a hurry. "I have to find a way to end this."

"End it?" said Gray from the doorway.

"I'll take the last of these clothes upstairs." Marabelle scurried away.

**

Gray knew one thing about his partner: when Madeline Sterling got cornered, she came up with outrageous plans and made them sound plausible.

This time her idea was foolish, dangerous, and smacked of a lie.

"It's a surprise attack," Sterling said as she finished ripping the sheets off the master bed. "I can snoop around unnoticed, gather information on Tom's business and his friends, ask questions about his wife's society acquaintances, and find out who sent Marshal Cooper after me in Norfolk. That's what we need to know. My instincts tell me Atlanta Investments is behind all this. Who is in Atlanta Investments besides J. D. Masterson? Who is J. D., for that matter? Once we find out about that company, we find the person who wants the Justice Tomorrow files, and we know who wants us dead. That's probably the same person or persons who destroyed Justice Tomorrow to stop our work."

"Listen to yourself," Gray said. "Surprise attack. Madness."

"The murders in the barn happened in Tennessee. People in Georgia aren't so worried about it."

"Every law enforcement officer and KKK Klavern in the world has an alert for you." Gray couldn't believe what he heard.

"At best I'm only a 'known associate.' It's you they want—and we don't even know if they've linked you to your alias," Sterling said and rolled her gaze away from him.

What wasn't she telling him?

"You told me the assailant in St. Louis said you had a bounty on your head. You, personally," Gray said.

"I don't think he meant me specifically." She waved the notion away. "The thug in Boston said he had orders not to kill me."

"Why was that do you suppose?" Gray asked. "Why would the first assailant in Boston say he had orders not to kill you, the second group of thugs in Philadelphia tried to kidnap, not kill you, but the man in St. Louis was ready to slit your throat?"

"I have no idea."

She did, however. He could see it in the flash of her eyes and in her slack jaw.

Instead of telling him, Sterling shrugged. "I wouldn't put much stock in what hired assailants tell you."

"Perhaps there was a change of leadership," Gray said, heat rising in his body and mind. "Maybe Tom wanted to protect you at one time, but now someone else is in charge."

"Makes sense," she said.

At least he knew part of her secret. Tom's protection mattered.

"Your theory makes it all the more important for me to visit Atlanta. Who is this mysterious new leader?"

"A perfect argument for you to stay away."

"Look, Gray, it's not as risky as it sounds. I can have my nails done in a salon or visit grocery stores near Tom's house and perhaps pick up gossip. I can spend time in the Atlanta library researching the companies and the men who appear to be Tom's friends," she said. "We could do that at the Morehead State library, but we don't want to risk someone here linking Georgia to you or me."

He looked at her sideways.

"I just feel like I can bring this to a close if I go to Atlanta." She walked to the door and dropped the sheets she was carrying. When she went downstairs she'd put them in the laundry.

"It's Tom. He is the key." Her insistence on going to Atlanta bothered him on a visceral level. He suspected her of having a fling with Tom in Crossville—his fault, if he was honest. He'd turned her away. Now he could not stomach the thought of her being near Tom Foster again.

"He's not the mastermind," she mused.

"Someone with bigger fish to fry . . . not that he isn't involved. I see him as a little ant in a bigger anthill."

Still defending Tom. Gray clenched his fists at the pain of her betrayal.

"Must you use every cliché in the world?" Gray snarled.

Sterling glared.

"Stay here. Heal, get well, catch our bearings. That's what you said." Gray paced the bedroom. "Remember what it feels like to be safe."

"I thought I was safe in Philadelphia and East Tennessee," she said. "I was wrong. I want to end this. I want to do something that will make these people back off both of us!"

Even in his jealousy, the idea appealed to him. God, no one knew how much he craved a normal life. He wanted all this to be over too, and Sterling had shouldered most of the burden of getting them this far. Instead of being grateful, he had hated every minute that he was dead weight and not her partner.

"I won't go near Tom unless I feel like I can do it safely," she said.

"I won't let you go," he said, stepping close to her.

"You don't get to tell me what to do, Gray. Not like that."

He blinked. The jealousy slunk into the corner of Gray's mind.

"I'm not telling you, Sterling, I'm asking you," he said, a backhanded apology that landed too late.

For a long moment they glared at each other. He felt his resistance crumble under the weight of his desire to have a measure of security and her pledge not to see Tom unless she could so it safely.

Sterling went to her duffel and searched for clothes to put in it. He sighed.

"Don't forget to contact the Secretary of the State's office for company records, if need be," Gray suggested, and realized that he'd once again bought into her scheme.

"I'll be careful, and I won't bring back any unwanted visitors."

Gray hugged her with his good arm, the warmth of her spreading through him.

"Don't be crazy enough to confront Tom alone, I'm asking you. Leave him to me."

She snuggled against him. "I hope I never have to see him again."

CHAPTER THIRTY-EIGHT: A TERRIBLE TINY TASTE

A week later Sterling drove an old white Chrysler sedan she bought on the installment plan from one of Marabelle's clients to Cincinnati, parked it in a city garage, and rode a bus around the city until she spotted a used car dealership. She got off, walked a few blocks back to the used car lot, and began looking at sticker prices on old cars.

A salesman finally approached her. "What's your budget, Miss—"

"Morgenstern. Avery Morgenstern. I've got two hundred dollars saved," Sterling said proudly.

The salesman whistled. "That much, well, let me see what I got for ya."

He showed her a 1953 Chevrolet with rust spots and a strange odor coming from the vent. She and the salesman drove it around to make sure it was running. For Sterling's purposes, it didn't have far to go, and that was probably a good thing.

She bargained him down to one hundred and fifty dollars total, hating every minute of the haggling.

"Now you sure you don't want to ask your daddy to look it over? I can hold it for ya," the salesman said again as she signed the papers using the fake driver's license she'd made. It was quite good if she did say so herself and she hated to waste it on a man who barely gave it a glance.

She held out her hand for the keys and drove straight to the airport where she parked in an airport lot and bought a roundtrip ticket to Atlanta and another to Charlotte. When she returned from Atlanta, she'd drive the junk car to the city parking lot where she'd left the white Chrysler she bought in Morehead and abandon the Chevy junker. She should be free and clear for the drive back to Belle's. If she felt someone following her in Atlanta she'd use the return ticket to Charlotte and ride a series of buses and trains until she could shake them.

Tom Foster's blood money was coming in handy.

What did she hope to find in Atlanta? Despite her assurances to Gray, Sterling didn't know. She wanted to see her daughter above all else.

The late August sun brought another hot, humid morning to Atlanta. Sterling's legs stuck to the seat of the nondescript sedan she'd rented at the airport. The weather made her hot and sweaty. More likely it was the terror of being so close to the men who tried to kill her that made her sweat.

She drove to a hotel that wasn't too far off the beaten path and checked in. The first thing she did was unpack the silver blond wig and shake it out. It had survived the trip fairly well. She hung up a tan linen pants suit that needed pressing and went to work.

Time to call the state and see what she could find out about Atlanta Investments. Let them trace her call if they could. She'd have disappeared by the time they discovered it came from her motel room and Tom would know the fight had come to his doorstep.

That was an intriguing notion: Tom afraid.

He'd been afraid at the barn.

The telephone book in her room showed no number for Atlanta Investments and the information operator couldn't find one either. Gray had suggested something she could try—she called the Secretary of State of Georgia to see if she could get her business done without going to the offices. After being put on hold and transferred to another line she struck gold.

"Atlanta Investments . . . incorporation papers . . . here it is. Incorporated in 1964." The clerk rattled off an address, which Sterling scribbled on a motel notepad. Her mind raced.

"Do you have the officers?" Sterling asked.

"Sure do. J. D. Masterson, president; Jonathan Cleary, vice president; Jackson S. Donaldson, secretary; and James Irwin Sr., treasurer. Board of Directors are Herbert Holcomb III, Bruce Wilson Roberts and Terrance Walter Roberts, Brian Foster, Jefferson Davis Pollack, and Tom Foster."

John Cofield's name was missing. Apparently, political leaders didn't invest in companies, at least not publicly. All those other men ran in the same elite circles, but a few of them were related in a way she couldn't pull into focus—until she did. Sterling rose to her feet, mouth and eyes wide open.

"You still there?" the clerk said.

Jonathan Cleary, Herbert Holcomb III, and Jefferson Davis Pollack were names she had read on evidence boxes crammed in Mrs. Woolworth's trunk the day she came to drive Sterling to catch a plane home. Those were names on Justice Tomorrow files.

"What does Atlanta Investments do?" Sterling had the presence of mind to ask.

"Oh, I couldn't tell you, darlin'," the woman said.

A zing of excitement ran through Sterling. She put on a blue dress that brought out the color of her eyes, gathered her new briefcase filled with pens and paper, and headed to Atlanta's main library. She told the librarian she wanted to research several men and learn what companies they owned. The librarian directed her to another department where old newspaper copies were on microfiche.

Hours later, Sterling had discovered from ribbon-cutting ceremonial photos and business titles on charity event pictures, and business stories that Atlanta Investments had bought Bartlett Containers and Cans Inc. in Atlanta, Golden Truckers outside Atlanta, and Blackstone Land Development in Macon. She already knew Atlanta Investments had bought Bellamy Warehouses in Albany. All the companies were related, but she couldn't think how.

She found several pictures of J. D. Masterson and studied the grainy photos. Short, stocky, dark hair, fat hands, and a face with massive wrinkles unfolding from his eyes to his chin, J. D.'s suit coat always hung like it was buttoned wrong.

The link between all the companies became clear when she learned Blackstone Land Development in Macon was a garbage disposal company.

She picked a local company, got in her rental car and drove on Peachtree to the address listed for Bartlett Containers. The office was in a tall grey building that bustled with people and sparkled with the wealth it housed. She parked on a side street, walked up the front steps and took the elevator to the tenth floor. Taking a deep breath, she opened the office door to find a beanpole of a man in red suspenders leaning over the secretary at the front desk and giving her instructions about a contract. His narrow blue tie dangled over stacks of papers. Despite the upscale exterior of the building, the Bartlett office smelled like cigarettes, dried sweat, and mold. A yellowed 1964 calendar hung askew from one thumbtack on the wall over an empty metal desk.

"Can I help you?" The secretary asked.

"I'm looking for the president of Bartlett."

"I'm Bruce Roberts," the man said. "What can I do for you, sweetheart?"

"I'm sorry, I was expecting a much older man."

Roberts grinned and grabbed his suspenders. "How can I help you?"

"I was hoping to talk about Atlanta Investments," Sterling said. "Perhaps you can tell me what Atlanta Investments does."

Roberts' eyebrows raised. "And you are?"

Sterling extended her hand across the railing by the desk. "Marsha Carpenter, *Atlanta Business News and Report*. I'm working on a story about Atlanta Investments and its trash empire."

Roberts burst out laughing and shook her hand. "Wait 'til I tell John he owns a trash empire."

Without thinking Sterling blurted out, "John Cofield surely knows what his money goes for."

"Every nickel." Roberts chuckled.

"Keeps his hands on it too, I bet." Her heart pounded and her palms grew sweaty.

"Good-bye, Miss Carpenter." Roberts turned back to the desk.

Sterling looked over the railing at the contract Roberts and his secretary were working on. The few words and names she read made her mouth go dry.

Roberts glanced up with a scowl, covered the contract, and said firmly. "Good-bye."

Bur Sterling had seen enough. Tom's garbage operation in Crossville, like Bartlett, was part of Atlanta Investments.

"How does the garbage dump in Crossville fit into this empire?"

Roberts frowned and grabbed onto one suspender with his right hand.

"MMS Land Management, I mean," she said. MMS. That was the second thing that made her cheeks flush in anger.

"Young lady, I don't know who you've been talking to. This is all propriety company information. Atlanta Investments is a private holding company, and I can't tell you anything."

MMS. Madeline Margaret Sterling.

"What a sonvabitch," she muttered.

"What's that?" Roberts demanded.

"Thank you for your time, sir." Sterling turned for the door, wanting to hit someone, preferably Tom Foster.

Against all Justice Tomorrow rules, Tom had taken over a garbage business that had threatened to destroy Crossville while they were on assignment. He apparently named it after her. That garbage operation brought trash from military posts into the middle of Crossville, one of the prettiest little places she'd ever seen.

She bet Grace didn't know MMS was named for Tom's ex-lover. She tucked that nugget into the back of her mind.

The other interesting thing Sterling learned was that Atlanta Investments was John Cofield's, a man whose name never appeared on public documents or in the press attached to anything but charity events and political activities. Or at least that's what Roberts' words told her.

Until now the most frustrating part of losing Kate was having no leverage to get her back, and no way to snatch Kate that would let her live in peace. She could sense the world tilting and spinning in a new direction.

She drove to her hotel and changed into something more casual than a dress and heels. Grabbing the cloth messenger bag she brought, she filled it with binoculars, a notebook and pen, her latest driver's license, and money. She hoped she would have more ideas after spending some time in Tom's neighborhood and watching his house.

Her first stop was the A&P supermarket nearest Tom's house. Since it was early afternoon, the time was ideal for finding shoppers picking up last minute items to cook for dinner. Young white women pushing carts crowded the aisles. The cashier bells rang, voices of employees hollered over the intercom for someone to come to the Meat Department, knots of women clogged the aisles to visit while shopping. No interesting gossip in the produce section that she could hear. Sterling tried striking up conversations with several of women at the meat counter to no avail.

Sterling tried another A&P store further away from Tom's home. It seemed larger, newer. The kind of place maids shopped for the staples in the morning and white women patronized for unusual items like garlic olives. Sterling pushed a cart down the frozen food aisle, picked up a carton of Coke, and a box of Cheerios, but found no one to talk with. Everyone seemed in a hurry.

She turned into the canned goods aisle and found two women in conversation. Sterling caught a word or two about babies. She grabbed a can of beans and asked if she could reach the peas for a woman who was even shorter than Sterling. The woman's face was pitted with acne scars, but she'd hidden most of them with make-up.

"Here's the peas." Sterling handed a can to the woman. "You don't want to use the Bird's Eye frozen peas?"

The young woman shook her head. "Not in my chicken rice casserole recipe."

"I never thought of that." Sterling tried to look fascinated. "Sorry to eavesdrop but I heard you talking about babies. I'm looking for a nanny—a beauty salon, a grocery, Catholic church, and everything. My husband and I may be moving here. Oh, I'm Lindsey Spencer."

"Ruth Ann Talley and my friend Mary Jo Bolton. Where y'all from?"

"Mississippi. A friend recommended we look for a house in this part of Atlanta. Do you know Tom Foster?"

Ruth's face brightened. She and her friend both nodded.

"I substitute in a bridge group with his wife," Ruth said.

"Grace, yes. Have you seen their new baby?" Sterling asked.

"Not yet. Grace acts like that baby might catch cooties from us. Mary Jo," Ruth turned to her friend, "wasn't I was just saying that Grace Foster hasn't shown anyone that new baby girl yet."

"Grace is being so careful with that child." Mary Jo laughed.

Sterling dropped her voice to a whisper and threw out a neutral but gossipy opinion, "I think Grace is having trouble adjusting to motherhood. Sometimes it's tough."

Ruth nodded at Mary Jo and pointed with her finger as if to say, "See, I was right."

"As long a time as it took Grace to have that baby girl, so I suppose she's overprotective. I am surprised she doesn't stay home with her more often instead of chairing this and running after that," Ruth said.

"Maybe she had a hard delivery. You know, those European doctors don't do things right sometimes," Sterling suggested. "She just needs time getting used to being a mother first instead of a wife."

"Oh, Tom will always come first," Ruth said.

"When he went away on business for six months, she like to lost her mind," Mary Jo said. "We all thought it must be a trial separation, you know."

"Separation? Huh! She'd kill him before she'd let Tom go," Ruth blurted.

Sterling didn't have to fake her shock.

"I'm being ugly. They're lovely people, really." Ruth hastened to add. She looked to Mary Jo for confirmation. "But it's no secret Grace will hardly let Tom out of her sight to go to work. Gracious, I shouldn't be talking like this. I-I need to finish my shopping. Nice to meet you, Lindsey."

"Same to you," Sterling said. "I hope we meet again."

"Don't pay Ruth any mind," Mary Jo said. "She's a real sweetheart. She and Grace got into it at the Ladies' Auxiliary Board at the Cathedral of Christ the King this morning over a new nursery and guess she's having a time letting it go. She didn't show her best side."

Sterling waved it off. "Think nothing of it."

"There is a little truth in what she said, though, about Grace being, ah, difficult of a late. Just when Tom needs a wife's loving support too." Mary Jo rolled her eyes.

"I did hear there was a little trouble with Atlanta Investments," Sterling confided.

"My husband had lunch with Tom, and he's worried about Tom keeping his company investors in line," Mary Jo said.

"Tom talked to my husband about it," Sterling lied. "Jon Cleary, Herb Holcomb, and Mr. Jefferson Davis Pollack . . ."

"Oh, not them. They're in. Old money, you know," Mary Jo said. "Tom's really going for the up-coming leaders of town."

"I should think Tom's father Brian and his father-in-law John Cofield would be helpful," Sterling ventured.

Mary Jo clucked. "I doubt John is doing anything since his stroke. I understand the poor man can't speak anymore or move his right side."

Stunned, Sterling managed to say, "Oh-h. My husband always liked him. I hadn't heard about the stroke."

"Happened right after Christmas. Or maybe it was January since it was right after my daughter's birthday." Mary Jo giggled. "When you have children, you know you keep track of things that happen by their milestones."

"I thought I was the only one who did that."

"Oh no." Mary Jo continued down the grocery aisle. "Nice to meet you."

"Same here," Sterling said, more than a little surprised by the women's frankness. So, Grace wasn't popular, Tom's Atlanta Investments business was shaky, and John Cofield wasn't the kingmaker she'd originally thought.

"Oh, try The Cuts and Curls Beauty Salon two blocks up if you need a shampoo and set," Mary Jo called over her shoulder.

By the time she left the A&P with a sack of canned goods and a carton of Cokes, Sterling's head swirled. She stopped by a liquor store for a bottle of bourbon before heading back to her motel. Her trip to the grocery had given her a lot to mull over.

**

Why had he agreed to Sterling's crazy scheme to go to Atlanta alone? Gray stewed and fretted as he tried to apply himself to fixing a broken lamp. He sat at the workbench behind the beauty shop and wondered how he had become the repairman for Paul and Marabelle. Still, Gray really didn't mind since he found the work relaxing— puzzles he could solve with his hands.

Gray's loft bedroom and tiny bath occupied one end of a long workroom behind the beauty shop. On the other end, a workbench and its rows of tools lined one wall. The rest of the workroom, which Gray largely ignored, contained costumes, head forms with wigs, floor racks of costumes, a wall of beauty supplies for the shop, and ceiling-to-floor drawers of make-up and chemicals that he'd never heard of.

Sun streamed through the curtains covering the workroom windows, and happy whistling drifted in from the shop.

He should be with Sterling. They worked better together. His rational mind told him Sterling was right: it would be suicide for him to go to Georgia, to go anywhere in the South. Even Kentucky was questionable.

Although he had relented and agreed to the trip, Gray doubted Sterling could find anything useful without getting herself killed. Her tendency to throw herself into a plan and discount the real dangers never ceased to terrify him, although he'd been hopeful she'd changed. She'd acted a little more cautious when the drunk boys attacked her car.

The thought of losing her made his mouth dry and blood pound in his ears. He plugged in the lamp and light flooded the workbench. His moment of victory faded in a hurry. The idea of living without Sterling was a nightmare he'd shelved while she was with him or when he was sick. Since she drove off, it consumed his daylight hours. He clicked off the finished lamp and set it aside.

Gray sighed and thought how much better Sterling had looked in the last few days. She walked straighter, not slightly bow-legged as he'd seen her once or twice during their flight. Color had come back into her cheeks. He never wanted to see her as sick again as she had been on the road. From the first time he saw her in that farmer's garage she'd been ill or injured, now that he thought back. She'd looked swollen—which he'd thought was a little weight gain. Now he decided it must have been something else.

Gray froze. He'd been too wounded to see what was in front of him while they were on the run. But now he could recall that she had looked haggard, lost, walked as though in pain, and drove sitting on a doughnut pillow. Bile lurched into his stomach.

Had she been raped?

How would he ever ask her about such a thing? He could barely think of it himself. The idea slithered away like an evil thought he should be ashamed of. Sterling would have killed any man who dared touch her like that.

She'd been sick. That seemed to fit better.

Gray put up the tools he'd been using. Why had she been so hell bent on going to Atlanta?

The blackest thoughts overtook him. Sterling might be going to see Tom. The man had a hold on her, some deep tie or pull that Gray couldn't fathom. He'd thought a lot about their time together in training camps and in Crossville. She'd never shown any interest in Tom, though. They had lived together, but that hadn't changed the way she acted about him. Gray had gazed at the house often at night and seen the lights from two upstairs bedroom windows blazing. He'd also seen the hurt in her eyes when he'd told her the truth: a Black man and a white woman would never have a future in America. No use to try.

He tried to be rational. Unemotional. Look what it had cost him.

Where Sterling was concerned, he couldn't be distant. Not any longer. On this, at least, Sterling was still willing to act recklessly and without a thought for what falling in love with him would mean.

Whatever hurt Sterling happened while they were apart, while he was in Mullinsville and she was hop-scotching around dodging assassins. Gray took down a screwdriver and pulled his next project across the workbench. What Sterling had done to save his life had only made things worse for Sterling.

What had she traded for his life and Silver's? That was the key to everything and the answer to that question would tell him all he needed to know. She said she'd given Tom case files from Justice Tomorrow to free Silver and him. Perhaps she'd discovered all the Justice Tomorrow files and what she exchanged would endanger other agents. She may have traded their lives for the lives of other agents.

He groaned. The screwdriver dropped from his hand.

No wonder she was so secretive. She would never tell him that an exchange like that happened. Maybe she even thought he'd condemn her for what she did.

He couldn't blame her for her choice. He'd tell her that when she came back. After all, the agents in the files might have escaped or were never revealed. He would soothe her guilty conscience when she came back.

If she came back.

**

Shielded by three Magnolia bushes that grew on the corner of the street, Sterling hunched down in the driver's seat to watch Tom Foster's house with the Korean War-era binoculars she borrowed from Paul. Tom lived up a gently sloping hill in a large, two-story brick with white columns lining the front porch. Climbing up the steps to his front door from the street would take seventeen and a half steps by her count. The half-step was the porch landing. She bet mowing the yard was a nightmare, and she also bet Tom didn't do it himself.

Tom lived in a neighborhood of houses where the owners hired Black men to mow their yards and trim their bushes. Sterling had driven around the nearby suburban park and through the neighborhood to get a feel for the area before she found a good view of the house.

Two Black women in maid's uniforms, one who looked barely out of her teens and the other old enough to be her mother, arrived at Tom's side door at six in the morning. Tom went to work at seven and Grace left two hours later. She was tempted to follow Tom to his office and demand her child back in a loud, messy scene. Instead, she waited to see who else came in and out of the household.

By ten she was growing uncomfortable sitting in the car on a residential street. Several maids with white children in tow had given her funny looks as they passed.

At eleven o'clock sharp, the younger Black woman tugged a stroller out Tom's side door and carried a baby outside to lay in the buggy. Sterling's heart nearly leapt from her chest.

Kate!

She had lied to Gray about why she really came to Atlanta. She came to see Kate.

With a glance at the clear sky, the young woman fussed over the baby a minute and started toward the park a block down the street. She must be Kate's nanny. With trembling hands, Sterling steered the car towards the far entrance of the park.

Sterling had already steeled her heart for seeing Kate from a distance. Maybe she could get closer.

Be careful what you pray for.

By the time the nanny and Kate reached the other side of the park, Sterling was sitting on a bench under a tree reading a magazine. She wore bell-bottom jeans and a striped shirt much like the ones she'd seen on several other women who walked into the park across from Tom's suburban home.

"Oh, goodness, a baby," Sterling cried as the nanny strolled by. "I love babies. Can I look? How old is she?"

"Four weeks." The nanny slowed.

"Well, I'll be." She was almost twice that, but four weeks would fit the timeline of Tom and Grace going to Europe and having a baby overseas. "She sure is a big girl for a month old."

"Her daddy is a big man," the nanny said, and it sounded practiced, like an explanation she'd heard others give.

For five minutes Sterling played with Kate's fingers and cooed at her. The little girl's smile brightened as though she knew her mother's voice. Sterling's heart soared.

She offered the nanny a seat beside her on the bench, the woman looked at her sideways.

"No, ma'am, thank you," the nanny said. "Missrus Foster tell me to walk Kate once around the park and bring her right back."

"Oh, well. I'm here from Boston visiting my sister. I'm waiting for her to meet me for lunch," Sterling said. "She's always late. Now I'm glad I was on time. I got to play with . . . Kate? That's her name?"

"You don't talk like you're from Boston," the nanny said, and Sterling gave her points for being observant.

"I originally come from Mississippi."

"You from Mississippi?"

"Tupelo."

"I got a passel of cousins in Jackson," the nanny said.

"Got some other kin in Vicksburg too," Sterling said. "Oh, this baby is so cute."

The nanny stayed a few minutes more while Sterling made goo-goo eyes at Kate and told a story about her grandfather's furniture company in Tupelo. Kate wore a long pink linen dress with pink booties. She managed to kick one off, and Sterling tickled the baby's soft toes gulping in the pleasure she got from touching her baby's toes. Kate giggled until the nanny chuckled, and soon all three of them were laughing.

"A baby's laugh is catching," Sterling said, aching to hold her daughter.

"Yes, ma'am, it shore is," the nanny agreed, but she fidgeted. "Been nice talking with ya, but I gots to take Miss Kate on home."

"Bye, Kate."

Sterling sat back on the bench and waited until Kate and the nanny were out of sight. Head held high she retrieved her car from down the street. Her hands shook so much she could hardly get the door open and drove to her motel. She managed to find her room, went inside, and leaned against the door with the rage and sorrow inside her churning into a vile mix. An idea began to grow in her darkness.

You lose any fight longer than four seconds.

It might last a few minutes longer than four seconds, but not much.

Sterling checked out the next morning, wearing her new pants suit and heels and carrying a briefcase. Before eleven o'clock, she took a seat on the same park bench and read a magazine. Her heart pounded as she hoped against hope that the nanny's morning walk was a daily habit. The aroma of fresh cut grass and the sound of children playing filled the air.

At the sound of footsteps, Sterling glanced up and smiled when she saw the young nanny stroll up with the buggy. The buggy shade was pushed back, and the baby fussed with the sun in her eyes.

"Well. Hello again," Sterling said.

"Still waiting on your sister, Missrus?"

Sterling laughed. "She came right after you left yesterday. Today she said she'd be here at noon on the dot. I came early to enjoy the sunshine. How is Miss Kate this morning?"

She leaned over the buggy, shaded the baby's face, and cooed to Kate. The little girl wiggled and giggled.

"I do declare, she shore seem to like you," the nanny said. "She smiles more for you than her own mama."

"I bet her mama dotes on her," Sterling said.

The nanny took a second too long to say, "Oh, she do."

The hard kernel of worry grew in Sterling's stomach. She sang a silly rhyme to her daughter and Kate kicked her arms and legs with a big smile on her face.

"You come to the park every day with this little cutie-pie?" She asked the nanny.

"Every day it don't rain. Miss Kate's mama say children gotta have sunshine, and she say to leave the buggy shade down when I stroll her. Hm-mm." The young woman shook her head as though she didn't think that was right.

Sterling licked her lips and forced a smile. "Does she look like her daddy or her mama?"

"She favor her daddy," the nanny said.

Sterling made silly faces to get Kate to smile, hardly thinking about what she said to the nanny. "Little girls love their daddies. I always did."

"Mr. Foster pure crazy about this child," the nanny said with some earnestness. "Sometime Mrs. Foster seem like she jealous of her own daughter."

When Sterling glanced over, the young woman's wide eyes showed that she was as surprised by what she'd said as Sterling was.

"What a lovely day." Sterling hurriedly turned back to Kate. "This is a nice neighborhood."

After a sigh of relief the nanny agreed, "Shore is."

Sterling made Kate giggle again.

"Oh, Lordy! Look at what time it is." The nanny wheeled the buggy around and started home in a rush. "I better get Miss Kate back into the house 'fore Miss Grace find out she still gone. That woman do have a temper."

"Take care of Miss Kate now, y'hear." Sterling said, relishing the last seconds of seeing her daughter.

But the nanny was searching for something frantically around the ground, in the buggy, under the baby and even in the buggy's hood.

Kate fussed and cried.

"Missrus Foster put a hat on her when we left the house," the nanny muttered as she walked. "And this child won't have none of it. Don't tell me I done lost it."

Sterling sat on the bench and put the book in front of her face until her daughter and the nanny were out of sight. She could hear Kate wail the all the way down the park path and her heart broke. A black void that held no shape or sound seemed to swirl around her in the middle of a bright summer day.

Be careful what you pray for.

Somehow she found her car and drove a few blocks away from Tom's house and the park. Suddenly she had to fling open the car door, lean out, and vomit. The pain of leaving Kate was unbearable.

Holy Mary, Mother of God, pray for me.

In her darkness, an idea floated into her head. She thought about it for a long time. It was crazy, but it could work. She had to break her promise to Gray and take a chance.

**

The address of Atlanta Investments turned out to be in the First National Bank and Trust building, Brian Foster's bank. Sterling wasn't surprised. She had figured the Fosters' criminal business partners would be kept close to home. Here it was, she knew it in her bones.

She almost turned and walked back down the stairs to the street.

Ideally, she would possess the evidence to convict these powerful men of murdering Blacks. In a 1965 Southern courtroom. Unlikely.

Even if she knew where Mrs. Woolworth stashed the Justice Tomorrow case records, she doubted the men would be brought to trial and convicted in Georgia.

What Sterling could do was threaten. Tom's backers were wanted for murdering Blacks in Georgia. Maybe John Cofield too. Even with Justice Tomorrow's security lapse concerning Tom's background, she doubted he would have been accepted as an agent if his father's name showed up in a case file. Sterling knew the organization had made a terrible mistake allowing Tom to join, but they didn't make many others. Brian was a kidnapper and extortionist, probably a dishonest businessman, but not a murderer.

In Atlanta, which bragged it was "the city too busy to hate," bad publicity about civil rights might be enough to scare an ambitious man whose backers were shaky and whose society wife wanted to head every committee. The city's business community need to maintain a veneer of tolerance to attract major companies and events to Atlanta. They wouldn't like the kind of publicity Sterling had to offer.

She was betting her life on it. Sterling licked her lips and fought to stop the flutter of fear in her stomach.

An impressive example of Neo-Classical architecture, the First National Bank's front door columns and portico took up half a block near the *Journal-Constitution* newspaper offices. A limousine disgorged four businessmen in blue suits as Sterling climbed the front steps. One of the men held the door for her.

"I'm looking for Mr. Tom Foster's office," she asked one of the men as they entered the grand lobby of the bank and headed for the elevators beside the small coffee and newspaper stand. She could feel her cheeks getting hot and her palms sweat. Her dry mouth made it hard to speak.

The man gave her an appraising look. "Third floor. I'll show you."

Sterling panicked. She'd promised Gray she wouldn't do anything foolish or reckless. What she was about to do was both.

"Thanks, but I want to buy a newspaper first," she said to the man. She went to the lobby newsstand with its other offerings of chewing gum, Tums, aspirin tins, candy bars, and Kodak film.

She had to stop shaking. She had to believe in herself again and forget, this one time, her promise to Gray.

Perhaps her plan wasn't as bad as it seemed on the surface. Tom claimed he still loved her and tried to warn her at the barn exchange site. She was counting on him to still feel that way and might even play on it. She also knew his ambition and greed were boundless, so a threat to his future would be potent.

"Today's *Constitution*," she told the woman behind the newsstand counter.

Time to call on her natural arrogance and instincts to pull off the bluff of a lifetime. She couldn't do it without being the person she had promised Gray she wasn't anymore. Her eyes scanned the bank lobby.

According to the directory on the wall, Jefferson Davis Pollack was bank vice president. A surge of anger spread through her.

A murdering vice president. Thank you, Saint Jude.

No more stalling.

When the elevator stopped on the third floor she got off and turned left. The outside glass doors at the end of the hall read: Atlanta Investments.

"Is Mr. Foster in?" she asked the secretary at the front desk.

"Do you have an appointment?"

Sterling shifted her feet on the plush, mint green carpet and thrust out her chin. "I've come about Madeline Margaret Sterling Land Management."

The woman looked puzzled. "I don't recall we have—"

Sterling set her briefcase on the edge of the desk and slipped the newspaper inside. "Tom will know it."

The secretary disappeared into Tom's office. Half a minute later he popped out of his office slack-jawed

"Tom, how nice to see you again. Fatherhood agrees with you," said Sterling as she swept passed him. On the way by she asked his secretary, "Would you bring us coffee?"

"Yes, do," Tom said and closed his door. "You were the reporter! Sterling, what the hell are you doing here? I told you to get lost, run . . ."

"I tried." Sterling sat in one of the chairs in front of Tom's mahogany desk and patted the push armrests. Her hands left damp fingerprints on the arms of the chair. She took a moment to peruse the gold-framed certificates of business awards, artful photographs of Atlanta, a lovely Monet print, and a family photo on the desk that included Grace and Tom, Kate, Brian Foster, and a broad-shouldered man with a mustache who must be John Cofield. She studied Cofield another second, memorizing the picture.

"I did try, Tom, but everywhere I turned there was a man following me, or a man trying to kidnap me. or a cop chasing me. Not much of a way to live. I like this better." Her eyes swept his office and the view outside his glass windows.

Tom collapsed in the chair in front of her with a groan.

"How is Kate?" Sterling asked, wishing she could shake Tom until his head fell off.

"Happy and well," Tom said. "She's the love of my life."

A knock on the door. Tom's secretary came in carrying a silver coffee service and two dainty cups that were the same ecru shade as the office walls.

"Just put it on the table," Tom said. His woodsy after-shave scent mingled with the smell of fresh-brewed coffee to turn Sterling's stomach. The secretary started to pick up the carafe.

"I'll serve," Sterling rose. The secretary hesitated but backed away and closed the door.

"How is Grace?" Sterling said as she poured the coffee. "How's such a high-powered woman adjusting to motherhood?"

"Jesus Christ, Sterling, is this what you came to discuss—Grace's political ambitions and child-rearing skills?"

"Perhaps later, if we have time. I am naturally concerned." Sterling handed him a coffee cup and saucer, proud that her hand was rock steady. "I put in two sugars. I presume that's how you still take it."

Tom set the saucer on the edge of the desk. "What do you want?"

"Call off the dogs. Tell your father, father-in-law, wife, housekeeper, pet sheriff or whoever's pulling the strings—to leave Gray, Silver, and me in peace. I don't want to have a single cop stop me for a running a redlight or a county sheriff look at Gray funny for the rest of our lives. We want to hold jobs, eat in restaurants, and take trips without fear. Silver wants to write, someday. I, for one, would like to walk down any street in America without worrying about one of your men pulling me into an alley like Marshal Cooper tried in Norfolk. Or those two amateurs who showed up in Boston."

The bits about Norfolk and Boston had an electric effect on Tom.

"I know nothing about that. None of it!"

"You better find out," she hissed. "I'm holding you and Grace personally responsible for everything. Personally."

"I tried to shield you, remember?"

"Somebody with a powerful reach wants our Justice Tomorrow secrets," Sterling said. "They have chased Gray, Silver, and me all over the South."

Tom's eyebrows drew together and his brow furrowed. "No. I-I didn't know ."

"The people who are worried about those files better leave us alone. If we so much as stub our toe, every newspaper and TV station in Georgia will get a packet of information from multiple lawyers in several states that details how investors of Atlanta Investments are under suspicion of murdering Black people in the civil rights movement."

"You're bluffing."

"With pictures. Remember how we used to get photographic evidence to go with our cases? Let's start with Jonathan Cleary, Herb Holcomb, and Mr. Jefferson Davis Pollack. Cleary used a knife in his killing two years ago. Three years ago, Pollack used a gun outside a Black church in Savannah, a revolver to be specific. Shall I go on? I haven't found your father's murder case, but there are so many Justice Tomorrow boxes to go through . . . You remember Justice Tomorrow? You know, all the friends and colleagues you left to die? That will be a good side story."

Tom closed his eyes and rubbed his forehead.

"I'm willing to leave you—and me if it comes to that—burned to the ground like Atlanta in the Civil War. Imagine what news stories about all this would mean to a fledgling operation like yours. Or to your reputation in a city that claims to be so ahead of the South in race relations. Tsk-tsk."

"Sterling, please!" Tom pleaded. "I'm trying to create a new corporation, free of the old men in town who—. I want to be part of the new Atlanta."

"Which means?"

"I want to cut my father, father-in-law, and all the old guard out of Atlanta Investments. I don't want to be associated with what they do."

"Because they're crooked?"

Tom said nothing.

"Everyone has kin they're ashamed of," Sterling continued and sipped her coffee. "My mother has a drunken uncle, for example."

"It's important for my future, for Grace and Kate's. I need to shove aside the older power brokers in Atlanta." Tom's voice sounded earnest and his breathing shallow.

"Who is J. D. Masterson? Besides, president of Atlanta Investments . . ."

"Nice fellow. Not real bright. University of Georgia drop-out . . ."

"I don't need his resume."

"J. D. is John Cofield's right-hand man. John uses J. D. to stand in when he doesn't want his own name associated with something in business and, ah, political dirty work."

"A straw man," Sterling said, remembering what Tom had once taught her about using front men to conceal the real buyers in some deals. "Would J. D. Masterson do something behind John Cofield's back?"

Tom snorted. "I don't think J. D. does anything without John's okay."

His secretary buzzed and asked Tom a question. While they talked, Sterling remembered something she'd almost forgotten. Gray heard a woman's voice. Was it Grace or someone else connected to John Cofield?

"Does John have a secretary or a lover?" Sterling asked when Tom finished talking. "Or does he pass his orders face-to-face?"

"Mrs. Talbot has been his secretary forever—why the hell should you care?"

"Mrs. Talbot?" Sterling asked.

"Fanny Talbot."

"Her name doesn't appear anywhere."

"She's a secretary, that's all."

"Really?"

"Yes. She's very efficient, has this sweet voice, and looks like somebody's grandmother—which she is. She did everything for John that J. D. didn't. Since John's stroke Grace's been the one to care for her father, even taking over some things Mrs. Talbot used to do," Tom said. His eyes narrowed. "What's going on here?"

She sipped her coffee, trying to absorb this new information. The silence made Tom fidget.

"Listen to me, Sterling. Grace and I— I have ambitions. Grace's father has the political influence to make it happen, so I need to separate our interests carefully," Tom said. "But in the end, a new Atlanta will rise. Stronger, more open to integration and equal rights. A city you would like."

"Yes, I get it," she said through pinched lips. "You want to be legit, aboveboard. No bad publicity."

"Kate will be part of that," he said. "I want to become governor."

"I want to stay alive!"

"Okay, okay." He fiddled with his skinny blue tie. "I will make your point to . . . those who need to know. But they don't control all the police or FBI."

Sterling guffawed.

"Not all of them. You know, the Shelby County sheriff in Tennessee thinks two Black men killed those men in the Memphis barn," Tom said. His eyes flashed. "These two men had wallets with aliases, but I know who they really are. Threaten me, and the police get an anonymous call on these men's real identities."

Sterling felt strangely calm. "The police still don't have Silver and Gray's real names."

"Not yet." Tom's mouth curled into a triumphant smile.

"Okay, tell them, Tom. And I will contact my lawyers. Or just wait twenty-four hours and they will contact the press on their own." Sterling said. "Then I'll come forward and tell everything I know. I'll even produce Kate's birth certificate."

Tom's smile faded.

"There's no need for all this huffing and puffing," she said. "I came here to make a deal."

"What deal?"

"Well, and get a little information." Sterling leaned closer. "Who killed the deputy, Tom? You and I both know I had Silver and Gray in my car and was long gone down the road. I saw at least two of your thugs in the car behind me."

"I figured one of you sneaked back."

"No, you didn't," she scoffed. "You saw how badly beaten Silver and Gray were."

"Sterling," he hesitated, "did you double back and shoot them?"

She scowled.

Her eyes fell on Tom's family photo. Suddenly a rush of wind blew, and a spiral of brambles gathered around her. She shuddered, tasted the red and yellow of anger, saw the voices talking idly in the hallway outside, and heard the sweat of Tom's fear.

"Sterling?" Tom stood, stepped close, and put his hands on her upper arms. "Sterling?"

The sting of the brambles remained as everything else vanished.

Before she could focus, Tom's lips captured hers as he had done so often in Crossville, the kind of kiss that had landed her in his bed. This time, it did nothing for her.

His shoulders slumped. His hands slid off her arms. For the first time, Sterling felt truly sorry for him. How could she ever have imagined she loved him?

"Bad timing," he said.

"Yeah." Her eyes fell to his shoes, and she sighed.

The picture of Grace at the barn flashed through Sterling's mind. She and Tom had gasped or cried when they saw the beaten bodies of Silver and Gray. Grace had stood poised like a cold marble Greek statue.

Sterling became so frightened for Kate her body trembled.

"It was Grace. Holy Mother of God," Sterling said, "she killed the deputy."

"No, no!" Tom drew back. "She was in the car with me. The whole time."

"I saw Grace get out of the car, leave you with Kate, and open the barn door," Sterling hissed through clenched teeth. The image of Grace struggling with the bar across the barn door had been seared into her memory. Even though she thought she saw Grace stepping into the barn, she couldn't be sure.

"Okay, okay. She did go inside the barn, but after a couple of shots, she came running out white as a sheet," Tom said.

"How many shots did you hear before she came out?"

"What? Oh, two." He licked his lips and glanced at the ceiling. Sterling recognized his tell at once. Tom was lying.

"Was Grace in the barn when the two men in the wrecked car walked back to the barn?" Sterling knew this had to be true based on what the former FBI agent hidden in the barn had told her.

"No. Well, for a minute, I guess," Tom said. "I heard the second shot, then she got in the car and screamed at me to drive, drive! She kept saying there was man in the barn with a gun. Someone she couldn't see."

"Did she tell that to the cops?" Sterling said. Tom seemed to be protecting his wife.

"We, ah, we didn't wait around for the police. We were supposed to be in Europe, remember," Tom said.

Were there four men in the barn? Or had Grace seen the ex-FBI man?

Although she had been frantic to escape, Sterling was fairly certain now that she'd seen Grace step into the barn once she had removed the bar across the door. Now Sterling imagined the scene inside the barn. "Grace stayed in the barn with one man when I drove off. After the men in the wrecked car walked back to the barn, there were at least three gunshots. Jibe with what you heard? Grace came running to your car in high heels? Why didn't she get killed?"

"She was safe in the car with Kate and me before the third shot," Tom said.

Third shot? He said he only heard two. How did he hear any shooting with his hysterical wife screaming inside the car? She let it go for the moment.

"Did she recognize the fourth man?" she said. "Could she describe him?"

"Tall, big-shoulders—he was in the shadows and all she could see was the gun anyway."

"Black or white?"

Tom shook his head. "She couldn't tell."

"What about the blood on her?" If Grace had fired a shot at close range, Sterling knew there would be some blood on her somewhere.

"What blood—?" Tom's mouth dropped open and he said nothing more for a second. "Sterling, I see what you're doing. You want to pin this on Grace because she is Kate's mother. But Grace's a good person. She loves Kate. Kate's happy."

"How far would Grace go to cover her secret about Kate?" Sterling asked. "Would she kill for you, Tom, for your chance to be governor?"

"The Grace I know is sweet, gentle, kind. I'm pretty sure she doesn't even know how to fire a gun."

Sterling paused, largely because Tom's description of Grace meshed with the impression Sterling had of the woman. Still, she couldn't let go of her voodoo vision. If what she was supposed to see wasn't Grace, who? Tom?

For Kate's sake she needed to stay close to Tom and Grace, to be sure her daughter was in good hands until she could figure out how to get her back.

Sterling's eyes flicked over the family photo again. Sick old John Cofield could not have been involved. But who did Cofield's dirty work? J.D. Masterson? Cofield's secretary Fanny Talbot? Grace? She heard a gust of wind and glanced at the photo again.

Brian Foster. What if I could separate Tom and his wretched father?

An idea sang to her. She pushed away the rush of caution that threatened to overtake her. Now was not the time to be timid.

"I want a piece of Atlanta Investments, Tom."

"You what?"

"I want your father's share. Right now. Call him," Sterling said. "After his shares are mine, I'll sign them over to you to act in my name and for my benefit, to be my straw man. Permission I can revoke at any time. Can you get that drawn up in a hurry? Like now?"

"We have a standard form for stock transfers—Sterling, can you pull that off?" Tom's smile reached across his face and into his eyes.

"Would that make you the majority stockholder?"

"Close."

"Knowing what you do about some of your other stockholders, wouldn't it be easy to have them vote with you on any issue?" she asked.

"What do you get out of this, Sterling?"

"A stake in your future."

He regarded her with a half-smile. "You want in my life but not in my bed."

"Get your secretary working and call your father."

With a grin, Tom rose, picked up his desk phone, gave instructions to his secretary, then called his father.

Sterling eased back into her chair, her heart thudding against her chest with such force she had to take shallow breaths. This was reckless, beyond foolish.

Tom sat down across from her again and toasted her with his coffee cup. "You are a marvel."

Sterling spotted a touch of gray in Tom's black hair and decided to throw him a bone. "Our daughter is proof of our love."

"I don't want any harm to come to you, Sterling." Tom took her hands and grinned like a man with newfound hope.

"If it does, Gray gets my shares of the company. He wants nothing more than to kill you and burn everything you touch to the ground. I'll take the company if something happens to him and come for Kate in court. What a scandal that will be."

Tom clenched his teeth with such force his jawline rippled. He dropped her hands. "I can only do so much to help."

A knock and Brian Foster came in, red-faced from his rush. "What the hell is the matter, Tom?"

"Hello, Brian," Sterling said.

"I'm sorry, I didn't see—son of a bitch!" The older man went slack jawed as Tom closed the office door. "What are you doing here?"

"Someone's been chasing her all over the map to kill her," Tom said.

Brian stared at his son. "Are you sure?"

Didn't he know? Sterling frowned, off balance by the sudden notion Brian wasn't in charge.

"Have a seat while I explain what's going to happen," she said and covered her surprise. "I want your shares in Tom's company. All of them. I will either share in this company's prosperity or destroy it. Consider it my life insurance policy."

Brian sat on the chair beside his son and made a tent of his fingers. "No."

"They'll stay in the family," she assured him.

He cocked his head, interested, but said, "No."

"May I borrow your phone?" Sterling said. "I want to call my Georgia lawyer and have him release some of the Justice Tomorrow files."

"You're bluffing," Brian said.

Sterling stared at him. "I will use the Justice Tomorrow files to destroy Atlanta Investments and dirty as many of the Cofields and Fosters as I can."

Tom nodded at his father.

A knock on the door. "Here are the contracts and forms you asked for." Tom's secretary handed over two thick folders and backed out.

"Young lady, I'm not going to . . ." Brian said to Sterling.

"She has details, bloody details, about three of our board members who murdered colored people. Like Jefferson Davis Pollack, your bank vice president? Proof enough to convict them, Dad. She has lawyers in several states ready to send a packet of information to every newspaper in the South. We could lose it all."

Color drained from Brian's face. "John, too?"

"That sick old man?" Sterling leaned back in her chair.

"Still runs Georgia," Brian finished.

"He has help, though, doesn't he?" Sterling asked. "Help that could be hit with a scandal so serious Tom and Grace couldn't get an invitation to a Boy Scout meeting, much less a society ball or a political meeting."

Brian's eyes darted to his son.

"Show him where to sign, Tom."

After a moment's hesitation, Brian finally scribbled his name.

"Stay long enough for my secretary to notarize the transfer then get out of my office," Tom said. "Tell anyone Sterling's here, dad, and you will never see Kate again. You have my word on that."

"You think you've won?" Brian glared at Sterling. "Huh! What kind of woman gives up her daughter for two nigras?"

Bile rose in Sterling's throat.

"Mary Lou," Brian cracked the office door and called to his secretary, "would you come in and witness this document?"

After the documents were properly signed, Sterling asked for a camera and when the secretary found one, had several pictures taken of her with Brian and Tom holding the agreement and a copy of the day's newspaper she had bought.

Sterling said, "Let's get this other one done, too."

Mary Lou brought in more legal forms papers that Sterling and Tom signed. Then the secretary took another picture of the three of them with the new document and the daily newspaper. Sterling took the whole roll of film out of the camera and said she'd get it developed herself as souvenirs.

"I'll send you a copy of the pictures, Tom," she said sweetly.

When she had notarized the transaction, Tom ushered Mary Lou out.

Sterling glanced over the papers and tucked her copies into her briefcase. "Partners?"

"Partners." He extended his hand, and they shook on it.

Brian snorted, shook his head, and started out.

"Not a word to anyone, Brian," Sterling said.

Tom's father glowered at his son.

"I just signed over half a million dollars to a whore," Brian said to Tom. "Hope she was worth it."

Sterling's face grew hot, and she knew all her freckles shone like dark diamonds.

When the door closed behind Brian, she asked, "How many shares does John Cofield own?"

"Not as many as we do." Tom grinned. "I owe you."

"I need some traveling money," she said. "I need to get out of here fast. I don't trust your father."

"He's made enough since Crossville to cushion this blow. He won't starve," Tom slipped a wad of bills from his wallet into her hand. "His pride's hurt. That makes him dangerous."

"I'll be careful."

"Sterling, I'm glad you're going to be in my life."

She shook her head. "I want Kate."

"A little safety is all I promise."

"Can you keep Kate safe? Knowing what you do about Grace?"

"Grace did nothing!" Tom drew himself to his full height. "Look, I will arrange for people to stop hunting you, Silver, and Gray. I thought I'd done that already out of love for you. This time I'll make sure."

"Good."

"But understand this, Sterling," Tom's tone sounded grim, "if you ever come for Kate, I will kill you myself."

Another knock. "Mr. Foster, you have a meeting in ten minutes."

"Thank you," Tom called.

"Remember, killing me, Gray, or Silver is not an option, Tom. Neither is ruining our lives. You know what bad publicity will do to investors, business partners, and anyone in Atlanta trying to sell this snake pit as the cradle of brotherhood," Sterling said. "They will scatter like chickens. You better pray we stay in good health for the sake of our mutual investment."

That's all she could get. Her heart screamed, but her bargaining position wasn't that strong. At least, not now.

His secretary cracked open the door. "Mr. Foster?"

"Thank you for your time, Tom. Tell Grace hello and kiss that adorable baby girl for me. She has the prettiest, curliest red hair." Sterling rose and left.

When she passed the secretary, Mary Lou stared at Sterling's hair. Her eyebrow raised on one side and a smile tugged at one corner of her mouth.

Sterling fluffed her curls and grinned back.

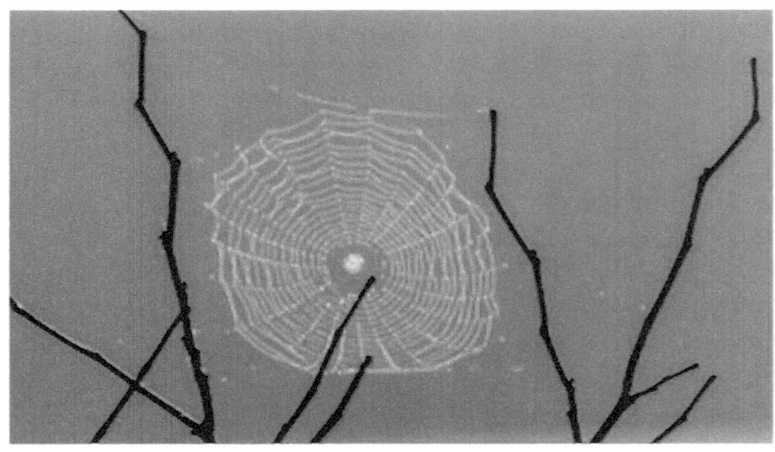

CHAPTER THIRTY-NINE: A RETURN

Outside the bank, Sterling ducked into a taxi that let her off at the Greyhound bus station. In the white women's public restroom that smelled of vomit, she changed into jeans, a paisley shirt, and put on the flaxen wig. Somehow, the thing didn't look as natural on her head as it had when Marabelle put it on. She walked out of the restroom and stopped.

Two men in sport coats ran through the terminal turning their heads as they went as though looking for someone. In a terminal full of Black passengers, she stood out. With more confidence in her step than she felt in her soul, Sterling strolled out of the restroom and left by the side door. She caught a taxi two blocks away and had it drop her off a block from where she'd parked her rental car.

At the airport she cased the departure gates, then used some of Tom's cash to buy a ticket for Chicago, the flight leaving out of the gate next to the one for Cincinnati. She took a seat in the waiting area for Chicago flight and got in line when that flight was called.

"Thank you for flying with us," the harried attendant said as she put the ticket Sterling handed her in her pile. Sterling stepped out of line just before entering the gate and moved to the back, pretending she'd forgotten something. Instead of returning, she slipped into the line for her Cincinnati flight, using the second half of the roundtrip ticket she'd bought.

Anyone who checked the paperwork would find she got on the plane to Chicago.

Perhaps her precautions were unnecessary, but Tom hadn't had time to call off all the hounds. It paid to remain overly cautious whether he kept his word or not. Those men in the bus station were proof of that.

Tom didn't know Silver was dead and she hadn't told him. The more she thought about it, the less she trusted him. She trusted Brian not at all. And, she had to wonder how a paralyzed old man continued to run Georgia politics. Perhaps he did it through his straw man J. D. Masterson and his daughter Grace Foster. Or his secretary, Fanny Talbot.

Tom was a weak, ambitious man. She always knew that about him, even when she thought she loved him. She'd left her daughter in his care. The idea gnawed her insides, but she didn't know how to fix it.

Yet.

As the airplane lifted off, Sterling replayed the scene in Tom's office and wondered if it was possible Grace really did kill those men in the Memphis barn. She didn't want to believe it. Grace seemed too ladylike to squash a bug, much less kill a man. Instead, Sterling imagined another scenario. Maybe the deputy killed the alleged drug dealers, as David Cohen had called them while she was in St. Louis, then tried to kill Grace with Silver's gun. Maybe Grace struggled for the gun and the deputy sheriff was somehow shot. That idea worked better for what Sterling knew of Grace than premeditated murder.

What kind of man was the deputy, what was he doing at the barn during this supposed drug deal, and how did he get Silver's gun? She needed to check out the deputy's life and history with the Shelby County Sheriff's Department in Memphis. What about the so-called drug dealers who died? What was their backstory? Who did they work for? What did the sheriff's ballistics report show, and what did the blood spatter patterns reveal?

If the killer wasn't Tom or Grace, the only other person she knew near the barn was the ex-FBI agent. He had lots of time to disable the three kidnappers and save Silver and Gray but didn't. That meant he didn't have a gun, a good opportunity, or the inclination. Like John Cofield and Brian Foster, the FBI man also had resources to use in tracking her. Cofield and Foster were wealthy men with Ku Klux Klan contacts, while he was a former lawman with friends in local, state, and federal law enforcement throughout the South.

On the other hand, the mysterious ex-FBI agent had saved her life in St. Louis.

With a sigh she snuggled in her seat, folded her arms, and closed her eyes. A lot of work still to do.

She needed Gray to help her solve this. All she had to do was keep pretending Kate was Tom and Grace's child and maintain the ruse that she'd exchanged a case file for him. She'd behaved like the Sterling of old and this time she'd gotten away with it. Never again. She had to convince Gray of that.

A longing for Gray washed over her. Sterling shelved all her questions to smile about being with him again. Her muscles relaxed and her thoughts turned to Kate. The baby's soft skin, little smile, infectious laugh, and those blue eyes that seemed to know Sterling.

Her seat back shook as the man in the row behind her rose to stand in the aisle. Suddenly he dropped in the seat beside her.

"Enjoy Atlanta?" the ex-FBI agent asked as he unfolded a magazine.

She jerked away. The man beside her wore a white shirt, a skinny red tie, a tan sports coat over dark trousers, and a bemused expression.

"I'm hurt you didn't visit while you were in town. I had to buy an expensive airline ticket to talk to you." He handed her a magazine.

She opened it and pretended to read, but her hands shook. "Who are you?"

"Al Morris the Fourth. Pleased to know you, Miss Madeline Margaret Sterling. Where you headed?"

She glanced at him sideways. "You pop up at the strangest times."

"Jest like your guardian angel."

Sterling wasn't getting an angel vibe from Morris.

The man squirmed to get comfortable against the seat back and fingered his mustache. "State warrant's been issued for our man and his brother in the name of their aliases. Not good, but not too bad . . . yet."

"You know that's bogus," Sterling whispered, wondering if he'd seen Kate from the hayloft and hoping he hadn't. "You saw me drive away with Gray and his brother."

"Fancy piece of drivin' too," Morris said.

"What happened to the white men in the car behind me?" Sterling said. "Did you shoot them?"

"You're a hard woman to like, you know that? I split before the gunfire. Yes, ma'am. I saw that fancy car of theirs light out of the barn then watched two of 'em walk back when they wrecked it. Quick as I saw my chance to get away after that, I took it. I was running through cotton when I heard—," he lowered his voice "—two shots and then, a third. When I heard the shots, I ran faster."

"Two, a pause, and a third?"

"So I said."

"Where was the couple in the Cadillac?"

"He sat in the car as far as I could tell. She was in the barn after two men in the car took off after you."

"She stayed with one of the kidnappers? What were they doing?"

"Talking. And before you ask I couldn't hear what they said. Made it hard to get out without being seen," Morris whispered. "Now, how long the Cadillac stayed where it was after I split, I don't know."

"If the two kidnappers were in the car chasing me, who else was there around the barn when you left?" Sterling could feel her excitement rachet up. "Our friend's wife says there was a fourth man in the barn."

Morris's bushy eyebrows raised. "Na, unless she meant me. Only folks there were the wife and the white man who stayed after the other two took off after you."

"The man in the Caddy said he heard one shot, a second, and then his wife came running out."

"Man's wrong. Two shots close together," Morris said. "A few seconds later, another."

"She could have been running after the first shot." Sterling tried again to remember the scene at the barn after she lost Kate.

"She'd have to be mighty fleet of foot to get to the car before that second shot." Morris glanced at his magazine.

Maybe Tom didn't hear any other shots. Or maybe he was lying to protect his wife.

Sterling swallowed a knot of fear. Morris could be lying.

267

Was Morris the man who ran from the back of the barn as Grace had told Tom? The sound of the shots came after Morris said he hightailed it out, according to Tom's version. Plus, the way Tom reported Grace's description of the assassin, Morris was too slender and short.

Holy Mother, was there really a fourth player in this drama?

That didn't make sense. Sterling shook her head and suddenly remembered Tom's tell, how Tom had licked his lips and looked at the ceiling when he told her about the number of shots he heard. His tell gave away his lie. She believed Morris' version of the shots and when they were fired.

"Mother of God," she breathed.

Panic nibbled at the edges of her mind. Could Tom have done it? Had he changed that much? Or was Grace that cold-blooded? The palms of Sterling's hands and the small of her back felt damp with sweat.

"Maybe there was someone else in the barn you missed," Sterling said.

"Unlikely. I mean, I suppose someone else might have walked in before you took off. After you saw me in the hayloft, I was afraid to move, to look out the window until the car roared outta the barn," Morris said.

The food cart rattled to a stop beside Morris. The stewardess asked, "May I serve you a turkey or ham sandwich? Something to drink?"

"A Coke, please." Sterling said.

"Turkey sandwich and coffee." Morris turned to Sterling. "Have a ham sandwich. You got to eat something."

"Ham, then," she told the stewardess.

They took their food and waited until the cart rumbled by before resuming their whispered discussion.

"Look, Mr. Morris, Tom's strictly a con man. His wife seems like she'd faint at the sight of blood."

Morris shook head once. "Don't you be blind to what that woman can do. She looks like a lady, but she comes from murderous stock."

Sterling lost her appetite for ham or turkey. Morris had just named what she feared in her heart of hearts. The woman who rocked Kate to sleep every night might be a killer. She glanced at Morris and wind roared in her ears. The thorns encircled her. She heard yellow, blue, and red colors and felt the sandpaper of her soul's weeping. In her pain the only thing Sterling could see was a country town like one of many she and Gray had driven through, the hills beyond it, and the bramble tunnel that gave her a peephole into the future.

"Hey!" Morris touched her arm.

Sterling blinked twice and grabbed her cold cup of Coke. "W-what makes you think our friend's wife is capable of—?" She couldn't bring herself to say murder.

"That's the way all the Cofields have done business for years. Now that he's old and sick, the daughter's stepping into his shoes for more decisions." Morris spread his hands apart. "How much of what she says or does comes from her dear old daddy is anybody's guess. Her daddy's roots are deep in the KKK, and he wields plenty of political clout from that. Plus, he's rich as hell. Huh! His opponents have been known to withdraw to nurse broken ribs. His businesses skate on the edge of legal. His daughter's learned everything she knows from him. They ain't a white or Black person in Atlanta who don't step aside for the both of them."

"Suspicions. That's all either of us have." Sterling said.

"Here's something. Those two men chasing you away from the barn? I found out about one." Morris said. "Worked for John's company, Golden Truckers."

"Cofield owns Golden Truckers?" Sterling grabbed her seat's armrests in a tight grip. "Can you find out more about the other men?"

"Hm-m. By and by," Morris said. "You and my man were in St. Louis. Where's his brother?"

"Dead."

Morris swore softly into a silence marred only by the roar of the plane's engines. "Nobody else knows that. Where, ah, is the man's brother?"

Sterling glared at him.

"O-okay."

"I want to hire you. I've got a little money," Sterling said. "Find whatever you can on the Fosters, their fathers, and known associates. I especially want to know about scandals, mistresses, anything illegal swept under the rug."

Morris took another bite of his turkey sandwich and wiped smears of mayonnaise from his chin.

"Lady, your money's no good with me," he said quietly. "Tell you what. FBI knows about everythin', but Justice Tomorrow is one group we never got a handle on. While I was an agent, we stumbled across some of the impressive work you and my man did in at least two states. Not enough for J. Edgar Hoover to get worked up about, though. That cracker was too focused on Dr. King. Interested me, though. I did some digging and discovered you both in Crossville doing the Lord's work. I quit around that time. Next thing I know Tom Foster's in my office begging me to find his good friends and see they doin' okay. I believed him, since he served with Justice Tomorrow. Now you tell me one brother's dead, and I brought his killers to the door. Na, your money's no good."

Sterling's eyes grew wide. She hoped Morris hadn't found out too much about what happened in Crossville. Then again, if the FBI thought that she and Gray were involved in killing the Crossville sheriff—even in self-defense—they would have been in handcuffs long ago.

"Why did you leave the FBI?" she asked and wrapped up her half-eaten sandwich.

"You gonna be hungry later if you don't finish that sandwich," Morris said. "I left because I wasn't going nowhere. White agents kept getting more money and getting promoted. I'm doing better on my own. Not rich like Foster got in Crossville, though."

"He saved the town from destruction and got Black farmers more for their land than they thought possible." She was giving Tom more credit for what happened than he deserved. Perhaps she couldn't bear to think she'd given herself to a total sleaze.

"Point taken," Morris murmured. "Still, I don't forgive and forget."

"He did work for Justice Tomorrow." Sterling hated herself for once again being in the position of defending Tom.

"Don't you think I checked him out?" Morris barked then lowered his voice. "Something happened to him in Crossville."

Sterling twirled her Coke.

"Know anything about that?" he asked.

"Money, I think. The allure of power?" Sterling poked her sandwich. "His father's got a hold on him."

"Could be he saved his father's ass. Brian Foster owed money to Cofield. Word is, most of that debt went away when Tom Foster married Cofield's daughter," said Morris. He bit off another piece of turkey sandwich with the viciousness of a lion attacking prey.

"Brian sold his son?" Her throat tightened. She folded her napkin on her airline tray with care.

"Hm-m-m," he said. "Girl, you stay outta sight. Bees are buzzing in Atlanta. You sure know how to stir up a fuss."

Sterling thought of Gray waiting for her in Morehead and warmth spread through her again. She and Gray would investigate the murders in Memphis and get him out from under a murder charge, but Morris could give them a head start.

"Can you get the coroner's report on the bodies and any police report of the Memphis incident? I want to know about the guns involved in the shooting and more about the connections any of the victims had to the Fosters or Cofield's close circle. like J. D. Masterson and that secretary he has," she said.

"Fanny Talbot. A useful idiot."

Sterling took out a pen and wrote one of her aliases, along with the Huntington, West Virginia Post Office Box number, in her magazine. She told him that she would check mailbox in a month or two.

He switched magazines with her and read a little. So did she.

"You kidnap the Foster's baby? That start all this?" Morris' eyes never left the magazine page.

Her hand slipped along the edge of the page she was reading. Her head didn't move. Blood from the long paper cut oozed onto the magazine, but Sterling didn't feel the sting.

"Jesus Christ." Morris grabbed her paper napkin to wrap around her palm.

"For a while," she said, "deal with me, not my friend."

Morris' bushy eyebrows shot up.

"He's still recovering." Sterling blinked back the useless tears.

"Hm-m-m."

"Do you have an office?"

Morris heaved a big sigh. "I'll find you."

She closed her eyes, folded her arms across her chest, and leaned against the window.

"Don't look for a while," she muttered.

Her stomach felt queasy. Had she put her faith in a man who could have killed three people? Even if he wasn't a killer, Morris could still be working with the FBI to lure Gray into a trap.

Or he could be a pipeline to information she and Gray needed. A witness to what really happened in the barn.

The cut along her palm burned and the ham sandwich sat like a brick in her stomach

CHAPTER FORTY: THE ACCUSATION

Gray saw a flashes of light outside, jumped off the workroom stool, and looked out the window. No Sterling. Paul's motion sensors must have caught another possum. Marabelle would complain again so Gray imagined the sensors would be back on his bench in the workroom by morning.

He returned to his stool and studied a machine that was supposed to billow smoke but only puffed. The screwdriver he'd chosen was too large, so he reached up for a smaller one.

The workbench in front of him ran the entire width of the room behind the beauty shop and down half the other wall. Mounted on the wall were tools of every size, shape, and function. When he first saw the setup, Gray imagined this was what heaven looked like. Until now he'd always been too busy studying or running for his life to tinker. After Sterling left, Paul discovered his interest and showed him a few tricks. Now he had a bench full of broken appliances and small machines to fix.

Gray glanced beyond the costumes and rows of make-up, to the loft Paul had originally built for his theater students. Now it was Gray's bedroom. He wondered if he'd get to sleep there tonight, if Sterling would get home and he could relax.

Gray's head jerked up from the smoke machine. Lights flashed in the driveway outside and a car crunched over the gravel between the house and Belles Beauty shop. He wiped his hands, hurried to a window, and swept aside the tan and blue curtains for the tenth time that night. In the house behind Sterling's car, a single lamp shone in the living room to show her the way upstairs.

He grinned. Sterling slammed the car door and picked her way across the road to the beauty shop. Her gait looked odd. Was she hurt? He flung open the workroom door. She wasn't limping, she almost seemed to be dancing.

The moment she crossed into the workroom, he swept her into his arms and kicked the door closed. His cast made the embrace awkward, but the kiss sprang from his heart.

When they parted, her eyebrows rose slightly, and her lips parted. The light in her blue eyes had changed. He'd never kissed her before, at least, not like that. As he moved to kiss her again, she met him with such force and urgency his senses reeled.

At last, he buried his face in her neck, kissed her collarbone, and groaned, "Christ, Sterling, you can't go off alone again."

"I think the trip was worth it." She laid her head on his chest. "I'm glad to be back."

He grabbed her hand. "What happened here?"

"Paper cut. I was reading a magazine," she said. "It's nothing."

Her whole body seemed to vibrate with a different energy.

"You look extremely pleased." Gray knew he was grinning like a fool.

"It was downright terrifying, but I think I got us breathing room. Tom's building a garbage dump empire with trucks, containers, haulers, storage, and more land for dumps. Really, I've got more questions than answers, but I also discovered at least three of the men on Tom's Board of Directors at Atlanta Investments have Justice Tomorrow case files. I told Tom I had lawyers ready to tell that story to the public if anything happened to you and me."

Tom. She saw him. Gray's body suddenly turned cold.

"You broke your promise. You went to see Tom," he said with a touch of bitterness. "God damn it, Sterling."

His words seemed to sting her. "I said I wouldn't take any crazy risks. I know this man and how he thinks. The risk wasn't foolish, especially since I went to Tom's office where he has to keep up a respectable front. I knew how the threat of bad publicity would hit him."

"Doesn't sound like much of a threat."

"Good enough. I got Brian Foster to sign over all the shares of his stock in Atlanta Investments to me as the price for my silence. Then I turned them over to Tom to be my straw man and vote the shares. His fortune is now tied to me. He knows you and I are willing to blow up the company."

Anger rose from Gray's stomach to his head. "Is he that dedicated to his new company?"

Sterling laughed. "You can't imagine how much. He wants to use the company as a springboard to the governor's mansion."

"Him?"

She nodded. "Tom and his men will back off, at least for a while. The cops—"

"You're in the clear with the cops," he said, "but they're still looking for me?"

"Warrants have been issued for your aliases—yours and Silver's. The good news is that they don't have your real names."

He expected it sooner or later, but the news deflated him.

"Gray, we'll fix it. I promise," she said. "I told Tom the cops had better back off too, but he claims not to have much influence with them."

Gray smirked.

"We have to find out who really killed those men to clear you. I've got some ideas." She took his hand.

They sat on a couple of stools next to the workbench under the harsh light of a desk lamp, and she filled him in on her trip. Gray felt the heat in his face. When she finished telling what she'd learned, his anger grew. He waited, hoping for the rest of it to pour out of her, the darkness that troubled her, shaded her eyes, wearied her to the core.

The omission, the part about betraying their fellow agents, never emerged. Gray dropped her hand.

He knew this woman, from the sound of her heartbeat to the fears that drove her, the ambitions she harbored, and the pain they shared.

But the nagging suspicion he'd always carried now hardened in him. The suspicion he'd had since Tom and Sterling had shared a house in Crossville, frustration at how much he had leaned on her, and a new streak of jealousy clouded his thinking.

"I was careful I wasn't followed back here. I think we can rest a little easier," she finished. Sterling got off the stool, made a pirouette and curtsied as though waiting for applause.

"You spoke to Tom? Face to face? In spite of what we agreed."

She touched Gray's shoulder and ran her hand softly down his arm. "We had coffee in his office."

"He went along with what you did to his father . . . and told you all this about his wife?" The implausibility of it rankled—did she think he was a fool?

"No, he didn't tell me all of it. I learned some things from women in the supermarket, from the nanny of Tom's daughter, from the owner of a warehouse company, and other things I inferred from what Tom didn't say—"

"You risked a trip to Atlanta to see Tom." Rage so filled his mind Gray couldn't think of anything else.

Her face sagged as though the joy holding it in place had drained away.

"Did you sleep with him?"

A gasp.

"Is that what you think? Is that what's important to you?" She wheeled for the door.

"Sterling . . ."

"Go to hell."

"We'll talk more in the mornin—"

She slammed the door.

Fists clenched, he watched her stomp across the driveway and into the house. He was still cursing when she turned off the downstairs light in the Carlson's home.

She only wanted to see Tom. Why else would she take such a chance? She lied to him.

As he walked back to the workbench, he punched one of the head forms on a nearby workbench and it careened onto the floor. The smoke machine that refused to yield its largest screw lay on its side, still waiting for him. He grasped the screwdriver he'd laid down when Sterling arrived and tried to concentrate on the machine.

The nuts and screws of the machine before him twisted in his mind to become Sterling and Tom Foster locked in an embrace he could not sever.

With a grunt he dropped the screwdriver and grabbed his head between his hands.

She might have made love with Tom in Crossville but what was passed was passed. That didn't bother him like the lie, the terrible risk, and the hundreds of dollars she spent to be with him in Atlanta. The betrayal stung him to his core.

Gray put the screwdriver back in its place on the pegboard wall with a shaky hand.

After all that had happened—it was unbelievable, unimaginable. that she wanted to see Tom. Gray gritted his teeth. His cast nudged a hammer on the workbench, and he swept it onto the cement floor.

God damn.

The clunk-clack-clunk noise of the hammer hitting the floor sobered him a little. He retrieved the hammer and hung it on the proper wall peg. After switching off the workbench light, he went over to pick up the head form from the floor and put it back on the shelf.

"Sorry, mate. Not angry with you," he said in the English accent he'd been practicing.

Gray turned on the light in the bathroom near the steps to his loft bed. He splashed water on his face and hands, soaking the front of his work shirt. Fuming and fumbling with the cast, he took off his shirt and pants and hung them on a hook behind the bathroom door. Before he climbed into the loft he surveyed the dark workroom at the rows of wigs on head forms. In the moonlight from the windows, they seemed to be turned away from him as though even heads stuffed with cotton couldn't bear to look at him.

Self-righteousness turned out to be a cold companion as he climbed the loft stairs to bed. A vision of Tom kissing Sterling appeared fuzzy in his mind. He couldn't remember another time when she had been less than honest with him. That's why her deception, her dark secret, stung so much.

Unless, he had jumped to the wrong conclusion about why she went to Atlanta.

He considered this as he rearranged the covers on the mattress. He'd been a jerk. No maybe about it. He'd acted like a hormonal teenager whose girlfriend danced with another guy. But he'd been so relieved that she was safe and fired by their kisses . . . he'd embarrassed himself and offended the woman who'd sacrificed everything to save him.

No excuses. He was lucky she hadn't decked him with a right cross.

When he flopped on his mattress, Gray settled into an unfamiliar feeling. Silver had always been with him, and Sterling too, for as long as he'd known her. He'd never been alone. Now his brother was dead, and in a moment of jealous insanity, he'd driven Sterling away. She'd been insulted, outraged. Hurt. Instead of unburdening herself to him, she kept her secret dammed inside her.

His stupidity had made that dam stronger.

Gray groaned and scrubbed his face with both fists. He turned on his side to count the nail holes in wall that the moonlight showed him, feeling small enough to crawl inside one.

What kind of apology could he give in the morning that would undo the damage he'd done tonight?

CHAPTER FORTY-ONE: NATURAL DISGUISES

Sterling didn't appear for breakfast, but after his classes Gray tried to adjust the motion sensors in the workroom and heard her laughter in the beauty shop. When he delivered extra towels to the shop, her face looked drawn. She was polite, but her vacant eyes spoke of despair.

Gray's heart sank. He had to get her alone and apologize her.

She spent the entire day in the shop getting to know the customers and learning to cut, color, and curl hair. Every time he peeked at her, she seemed almost light-hearted, bantering with customers as she watched Marabelle's every move with the scissors or a hairbrush.

"Cut vertically when you cut sections of hair then check the cut horizontally," Marabelle said as Sterling combed out the strands of white hair in her hand and grasped the scissors. "Don't you give Clara here a crew cut."

"No, no!" The old woman seated in the beautician's chair waved her arms.

"I could show you how to wear a crew cut with style," Sterling teased.

Clara laughed and patted Sterling's arm. "I bet you could, honey."

At the end of the day, Marabelle sent her from the shop to get supper started, leaving the clean-up to Gray and herself. Gray swept, something he had become good at, while she restocked towels and hair products. When she finished, Marabelle collected the money from the cash register and locked it in a workroom safe.

She started back through the blue door back to the shop, then stopped to lean on the frame.

"You have a fight?" Marabelle asked. "No, nope. None of my business. Forget it."

"I was an ass," Gray said.

"A man actin' like an ass? Get outta town."

"I have to fix it."

"Soon. Her kind of pain's contagious."

Gray put the broom away and headed across the drive into the kitchen.

Sterling didn't glance at him when he entered. A pile of potatoes lay to the left of the sink, ready to peel and put in the pot beside her. She stood over the sink stringing green beans, cutting out the black spots, and rinsing the beans off.

Gray came beside her, took a knife, and peeled potatoes. Two, three, four peeled potatoes hit the water in a tall pot. The skins flew into the garbage can. The fresh green beans snapped in Sterling's fingers.

He'd never seen her like this. She stared at the beans in her hands as she stringed them and tossed them in a pot with the repetitive motions.

"I'm sorry, Sterling. I have nothing to excuse what I said."

"Please cut those potatoes into quarters before you put them in the pot," she said.

"I was wrong. I'm sorry. I was an ass." He cut the potatoes up and tossed them back in the water.

"You were wrong, you're sorry, and you are an ass." Each word sounded the same. Each motion seemed like it was the same as the one before. She seemed to have divorced her mind from her body.

"You're hurt. I know," Gray said, his heart cracking.

"I took that calculated risk for you. For both of us and our future."

"You have a right to be angry. What can I do to make it better?"

She finished with the beans and turned to him. "I forgive you."

Somehow, he didn't think it was that simple.

"I understand—," he began in a reasonable tone.

"I doubt you do, Gray," she said. "I forgive you, but I can't trust you. Last night you told me in no uncertain terms that you didn't trust me either."

Her words hit him like a gut punch.

"I thought we were back to the partnership we shared, the one where we understood one another. In the woods, when those boys came? I lay in the front seat of that car while they tried to get in and told myself to be still and wait for you. I heard the truck roar and knew I was safe."

He waited while she grabbed a breath and steeled himself.

"But I can't trust you to look at things in a logical way anymore, not the way I always did." She laid down the knife and stared at the "Home is Where the Heart Is" plaque on the wall.

She grasped the edge of the sink to steady herself. He watched the blood leave her knuckles.

"I'm alone in this," she whispered to the plaque.

"No, Sterling . . ."

"You need more time to heal," she told him and returned to the beans.

"Do I smell beef roast? Boy, I'm hungry." Paul walked into the kitchen from his first lecture classes of the semester and slung his book bag on the table inside the door. "Where's Marabelle?"

"She's, ah, still in the shop," Gray managed to say.

"Hello, Paul." Sterling gave him a small smile.

"Teaching is hungry work," Paul said. "How was your day, Sterling?"

"I can't cut a straight line."

Paul guffawed. "Give it time."

"That's just what I told Gray." She put the beans on the stove to cook.

"I'll set the table," Gray offered.

"Gray, what happened in Sharpsville in January 1960?" Paul had the irritating habit of drilling him on South African history, geography, and politics.

"Police killed sixty-nine people and wounded two hundred who were peacefully demonstrating against Pass Laws for Africans," Gray said. "The pass laws are part of apartheid and said which areas a person was allowed to move through or be in without being arrested. They still exist but I doubt anyone will ask me about that."

"Who is the leader of the Republic of South Africa?" Paul said.

Marabelle came in, washed her hands, and stirred the beans.

"Prime Minister Hendrik Verwoerd, architect of apartheid." The quiz, which Gray found to be a blessing tonight, continued as Sterling finished making dinner. She emptied the boiling pot of potatoes, added butter and milk, picked up the masher, and went to work turning them into mashed potatoes. The work seemed hard for her, her movements awkward and stiff as though her bones ached.

"My favorite feature of my homeland?" Gray said with his eyes on Sterling. "I love the Drakensberg Mountains, which my people, the Zulus, call the Barrier of Spears."

"Bravo," Marabelle said. "You sound like a native."

The oven buzzer went off. Sterling removed the roast, placed it on a platter and carried it to the table. Gray started to help, but she brushed by as though he weren't there.

"I imagine folks will only ask you what you eat in South Africa," Marabelle said.

"Corn and corn dishes, mostly," Gray said.

Sterling put the green beans and the mashed potatoes into serving dishes and added serving spoons to each. The bowls shook in her hands as she set them on the table.

"Looks like dinner's ready," Paul said rubbing his hands together. "I'm starved."

When everyone was seated at the kitchen table, Sterling said, "If you'll excuse me, I'm not hungry."

"Bad sign when the cook won't eat her own food." Marabelle gestured to the chair next to Gray.

Sterling slid into the seat. Gray hung his head.

"How was your day as a beautician, Sterling?" Marabelle asked as Paul passed the roast.

"Your customers are nice." Sterling pushed mashed potatoes around her plate.

"You did a good job," Marabelle said, "Nobody went home scalped."

Everyone at the dinner table laughed. Sterling's crooked smile seemed forced. The smile of someone who wasn't present at the table but far away.

THE PRICE OF THE FUTURE

"How were your lecture classes?" Marabelle asked her husband. She passed him the green beans and glanced at Gray.

"The kids get younger every year. One day I'm going to walk into the lecture hall and my students will be in diapers," Paul said.

Gray and his two hosts laughed. Sterling chuckled weakly.

"I'm looking forward to having an audience for my English accent tomorrow," Gray said.

"Your performance tonight has been wonderful so far." Paul applauded, Marabelle joined him, and Sterling scooted back from the table.

"Gray always gives an excellent performance," she said. "Excuse me."

The remaining diners fell silent as she took her plate to the sink and went upstairs. Marabelle turned to Gray with an upraised eyebrow. He carefully carved his slice of roast into six pieces. Perhaps he should leave her alone for a few days and try again later. He put down his fork. His appetite had left him. His stomach was too filled with sour regret.

Marabelle was right, Sterling's pain was infectious.

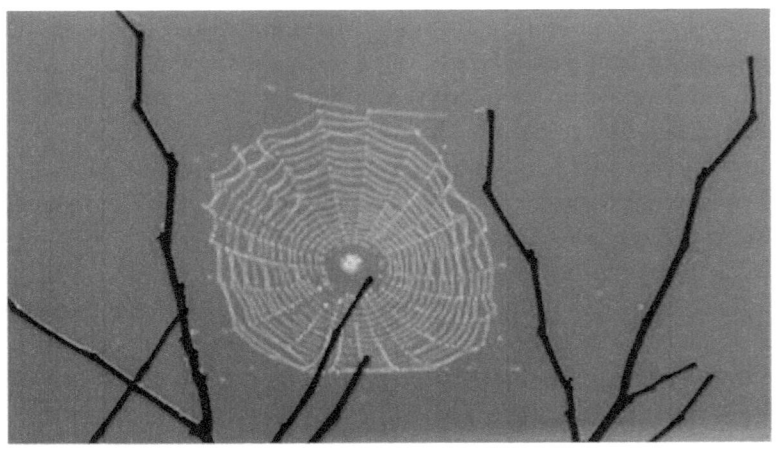

CHAPTER FORTY-TWO: A WAY FORWARD

For the next two days Gray watched Sterling walk through her day with eyes that showed nothing: flat, blank spaces that held no light.

More troubling, Marabelle reported Sterling curled up in a tight ball on her bed, covers over her head. Judging from the circles around her eyes, Sterling wasn't sleeping. Neither was he.

What does she want from me?

He prepared a new apology. That much sadness and pain must come from another source—it couldn't be just his stupidity. One day she'd tell him about the Justice Tomorrow agents whose lives she'd exchanged for his, and he would never mention he'd already guessed.

One day when she was ready. Or thought he was ready.

**

When she heard Gray's footsteps outside the kitchen door two days later, Sterling stiffened in front of the kitchen sink where she stood shucking corn. He opened the door and said her name.

She stripped the green husks with vicious rips that mimicked her shredding heart and tossed them in the garbage, scrapped off the silks with her fingers, and dropped the corn in a pot ready to boil. Tomatoes had already been sliced onto a plate and a solitary fly buzzed over it. Butter beans bubbled on the stove. The smell of chicken roasting in the oven filled the kitchen. Sterling wiped sweat off her forehead with the corner of her apron.

"Paul and Marabelle need better air-conditioning," she said.

"Sterling, I've been thinking about what you said. I'm irrational when it comes to anything about Tom Foster," Gray admitted. "It's a flaw, a blind spot, but I don't know how to overcome it. It's like a fire inside me."

"Tom and his relatives have caused you a lot of pain. They cost you a brother. I know something of loss and pain myself."

Unlike Gray, however, Sterling had filled with new determination to get her daughter back—she would come up with a plan that Tom would find attractive now that she owned part of his company and his future. His love of power and money would get her what she wanted, she just had to get the right information. But it had to be soon.

"I had no call to strike at Tom through you," Gray went on. "You faced an unimaginable choice and came for me with no regard for yourself. You alone carried the load of that decision and our safety for weeks. You are half my soul. I knew all that even as I hurt you."

Panic sizzled through her like an electric shock. One eyebrow raised. "Choice?'

He took her upper arms and drew her close. "I wasn't there to voice an opinion about the ransom decision you had to make. It would take a lot of gall for me to condemn you for whatever you decided."

Heedless of the corn silk floating from her hands to the floor, Sterling dared to search his eyes and his face to see if he had somehow learned about her daughter. Had he read her mind? Ever since she returned from Atlanta she'd been wrestling with how to get Kate back, whether the Fosters were killers, and how to gather enough leverage to force Tom into some kind of arrangement for Kate. Had she slipped and said something aloud?

"Seeing patterns, hearing then finding holes in stories is not my strong suit. Facing the unpleasant truth is your forte. Sometimes I can't see what is in front of me," she said. "We are so much better together. But not if we doubt each other."

He pressed his forehead against hers. "I'll be ready for whatever you want to share. Meantime, I'll focus on what we have. A good partner would have done that already."

"I'm afraid," she whispered. "I doubted myself in that bank in Atlanta and I nearly ran. I may not have guaranteed our safety, but I got something from Tom. These voodoo spells frighten me, the idea that people are probably still after us terrifies me, and the real possibility that I failed at everything, keep me up at night."

"I'm sorry I let you down," he said. "As long as I'm here you don't need to be afraid."

"You should hate me for what happened to Silver. You have no idea how badly I screwed up everything," she said. The lump in her throat threatened to choke her. "I should have taken Silver to a doctor—"

"If it's anyone's fault, it's mine. It's always in the back of my mind, eating at me. He didn't want it, I know that. I may have been hurt, but I knew taking him to a Memphis hospital would be a certain death sentence. The police would treat him like a cop killer," Gray said. "You must know that too."

A cop killer was how the police would treat Gray now if they discovered him.

"We have a lot of work to do to clear you," Sterling said. The truth of it chilled her.

"I want the detective agency we dreamed of when we were Justice Tomorrow agents," Gray said.

Sterling turned down the heat on the beans. "Sterling Brothers Limited?"

"I still like A White Chick and Two Brothers," he said.

She grinned and so did he. The weight in her chest eased.

"Gray, we need time for scabs to form over all our wounds before we can think about getting more. Meantime, I'll be a beautician and you'll be a student."

She felt different. More focused, more cautious, but filled with hope at last. She would rethink and test her idea to get Kate back until she was sure it would work. She and Al Morris would pool their resources to discover who killed Justice Tomorrow and Silver. Only then would she return to Atlanta. What she'd tell Gray then, she had no idea.

But right then she didn't think he could bear knowing the price of their future together.

"Until you're ready to tell me what eats at you, you do what you must," he said. "I'm your partner, not your keeper."

She put her hand over Gray's heart.

"Just don't do anything stupid, Sterling."

She kept a straight face until he rolled his eyes.

THE END

A NOTE FROM THE AUTHOR:

Thank you for reading *The Price of a Future*. If you liked it, please drop a review on Amazon, BookBub, Goodreads, Storygraph, or wherever you find your books. Reviews are the lifeblood of authors. Thanks.

I would love to hear from you at www.jrflaum.com or Threads at @jrflaum or Bluesky at @jrossflaum.bsky.social or on my Facebook page at https://www.facebook.com/WriterJackieRossFlaum

Please enjoy the first chapter of the next Sterling Brothers Ltd. III story: **Wigs, Mustaches, and Other Disguises**.

Wigs, Mustaches, and Other Disguises

CHAPTER ONE: THE ELECTION

A gust of wind hurled dead leaves against the glass window of Belle's Beauty Shop. Startled, Madeline Sterling looked up and caught a whiff of something foul. Her nose wrinkled and her eyes flew from the strand of white hair she was trying to twirl on a roller to the parking lot out front.

"Ouch! Honey, I know you're still learnin,' but the first lesson is don't pull the customer's hair out." Clara Turner glanced outside the picture window and stiffened. "Oh no. No-no!"

Terror sizzled through Sterling. The hair she'd been trying to get around the roller fell from her fingers. The former murder investigator dropped behind the chair for cover as a bramble wall grew from her feet and swirled around her.

Voices chattering and hair dryers blowing became swirls of purple, yellow, and pink in Sterling's head. She saw voices of people in the shop. Fear clawed through her like a pack of feral cats. With a herculean effort, she reversed the narrow-tailed comb in her hand to use as a weapon.

How had the killers discovered her in Morehead, Kentucky?

I don't have them! I don't have any files from Justice Tomorrow! Leave us alone!

Sterling thought she had screamed it aloud, but no one in the shop seemed alarmed.

Her partner, Justice Tomorrow investigator Socrates Gray, appeared at Sterling's elbow with a stack of white towels, his eyes wide. She tried to warn him, but her lips wouldn't move.

"It's fine," he whispered.

The bramble wall vanished. Her mixed up senses righted. What she had dubbed her voodoo spell had ended.

"What in tarnation?" Clara leaned over the arm of the chair and gaped at the petite young woman hunkered behind her.

Shame washed over Sterling.

"Dropped something." She held up a pink plastic hair roller as she rose, feeling light-headed. Gray picked up another roller and handed it over with a knowing smile.

"Oh, honey, relax. It ain't that ex-husband of yours," shop owner Marabelle Carlson said from across the room.

"Yeah, I know," Sterling said, keeping up the lie she and Marabelle had told Belle's customers.

"Clara's acting a fool," Marabelle added.

The shop chatter resumed.

"Bertha Johnson out there's a menace. I don't want her in here pestering people for votes," Clara said in an apologetic tone that grew more heated. She pointed out the front window. "That woman ought to be in jail for murder instead of running for County Judge of Rowan County."

"Miss Clara, what a terrible thing to say," Sterling said. She patted her bleached blond curls, then used shaky hands to brush hairs off the black plastic cape around her client. "Tell her no if she bothers you for your vote."

"You don't tell Bertha no," declared a woman waiting to get the white in her hair dyed brown.

"That's a fact," added another customer.

Gray placed some towels in Sterling's station cabinet and moved to the next one. He left the door open, and she closed it with a practiced nudge of her hip.

A coed getting a manicure followed Gray with her eyes, showing the same admiration that Sterling had seen from other women during the four years she and Gray had worked together. With broad shoulders, brown eyes deep as the Kentucky forests, and light brown skin, Gray had a lot to admire. Currently he spoke with a sexy British accent since he was posing as a South African foreign student.

"Bertha killed my neighbor over this darn election," Clara concluded.

The shop talk hushed again. Someone harrumphed.

"You mean that lady? Oh no." Gray hurried to the front picture window, scrunched up his face, and gestured outside at a stocky, middle-aged woman with stark black hair. She battled a stiff breeze in her attempt to secure flyers on parked vehicles.

Gray shook his head. "Madam, I do not believe she could pull off such a deed. She does not appear competent to place paper on automobiles."

Belles' patrons giggled.

The sight of Bertha stretching over car and truck hoods to slip flyers under windshield wiper blades mesmerized Sterling. Once or twice the candidate's dress hem rose to such precarious heights, it was like watching a train wreck—the sight was so awful Sterling couldn't look away. Several flyers got away from Bertha and sailed across the road.

Bertha's shoulders sagged, then she headed for the shop. She halted, scowled at the large peace sign on one wall, the Power to the People symbol on the other, and walked up the steps. A few fall leaves rushed in as she opened the door. She posed in the doorway, and fresh mountain air replaced the odor of shampoo, conditioner, and permanent wave solution in the shop. When no one greeted her at once, she shut the door with a bang.

"Bertha! Didn't know you had an appointment," Marabelle said. The forty-two-year-old shop owner stopped rolling a perm and moved across the floor as graceful as a deer and just as fast.

"I wanna drop off my campaign poster, Marabelle." Bertha jutted out both her chins. "For your big old window."

Sterling faced the rear of the shop. She didn't like working out on the floor where everyone could see her, but Marabelle had overbooked. Marabelle's husband Paul had even been pressed into service as a manicurist. Before she looked away, though, Sterling noticed Bertha's frizzled hair a needed conditioning treatment. Maybe she'd gotten the hang of being a beautician instead of a murder investigator.

"Ouch!" Clara grabbed her head again.

"Sorry, Miss Clara," Sterling said.

Bertha whirled toward the cry like a hunter stalking prey. "Why, there's Clara. Ethel Dickerson—getting that gray hair permed? Ruby Tolliver, that you?"

The candidate left Marabelle standing helplessly at the front door while she glad-handed the entire shop. She even tried to shake hands with the woman who was having her nails painted.

At last Bertha paused to examine at the psychedelic colors in the shop and the life-sized portrait of Jimi Hendrix on one wall.

"Hollywood hippies," she muttered.

"Now, Bertha, you know you're thrilled to have me home from California," Marabelle teased.

"Ho-lly-wood," Bertha repeated like a curse. "At Belles."

Belles had stood as an unchanging oasis on Route 60 for women of the farm community that Morehead State College was transforming. The college had swallowed homes in Morehead and spit out offices. Ladies' apparel stores had become boutiques with short skirts. Young people were marching through Morehead with signs reading, "Get Out of Vietnam." Through it all, Belles had remained the same white painted cinderblock building with the same white gravel parking lot and the same attraction—women came in frazzled and left feeling good.

Then came Marabelle, whose name fit the shop but whose ideas in décor shocked older folks in the community. Regular customers reeled at the peace signs and the sheriff stopped by to see what was going on, but college girls began coming.

Bertha grabbed the latest *Cosmopolitan* in the reception area and read the yellow cover promising articles on women's sexuality. Her jaw dropped quicker than the magazine from her hand.

"Peace and love." Paul watched Bertha's moves with amusement and adjusted his wire-rimmed glasses. He finished painting a co-ed's nails with a flourish.

The young woman laughed.

"Hi there." Bertha pounced on the co-ed with a full-voltage smile. "I'm running for County Judge, and I'd appreciate your vote."

The coed blinked as though waking from a pleasant dream into a nightmare.

"No, nope, no." Marabelle stepped between them.

"Will you at least put up my poster?" Bertha said.

"No posters in the window."

"You got one for the Morehead State's Little Theatre," Bertha whined.

"Paul's head of the theater department."

"I get my hair done here."

"Not lately. Your roots are showing."

"I'm too busy to come in. I need everybody's vote for this race. Yours too." Bertha cast a longing gaze at the picture window where drivers on the two-lane as well as shop patrons would be sure to see it.

"H-how you gonna be County Judge, run the Foothills public housin' apartments, and the new Plantation ones," Ethel called out.

"Why, those new senior apartments almost run themselves." Bertha winked at her. "Vote for me, Ethel, and get moved up on the list to get in the new place."

Indignation skittered up Sterling's spine.

"Bertha, come in when you get time and I'll give you a deep conditioning on the house," Marabelle offered in desperation.

"Well, I tried," Bertha declared. "You're gonna have to pick a side, though."

Marabelle shrugged.

Before she disappeared outside, Bertha hollered: "Vote for Bertha and Get Your Money's Worth!"

The awful slogan—or the slamming door—made the beauty shop patrons flinch.

"Hateful old woman! Poor Lurleen Carter," Clara spewed.

"Bertha Johnson is one of the kindest, most thoughtful people I know. She don't want it told, but she pays the rent out of her own pocket for some folks at Foothills," said a woman. She waited for Marabelle to take her money for a shampoo and set, then adjusted her car coat, and flounced out in a huff.

"Clara, you don't know that anybody killed Lurleen," muttered Ethel. "It was an accident."

"Huh," Clara harrumphed. "Lurleen said she told Bertha she wouldn't vote for her, then the fire happened. Her front door stuck—or someone made it stick."

"Oh, Clara . . ." Ethel began.

"I saw that Bertha's idiot nephew Willie kneeling at Lurleen's door the day of the fire." Clara glanced up at Sterling. "I told the sheriff, but that man is shiftless."

"Come on, people don't kill over an election." Sterling finished rolling Clara's hair.

"Huh! Politics around here is a blood sport—always has been," Clara said.

"Twenty people got killed back in the 1800s over politics," observed Ruby, the white-haired woman who wanted to be brunette again.

"That's a fact, Ruby. But Ethel's right, Bertha doesn't usually kill people," Clara said.

Ethel protested, "That's not what I said."

"Her weapon is refusin' to fix people's toilets," Clara went on. "Or never spraying their place for bugs."

"Now, Clara." Ethel admonished again.

"You know the exterminator never came around your place or mine," Clara told Ethel. "Thank God it's fall, and the bugs aren't as bad."

Ethel didn't argue about the pests, but repeated, "Nobody killed Lurleen."

"If you saw Miss Johnson's nephew jamming the door so Lurleen Carter would die in a fire, that would be a motive for murder," Sterling said. "And you'd the next victim, Miss Clara."

Gray glared at her.

"Not that you have anything to worry about," she amended and gave herself a mental kick.

She heard Gray's exaggerated sigh as he swept hair clippings into a dustpan, his way of reminding her that she had promised to be more careful.

"Miss Clara," he said, "I am interested in how Americans conduct their elections. How would Miss Bertha know if you voted for her?"

Sterling dabbed at her nose with a tissue from her apron pocket, grateful to Gray for covering for her. Again.

"With absentee ballots, it's a sure thing, Gray." Ethel lifted her head from the shampoo bowl where Marabelle prepared to rinse the perm solution from her hair.

"Who's in a red Ford Falcon?" A woman in glasses opened the front door and jerked her thumb toward the parking lot. "Taillight's busted. There're pieces all over the gravel."

Clara moaned and covered her face with both hands.

"Don't fret, Miss Clara." Sterling said. "Paul probably has a spare one someplace. He's got everything from a fish tank to an oxygen tank."

"Sure do, Miss Clara," Paul said as the coed paid him for the manicure. "I'll go look for it and call you." He patted her shoulder as he walked out the back of the shop.

Marabelle finished rinsing, patted the tiny rollers in Ethel's hair with a towel, and shook her head sadly at Sterling. Everybody knew Clara struggled to find a dime. Marabelle gave her a free shampoo and set for letting Sterling practice on her. Clara kept her dignity, and Sterling had someone who didn't complain when her scalp burned, or her make-up resembled a Picasso painting.

"I hear voters won't turn out for this election 'cause it isn't a presidential year," Ethel babbled, acting too cheerful. "Whoever has the most kin's gonna be the next Rowan County Judge."

"Sounds like it's a tight race," Sterling muttered. She'd been feeling safer and calmer than she had in weeks until all the talk about crooked elections and murder twisted her stomach back into knots.

"The man running against Bertha is a good man. Bubba Parker goes to my church. He owns the gas station and feed store on Route Sixty and does his own taxes," Clara said. She had been a bookkeeper and appreciated those who knew their numbers.

"Come on, Ethel, got a hot seat for you." Marabelle pointed to the tall dryers and Gray pulled back two of the hoods. "Over here, Clara. I put the new Good Housekeeping out for you."

Two hair dryers began roaring.

The front door opened, more fresh air flew around, and a woman wearing a blue and white scarf on her head walked in. Marabelle waved at her and made her way to the front.

"Are you Dolores Stephens? Hi there, I'm Marabelle. Come on and have a seat." She escorted her customer to the back and patted a beautician's chair.

"Does seem strange Lurleen's apartment caught fire," Ethel went on as she hobbled to the dryers on arthritic knees. "She was real careful about fires 'cause she was in a wheelchair."

Gray adjusted the height of the dryer to suit Ethel.

"She was the first colored person to move into Foothills. I wonder if that had something to do with the fire," Clara muttered before the hair dryers blew all talk away.

"Whatcha got under this pretty scarf, Dolores?" Marabelle helped her new client settle under a plastic cape.

The woman removed the scarf to reveal a mass of out-of-control black curls.

"My gracious," Marabelle gasped.

"I'll be honest, I've been everywhere. Ashland. . . Lexington. . . Louisville," Dolores said. "Someone told me you knew how to cut curly hair."

"My cousin over there has the same blessing. . .or curse, dependin' on your point of view." Marabelle's comb pointed to Sterling, who had been introduced around town as a distant cousin from North Carolina.

"You know, Lurleen's son works at our tobacco barn during the season," Dolores said as Marabelle slipped a cape around her neck. "Now that I think on it, Luther ranted something about the County Judge's race and the fire. I never put any stock in it."

"You think it'll rain?" Marabelle said.

Her customer took the hint. "In the afternoon, maybe."

Marabelle finished cutting and styling the curls without another word about the County Judge's race, so the shop talk turned to grandchildren and girls' short skirts in school. When Dolores rose to leave, she preened and pocketed her scarf.

Gray met her behind the cash register. "Pardon me, madam, but I wish to learn about American elections. Would y'all—I mean—would the son Luther's claim, if true, be coercion and fraudulent voting practices in this County Judge election?"

"Our elections are honest and fair in the US of A and Rowan County. I should know. I'm on the Election Board." Dolores clawed inside her purse, came up with some dollar bills, and thrust them on the counter. "That stuff about Lurleen was just a grieving son talkin' and that's all there is to it."

"Thank you, madam," Gray said.

"I'd like to make an appointment for next month. November first? Don't want to get too close to Election Day. That's the seventh," Dolores said.

Gray opened the appointment book, wrote the Dolores's name in the noon slot, and thanked her for coming.

When he turned toward the dryers where Ethel and Clara sat reading magazines, Sterling gave him the evil eye to remind him they were not hunters anymore, they were prey. Chased by killers seeking Justice Tomorrow murder case files, they'd found sanctuary at Belles three months ago. While she held some hope the hunt had been called off, they couldn't afford to do anything that would bring them attention.

"Hey, you two, finish for me? I'm headed home." Marabelle pulled her long hair into a ponytail and unlocked the blue door to the workroom. The workroom door out back faced her house.

"Yes, madam," Gray said.

Beyond the blue door, Marabelle and Paul stored wigs, grease paint, fake eyebrows, and other tricks of disguise and illusion that had made them famous as Hollywood special effects and make-up artists. On one long wall, Paul had built a workbench with a pegboard to hold all his tools. Since his theater students occasionally stayed overnight to work on props for a show, Paul had added a full bath and a loft big enough for a double bed mattress. It was a perfect arrangement for Gray after he and Sterling fled those who destroyed the secret civil rights group Justice Tomorrow and sought their murder case files.

Sterling brought Clara from under the dryer and started to unroll her hair.

"Let Gray try it," Clara said. "He needs to learn."

Gray's eyes darted back and forth from Clara to Sterling.

"Can't be that hard, come on," Clara said. Ethel's hair dryer shut off and she rose from her seat.

"Make-up and hair styles are part of the dramatic arts you came over here to learn," Sterling said. "Go on. I'll finish Miss Ethel."

"May I work on a white woman?" His voice dropped to a whisper. "Out on the floor?"

Ethel glanced around the empty shop as she hobbled to a chair. "Nobody here to care."

Gray's forehead furrowed, but he opened a cabinet drawer, took out a comb and brush, and began work on Clara's hair. Sterling finished with Ethel's style while Gray brushed out Clara's curls.

Sterling walked Ethel to the front, smiling as she shut Gray's cabinet drawer with one hand as she went. Socrates Gray had never shut a drawer, door, or cabinet in his entire life, according to his younger brother. The memory of Gray's dead brother squeezed her heart.

Gray teased Clara's hair with a comb and finished in clouds of hairspray.

Sterling cashed Ethel out, waved goodbye, and stood in the doorway, admiring the mountains and acres of farmland across the two lane. In the setting sun, the fields seemed golden, and the hills painted dark blue with flashes of color. She liked the Kentucky hills from a distance. While they were on the run, she and Gray had hidden in a dozen forests all over the South. She had the bug bite scars to prove it.

Something stirred on the fringe of Sterling's sight, a dark figure that blended into the shadows near a truck in the parking lot. Her heart leapt, her mouth opened to cry out, but the figure vanished. Another imaginary assassin. At least she didn't drop to the floor again. Sterling eased her breath out. She had to stop conjuring trouble; she had to figure out a way to control these voodoo spells that mixed her senses.

Ethel's car taillights disappeared around a treacherous bend in the road toward Foothills.

"Sterling? What do ya think? I might go dancin' tonight." Clara turned around and swayed her hands in the air.

"You look nice. Gray did a fine job." Sterling smiled at her favorite customer and adjusted the collar of Clara's pink blouse. "Next week?"

Ten minutes later, Clara walked out of Belle's humming.

Pink. Sterling never saw that color without remembering a pink baby blanket as it floated in the breeze and fell into the Mississippi River.

Clara got into her Falcon.

Sterling sagged against the front door frame. Her feet ached from standing all day, but her heart hurt more. She drew in a ragged breath, longing to stop being sad and afraid.

She locked the shop door, pausing to watch Clara drive off in the dusk. Suddenly, the vision she had imagined standing next to a tree morphed into a man who climbed into a pickup and sped down the road behind Clara.

Look for **WIGS, MUSTACHES, AND OTHER DISGUISES** on Amazon and other fine booksellers

www.ingramcontent.com/pod-product-compliance
Lightning Source LLC
Chambersburg PA
CBHW020411260626
47156CB00007B/2327